Praise for Margaret Truman and her Capital Crimes mysteries

"Truman has settled firmly into a career of writing murder mysteries, all evoking brilliantly the Washington she knows so well."
—*The Houston Post*

"She's up-to-the-minute. And she's good."
—Associated Press

"Truman 'knows the forks' in the nation's capital and how to pitchfork her readers into a web of murder and detection."
—*The Christian Science Monitor*

"An author whose inside knowledge of Washington is matched by her ability to spin a compelling mystery plot."
—*Crime Times*

Also by Margaret Truman

FIRST LADIES
BESS W. TRUMAN
SOUVENIR
WOMEN OF COURAGE
HARRY S TRUMAN
LETTERS FROM FATHER: THE TRUMAN FAMILY'S
  PERSONAL CORRESPONDENCES
WHERE THE BUCK STOPS
WHITE HOUSE PETS

IN THE CAPITAL CRIMES SERIES
MURDER AT THE WATERGATE
MURDER IN THE HOUSE
MURDER AT THE NATIONAL GALLERY
MURDER ON THE POTOMAC
MURDER AT THE PENTAGON
MURDER IN THE SMITHSONIAN
MURDER AT THE NATIONAL CATHEDRAL
MURDER AT THE KENNEDY CENTER
MURDER IN THE CIA
MURDER IN GEORGETOWN
MURDER AT THE FBI
MURDER ON EMBASSY ROW
MURDER IN THE SUPREME COURT
MURDER IN THE WHITE HOUSE
MURDER ON CAPITOL HILL
MURDER AT THE LIBRARY OF CONGRESS

MURDER IN FOGGY BOTTOM

Margaret Truman

FAWCETT BOOKS • NEW YORK

A Fawcett Book
Published by The Ballantine Publishing Group
Copyright © 2000 by Margaret Truman

All rights reserved under International and Pan-American Copyright Conventions. Published in the United States by The Ballantine Publishing Group, a division of Random House, Inc., New York, and simultaneously in Canada by Random House of Canada Limited, Toronto.

Fawcett is a registered trademark and the Fawcett colophon is a trademark of Random House, Inc.

www.ballantinebooks.com

ISBN 0-449-00196-2

This edition published by arrangement with Random House, Inc.

Manufactured in the United States of America

First Fawcett Books Edition: February 2002

10 9 8 7 6 5 4 3 2 1

For Clifton, my husband
of forty-three years

MURDER
IN
FOGGY
BOTTOM

Foggy Bottom

A Washington, DC, neighborhood that was built on a low-lying swamp, at one time home to a glass factory, a large brewery (now the Kennedy Center for the Performing Arts), and some of the city's worst slums . . . it was named either for the miasmic fogs that once enveloped it, or the hazy foreign policy of one of its most visible current residents, the U.S. State Department.

Now a relatively quiet but trendy residential area with housing prices to match, it is also home to the Watergate hotel, apartments, and office and retail complex; George Washington University, the city's second-largest landholder after the federal government; the Corcoran Gallery of Art; and the omnipotent Federal Reserve. The Organization of American States, at Seventeenth and Constitution, is located precisely at the geographical center of the District of Columbia.

Murder is uncommon in Foggy Bottom.

But a few occur now and then.

Part One

1

The corpse was well dressed. *Washington Post* reporter Joe Potamos looked down at the body behind a bench in the pocket park in front of the hotel at E and K Streets, on the eastern edge of Foggy Bottom. The victim was a white male with neatly trimmed and combed salt-and-pepper hair. His suit was blue, shirt white, tie gray with small red-and-white flags.

"Canadian," Potamos said to a tall, boxlike man writing in a small notebook.

"Huh?" Peter Languth muttered as he continued to write.

"Canadian. Those little flags are Canadian," Potamos said. "The red maple leaf in the middle and those red blocks on each side. You don't know that?"

Homicide detective Languth stopped writing and turned to look down at Potamos. Languth was six feet four; Potamos topped out at five-eleven. "You get off on flags, Joe?"

Potamos shrugged and started writing in his own long, slender, spiral-bound notebook. Uniformed officers stretched yellow crime-scene tape around the scene. A late-arriving EMS team knelt next to the body. Pressing in for a

5

closer look were a half-dozen homeless men for whom the park passed for home in summer. One of them had alerted a passing squad car to the dead man's intrusion.

"Get back," Languth growled at them. In the humid atmosphere of the nation's capital, the heavy air pressed down like a rubber blanket, capturing the men's pungent body odor. "You guys ever hear of a shower?" Languth asked, wrinkling his bulbous nose.

"The hot water stopped working in my mansion," the youngest of the homeless men said.

"Call a plumber," Languth said.

Potamos hoped he wasn't contributing to the bouquet of the moment. He'd been wearing the same blue chambray shirt two days in a row, and hadn't gotten around to getting last summer's lighter-weight clothing back from the cleaners. He itched under the weight of his gray tweed jacket.

"Sit over there till I want to talk to you," Languth told the odd assortment of men, pointing to a bench a few feet away. To a uniformed cop, he said, "Make sure nobody leaves."

Potamos arched his back against stiffness and yawned. Eleven-twenty. He'd dozed off in front of the television set in his one-bedroom condo in Rosslyn, Virginia, just across the Potomac from the District, when the call came from his editor telling him to get to the park. Such a call wouldn't have been made a few years ago, when the State Department was his beat, and crime reporting was only a memory. But that was *then*.

"Whadda you see?" Languth asked one of the EMS technicians who'd left the body to come to where the beefy, balding detective stood with Potamos.

"Something in the ribs, right side."

"No weapon?" Potamos asked.

6

Languth scowled. "You see any weapons, Joe? You see something nobody else does? Except flags?"

Potamos nodded at the bench where the vagrants had gathered, smoking cigarettes and passing a brown paper bag among them. "You check them out?" he asked.

"Joe, write your goddamn story and leave the investigation to me."

"Just asking. I thought I'd let a few facts slip into the story."

"Well, don't. How's it feel getting down and dirty, Joe, hanging around real people after being a media star? You used to cover this neighborhood, right?"

"Don't start with me," Potamos said, feeling the familiar anger bubble up inside. He visualized a tranquil, sun-drenched beach and drew slow, even breaths, the way he'd been taught in the anger-management course he'd been forced to take after the incident that had cost him his State Department assignment. And the inherent perks and prestige that went with it. State wasn't exactly the White House, where something big seemed to be popping every day, but some of the stuff was important. A real story broke now and then—Bosnia, Israel, Rwanda . . .

"Hey, you, get over here," Languth yelled at the homeless men.

Calmer now, Potamos listened as they gathered around the detective, who said, "Okay, what'd you lovely ladies see here tonight?"

Twenty minutes later, after it was clear that the men were hear-no-evil, see-no-evil, the well-dressed body was removed. Photos of the body had been taken from many angles; the homeless men had given their nonstatements, names, and addresses—"Bench Number Three," the young wise-guy vagrant cracked—a search of the immediate area had been conducted; and the crowd that had gathered had wandered away.

7

"Buy you a drink?" Potamos asked Languth.

"No."

"Suit yourself. What was in the deceased's wallet?"

"Money, credit cards."

"So, it wasn't a robbery gone wrong."

"Brilliant deduction."

"Who is he?"

"Ever hear of next of kin, Joe?"

"I'll hold it until you say it's okay."

"Yeah, right."

"You know who you remind me of, Pete?"

"Who?"

"Willy Loman."

"Who's he?"

"*Death of a Salesman.* Maybe just death. You ever see it?"

"No. Is it out on video?"

"Thanks for the usual wholehearted cooperation, Pete."

"Always a pleasure, Joe. How come you never offer to buy me a drink when I'm off duty? Say hello to your buddy Bowen."

The anger welled up again as Potamos watched Languth slowly walk away, big body moving side to side beneath his black raincoat, like an aging waiter with aching feet after a long shift. He went in the Lombardy, ordered a drink at the small bar, and made a few calls from his cell phone in search of additional information, including one to the Canadian embassy: "This is Joe Potamos from the *Post*," he told the night-duty officer. "There's been a murder in the park across from the Lombardy Hotel; looks like the victim might be Canadian. What? No, I don't know who the victim was but I figured maybe somebody from your embassy was supposed to be there tonight but didn't show up and . . . Huh? A man, middle-aged, nicely dressed, wore a tie with little Canadian flags on it and . . . Huh? No? I just thought I'd give it a try. No, I don't know his name. Yeah, thanks." He tried to reach a contact in the coroner's office in the hope of getting an ID on the deceased but was told he was away on vacation. He silently cursed Languth for not at least giving him a name, then filed the story, what little there was of it, and went to his condo in Rosslyn, where Jumper greeted him as though he were a raging success. He called Roseann at her apartment on Capitol Hill. Most nights, Potamos and the dog stayed there. But Potamos had kept the condo in Rosslyn as a gesture of independence, and as a refuge, especially when anger and frustration got the better of him, and Roseann, knowing how volatile he could be, never urged him to give it up. Smart girl, Ms. Blackburn. When he got in these moods, which she called his "vapors," he wasn't fit company for anyone, except the dog. It was the other times that had attracted Roseann to him, times when he could be tender and loving and funny and . . .

This was definitely a night full of vapors.

"I tried you earlier," she said.

"Everybody was trying tonight, it's a trying night out there," he said. "I was on a story. A homicide."

"Where?"

"That park in front of the Lombardy Hotel. How was your gig?"

"All right." She worked Washington's upscale rooms and private parties, with an occasional real gig when one came up. Jazz was her love; playing show tunes on the piano at fancy affairs was her income. "You okay, Joe?" she asked, knowing he wasn't.

"No, I'm not okay, Roseann. Instead of covering a murder, I'd rather commit one. Pete Languth was there."

"Your dear friend from law enforcement?"

9

"My fat cop friend."

"You don't want to kill a cop, Joe."

"How about Bowen? Anybody knows him'd give me a medal."

"You shouldn't say such things on the phone. It might be tapped. This is Washington."

"I hope it is. Tapped, I mean. Hey, anybody listening, I would like to kill George Alfred Bowen. Slowly." He sighed, said to her, "Ah, you've heard all this before. Potamos, the original broken record. Oops, CD. Showing my age. Sorry I didn't call before I went out. See you tomorrow?"

"If Jumper lets you." She often said he liked the dog better than he liked her, which he had to admit was occasionally true; not just better than her, of course, better than the whole human world at large.

"I'll talk to her about it. Look, Roseann, sorry that I'm down. Sometimes—well, sometimes it seems to pile up, you know? I'll get over it, always do, huh?" He laughed. Roseann smiled on the other end of the phone, seeing his face, the crooked grin, healthy white teeth made whiter against his dusky complexion, knowing he was feeling sorry for himself and that he disliked people who felt sorry for themselves, and feeling a little foolish for whining and wishing he hadn't.

"Joe, I understand. I really do. And excuse the comment about Jumper. Just kidding."

"Yeah, I know you were. I'd come over but it's late and—"

"Get a good night's sleep, Joe. I love you."

"And I'm glad you do. Good night, Roseann. See you tomorrow."

Roseann hung up, sat back on the couch, and absently played with an errant strand of her lustrous hair. Her feelings at the moment were ambivalent; Joe was good at creating mixed emotions.

On the one hand, she'd settled into the reality that being in love with the changeable—*that's* an understatement— reporter came with some baggage, his, and hers, too, of course. They'd met when Joe was a hotshot general assignment reporter for the *Post,* covering the murder in Georgetown of Valerie Frolich, the daughter of a powerful U.S. senator. It hadn't been love at first sight. He was handsome enough to turn her head, but his quirky personality was readily apparent on their first date; he was skeptical of everything, bordering on cynical, opinionated, talkative in spurts, silent for long periods. Not an easy person.

Then again, Roseann had never considered herself a prize catch either. Since being labeled a prodigy when she was eight—she later wondered whether her piano teacher said that to encourage her mother to keep writing the weekly checks—she increasingly immersed herself in her music, although not always in the direction of classical performance, to the chagrin of her teacher. She began listening to jazz in her teens, her father's record collection the prime source, and gradually applied her classical training to that distinctly American art form, the two not wholly incompatible.

In a sense, music increasingly became an introspective substitute for the more social pursuits enjoyed by her friends. Roseann once told her therapist, "I sometimes think I accompany life on the piano rather than living it."

Which was true. She was able to smoothly fend off the advances of men—there were many, several even desirable—by offering her career as an excuse: "Sorry, I have a lesson." "Sorry, I'm due at a rehearsal." "Sorry, I'm in the middle of writing an opera and can't break my momentum."

Until Joe came along, who, she reasoned early in the relationship, had as many problems as she did, which made them soul mates who often understood each other's foibles and fractures, and who knew when to back off, ease up, put their heads under the covers until the storm passed.

Like tonight.

She slept soundly.

2

Two Days Later
New York

Harry Syms turned off Highway 684, stopped for a red light, then turned left onto the access road leading to Westchester County airport, approximately fifty miles north of New York City. Seated next to him was his wife, Hope, and their two children, Janet, age six, and Jill, age eight, who were safely buckled in the back of their new green Plymouth Voyager minivan.

"I wish I could come with you," Harry said.

"It's better this way," Hope said. "With your Kamerer negotiations heating up and all, I understand. Besides . . ."

Syms was a corporate attorney whose company was in the midst of buying a competing firm.

"There's always some negotiation or meeting," Harry said heavily. "Maybe when it's wrapped up I can grab a few days and join you."

"No," Hope said. "Use the time to work and to . . . well, to think some more about—"

"We're here," Harry said, cutting her off. He stopped in front of the new terminal, a reflection of the rapid expansion of the regional airport, which chagrined those homeowners over whose houses the noisy, turboprop commuter planes flew. And now jets regularly operated from there. What was next, the Concorde?

He pulled luggage from the minivan as Hope unbuckled the girls. "You two young ladies look beautiful," he said, beaming. They shared their mother's blond genes and freckled cheeks. They wore matching frilly blue-and-white dresses, dresses designed especially for a trip to Grandma's.

Harry noticed that Jill wore a thin gold necklace with a tiny four-leaf clover at its end. He asked his wife, "You're not wearing the flying necklace?"

"No," she said, smiling. "Jill wanted to wear it."

The "flying necklace" had belonged to Hope's mother, who'd been a travel photographer of some note before retiring. She viewed the necklace as her good luck charm whenever she flew, which was often, and passed it on to her daughter.

"Don't lose that," Harry said to Jill. "It's mother's."

"I won't," Jill said.

"I'll take it back from her as soon as we arrive," Hope whispered to Harry.

"We'll bring you a present," said Jill, hugging her father.

"Great! Make it a big one. Hey, what about you?" he said to Janet. "Don't I get a kiss and a hug?"

She allowed him to kiss her cheek.

"They're so excited," Hope said.

"They should be. Make sure everybody drinks plenty of water when you're traipsing around DC. You know what it's like there in the summer."

"We'd better get inside," Hope said.

Syms enjoyed flying out of the smaller, regional airport, a half hour's drive from their home in Bedford Hills, or seeing people off from it. There was less of the traffic madness associated with taking a flight from LaGuardia or Kennedy. He waved to a security guard—

14

"Back in a minute," he shouted pleasantly—and carried the luggage inside the terminal to a short check-in line. "Flight's on time," he said after checking a departure board.

"Go on, we're fine," Hope said. "Don't be late to your meeting."

Harry took her arm and pulled her aside, away from the girls and others in the line. "Look," he said, "I know you're upset, and I don't blame you. But going to your parents' place isn't the answer."

"Harry, we've been over this a hundred times. I just need to be away for a spell to help me sort this out."

"Wouldn't it be better if you stayed and we kept talking it out?"

"Maybe, maybe not, I don't know. All I do know is that I have to clear my mind. A couple of weeks with Mom and Dad will help, I'm sure, and the girls will love it." Her eyes filled, and she quickly ran fingertips over them to keep the tears from spilling out. "We'll get through this, Harry. I know we will. If I didn't believe that, I wouldn't be talking about just a few weeks away."

He looked into his wife's eyes and swallowed against tears of his own forming. "You know I love you," he said, "more than anything in the world."

She nodded.

"Let's not let my stupidity ruin the good thing we have going together, you, me, them." He nodded to where the girls were giggling at something the man in front of them had said.

"Go," she said. "I'll be fine." She managed a smile, which sent a current of relief through his body. Then she kissed him and said, "I love you, too, Harry. Everything will be all right." She meant it. Although there would be the requisite period of recriminations, and should be, her determination not to allow a single indiscretion to take away what they had built as a family was as strong as her husband's.

They rejoined their daughters and he kissed both girls again. "Call tonight," he told Hope.

"I will."

"You girls be good and do what Mom says. But not when she says get lost."

"Those are a fine-lookin' couple of young ladies," the grinning, chubby businessman ahead of them said, Alabama coating his words.

"Thanks," Syms said.

"First time on an airplane?" the man asked.

"No," Hope answered. "They even have their own frequent flier accounts." To Harry: "Go!"

"Call."

"I will, I will."

Syms backed away, waving, and almost tripped over a suitcase belonging to another passenger. He left the terminal, got in his car, and headed for his meeting at company headquarters in White Plains, torn, wishing he'd been able to get away and accompany his family—wishing Hope had wanted him to, yet ready for the short separation. His in-laws were nice people, no bad mother-in-law jokes for him. Maybe when the negotiations were over he'd just get on a plane and surprise them. Even though Hope said she didn't want him there, he thought she'd like it if he arrived unexpectedly.

At least he hoped she would. He'd have to think that through. No room for more missteps at this juncture.

As Syms turned back onto 684, Al Lester looked up at a twin-engine Saab turboprop taking off from the airport. It passed directly over him, low, engines whining at full throttle, and banked left to the west, a standard takeoff pattern when the wind blew from west to east.

Lester, sixty-eight, was enjoying his retirement, finally having time for his passion: fishing the lakes, streams, and reservoirs that were, perhaps surprisingly, plentiful in Westchester County, Manhattan's primary source of potable water. Minnesota might be the land of ten thousand lakes, but New York State and Westchester within it were no Sahara. But you couldn't just go out and fish the reservoirs. It took a special license from New York City's Bureau of Water Supply. Among many restrictions was a prohibition on powerboats. You paddled or didn't fish. Lester believed in fishing regulations and followed them faithfully, knowing that the licensing requirement had been initiated during World War Two, when it was feared a foreign power might poison the city's water supply. No such fear existed today, but still having to obtain the special license kept the number of fishermen down, something he approved of. Al Lester wasn't a social fisherman. He liked to fish alone.

He'd left the house at six after Nancy had made him a hearty breakfast. The key to still getting along fine after forty years of marriage was, as far as Al was concerned, understanding and respecting each other's needs. His days were spent fishing; she enjoyed tending to their flower garden and reading the dozen or so romance novels that seemed to arrive weekly from a book club. Many of their friends had moved to Florida or North Carolina, in search of cheaper living and more consistently moderate weather. Those states had their attractions, including a usually benign climate—except when it turned terrifying—but there would be no such move for Al and Nancy Lester. "Like signing your death certificate" was the way he saw it. Bring on the change of seasons, including snowy winters. It kept a man alert and alive. And no early-bird specials at the local eatery in this couple's future. Nancy could cook . . . and liked it.

He had just reached his favorite spot in Webers Cove when the Saab aircraft roared into the sky above, causing him to mutter a curse. There would be a dozen more departures that morning to intrude on his quiet, solitary pleasure, just him in his canoe, and the birds, and the fish that would rise to his lures—or at least flirt with them. He watched the plane disappear into puffy clouds to the west, tossed out his line, secured the rod between his knees, lit his pipe, and settled back.

"Been living in the DC area for thirty years," the cornpone businessman said to Hope Syms as she and her daughters settled in their seats for the trip to Washington. The Canadian-made, high-wing, twin-turboprop Dash 8 was fully booked, the thirty-six passengers seated in two rows, two seats to a row. Hope and the youngest child, Janet, sat together. Directly across the narrow aisle were Jill and the businessman, who'd introduced himself as Wally Watson—"Plastic extrusions, household gadgets," as if they were all part of his name. He was a jolly type who made the kids laugh; his grandchildren were older, four of them, three boys and a girl. He'd been in New York on a selling trip: "Hardware stores, not many in Manhattan, department stores. The buyers all know Wally Watson." Eight-year-old Jill had been assigned to the aisle seat but wanted to be next to the window, and Watson had happily switched with her.

The sole flight attendant came down the aisle checking that seat belts were fastened. She stopped and smiled at the kids. "Welcome aboard," she said. "First flight?"

"No," Hope said in response to what was the standard question. "They're both old-timers."

"Glad to hear it," the flight attendant said. "I'll be back once we're up with Cokes and pretzels."

"Mommy, this plane is so *s-m-a-l-l*," Jill said.

18

"Big enough to get us there," Hope said, thinking that their children had become spoiled traveling on large jet aircraft. This would be a different experience for them.

The captain spoke over the PA system: "Welcome aboard, ladies and gentlemen. Nice to have you with us today. We'll be taxiing out in a few minutes. Shouldn't be any delays in getting off. Flight time to Reagan National Airport is an hour and twenty minutes, get us there right on time. Weather looks good all the way so we should have smooth sailing. Washington's hot, though, forecast to get up into the nineties."

Jill Syms made a face and said, "Ugh!"

"Grandma's house is air-conditioned," Hope said, "and the car. We'll stay cool."

The aircraft's Pratt & Whitney engines came to life and the Dash 8 slowly left the boarding area and headed for the runway, an east-to-west takeoff into the wind, blowing in at eleven knots. In the cramped cockpit was Captain Robert "Red" Sutherland and First Officer Wendy Johnson, one of a growing number of female commercial pilots advancing their airline flying careers by piloting smaller, commuter aircraft. They reached the active runway and turned onto it. The tower controller's voice crackled in their headsets: "Dash three-three-seven, you're cleared to roll."

"Roger. Three-three-seven rolling."

Johnson advanced the throttles. The engines responded, the four-bladed props cut into the air, and the craft moved forward, gaining speed as she kept it glued to the runway's white center stripe while monitoring the air speed indicator. The plane reached the predetermined speed for liftoff.

"Rotate," Captain Sutherland said.

Johnson pulled smoothly back on the yoke and the ground fell away. In the passenger cabin, Jill Syms gave out an exuberant yelp. Wally Watson laughed. Hope took her daughter's hand and squeezed. As often as she'd flown, she was never completely comfortable in a plane despite her mother's good-luck necklace, and would be glad when they touched down safely at Reagan National.

Harry Syms sat in his company's conference room with colleagues, as well as lawyers from the firm about to be willingly gobbled up.

"How's the family?" he was asked.

"Great. Hope and the kids are in the air right now on their way to Washington. Her mom and dad live there."

"Playing the bachelor game for a few days, huh, Harry?"

"Yeah." He laughed.

"Nothing like a trusting wife."

The comment nettled Harry but he didn't respond. The idea of ever cheating on Hope had always been anathema to him. As far as he was concerned, he'd gotten lucky when he met and managed to woo Hope Martin into becoming Mrs. Harry Syms. And there were the girls. A man would be a fool to do anything to jeopardize a family like that.

A fool like him, he thought. One extra drink at the Chicago convention that impaired judgment, falling into that silly eye-gazing game with the stunning brunette attorney, full, red lips and lush figure, liking that she laughed at everything he said, enjoying touches on his arm and back. Another drink. Ending up in her hotel room. The mad, frantic shedding of clothes and the twisted sheets and the rapid rush and pleasure of it, followed immediately by a vision of Hope and the kids at home and what would happen if she found out and was this worth it and how can I make it go away and pretend it never happened and . . .

He was lucky Hope hadn't walked out with the kids when, weeks later, that woman, whose name was Kay and whom he had been ignoring, called and demanded she speak with him. When his wife pressed her for identification, the lawyer shouted, "I'm the woman who slept with your husband in Chicago. Put him on!"

Real-life *Fatal Attraction*. Not much attraction left, possibly fatal.

When Harry came home from work that evening, Hope confronted him. "She's demented," Harry said initially. But Hope's questions persisted, and Harry said, "Just a drunken fling. Stupid. God, I'm sorry. Believe me, it'll never happen again."

"So, where are we, Harry?" someone at the White Plains meeting asked.

"What?" Harry said. "Oh, sorry. My mind was somewhere else." He pulled a thick file folder from the briefcase at his feet. "What say we get down to business? Be due diligent and all that."

Hope Syms, too, was having similar thoughts about her marriage and family as the plane climbed. It passed low over cars on Highway 684 and continued in a westerly direction, its course dictated by air traffic control. The highway fell behind and the aircraft crossed the shoreline of Rye Lake. Beyond it was a larger body of water, the Kensico Reservoir.

Below, fisherman Al Lester's reverie was interrupted by the sound of the Dash 8's fully throttled engines. He looked up as the aircraft banked and passed directly above his canoe, its left wing dipping as though tossing a greeting. Lester mumbled something less welcoming in return. He continued to watch as the plane reached the far end of the lake and maintained its climb attitude over a vast, undeveloped wooded area to the south of the

21

reservoir. He returned his attention to his fishing line, giving it a few jerks to prompt the lure into a seductive jiggling action. Then, he took a final look up at the Dash 8. What he saw stunned him, froze him, caused his hands to involuntarily shoot up to his face. The fishing rod flew out of the canoe, and his favorite fishing hat, with dozens of hooks and lures dangling from its crown, went into the water.

The sight had such a potent impact on him that he thought for a moment it might have been an apparition— *hoped* it was—a special effect from one of those damnable action-packed movies or video games popular with young people. The plane's silver, sleek profile split apart. A vivid orange ball erupted where the left wing joined the fuselage, and the faint sound of an explosion reached Lester's ears a second later. The fisherman watched as the wing separated from the aircraft and began a slow, topsyturvy descent to earth, followed by the rest of the plane, silently twisting and turning against the blue sky, the only sound the breeze on Rye Lake and the beating of Lester's heart. He saw other things falling, too, smaller things— bodies came to mind; he closed his eyes and lowered his head.

When he opened his eyes, it was over except for a lingering wisp of black smoke dissipating into the atmosphere. There was a second when he thought it hadn't happened, that he'd had a fleeting daydream or a ministroke. He immediately knew neither had been the case. He may have had a pacemaker installed two years ago, and his right knee might ache from arthritis, but Al Lester's eyesight was good, remarkably good for his age; he'd been told that only last week by his optometrist.

No, what he'd witnessed was only too real. It had happened. One of the planes he so often cursed for their noise had exploded in midair and fallen to the ground, gone silent, along with whoever was on board.

It was the *other* thing he'd seen that was so unreal.

3

The cold front that had sent some advance clouds into Westchester County was already firmly established in the Pittsburgh area when Max Pauling arrived at a private airport west of the Steel City. Rain had come down in buckets earlier that morning, but things had improved by the time he'd filed an IFR—Instrument Flight Rules—flight plan with the crusty airport operator. Flying out of such a small airport could have been done under Visual Flight Rules, but Pauling was headed for Washington, where he'd have to negotiate that area's sophisticated air traffic control system. Besides, he was proud to have earned his IFR license, and flew under instrument rules as often as possible to keep his skills sharp.

He left the flight operations center, as the shack with peeling yellow paint was known, and went to where he'd tied down his Cessna 182S two days earlier. He'd purchased the single-engine, fixed-gear plane a year ago from a Maryland flying club shortly after returning from a seven-year stint in Moscow. There he was ostensibly a member of the Trade and Commerce Division of the U.S. embassy, but in reality was on assignment for the Central Intelligence Agency. He'd been called back to Washington to join a special task force in the State Department's Counterterrorism Division—Russian desk, a joint effort with the CIA. Officially, he was now an employee of State; unofficially, he reported to two masters, Army Colonel Walter Barton, State's director for counterterrorism operations, and his boss and friend at the CIA, Tom Hoctor. It was, as far as Pauling was concerned, a clumsy, convoluted arrangement, but not at all unusual in the murky, often unfathomable, seemingly unintelligent world of intelligence, Washington style.

Pauling sat in the Cessna's left-hand seat and checked that the magneto switches and mixture control were off and that the throttle was closed. After securing his overnight bag on the right seat with the seat belt, he got out and did a slow walk-around, visually inspecting the aircraft's exterior for loose parts, dents in the prop, and for any signs of leaks on the ground. He manually manipulated the control surfaces on the wings and tail assembly to ensure they moved freely, then confirmed the fuel gauge readings with a dipstick and drained a small amount of fuel into a clear plastic tube to see if it was free of water and other contaminants. He undid the tie-downs, took another look at the brightening sky, and was about to get back into the plane when "Hey, Mr. Pauling!" stopped him.

A young man in greasy coveralls yanked off earphones attached to a Walkman as he approached. His name was Juan, and he worked for the airport's owner and operator. Pauling knew him from having flown in and out of the airport dozens of times. Pauling often visited his two teenage sons, who lived in Pittsburgh with Doris.

"Juan, my man," Pauling said. "What's up?"

"You hear?"

"Hear what?"

"The accident. A plane went down this morning."

"Commercial flight?"

"Yeah. In New York."

"Kennedy? LaGuardia?"

"No, some small airport up in the boondocks. West-chester or somethin' like that."

"That's hardly the boondocks, Juan. How bad?"

Juan shrugged. "They didn't say. I was listening to music when the announcer came on with a news bulletin."

"Sorry to hear it. Thanks for replacing that mag for me."

"Hey, happy to do it, Mr. Pauling. See you next time. Safe flight."

Juan watched Pauling climb up into the left-hand seat of the Cessna. Of all the private pilots who flew in and out of the small airport, Max Pauling was, as far as Juan was concerned, the most professional. Other pilots looked like what they were, average citizens enjoying the hobby of flying. Pauling had the look of a pro, a military pilot about to take off from a carrier deck, or a veteran commercial captain getting ready for a transatlantic flight in a jumbo jet. He dressed differently from average private pilots, who flew in and out of the airport wearing sports jackets, Bermuda shorts and T-shirts, or suits, even occasional tuxedos when they were coming in to attend fancy parties. Not Pauling. Although he was a civilian pilot in a small, single-engine aircraft, he always wore a green jumpsuit from his military days, and his favorite item of clothing, a tan Banana Republic photo-journalist vest with twenty-six pockets—"My answer to a woman's purse," he was fond of saying when asked about the vest. He approached his preflight check with precision and purpose. He even *looked* like a professional or military pilot: square face and close-cropped hair, lots of wrinkle lines from peering into the sun, obviously a sturdy guy, fit beneath the jumpsuit.

Pauling's demeanor, too, impressed the impressionable

Juan. He was easygoing and always courteous, something Juan couldn't say about some of the demanding, unreasonable amateurs he met on the tie-down line.

Strapped in the left-hand seat, Pauling set the throttle at half power and leaned out the open window to shout "Clear!" to alert anyone in the vicinity that he was about to start the engine. He turned the key; the engine and prop cranked over easily. Pauling waved to Juan, who threw him a smart salute—good kid, Pauling thought—and squeezed the throttle forward just enough to break inertia and to begin his taxi to the end of the thousand-foot macadam strip, the airport's only runway. He tuned his radio to the ground control frequency and announced into the handheld mike, "Cessna three-three-nine Alpha rolling."

"Okay," the airport owner rasped from the yellow shack.

Pauling held his toes on the brake pedals as he advanced the throttle all the way to the instrument panel, then released it. The Cessna jerked forward, gaining speed, until the natural lift created under the curved wings was sufficient for Pauling to pull back gently on the yoke.

Procedures at the airport called for a right turn as soon as it was safe to avoid flying over a housing development. He banked right, leaned out the fuel mixture once he'd reached his announced cruise altitude, set the throttle to 75 percent power, and settled back for the two-hour flight to Washington.

He flew most of the trip on autopilot, adjusting the Cessna's heading and altitude when instructed to do so by ground controllers. This was prime time for Pauling, alone in his little plane, his pride and joy, above the stresses of daily life on the ground, at work, and in his personal life. It was what fishing was for some men. He did his best thinking when in the air, indulged in his most fertile and useful reflections.

This most recent visit with his ex-wife and sons had been like most visits since their separation and subsequent divorce four years ago—practiced civility by the adults, guarded behavior by the sons to avoid the appearance of taking sides. The only potential for a fissure in their adult politesse was when his older son, Rob, asked when he and his brother could go flying with Dad.

"Don't even ask," Doris said.

"Dad's instrument rated," Rob said. "He's as good a pilot as any airline captain."

"I wouldn't say that," Max said.

"I don't care how many licenses he has, he flies that silly little plane that a stiff breeze could blow over. You're not going up with him."

Years earlier, Max had taken offense at her stance, silently considering it an assault on his ability and, yes, his manhood. But he no longer argued.

"You live with Mom and you do what she says," he told them, glancing at Doris for approval. "When you're older and making your own decisions, there'll be plenty of time to fly together, maybe even get you started on flying lessons of your own."

Another glance at his wife brought a stern look in return. He smiled, and she resumed basting that night's dinner, as if the ham were him.

He'd never blamed Doris for filing the divorce papers while he was in Moscow. Once he'd joined what they once called the Company—the CIA—he was barely home, certainly long enough to father two kids, but that hadn't taken long. The marriage had quickly become one in name only, he off on secret ventures to exotic places, she running a house, paying the bills, and bringing up two energetic sons without him around to help. In a sense, it was a relief when he learned she was divorcing him. He didn't contest it, nor did he attempt to make a case for custody. He wouldn't have been any better a father than he'd been a husband. The boys needed a full-time father and a mother; whatever Doris's feelings for him, her love of their sons was profound.

Later that night, he and Doris sat alone on the screened porch at the rear of her house. Max knew she enjoyed being with him, and he liked sitting with her. Romantic love was a thing in their distant past; there had never been any talk of giving it another try. But there was a comfort in spending time with someone you knew intimately, and with whom you'd shared a good hunk of your life. No need for posturing, no putting silly spins on things when the other person knew the truth.

"How's Washington?" she asked.

"All right."

"Must be blah after romantic Moscow."

"*Romantic* Moscow? You've never seen the leftover Soviet Union."

"I understand Russian women are very beautiful—and seductive."

Where was this going? he silently wondered.

"They are beautiful, almost as beautiful as American women."

"Does that include me?"

"I *meant* you."

"Thank you."

She looked away from him and placed the knuckle of her right index finger against her lips. Max knew what that meant; there was something she wanted to tell him but was debating whether to do it.

She looked at him again. "Max, I've met someone."

"You have? Who?"

29

"Someone at work. A nice man."

"An accountant?" She worked in a large accounting firm.

"Yes."

"A solid citizen. Accountants are solid."

"Dull, you mean?"

"I didn't say it. I mean dependable."

He saw her smile in moonlight filtering through the screen. "Look, Doris, if you've fallen in love with a nice guy, I'm happy for you. I really am. All I care is that he's good to the kids if you end up marrying him. He's what, divorced, widowed, never married?"

"Divorced. He has two daughters. They're about the same age as Rob and Joe."

"Sounds like it has all the makings of a fifties sitcom."

"Which you never enjoyed."

"On TV or in real life?"

"Both. The role of husband and father was beneath you."

"I wouldn't put it that way, Doris. I had other things on my mind."

Her laugh was not sarcastic. "Other things. God, Max, you really do love what you do, don't you?"

"Shouldn't I? You're supposed to love what you do."

"Which is supposed to include being a husband and father."

"I wasn't bad—when I was around."

"Max, even when you were around, as you put it, your mind was in some dark alley in Beirut, playing the bad guy, wondering whether the real bad guys would get on to you and put a bullet through your brain. I—"

"Are we about to get into an argument? There's no need for that. We're not married anymore. You knew what I did for a living when you married me."

"No, I didn't. That was against the rules. 'Sorry,

30

honey, but I'll be away for six months, can't tell you where or why, I'll miss you, take good care of the kids—' "

"I don't want an argument, Doris."

"Nor do I. I married you, Max, because you were the most charming man I'd ever met, not that I'd met many charming men at age twenty-four, but you were smooth. Part of the job description, isn't it?"

Max said nothing.

"I suppose I just want you to know yourself and not have any illusions about who Max Pauling is. And I understand, I really do. There are men who marry and father children and mean well, but who have a pull in some other direction that overrides changing diapers and helping with homework and attending school concerts and parent-teacher meetings."

"I agree, Doris. You're right. A PTA meeting can't hold a candle to a cloak-and-dagger meeting in some Moscow alley with a half-crazed Russian mafioso. And as for school concerts, grade-school music teachers either have a special place in heaven or they end up serial killers. No, Doris, my adrenaline did not flow when the kids were squeaking on their clarinets. I'm glad you've met your accountant."

"You're being facetious."

"No, I'm not. Being married to a solid citizen is—"

"Don't jump ahead too far, Max. We've just been dating a few months."

"Well, however it turns out, know I just want the best for you and the boys."

"You always have, and I appreciate it. You? No Mrs. Max Pauling number two in the future?"

"No. I have my work and my plane and—"

"Don't kid a kidder, Max. You aren't saying that the handsome, rugged ex-Marine I married doesn't have

31

women falling all over him? I read there's at least four women to every man in Washington."

"Can't prove it by me. Does your friend own a plane?"

"No, thank goodness."

"Then we probably won't have anything in common except that we fell in love with the same knockout woman. If I get in trouble with the IRS, will he help me?"

"Think I'll get to bed. Good night, Max." She came to where he sat, kissed him on the forehead, and left him alone to sit in the still darkness for another hour before going to the guest bedroom, where he stood in front of the mirror staring at the face peering back at him. From his perspective, he hadn't changed much from his Marine days in 'Nam, although there were the dozen or so crevices lining his face that hadn't been there, and the skin under his eyes sagged a little, and some silver had crept into his brown hair and—he hadn't lost any hair; there was solace in that, and he kept fit through regular workouts, including weights. His Marine uniform still fit.

But time marched on, as it was said, and Pauling knew it. His sons were on the verge of becoming men; his wife, still attractive, was not the dazzling young gal he'd married, and seemed interested in settling down with a middle-aged accountant with two teen daughters. On top of that, he, Max Pauling, had been relegated to a desk job, put out to metaphorical pasture. What next?

He slept fitfully.

He realized as he approached Washington that he'd been so immersed in his thoughts about Doris and his sons that he'd forgotten there had been a commercial aviation accident in New York. He turned on the plane's AM radio and tuned to a Washington all-news station in search of a quick update before having to negotiate air traffic control. He sat through a movie review and a story about a murder-suicide in Rockville, and was about to turn off the radio to avoid its distractions when a newscaster came on:

"We reported earlier that a commuter airliner has crashed in Westchester County, New York. The downed flight, we're told, was bound for Washington and carried a full passenger load, including area residents. Stay tuned for further developments in this breaking story."

"Damn!" Pauling muttered as he clicked off the AM radio and focused in on his approach instructions. Traffic was heavy and he had to hold for fifteen minutes, but eventually landed and taxied to the side of the airport reserved for private and corporate aircraft. It cost him what he considered a small fortune to tie down there, but he never toyed with going to a less expensive, private facility out in the country. He liked being around a major airport, enjoyed conversations with professional pilots and serious amateurs like himself.

He walked into the flight planning room to close out his IFR flight plan and was in the process of doing the paperwork when another private pilot he knew came up to the desk.

"Coming or going, Max?"

"Just flew in. I was in Pittsburgh visiting my ex-wife and kids. You?"

"Going up to Maine to do some bass fishing. Weatherby's Lodge. Know it?"

"No. I haven't been fishing in years. I caught the news about the accident. You have anything new on it?"

"The *accident*? Make that two."

Pauling slowly turned and looked quizzically at his friend. "Two?"

"Boise, Idaho. Just heard it five minutes ago."

"Two in one day? What was the equipment in Boise?"

"A Dash 8, I think. Commuter flight out of a regional there."

Pauling drew a deep, distressed breath, signed his completed flight close-out form, slid it across the counter to the duty officer, and picked up his overnight bag. To his aviator friend, he said, "Safe flight."

"Maybe I ought to check how the planets are aligned today, along with the weather."

"Not a bad idea. Two in one day. Take care."

Pauling drove to his apartment complex in Crystal City, Virginia. The fifteen-minute drive was nothing more than a blur, as though it hadn't happened. All he'd thought about, the only vision he had, was of a twisted, burning, crushed aircraft strewn over countryside, or suburb or city, body parts sprawled everywhere, acrid smoke searing the throat and nose, and, if lucky, a painful cry from someone who'd survived. He'd once been at an aircraft crash site, and the scene was forever etched in his memory.

His phone was ringing when he walked through the door, and the digital readout on his answering machine indicated eight messages had been left. He picked up the phone.

"Max, it's Colonel Barton."

His boss at State was military through and through, always referring to himself by rank, never Walter or Walt, which annoyed Pauling, like a doctor who insists on being called Doctor but uses his patients' first names. It wasn't the military thing that bothered Max. He'd liked his tour of duty with the Corps even though it meant Vietnam, and he respected the need for a clear chain of command, all the rules and regulations, the need to forbid fraternization between officers and enlisted men—and women. It had to be that way if you were going to win wars. Pauling always felt a sense of silent pride whenever he saw young men and women in uniform riding the Metro to and from the Pentagon, no rings in the nose, ear, or lip, no scraggly beards, but clean-cut and erect and proud. Or ready to be proud once they'd proved themselves.

So it wasn't Barton's military bearing and mind-set that bothered Pauling. It was the man behind the uniform, more politician than officer. Lots of them in Washington.

"Hello, Colonel. What's up?"

"I've been trying your cell phone."

"Batteries must have run down." Truth was, Pauling had turned it off when he left for the weekend.

"I need you here right away."

"I'm on leave . . . Colonel."

"You *were* on leave, Max. Can you be here in a half hour?"

"Yeah, I suppose so, but what's so important?"

"A half hour."

Pauling held the dead phone away from his ear and said something decidedly not official—and certainly not military.

4

**That Same Day
New York**

First to reach the Dash 8 that had crashed less than three minutes after taking off were two New York State troopers, who arrived in separate marked cruisers. At first, they weren't sure where the plane had gone down. They could see smoke when they'd first gotten the call while patrolling 684 and headed in that general direction, but it wasn't until a homeowner a mile from the crash scene called 911 to report "some sort of accident" that they were able to home in, converging in front of the caller's house and setting off on foot down a hiking trail leading to the shoreline of Kensico Reservoir.

When they reached the downed aircraft, they were stunned by the carnage spread out before them. The fuselage of the Dash 8 must have exploded upon impact, sending passengers, and parts of passengers, flying in all directions. The troopers started toward what appeared to be the largest intact portion of the plane, but one of them suddenly stopped and recoiled. A few feet in front of him was a man's torso, the lower portion of his body missing.

"God Almighty," the younger of the two troopers said, squeezing his eyes closed. He'd seen fatal auto accidents up close on the state's highways, but this was beyond anything he'd ever imagined.

"Nobody survived this," his colleague said quietly. They stood side by side, not moving, saying only those things that tend to be said when there is nothing meaningful to say, hearts pounding, smoldering wreckage and brush ignited by the flames hissing in the background.

The senior trooper pulled his radio from his belt and spoke into it: "Troopers Mencken and Robertson at scene of airliner crash. A couple hundred yards up from the reservoir, the Kensico. It's a . . . it's a mess. No apparent survivors."

The voice in his ear said, "I read. Secure scene. Nobody near it until you're relieved."

They looked at each other before splitting up, one staying where they'd been, the other slowly, carefully circumventing the apparent perimeter of the crash site to take up a position on the opposite side.

FBI Special Agent Frank Lazzara had been appointed agent in charge of the White Plains field office only a month earlier after serving three years with the Bureau's organized crime unit in Manhattan. At first, he resisted the reassignment because he considered it a demotion. Working organized crime in New York City was where the action and visibility were. White Plains? In suburban Westchester County?

But when his boss and mentor explained over dinner one night that the mob was in the process of shifting many of its more lucrative operations out of the five boroughs and into smaller but still sizable cities in New York and Connecticut—they'd already established a stranglehold on the carting industry in Westchester—and that the Bureau considered White Plains and adjacent cities and towns to be future hotbeds of mob activities, Lazzara changed his view of the new posting. He had started the reverse commute from Brooklyn, where he and his wife and their one-year-old child lived, and spent much of his first month in the new office being brought up to speed on pending cases and getting to know other special agents who'd be working under him.

He was poring over a thick file that had been compiled on mob-connected carting companies in the county when another agent entered the office.

"Frank, there's been a commercial airline accident."

Lazzara looked up, wondering why he was being told.

"It's local," the agent said. "A commuter plane out of Westchester airport. A Washington flight."

Lazzara sat back and frowned. He'd flown from Washington into Westchester the previous day after a round of meetings at the J. Edgar Hoover Building.

"Any survivors?" he asked.

A shrug.

"Where did it come down?"

"Out near one of the reservoirs. Joe is monitoring it."

Lazzara left the office and went to where Special Agent Joe Pasquale sat in the midst of communications equipment.

"The accident?" Lazzara said. "Where? What reservoir?"

"Near the Kensico Reservoir. Plane crashed on takeoff. There's been another."

"Another what?"

"Another aircraft accident. In Idaho."

"Not a good day for the airline industry. Or for a lot of people. Any details on that one?"

"Only a few. Just happened. About the same time. Commuter, too."

"Frank, Washington on the line," Lazzara's secretary said.

He returned to his office and picked up the phone: "Lazzara."

His supervisor said, "Send everybody you've got out to the scene of this airline accident near you."

"Everybody? Okay. Special instructions?"

"Yes. Put a clamp on everybody there. No statements to the press. No statements to anyone."

"Yes, sir. I just heard another commuter plane went down in Idaho."

"You heard right, but no comments on that, either."

"Criminal acts involved?" Lazzara asked, trying to determine whether his agency would be in charge of the investigation.

"Let's assume there are until we know otherwise."

Lazzara called the four special agents who were on duty that morning into his office.

"What's up?" Pasquale asked.

"The plane accident. Get a fix from the locals where it went down."

"State police just called in, Frank," his secretary said. She handed him a piece of paper on which she'd written information on the downed plane's location.

"Let's go," Lazzara said.

Notification of the downed Dash 8 in Westchester County had come through earlier via the communications center at the National Transportation Safety Board's headquarters at L'Enfant Plaza. It was forwarded to their Office of Aviation Safety, where that day's standby instant-response team, known as a "go team," which included experts on airframe and power-plant analyses, human performance, radar data, fires and explosions, and witness statements, was alerted to make ready to fly to Westchester County airport. Other calls were made simultaneously to NTSB's Northeast regional office in

Parsippany, New Jersey; the de Havilland Corporation in Ontario, Canada, the Dash 8's manufacturer; the airline; the Federal Aviation Administration; and to FBI headquarters. The NTSB public affairs duty officer was brought into the loop to be ready to handle media and public queries. The initial team that would rush to the accident scene would soon be augmented by designated parties not directly affiliated with NTSB, but who could give the lean-and-mean agency needed expertise. With only four hundred employees, the chairman of NTSB had proudly testified at a recent congressional budget hearing, his agency was "one of the best buys in government." They investigated more than two thousand aviation accidents each year, as well as five hundred other transportation mishaps, and had issued more than ten thousand safety recommendations since NTSB's inception in 1967, "at an annual cost of fifteen cents per American citizen."

The team flying to Westchester would be led by Peter Mullin, one of eight NTSB vice chairmen and a thirty-year veteran of aircraft accident investigations, a commercially rated pilot with thousands of hours in the cockpit, and whose reputation for running a tight ship at accident scenes was well known. His team assembled at Hangar Six at Reagan National, where NTSB maintained its own fleet of aircraft. Mullin, a tall, angular, balding man who walked slightly hunched to accommodate a bad back, grimaced as he took the right seat in the Learjet 45 twin-engine jet aircraft with NTSB markings. A full-time bureau pilot slipped into the left seat. Seated behind them were six members of the initial instant-response team. The engines had just come to life when Mullin was called on a radio channel linking the aircraft to NTSB headquarters.

"Peter, there's been a second accident."

"Where? Commercial? A jumbo?"

"Boise. Another commuter flight."

Mullin set his jaw, turned, and told the others of the news, then got back on the radio: "What's the status in Boise?"

"Vague. Denver's got a team ready to go."

"Good. Keep me posted." To the pilot he said, "Let's move!"

They were given priority takeoff clearance ahead of a string of commercial jets and were airborne within minutes. They'd reached their cruise altitude when Mullin was again contacted on the NTSB reserved radio channel. "Peter, you're not going to believe this but there's been a third accident involving a commuter plane."

"You're right, I don't believe it. Where?"

"San Jose. A Saab 34."

"Status?"

"Unknown. The Gardena office is on it."

"Three," Mullin grumbled.

"What?"

"I said *three,* goddamn it!"

"Peter, there's an eyewitness to the San Jose incident who's come forward."

"Oh?"

Mullin listened silently to what his assistant at headquarters said.

"Tell Gardena to stash him away. We don't need unsubstantiated stories like that getting out."

"It's a woman."

"What the hell difference does that make? Stash *her* away."

"Okay, Peter."

"What's up?" a team member seated behind Mullin asked after he'd ended the radio transmission.

"Another commuter plane down, a Saab, San Jose."

There was silence in the aircraft. Someone broke it by saying, "Three? Can't be a coincidence."

"No, it can't be, especially if an eyewitness in California has twenty-twenty eyesight and isn't too whacked out."

He used the same cleared frequency to reconnect with headquarters. "This is Mullin. I'm on my way to New York to investigate the downed plane there. Give me Poe."

Poe took the call and listened intently to what Mullin had to say. "Thank you, Peter," he said, ending the conversation with his thumb on the cradle's plunger, then dialed another number.

"Federal Bureau of Investigation. How may I help you?"

"This is NTSB Vice Chairman Poe. Put me through to the director's office. It's an emergency."

5

Potamos was in that indeterminate stage between sleep and wakefulness. He wondered what he was doing in a powdered wig, dancing in Austria. Roseann had taken Jumper for her morning walk and now sat at the piano in the living room struggling through Viennese waltzes to play at a cocktail party that evening at the Austrian embassy. Ordinarily, Potamos enjoyed hearing her play, but not when he was trying to sleep, and not waltzes by Strauss. Billy Joel, maybe.

He'd been up late the night before, which wasn't unusual. Potamos was a night person, which was fortunate considering that Roseann was a musician who usually worked at night. If he wasn't out on an assignment, he stayed up late anyway watching old movies on TV, or indulging his recent passion of surfing the Internet, the small screen beginning to win out over the tube.

This was a scheduled day off. Late yesterday, he'd filed a longer story on the body found in the park after gathering information about the deceased, digging into sources more giving than the cops. The murdered man's name was Jeremy Wilcox, age forty-seven, attached to the Canadian embassy in its trade and commerce office. A

43

diplomat. No suspects. Wilcox's father had come from Toronto to claim the body but had been told it would have to remain in Washington until further forensic tests had been conducted. Jeremy Wilcox was single—forty-seven years old and never married. Gay? Not a very enlightened reaction, Potamos knew, but one that came to mind.

Potamos himself had been married twice. Ungay and unhappy.

Wife number one was Patty Kelly, an Irish Catholic ("Don't tell me," Potamos had said when they met) with fair skin, blazing green eyes, and a field of freckles splashed across her pretty cheeks. Potamos had just graduated from New York University with a degree in journalism, a proud moment in the Potamos family. His father owned a quintessentially Greek diner in Queens and routinely told customers that his son, Joseph, was about to win a Pulitzer Prize even though he hadn't landed his first job.

When he brought Patty Kelly home to meet the folks, his father awarded him no prizes. He took him out in the yard and said, "If you marry someone who is not Greek, you are no longer my son." He maintained that posture through two grandchildren, although Potamos's mother and two sisters kept in touch.

Joe and Patty tried marriage counseling before officially calling it quits. The sessions with the female therapist, six in all, found each of the warring parties expressing opinions about why the marriage wasn't working. For Patty, it was Joe's love of his job to the exclusion of her and the children, his family's dislike of her, even his disinterest in dressing better. Joe's take on the failing marriage was Patty's lack of interest in sex, her hatred of his family, her choice of friends, and her harping on how he dressed. By the sixth session, the therapist came to the conclusion that they'd be better off separating and divorcing, although she refrained from suggesting it. Just another case of two people who shouldn't have married each other in the first place.

Patty became a Unitarian-Universalist before the divorce, which salved her Catholic guilt. Joe's father softened when they divorced, although it became Potamos's mother's turn to be anguished when Patty moved to Boston and visits with the grandchildren became less frequent.

Things settled down in Potamos's life until he fell in love with Linda, a bright, vibrant, intense, occasionally hysterical Jewish woman who worked as a secretary at the CIA. That marriage lasted four months after he discovered she was cheating on him. That her lover was another secretary at the agency named Gertrude gave Potamos a certain comfort; at least he hadn't lost out to another guy. The divorce was routine and quick, without kids to complicate things as there had been in marriage number one.

When his father was diagnosed with terminal cancer and told he had no more than six months to live, he summoned Joe to New York and handed him a check for $100,000: "Take it now. It makes no sense to wait until I'm dead."

Potamos used the money to buy his one-bedroom Rosslyn condo. On the day he closed on it, he made a silent pledge: He'd never marry again. So far, so good, although there were times with Roseann when his resolve threatened to wilt. She was good-looking—but weren't they all?—slender and small breasted, with long, strong fingers, a pianist's hands. She wore her blue-black hair short and swept back at the sides, exposing the graceful line of a lovely neck. Her makeup was applied with a deft hand, just enough to add the proper touch of color to her naturally pale face. Well, maybe someday ... maybe not.

Although he'd buried his head beneath the pillow to muffle the incessant one-two-three rhythm of the waltzes, he heard the phone ring. Roseann entered the bedroom. "It's for you, Joe. Gil Gardello." Gardello was Potamos's editor at the *Post*.

Potamos moaned as he kicked Jumper off his legs, dragged himself from bed, and went to the phone in the kitchen.

"Yeah?"

"Joe, you hear about the plane that went down in New York?"

"No."

"Was DC bound. Locals on board. No survivors."

"Gee, I'm really sorry to hear that. What the hell does it have to do with me?"

"As soon as we get a passenger list, I want you to contact family members, get their reactions."

"Jesus! What's this—TV time? You want me to ask some wife how she feels about her old man dying in a plane wreck?"

"Be subtle, gentle."

"Not me, Gil. Send some breathless intern."

"Be here in an hour, Joe."

"I'm not asking those questions."

"An hour. Better still, a half hour. No point in washing up, the way you dress." Gardello hung up.

Roseann, still in a film of nightgown, returned to the piano.

"I got to go," Potamos said.

"On your day off?" she said, still playing. "Sorry."

"At least I won't have to hear you play those apple strudel songs."

Her response was to play louder and with greater

flourishes. He closed the bathroom door, showered, got dressed in his fashion, and left the apartment to the strains of "Wine, Women and Song."

6

Within an hour, hundreds of people had converged on the area where the Dash 8 aircraft had crashed after taking off from Westchester County airport. State and local police, airport and airline personnel, volunteer fire departments, ambulance corps technicians, elected village officials, and Special Agent Frank Lazzara and his three colleagues looked out over what had once been a tranquil wooded area a hundred yards from the reservoir. A police helicopter hovered low overhead, its incessant chopping sound making conversation difficult.

There was understandable confusion. Lazzara had been alerted that the NTSB contingent would be arriving shortly. Unless there was suspicion that the plane had been brought down by a criminal act, NTSB would control the scene and the ensuing investigation.

But in the absence of NTSB officials, Lazzara took charge, ordering uniformed police to further secure the area as far up as where the troopers who'd originally answered the call had parked their vehicles, and instructing medical and fire personnel to search for survivors, no matter what. There was always a chance. Those earthquake victims buried under rubble until—

His cell phone rang.

"Lazzara."

"Frank, it's Will." Wilfred Fellows, Lazzara's second in command at the White Plains office, had been out of the office when the call came to head for the crash scene. "I think you ought to know there's a third plane down."

Lazzara was speechless.

"California, outside San Francisco. San Jose. A commuter plane like the others. There's an eyewitness to it. . . . You there, Frank?"

"Yeah, I'm here. Three. This eyewitness. Credible?"

"I don't know. A woman. I just got a call from the San Francisco office."

"What's she say?"

"She claims she saw something hit the plane after it took off."

"Something hit it? Like what? Another plane? An asteroid?"

"That's what they told me. Thought you'd want to know."

"Yeah, thanks. We'll need more agents here. It's thickening up. Call Manhattan, get them to dispatch some."

"Shall do."

Lazzara pushed the off button and slipped the small phone into his jacket pocket. As far as he was concerned, the question of whether there was criminal involvement was now a no-brainer. Had the Dash 8 been the only plane down that day, he would have been slow to come to that conclusion, and would have taken NTSB's lead once its officials had made their preliminary evaluation.

But the Dash 8 hadn't been the only commuter aircraft to fall from the skies that morning. Two others had. There had to be a connection among the three. *Had to be.* Only a naive fool would even consider the possibility that three well-maintained, professionally piloted commercial aircraft had, within four hours, in good weather (if Westchester was any indication that morning), fallen to earth due to natural causes—mechanical failure, pilot error, air traffic control mistakes, metal fatigue, fuel tank explosion, or other noncriminal causes of aircraft falling from the sky.

He wasn't happy with what Fellows had told him about the California eyewitness. He hadn't worked aircraft accidents before, but having followed every aspect of the TWA 800 accident over Long Island, he was well aware that the missile theorists, for example, were less than credible—a generous lay psychological evaluation.

A young volunteer fireman came up to him. "There's nobody alive," he said.

"What's that?" Lazzara asked, referring to something the firefighter held.

"A necklace. Found it over there." He pointed. "Must have belonged to a passenger." He handed it to Lazzara, who fingered the four-leaf clover.

"A good luck charm," Lazzara said grimly. "Some luck." He handed it back to the firefighter—"Give this to the NTSB people"—and turned as several men arrived. They wore blue windbreakers with NTSB emblazoned in yellow on the back.

"Frank Lazzara, FBI," the special agent said, extending his hand to the leader.

"O'Connell, NTSB, Parsippany. Any survivors?"

"Negative so far. I'm afraid it'll be negative forever."

O'Connell looked back up the trail he and his people had used to reach the scene. "We'll need a bulldozer to widen that out, get a road down here."

The mayor of a nearby village overheard the comment and said, "I'll arrange it right away."

Lazzara took O'Connell aside. "You'll be heading the investigation?" he asked.

"No. Pete Mullin from Washington should be here any minute."

"You've heard about the other two," Lazzara said.

"Yeah."

"There's got to be a link."

O'Connell shrugged. "To be determined."

"Got to be," Lazzara repeated. "What were the other planes?"

"Another Dash 8 in Boise, a Saab 34 in San Jose."

"Saab? Like the car?"

"Yeah. A commuter plane operated by a regional carrier."

"Survivors?"

"None reported."

Lazzara pondered whether to mention the eyewitness report. O'Connell spared him that decision. "An eyewitness in California says she saw something hit the Saab shortly after takeoff."

"I heard that. Play for you?"

Another shrug.

Peter Mullin and his experts came down the narrow hiking trail, followed by volunteers from the Westchester Red Cross office. Mullin had been glad to see them. Having investigated dozens of aircraft accident scenes, his respect for the Red Cross and its support was unbridled. Sometimes, it was only the coffee and encouraging good cheer dispensed by the dedicated volunteers that kept him and his people going through the night.

Mullin was greeted by O'Connell, who introduced Lazzara to the lead investigator.

"Any witnesses?" Mullin asked.

"Not that I know of," Lazzara said. "We have more agents coming from the city. I told the local police to start canvassing houses in the area."

"Good."

The combined NTSB teams from Parsippany and Washington fanned out to examine those areas of the wreckage of particular interest to them, taking pictures as they went. EMS personnel brought the first empty body bags down the hiking trail, and a pastor from a local church arrived on the scene. Mullin thanked the clergyman for coming, but told him he'd have to bestow any blessings from a distance. No one not directly involved in the investigation was allowed beyond the perimeter established by uniformed officers.

Lazzara trailed after Mullin as he slowly, cautiously walked among the twisted, charred wreckage and bodies and body parts, which seemed to Lazzara the product of the bizarre and warped imagination of a macabre performance artist—meant to shock rather than inspire. They stood side by side and looked down at a teddy bear spotted with blood.

"Kids are the worst," Mullin said.

"Yeah. I have one. A year old."

Mullin turned at the sound of his name. Two state troopers new to the scene stood at the foot of the trail. Between them was a fisherman wearing a tan fishing vest with multiple pockets over a tan shirt with still more pockets.

"Who's this?" Mullin asked a trooper.

"He says he saw the accident."

"You did, sir?" Mullin asked.

"Yes, I did," Al Lester said. His round face was flushed with excitement and anxiety, and he spoke rapidly. "I saw it happen. I was out in my boat—"

"Maybe we should go someplace else to hear what the gentleman has to say," Lazzara suggested.

Mullin nodded, and he and Lazzara led Lester up the trail to a small break in the trees.

"Now, sir," Mullin said, "tell us what you saw."

Lester looked back and forth between the two men and frowned.

"I'm Peter Mullin, from the National Transportation Safety Board," Mullin said, realizing that an introduction was needed. "This is FBI Agent Lazzara."

Lazzara extended his hand to Lester. "Frank Lazzara, special agent in charge of the White Plains office." Lester took it, did the same with Mullin's.

"I was out in my boat. I fish most every day, bass mostly, sometimes trout—depends on what lure I use, things like that."

"I do some fishing myself," Mullin said. "You saw what happened to the plane?"

"Yes, I did. Oh, yes, I certainly did."

Lazzara and Mullin waited for him to continue.

"It blew up right where the wing joins with the body. What do you call it, the fuselage?"

"Yes," Mullin said.

"Plane took off right over my boat. It's a canoe, actually, an old aluminum one. Grumman canoe. They don't make them anymore."

"And?"

"I watched the plane all the way. I guess I always watch 'em taking off 'cause I don't like the noise. I watched him all the way until . . . until it blew up."

"You say it blew up," Mullin said. "What side of the plane?"

Lester maneuvered his body to come up with the proper angle. "It was—let's see, it was the left side of the plane. He was making a left turn, it looked like to me. Yes, it was the left side."

"There was an explosion?" Lazzara asked.

"Yes, sir, right where the wing fits into the fuselage."

"How large an explosion?"

53

"Pretty big. Well, not so big, maybe, but pretty big, big enough to knock the wing off."

"What color was the explosion?" Mullin asked.

"Red, yellow. I told the troopers about the missile I saw."

Lazzara and Mullin looked at each other.

"I know," said Lester, "I probably sound like some nut who doesn't know what he saw. Well, I don't see things, and my eyesight is pretty damn good. It was a missile or something like a missile that went up and hit the plane."

"Did you see where it came from?" Lazzara asked.

"Not really; from the woods somewhere."

"You're absolutely positive that you saw a missile come from the woods and hit the plane?" Mullin said.

"Yes, sir. That's what I saw."

Lazzara said, "Mr. Lester, who else have you told about this?"

"Nobody, not even my wife. I was going to call her but I saw the troopers after I came up from the water and told them. They brought me right here."

"So you told the troopers about the missile?"

"Yes, sir."

"And no one else."

"No, just you two gentlemen."

Lazzara glanced at Mullin before saying, "Mr. Lester, I'm going to arrange for you to be taken to a . . . to a command post where we can discuss this further." To Mullin he said, "Has a command post been established?"

"The airport, a vacant hangar."

"We'll take you there, Mr. Lester. We can talk better. That okay with you?"

"I'd better call Nancy."

"Your wife?"

"Yes."

"You can do that, but you can't tell her what you saw this morning."

"Why not?"

"Just procedure, sir. You can tell her tonight after we've gotten your official statement."

"I suppose I don't have any choice."

Lazzara didn't reply.

They escorted Lester to where two of Lazzara's colleagues stood. Lazzara instructed them to take the witness to the airport and stay with him in the hangar that was being used as a command post. Before they left, he said, "Mr. Lester will want to call his wife. That's fine, but he knows he's not to tell her anything about what he saw." He turned to Lester. "Why not just tell your wife that you witnessed the plane accident, are giving a statement to the police, and that you'll be home later in the day?" The agents nodded; they understood that what Lazzara said was, in fact, an order.

Mullin and Lazzara watched them leave.

"Two eyewitnesses, in two different accidents, claim missiles brought down the planes," Lazzara said.

"Doesn't mean it's true," Mullin said. "We had hundreds of witnesses who claimed they saw a missile hit TWA 800. They were all wrong."

"That was one plane. This involves two, on two coasts. You aren't ruling out the criminal element, are you?"

"It's on the table along with every other probable cause, but until there's some confirmation, I'd prefer it not be bandied about in the press."

"No argument from me, but that's wishful thinking. How do you want to handle the interview with our fisherman friend?"

"Do it jointly, get it down officially."

"Okay. Ready?"

"No. Hold him for a few hours. I can't leave here yet."

Lazzara walked away. Mullin started back to where his team was examining wreckage, and where EMS was removing the first of the bodies. His expert on metals was on his knees looking closely at a shaft of metal three feet in length and a few inches wide.

"What's that?" Mullin asked.

"Not sure, Pete, but it's not part of the plane. There's a smaller, similar piece over there."

"No idea what it is, where it came from?"

"Could be a piece of a weapon of some sort."

"Weapon?"

"Yeah."

"A missile?"

The metals expert looked up at Mullin and winced. "I'm no missile expert, Pete. But I'd say it's a possibility."

7

Mike McQuaid, special assistant to the president of the United States—on terrorism—prepared to leave the Situation Room on the first floor of the White House. He hadn't wasted time changing into more formal clothing after receiving the FBI call at his Maryland home. He wore the same khaki pants and red-and-white-striped short-sleeve shirt he'd had on when the call came through. He'd spent the past fifteen minutes calling members of CSG, the Coordinating Security Group on terrorism, setting up a video teleconference between the involved agencies—the State Department, the Joint Chiefs, Secret Service, the Pentagon, and Justice. Because aircraft were involved, the FAA was included on the list.

"Mike, the president wants you," an aide said after answering a phone.

"Keep things moving," McQuaid said.

He was ushered into the Oval Office, where Anthony Cammanati paced.

"Everyone in the loop?" Cammanati asked. National Security Advisor Cammanati was a squarely built man with heavy black eyebrows and a permanently creased, broad forehead. His physical appearance, including his navy-blue suit, white shirt, and tie, set him apart from the fair-skinned, redheaded, slender, casually dressed McQuaid.

"In the works," McQuaid replied.

Both men straightened as Lawrence Ashmead, president of the United States, entered the room. The door was closed behind him and he went directly to his desk. As usual, he was in shirtsleeves, wide, red suspenders, and a nondescript blue tie. Ashmead was known as a hands-on president, less statesmanlike and presidential than his predecessor. To a fault, some on his staff felt: He'd been governor of Missouri before capturing the White House, and ran things too much like a governor, micromanaging rather than viewing the proverbial larger picture. But he was liked and respected by most; those who'd ended up on the receiving end of a sizable temper were the exception.

He looked at McQuaid and Cammanati with probing eyes. "So, tell me," he said.

McQuaid brought him up to speed on the three aviation accidents, using half-formed sentences, the bulleted approach he knew Ashmead preferred.

". . . spoken with all the involved agencies, Mr. President. Vice Chairman Poe at NTSB confirms two eyewitness claims—missiles hitting the planes, California and New York—but no tangible evidence. The lead investigator . . ." he consulted his notes ". . . Peter Mullin—they found metal fragments at the New York scene that could have come from a missile—on their way to the Pentagon for analysis. FBI agents on the scene in New York confirm the eyewitness account."

"Confirm it! It *was* a missile?"

"No, sir, sorry. They confirm that the New York eyewitness *claims* he saw a missile hit the aircraft."

"What about Idaho?"

"No eyewitnesses there, sir."

"What's the possible link between them?" Ashmead asked, more of himself than the others. "If those three planes were shot down by missiles, there has to be a reason. Who was on them?"

"We don't have passenger lists yet, sir," McQuaid said. "They're being officially withheld until next of kin are notified. We're working with the airlines."

"Government officials on the planes? Businessmen from the same industry? Scientists? Mobsters in witness protection? Somebody with a new insurance policy for a couple of million? Christ, people don't target three planes in three different parts of the country—and on the same day—unless there's some common denominator."

"We'll know more when we have passenger names and backgrounds, Mr. President."

"How much of the missile theory has gotten out?"

"The press? The FBI and NTSB are keeping a lid on the eyewitnesses, but it's already been leaked."

"How? Where?"

"CNN. They went with the rumor story ten minutes ago."

"How'd they get it?"

Shrugs from McQuaid and Cammanati.

Ashmead punched a button on his phone: "Send Chris in here."

A minute later Ashmead's press secretary, Chris Targa, entered.

"What's being reported on the aviation accidents?" the president asked.

"It's the lead story, Mr. President. No surprise, with three commercial planes down the same morning. Got to be a first."

Cammanati started to ask something of Targa but stopped.

"The missile theory," Ashmead filled in, not prone to keeping things from his press secretary as were other presidents. "Are they talking about eyewitnesses saying they saw missiles hit the planes?"

"CNN is, sir, but they're couching it. 'Unconfirmed reports,' 'alleged sightings,' that sort of thing."

"What kind of planes were they?" the president asked. "All the same make and model?"

"No, sir," McQuaid answered, again referring to notes. "Two Canadian-made Dash 8s, one Saab 34, Swedish-made. Three different airlines."

"So whoever shot missiles at them wasn't out to cripple a particular aircraft manufacturer or airline."

"Evidently not, sir," said McQuaid.

The president asked to be kept abreast of any news reports playing up the missile allegations, and dismissed Targa and McQuaid. Alone now with Cammanati, who'd been a boyhood friend, Ashmead sat back and twisted his mustache—he was the first man with facial hair to sit in the White House since Teddy Roosevelt. "It's terrorists, isn't it, Tony? There can't be any other explanation."

"I'm afraid you're right, sir, and if it's a foreign group, state sponsored, we've got a war on our hands."

"Call a meeting." Ashmead looked at his watch. "Six this evening. Appropriate Cabinet members, FBI, Justice, our counterterrorism people."

"Poe from NTSB?" Cammanati asked.

"Sure, but it looks like a criminal act. FBI's show now."

"The Bureau and State's counterterrorist people are meeting as we speak, sir."

"Good. Coordinate this effort, Tony. Assemble a team. Use anybody you need, pull 'em off whatever they're doing. That's from me."

"Yes, sir."

Max Pauling was running late. He entered the huge, square, nondescript, singularly unattractive government-issue gray box known as the State Department from C Street, passed through the Diplomatic Lobby, displayed his credentials to the security guard, and went directly to Walter Barton's—*Colonel* Walter Barton's—office in Room 2507.

"They're meeting in Room 3524," a Barton aide said immediately.

Pauling bounded up a back stairway and went into the small conference room where his jingoistic boss and a dozen others had gathered.

"Max," Barton said as Pauling took a folding chair and pulled it up to one of two tables already occupied. "Now that we're all here, let me brief everyone on what's known to date. Three commercial aircraft down, the incidents occurring within hours of each other. Locations—Westchester County, New York; San Jose, California; and Boise, Idaho. Passenger fatalities, thirty-six in New York, thirty-one in California, and eleven in Idaho—seventy-eight in all. Plus a crew of three on each aircraft. Cause of accidents unknown. Eyewitnesses claim to have seen missiles hit the planes."

"In all three incidents?" someone asked.

"No, in California and New York. No eyewitnesses in Idaho, at least that we know of."

Pauling said, "If there's any truth to these eyewitness sightings, we've got terrorists armed with missiles, an internal enemy nation or rogue group within a friendly nation. I understand all three aircraft were taking off when they came apart."

Barton turned to an assistant who'd been monitoring preliminary reports from NTSB. "Correct," she said.

"They knew something about flying," Pauling said, "positioned themselves upwind, knew planes always take off into the wind." He sat back and focused on his thoughts while others tossed about theories. These missile-toting terrorists weren't amateurs, not with what the missiles must have cost. They went for premium prices on the black market, no holiday sales at Kmart.

The meeting was interrupted by a senior advisor to the secretary of state, who drew Barton aside. "Cammanati just called, Colonel. The president's holding a meeting at six. Secretary Rock will be attending. She wants a briefing at five-thirty before she heads over there."

"Okay," Barton said.

Barton's aide assigned to monitor NTSB returned to the room. "NTSB just got a report from its Denver office on the Boise incident," she said. "Fragments found at the scene point to the use of a missile. Evidence is being flown in as we speak."

"What do we know about the missiles?" Pauling asked. "American Stingers, foreign-made?"

Barton shrugged. "I'm meeting with Harris at the Bureau at three. I'll know more then." Harris was Barton's counterpart at the FBI's counterterrorism division. "In the meantime, we're on twenty-four-hour alert. Coordinate your movements through Ops. Nothing for the press. *Nothing!*"

"Does the president or Secretary plan to make a public statement?" Barton was asked.

He ignored the question. "Let's get cracking."

Pauling watched the others in the room get up and head for their respective offices. Since coming over to State from the CIA, he'd been impressed with the organizational structure and smooth teamwork within the agency's departments. There was a more clearly defined chain of command and a smoother interplay between departments than he'd experienced at the Company. He wasn't quite as sanguine about some of the larger political and diplomatic decisions made at the top, like the gloved-hand approach to nations run by dictators and deemed important, at times, to America's foreign policy, while a harder line was taken with countries whose loyalty to the American diplomatic agenda was solid.

But lofty decisions weren't part of Pauling's job description. Before this new assignment, he'd been an agent, an operative, a "spook," and loved it. Why wouldn't he? You were sent on an assignment, handed enough untraceable cash to buy a small country—or at least its leader— and instructed to tell no one where you'd be or how long you'd be there.

"I'm leaving tomorrow on an assignment, Doris."

"Where are you going? How long will you be gone?"

"Can't say."

There was the requisite icy stare as you packed your bag in the bedroom where you'd made love the night before. The kids asked, too, where Daddy was going, and you answered with a pat on the head when they were little. Once they got older, they didn't bother asking because they knew there wouldn't be an answer.

Hugs and kisses when you were leaving. A modicum of guilt, tempered by the excitement of the assignment, another important one, national security, defending their way of life, someone has to do it—plenty of rationalizations at the ready. The waves good-bye—"I'll be in touch"—when you knew you probably wouldn't be. Then, the relief when you were on your way, alone, pumped up, anxious to do what you'd trained for and were good at. Of course he loved it, like almost every other spook.

Now, since coming to Washington, he spent most of his time behind a desk in the Department of State analyzing information gathered by a variety of sources, including people doing what he'd happily done while in Moscow and elsewhere, and filling in gaps from his personal experience and knowledge. As far as he was concerned, he'd been booted upstairs, and was in the process of giving credence to the Peter Principle.

He wandered down to Room 2109, the nerve center for State's public affairs and press operations, where a bank of television monitors were tuned round-the-clock to CNN and MSNBC. All personnel there were also on a twenty-four-hour cycle, tearing stories off the wire service machines, taping relevant TV news and other reports, and at the moment fielding calls from the press and the public about the unfolding story of three aircraft crashing that morning.

"Can you believe it?" a young PA employee said, pointing to one of the monitors:

"CNN has learned from a highly placed source that the planes were shot down by missiles launched from the ground near the three airports. The president, we're told, has scheduled a meeting of Cabinet members and other top administration officials. Meanwhile, the FBI's antiterrorism unit has issued an alert to state and local law enforcement officials across the country to put into effect contingency plans formulated following the World Trade Center and Oklahoma City bombings, and airports have elevated their security systems to top-readiness status. Stay tuned for further information as CNN receives it."

Two of the networks had broken into their normal afternoon programming to issue brief reports on the situation, but had gone back to their soap operas. The third network ended its breaking news with soft drink and feminine hygiene commercials.

"Who the hell would do such a thing?" the young woman said, shaking her head. "They killed innocent civilians and kids, people minding their own business—or too young to have any business."

Pauling's beeper went off. It was Barton. He left the press area and went back to the office. Barton held up his hand to keep Pauling from entering, wrapped up his meeting, then waved Pauling in.

"Any new information?" Pauling asked.

"Close the door."

Pauling did as instructed and returned to the visitor's side of the desk. Barton stood behind it, erect, stomach flat, chin jutting, hair perfectly trimmed to conform to his temples.

"Got your bags packed, Max?"

"Haven't unpacked yet. I flew up to visit my ex-wife and sons."

"I'm not talking overnight. I want you in Moscow."

"Would it be out of order to ask why?"

"The missile fragments from the Westchester incident arrived at the Pentagon, although the FBI's labs did the testing. Took them a half hour to determine it's Russian-made, a SAM, probably an older model of the Grail SA-7."

"Those missiles were introduced, what, more than thirty years ago."

"I thought you might appreciate things improving with age, Max."

Pauling smiled. Barton had his cute moments. "The Russians are shooting down our commuter airlines with nearly obsolete missiles?" Pauling said.

"Somebody is, and if this initial evaluation holds up, they're using weapons out of the old Soviet Union."

Pauling lowered himself into a chair and slowly,

pointedly exhaled. "Same with the other two accidents?" he asked Barton, who'd relaxed into parade rest, adopting what would pass as a starched slouch.

"Undetermined as yet."

"What do you want me to do in Moscow?"

"Be there in case you're needed."

"Just 'be there'?"

"On hand. First, pick up on some of your former contacts with Russian businessmen, more specifically, arms dealers."

"What makes you think Russian arms dealers sold these particular missiles, Colonel? Thousands of vintage Grail missiles have been manufactured and sold to every dictator, so-called freedom fighter, and head case in the world. They could have come from anywhere."

"And there's usually a trail. With bits of paper. What's the saying—'Follow the money'?"

"What about domestic terrorist groups?" Pauling asked. "No one's taken credit for the attack?"

"If the Bureau knows, it's not sharing it with us—yet."

"Who do I report to in Moscow?"

"Your old friend, Lerner."

"At the embassy?"

"You're back wearing your trade and commerce hat, which should make you happy. You've been grousing ever since you got here about sitting behind a desk. No one knows how this event is going to play out, Max. Whether the planes were brought down as part of a conspiracy by a domestic terrorist group, or this represents the actions of a foreign power, the ramifications are immense, especially if it involves the Russians. If those missiles came out of Russia, and their so-called government played any role, no matter how tangential, Congress and the administration will want blood."

"The Russian government may be screwed up big-time, Colonel, but it's not dumb enough to sanction the sale of missiles to terrorist organizations here."

"Of course not, but those missiles had to find a way out of the country. A skid somewhere had to have been greased. First task: Find out who greased it."

Pauling stood and went to the door, turned, and said, "You're right, Colonel. I hate sitting behind a desk. I'll send you a postcard. I'll leave right away."

"No, Max, check in with Tom Hoctor at the CIA first."

"Hoctor? I thought I was reporting to Bill Lerner."

"You are, but Hoctor's running the show from here. I spoke with him an hour ago. He expects you at Langley at ten tomorrow morning. You'll get a briefing from the missile guys, the arms trade, the rundown on what's been going on in Russia recently."

"There hasn't been any good information coming out of Moscow since I left."

"Your modesty is overwhelming, Pauling."

"Anyone *else* I'll be working for? I don't like reporting to a committee."

"Ten in the morning, at Langley. Thanks for coming in."

"Wouldn't have missed it."

8

That Afternoon
George Washington University

Jessica Mumford tried to get her students in post-Soviet Russian-U.S. relations back on track but was losing the battle. By the time they'd arrived at the three o'clock class in GW's School of Diplomacy and International Relations, the only thing on their respective and collective minds were the day's airline tragedies and the unconfirmed reports that missiles had been involved. Professor Mumford could have dictated an end to that discussion and insisted upon returning to the subject of the lecture—the Duma, Russia's lower house, and the new structure of power within it—but she decided doing so would only result in the students missing the salient points of the lecture.

Her fifteen disciples that day proffered many theories, all based upon speculation, an exercise for which Jessica had little patience. Since becoming an adjunct professor of diplomacy and international relations at the university, she'd taught what she believed—that too many of the country's diplomatic decisions and actions or inactions were rooted in supposition and conjecture, rather than formulated from verifiable international reality. Facts!

Focused decision making based upon them. These were her mantras.

When at her full-time job as an analyst specializing in post–Cold War, post–Soviet Russia at the Department of State, she applied that belief to auditing the volumes of information crossing her desk each day. Some of her less methodical colleagues found her approach to be mildly annoying at times, and downright abrasive at others. A Siberian expert in the department once remarked to an associate, "No wonder her husband walked out on her. You say 'I love you' and she'll want to know what you base it on."

"Shame," said his friend. "She's good-looking. I wouldn't mind a little of that myself."

"Probably sex by the book. She's got a computer for a heart."

Jessica was aware of the assorted attitudes but dismissed them. Reacting would, she knew, only dignify them. She also wasn't displeased that there was speculation about her personal life. Let them fantasize how she spent her time away from State, who she had dinner with, what movies she saw and enjoyed, the men she slept with. If compartmentalism was now in vogue in Washington since the Clinton years, she was all for it.

She ended the class a few minutes early and issued an admonition to her students the way a judge would to a sequestered jury being dismissed for the evening: "Don't jump to conclusions until you've heard all the facts. Remember, we don't know whether the planes were downed by missiles. We don't know whether, if they were, the missiles were foreign or domestic. We don't know whether it's organized terrorism or miscellaneous madness. We don't know who or what, only where and when. Why is an even bigger question. One thing no one needs is knee-jerk finger pointing at groups or individuals. See you next week."

As she watched them leave the room, she experienced a sense of pleasure and purpose. Some of them, ideally the best and the brightest, would go on to play important future roles in how the country conducted its relations with other nations—friend, foe, or the conveniently neutral. If she could help shape them into persons who viewed their world realistically, and humanely, her efforts in the classroom would be more than validated.

She packed up and stopped in an office she shared with other adjunct professors. Her boss at State had called earlier that day about the aircraft crashes and told her to be ready to report at any time. She'd mentioned she had a class to teach in the afternoon. "No need to cancel," he'd said. "Now."

Jessica sat down at the nearest phone and quickly dialed his number.

"It's Jessica. I just dismissed my class. Need me?"

"No, but keep your beeper on."

"What's new?"

"Looks like a missile, Jess. Little doubt about it."

"Any suspects?"

"No. I got from Colonel Barton in Counterterrorism that the missiles might be Russian-made, old Soviet SAMs."

"SAMs? Surface-to-air?"

"Uh huh, but that's not official. You'll be at home?"

"I'm heading there now."

After checking her mail, Jessica looked for a cab to take her to her apartment in Columbia Plaza, on Twenty-third Street, almost directly across from the State Department building. Mackensie Smith pulled up in his blue Chevy sedan and rolled down the window. "Jessica," he called, "need a ride?"

"On my way home, Mac."

"Get in."

Mac Smith and his wife, Annabel Reed-Smith, had become Jessica's friends two years ago after Mac delivered a guest lecture on international criminal law to her class. Smith had been a top-flight attorney in Washington until his wife and only child were killed in a head-on collision on the Beltway. He lost his passion for the rough-and-tumble world of the criminal courtroom after that, closed his practice, and joined the faculty of GW's esteemed law school.

Annabel, a matrimonial attorney when she and Mac met, had been toying with the idea of giving up her own practice to open an art gallery specializing in pre-Columbian art, a subject she'd fervently studied since her undergraduate years. With her husband's encouragement, she took down her shingle, found space in Georgetown, and successfully launched her dream.

Because their individual interests and circle of friends cut across many lines, the handsome couple's names appeared frequently on invitation lists, which they carefully parsed to leave themselves enough private time alone to enjoy their new apartment in the Watergate—and to enjoy each other.

Smith had the radio tuned to all-news station WTOP as Jessica got into his car.

"The investigation into fatal crashes of three commercial airliners this morning, including one headed for Washington from New York and carrying an undetermined number of area residents, is continuing. Information from reliable anonymous sources at various agencies gives growing credibility to eyewitness reports of missiles hitting two of the planes shortly after they'd taken off. All three planes were smaller, commuter-type aircraft. The death toll in the three accidents is eighty-seven. The Washington-bound airplane carried thirty-six passengers and a crew of three. The FBI is scheduled to hold a press conference within the hour about this multiple, unprecedented tragedy. We'll bring that to you live. Stay tuned!"

A jazzy recorded promo for the station caused Mac to turn off the radio. "They keep pounding away with what we already know."

"They have all those hours to fill."

"You hear anything new, Jess?"

She considered mentioning what her boss at State had said about the missiles possibly being Russian-made but knew she shouldn't. "No facts," she said. "How's Annabel?"

"Fine. What's your read on the accidents?"

A shrug from Jessica. "Without knowing who was on those planes, it's impossible to conjure a motive. Maybe even knowing that won't provide any answers."

"Missiles," Smith said more to himself than to her as he pulled up in front of the apartment complex. "Shades of TWA 800 and the missile theorists."

"With a big difference, Mac," said Jessica. "In the TWA case, most missile theorists speculated it was an accident, remember? A Navy exercise gone awry. If *three* missiles were used, that's no accident."

"I suppose we'll find out soon enough. Annabel and I are planning a dinner party a few weeks from now. Annie will call. Hope you're free."

"Depends how this crisis plays out, but I'd love to come."

As she was about to get out of the car, a twin-engine commuter plane taking off from Reagan National Airport flew low over them and disappeared from view behind a building.

"I wonder what the passengers on that plane are thinking," Smith said.

"Hopefully, more pleasant thoughts than I'm having," she said. "Thanks for the lift."

"Can I go home now?"

Al Lester sat at a folding table in an empty hangar at Westchester County airport. Dozens of law enforcement, NTSB, and medical personnel milled about. The retired fisherman sighed. Bell Atlantic telephone technicians had installed an emergency bank of phones on another table in a corner of the cavernous building. Across from Lester sat Peter Mullin, NTSB's lead investigator, and FBI Special Agent Frank Lazzara.

"Of course you can go, Mr. Lester," Lazzara said. "You were free to go any time you wanted to."

"I sure didn't feel that way."

"Sorry if we misled you, but you should know that the information you've given us has been valuable," said Mullin. "We do have one request, however."

"Not to talk to anybody," Lester said.

"That's right," Lazzara said. "The press are all over the airport, Mr. Lester, and you know what they're like. They'll take anything you say and twist it, blow it up to suit their own purposes. If it was a missile you saw—"

"That's what I saw," said Lester. "No doubt about it."

"And we don't doubt you," Mullin said. "But it's important that we not get people panicked until we have all the facts, until we really know why the plane crashed."

Lester stood and stretched; his back ached, so did his knee. "I've been hearing what's going on around here," he said. "This wasn't the only plane that went down, right?"

Neither Mullin nor Lazzara responded.

"You don't have to worry about me and the reporters," Lester said. "I don't have any use for them. Buncha lyin' buzzards."

Lazzara laughed, stood, and put his arm around Lester's shoulder. "That's right, Mr. Lester. A bunch of lying buzzards. Keep that in mind when they start asking you questions. I'll have someone drive you home."

"No need. Nancy's somewhere out there waiting for me."

"Well, I'll walk you out and help you find her," Lazzara said, his hand still slung over Lester's shoulder, as if he were a buddy. "Thanks for all your cooperation. Hope you have better luck fishing tomorrow."

Nancy Lester stood by their car a hundred feet from the hangar, behind a barrier of stanchions and orange ropes that had been established to keep bystanders away from the command center. When she saw her husband approaching, accompanied by another man, she came to the rope and waved. A uniformed patrolman stepped in front of her.

"It's okay," Lazzara said, flashing his Bureau badge at the cop, who lifted the rope for them to duck under.

Nancy Lester hugged her husband. "Are you all right, Al? What's happened? Why are you—?"

"I'm fine, Nancy. Oh, this is Agent Lazzara from the FBI."

"FBI? What have you done?"

"I didn't do anything, Nancy. I had to give them a statement, tell them what happened to that plane this morning. I think I probably solved everything for them."

Lazzara smiled. "Your husband's been very helpful, Mrs. Lester. Well, you two get on home and enjoy some dinner. Nice meeting you, ma'am. Good night, Al. Pleasure meeting you."

Lazzara watched them walk hip-to-hip to the car, Al Lester's arm about his wife. The agent smiled. Nice guy, nice couple. They reminded him of his own mother and father.

His pleasant reverie was short-lived. He returned to the hangar, where things distinctly not as pleasant were taking place, including the arrival of the dismembered bodies of the passengers and crew of the Dash 8.

9

Jessica kicked off her shoes as she came through the door of her apartment and dropped her heavy briefcase on her way to the bedroom. She quickly got out of her pale yellow linen suit, mauve blouse, slip, and panty hose, pulled on a crinkled purple-and-pink lightweight jogging suit, and went to the second bedroom, which functioned as a home office. The digital readout on her answering machine indicated two messages. She listened to the first: "Jess, it's Cindy. I'm in shock over what's happened to those planes. You must be, too. Give me a call when you get in. Dying to talk about this weekend. Weather's supposed to be magnificent."

Jessica returned the call.

"You're back," her friend said. "Your teaching day?"

"Yup, although I didn't get much teaching done. All they wanted to talk about were the aviation accidents."

"Accidents?" Cindy said. "Try murder."

"I'm not sure—"

"Some sick fiends shot them down with missiles."

"About this weekend, Cindy, I'll have to play it by ear."

"Because of the missiles?"

76

"Yeah, because of the missiles. We're on twenty-four-hour call."

"You've *got* to make it, Jess. Perfect weather. It's rained the past two weekends. Horace called me last night. He was out at the Maryland shore yesterday and says he saw a least bittern."

"Really? That's an unusual sighting, almost as unusual as the piping plover."

"I won't take no for an answer about the weekend, Jess. Everyone's going to be there."

"I'll try, Cindy. Have to run. Other calls to return."

Jessica leaned back in her office chair and allowed her gaze to play over the wall above the desk. It was covered with color pictures of birds she'd photographed on ornithologic trips over the years. An inveterate bird-watcher and, in recent years, photographer, she had been searching for rare species since she was a teen growing up with her parents and two brothers in New Hampshire. Hers was, as her mother often said, a "bird-friendly home"—a half-dozen feeders hung from nearby trees, and an especially large one was suspended right outside the kitchen window. Jessica watched the comings and goings of dozens of varieties of birds the way other teens watched television, fascinated with their habits and mannerisms, their alertness, their distinctive songs and sounds, and the frantic flapping of wings when vying for perch space.

In springtime, the birdhouses her father built became homes for new families of birds—wrens and finches and English sparrows. Once, a nesting pair of Baltimore orioles, who'd ventured farther north than Jessica's well-worn bird book said was normal, arrived and built their drooping nest in a large elm in the backyard. Jessica spent hours watching them create their home and feed their young, carefully noting everything through powerful binoculars bought for her as a birthday present.

She'd carried her love of birds into her adult life, finding time at college to spend days in the fields and woods, binoculars and camera ever-present around her neck, her bird book (a new one given to her as a high school graduation gift) in the large pocket of a safari jacket she always wore when enjoying her hobby. There was a time when she considered pursuing a career in biology or ornithology, but a parallel fascination with geography, history, and current events tipped the scale in favor of an undergraduate degree in history, a master's in diplomacy, and a serious stab at a Ph.D. in international relations; she was a thesis away from being granted it.

These days, working and living in Washington, DC, her most treasured personal time was spent out of the city searching for birds she'd not spotted before and that would be checked off in her book (another new one as a college graduation present). And there were trips to other parts of the country with a national bird-watching group to which she belonged.

The unpleasant realization that she would not be out with her friends that weekend caused her to frown as she went to the kitchen and poured herself a glass of grapefruit juice and turned on a small TV set on the counter. It was tuned to CNN; the FBI press conference had just begun. The agency's director, a former judge who didn't look old enough to head the nation's preeminent law enforcement agency, was introduced and stepped to the cluster of microphones. He spoke bluntly and without emotion.

"This morning, three civilian airliners crashed in three different parts of the country. It is an unprecedented event in the history of domestic commercial aviation. The crashes occurred in New York, California, and Idaho. A full and thorough investigation by all involved agencies is under way to determine the causes of these crashes. The Federal Bureau of Investigation is working closely with officials from the National Transportation Safety Board in this effort.

"As is generally the case in the early stages of such an investigation, unsubstantiated rumors are floated, and unsupported conclusions are reached before the facts are brought to light. Every lead, no matter how seemingly insignificant, will be examined, and every avenue of investigation, involving every appropriate investigatory agency, will be pursued.

"Thank you."

Reporters hurled a barrage of questions as the director stepped away from the mikes. His place was taken by a public affairs spokesman: "Please understand that because the investigation is in such an early stage, it would be inappropriate to attempt to answer your questions at this time."

One especially loud reporter shouted, "Why is the FBI holding this press conference and not the NTSB?"

The Bureau spokesman stopped, turned, seemed about to reply, then left the platform, trailed by a cacophony of other questions.

Jessica snapped off the set. The answer was obvious: It must have already been established that criminal acts were involved in the plane crashes. That put the Bureau squarely in charge.

She went to the living room, stretched out on the couch, and closed her eyes. The ringing phone woke her.

"Hello?"

"Jessica? I was getting worried about you."

"Why?"

"I left a message. When you didn't call I—"

"Mea culpa. I got your message and forgot to call back. I was watching the FBI press conference."

"So was I. I've been in meetings about it."

"I don't wonder. What's new?"

"Nothing you haven't heard on TV. Look, I'm heading out of town in a few days, not sure how long I'll be away. How about dinner tonight?"

"I'm on call, but there's always my trusty beeper, provided the restaurant hasn't banned them along with cell phones."

"In DC? Nah. Primi Piatti? Seven?"

"Sounds good. Where are you going?"

"I'll fill you in at dinner. Seen any new birds lately?"

"I'll save that for dinner, too."

Celia Watson sat sobbing on a couch in the living room of the home she'd shared for more than thirty years with her husband, Wally—she preferred to call him Walter and always had—and their two daughters and a son. The call informing her that her husband had, in fact, been among the fatalities on the plane that crashed outside Westchester County airport had come only five minutes ago. It perhaps shouldn't have been such a shock for her. She knew he was scheduled to catch that particular flight because he'd called from the airport. But there was always that chance, wasn't there, that something had caused him to miss the flight? She'd heard stories like that before.

But while there had been time to accept the likelihood that he'd gone down with the plane, hearing it officially was very different. She cried into her twenty-year-old son's shoulder, saying over and over, "Why, why, why?"

Joe Potamos had been called by his editor on his cell phone once the names of passengers on the downed

Dash 8 had been released and told to get to the Watson home for a statement. He sat in his car for a long time in front of the nicely maintained middle-class house on a pretty street in northern Virginia. He considered calling Gardello back at the *Post* and telling him he wasn't about to ask any widow how she felt about her husband burning up in a plane crash. But that would have been impetuous; one of the things his anger management counselor kept repeating was that Potamos had to gain control of his hasty nature.

He looked in his rearview mirror and saw a remote truck from a TV station pull up, which prompted him to get out of the car, go up the walkway bordered by pansies and impatiens and marigolds, pause at the door, then knock. A young man answered.

"Look," Potamos said, "I'm really sorry to intrude on you and the family in this moment of intense grief and pain, but I'm Joe Potamos from the *Post* and I was wondering whether you or Mrs. Watson would like to make a statement."

"You've got to be joking," the son said.

"Hey, I know this is an imposition but I'm just doing my job. What's the . . . what's the mood here?"

"You creep, you sadistic son of a bitch," the son said, and slammed the door in Potamos's face.

He returned to his car, started it, thought, Sometimes I hate this job. But it's nice to be hated. He mouthed an opening line to the story: "The mood at the Watson family's home was joyous and happy, like a celebration. 'We finally got rid of the fat, old bastard, and can live like kings off the insurance.' "

Bile stung his throat. He spit out the window, pulled away, and headed back to the District.

* * *

". . . and so Jessica was waiting for a cab and I drove her home."

Mac Smith was with his wife, Annabel, on the terrace of their Watergate apartment. The sun was setting over the Potomac, creating a warm orange glow to the end of a sunny yet emotionally gray day in the nation's capital. Their Great Dane, Rufus, slept at their feet.

"How is she?" Annabel asked, sipping from the Gibson Mac had made.

"Seemed fine. We talked about the plane crashes and this rumor about missiles bringing them down."

"Still just rumor? I haven't caught up on the news."

"Evidently."

"I like Jessica," Annabel said. "Shame how her marriage to that FBI guy worked out, or didn't. I wonder if she ever sees him."

"Not something I'd ask," said Mac. "Probably not. He was an undercover specialist, remember?"

"Sure, I do. The last time I saw her, which was a month ago or so, she said she was seeing someone from the State Department."

"Work is the best place to meet someone, they say."

"We didn't meet at work."

He chuckled. "Probably wouldn't have liked each other if we had. When you told me you were a lawyer, too, at that embassy party, I thought, What a shame."

"Why?"

"I never liked lawyers."

"I'm glad you didn't hold it against me."

"So am I. Besides, you weren't like most lawyers. Is Jessica still roaming the hills and meadows?"

"Yes. She talked about birds a lot more than the guy from State she's seeing. It's such a passion with her."

"Maybe that's what happened with her first marriage.

82

It's not that passion is for the birds, but maybe she felt too much passion for them, not enough for her husband."

"Mac, that's unworthy of you."

"Just speculating. Another drink?"

"Thanks, no. Oh, look." She pointed at a bird that flew by the terrace. "How pretty. I'm crazy about birds."

"Don't start."

She giggled and squeezed his hand. "You're the only bird I care about. You're like a . . . like a cardinal."

"Not an old crow?"

"Or an eagle. What do I remind you of?"

"A . . . I don't know much about birds. But you're a . . . a . . . a canary. A flamingo. A beautiful robin. Ready for dinner?"

"Yes. The drink was excellent. What are you in the mood for?"

"Duck? Quail? Pheasant under glass?"

"Pasta."

"Sold. Let's go."

10

Jessica arrived at Primi Piatti early; she was early to most appointments.

"Ah, Ms. Mumford," said the maître d', "what a pleasure to see you again." He led her through the large, Art Deco room to a table for two in a far corner, held out her chair, and asked if she'd like a drink while waiting for her dinner companion.

"A Negroni, dry, please."

"The usual," the maître d' said.

Jessica laughed. "I didn't realize I'd ordered enough Negronis here for it to be the *usual*."

"I didn't mean—"

"Of course not," she said, waving her hand. "I just found it amusing."

A few years ago, "the usual" for her would have been an extra-dry martini, straight up. But after spending a week in Florence and being introduced to the Negroni—a martini with the pleasantly bitter taste of the aperitif Campari—she'd ordered them ever since.

She tasted her drink and looked at her watch. He was late; no surprise. He'd made the reservation for seven; it was a quarter past. Then, she saw him enter. Escorted to the table by the maître d', Max Pauling leaned over to kiss her on the cheek, slipped into the chair opposite, and said, "Sorry I'm late."

"For you, this is early," she said pleasantly.

"Having your usual?" He nodded at the drink.

"Yes," she said, thinking: I give up. "They're good here. The splash of club soda in summer makes a difference."

"So you always say."

Pauling ordered a Bloody Mary without the vodka—a "Virgin Mary" in America, a "Bloody Shame" in England.

"On the wagon?" she asked.

"For tonight. Hate to dull the senses when I'm with you."

They raised their glasses and touched rims.

Pauling took her in and liked what he saw, as he always did. He considered Jessica Mumford a strikingly beautiful woman, although such an evaluation, he knew, was highly personal, the eye of the beholder and all that.

He'd first seen her a year ago across the John Quincy Adams State Drawing Room, one of several opulent diplomatic reception rooms on the eighth floor of the State Department. The rooms, wonderfully handsome compared with the building as a whole, house one of the nation's greatest collections of American antiques and antiques accessories, valued at more than $50 million. The rooms' perpetual renovation and the addition of rare items were funded by wealthy members of State's Fine Arts Committee. A paid curator manages what is, in reality, a museum.

Pauling had been back from Moscow only a few months and was still getting his bearings at State when he attended the reception for the new Russian minister-counselor of trade assigned to their embassy. He didn't know many people, and spent the first half hour browsing the room's treasures under the watchful eye of a dozen uniformed security guards—a precious Philadelphia highboy, yellow-and-red-damask-covered eighteenth-century furniture, rare Oriental rugs, and three huge crystal chandeliers. He'd stopped to listen to what the string quartet was playing—a Russian piece he'd heard at Moscow concerts, a Borodin theme based upon an Asian melody?—when he saw a woman talking with a trio of Russian diplomats wearing dark suits and dark expressions. He was instantly attracted to her, a visceral reaction; she was an inch taller than the men surrounding her, with blond-and-silver hair worn short and wet, high cheekbones, a nose long and fine and slightly arched, a clean purity to her profile. He wouldn't have moved to her if she hadn't glanced across the room and locked eyes with him, as though sending a signal that an overture would not be dismissed, provided it was an intelligent one. Not a woman who suffered fools easily, Pauling thought, but this fool will try, as he navigated knots of people and stopped a dozen feet from her and the Russians. She graciously concluded her conversation and came directly to him.

"Hello," he said.

"Hello," she said, a smile passing across her lovely face. "Buy me a drink?"

"The price is right," he said.

"A Negroni," she said. "Dry."

"You like to challenge bartenders?"

"I *love* to challenge bartenders, and others," she replied.

Drinks in hand, they moved to a relatively quiet corner of the room.

"I'm Max Pauling," he said.

"I'm Jessica Mumford. You work at State?"

"I think so. I've been here a month."

"What division?"

"Counterterrorism, Russian desk."

"You work for Barton then."

"*Colonel* Barton."

She winced. "Yes, *Colonel* Barton. Where did you come from?"

"Moscow. I was with the embassy, a trade rep."

Her expression said she knew what he really did in Russia.

"You?" he asked.

"An analyst, Russian section. I also teach at GW."

"Took some courses there before I went to Moscow."

"Not one of mine."

"No. I would have remembered . . . you."

"Especially if I'd flunked you."

"I'm not used to failing."

"No, I don't imagine you are."

As they spoke, he found himself intrigued with her manner. There was an unmistakable near-arrogance, although a better term might be confidence, and lots of it. At the same time, there seemed to be a playfulness behind her questions and comments, testing him, putting him on trial; conviction or acquittal, he knew, wouldn't be long in coming. He decided to preempt being flunked.

"Want to get out of here and go somewhere for dinner?"

"That depends."

"Depends on what, my choice of restaurant?"

"Depends on whether there's a Mrs. Pauling at home thinking her husband's working late."

"There isn't. Is there a Mr. Mumford doing the same?"

"No."

"Then we've cleared the hurdles. French? Italian?"

"British, some German on my mother's side."

"I meant—"

87

"I know what you meant. Steak. I'm in the mood."

"Morton's?"

"I'm beginning to like you—Max."

That was eight months ago. There had been plenty of dinners, and an occasional weekend away in the country when she wasn't chasing the elusive prize bird with her friends, whom Max considered flaky but nice enough. He'd declined invitations to join the club. His bird was his Cessna 172, which he flew most weekends, even enticing Jessica to go up with him a few times.

"Your pleasure?" he asked after they'd gone through the motions of examining Primi Piatti's menu.

"Red snapper," she told the waiter, "grilled thoroughly."

"Ossobuco," Pauling said.

"So, where are you going?" she asked after they'd chosen a wine.

"Moscow."

Her naturally arched eyebrows went up even higher. "The planes today?"

He nodded.

"Why?"

"Why am I going to Moscow? Colonel Barton told me to."

"Because the missiles were probably Russian."

He smiled. "You have sources."

"Of course. Barton told my boss."

"Loose lips sink ships."

"Ashmead is speaking tonight."

"I know. He had a meeting at six. The secretary was going to it."

"What will you do in Moscow, Max?"

"Try to find out who handed over the missiles and in whose hands they ended up, provided they really were

Russian. Actually, Barton told me to just be there in case I'm needed."

She fell silent.

"Hear anything from your ex?" Pauling asked as their salad dishes were cleared.

"Skip? Scope?"

" 'Scope'?"

"That's a code name Skip used years ago when he was working undercover." She laughed gently. "Better than 'Meathead,' which I sometimes called him. Have I heard from him lately? No. He's probably in disguise, working underground somewhere." Her former husband, Donald, or "Skip," Traxler, was an FBI special agent who'd spent most of his career with the Bureau working in a special covert operations unit.

Pauling laughed.

"What's funny?"

"Something you said shortly after we met. You said the problem with the marriage was that Skip worked under too many of the wrong covers."

"Did I say that? It's true. Of course, there was more to it than uncovering other women. His machoness—is there such a word? There should be—I wasn't a willing contributor to his machoness."

"You were too strong a woman."

"I was not a subservient woman."

"So I've noticed."

"Besides, we weren't cut from the James Carville–Mary Matalin mold. Skip's a raving right-wing conservative. Maybe you've also noticed I'm more of a knee-jerk-liberal model."

"Uh huh."

"I'm surprised the marriage lasted as long as it did, almost two years. Out of that time we were together, maybe, two months. It could have ended on our wedding night. When are you leaving?"

"A few days, but I'll be out of town before I head for Moscow."

"Oh? Where?"

His answer was to ignore the question, no surprise to Jessica. It was always that way with the men in her life—mysterious trips, questions ignored, living in the shadows.

"How's *your* ex-spouse?" she asked.

"Fine. The boys are getting older, almost young men now. Doris is dating a nice accountant. Coffee? Dessert?"

"There's no accounting for taste. Probably a good idea. Let's go back and have a going-away party for you, but not too late. I have a feeling tomorrow's going to be a busy one."

"I'll set my wrist alarm."

"Have I bruised your machoness?"

"Bruise me anywhere you want, Ms. Mumford."

Later that night, after he'd left her apartment, she lay awake in bed for a long time smelling him, feeling the cool dampness of the sheets where their sweat had pooled, enjoying the slight soreness between her thighs.

But her thoughts weren't unmixed.

She'd fallen in love with Skip Traxler, the handsome, young FBI special agent who lived his penumbral life on the edge, always in the shadows, always away on some assignment he couldn't discuss with her, and probably wouldn't have even if he could. She never knew who would walk through the door when he returned from an undercover assignment: the idealistic special agent, or "one of them," a man acting and thinking like the lowlife he'd infiltrated, an actor unable to get out of the role upon leaving the stage after a performance. She knew that was common with all law enforcement people who went underground to get the goods on the bad guys. The Bureau had a special psychological unit specifically to help agents in that situation. A nice idea, having a shrink handy when your husband emerged from the nether lands acting like a Mafia capo or Arab wheeler-dealer. Maybe she should have seen a shrink, too. Once, when he'd come home after spending two months with an Irish gang in New York, his demeanor for weeks was distant and cold, frightening in its intensity. He'd been given the customary leave after emerging from underground— "decompression time," it was called—and spent it looking like the gang member he'd become, never even attempting to shed that guise and return to being Special Agent Traxler—until he received orders to report to Quantico for three weeks of special training. She was glad to see Skip go that time, relieved that his menacing presence had been removed from her life if only for three weeks. *Menacing.* Her fear of her husband grew each time they were together, an unstated, unsettling threat he exuded without acting it out with her, laying dormant like water close to the boiling point, simmering, never bubbling over but the hissing and steam offering evidence that it was there.

The divorce was easily accomplished, uncontested, no kids to fight over, separate bank accounts that stayed that way, divvy up the cars, sell him her half share in the West Virginia cabin they'd bought as a vacation retreat, sign the papers, I wish you well. No happiness that her first marriage was short-lived and over quickly, but a profound sense of relief in its place.

Now, it was Max Pauling in her life, and bed, ex-CIA operative in Moscow, independent to a fault, good-looking and rugged and manly without flaunting it, going back to his sub-rosa life in Moscow for God knows how long, living dangerously and loving it, loving it more than her, she knew.

Why am I drawn to such men? she wondered as a jet from Reagan National screamed over the apartment building, causing her to flinch. She sometimes knew the answer, although was reluctant to admit it even to herself. The fact was, she lived what she considered a dull life, desk-bound and classroom-bound, spicing it up by pursuing little winged creatures and marking them off in the latest edition of *Birds of North America,* analyzing information at State each day that had been gathered by more adventuresome souls.

The pension. Was that all there was to look forward to? There were worse things—or were there?

The phone rang.

"Jess, things are heating up here. We need you."

"I'll be right there."

Forty minutes later she was at her desk reading secured reports from the embassy in Moscow regarding the Russian government's reaction to the initial charge that the missiles had been manufactured there. Dry words on dry paper. Indignant reactions by Russian officials, transcripts of Russian radio and television broadcasts, newspaper stories, long, verbose analyses from embassy "experts"—plenty of material to wade through. It was her job to read them once, twice, then read them through again, trying to discover any clues in what was said or, just as important, not said, and to write up her discoveries, speculations, insights into brief, pithy reports and, sometimes, longer analyses. She was good at this, reading between the lines, and behind them, and she knew it, which didn't help when the paper traffic turned from stream into flood at times like this.

"Coffee?" she was asked by a colleague.

"Thanks, yes," Jessica said, "God yes," wishing she were back in Primi Piatti working on a second Negroni.

Part Two

11

The multiagency meeting took place at two in the FBI's seldom-used Strategic Information and Operations Center, a secure command center. Present were representatives of the FBI, the National Transportation Safety Board, and the CIA; the White House's national security advisor, Tony Cammanati; Colonel Walter Barton, director of the State Department's Counterterrorism Division; the FAA's second in command; and the Justice Department's assistant attorney general in charge of liaison with city and state law enforcement. The rectangular table at which they sat was surrounded by classified computers and communications equipment.

Joe Harris, the FBI's counterterrorism chief, chaired the meeting. "Let's go around the room," he said. "Give us what you have so far."

NTSB's Peter Mullin led with an update of his agency's portion of the investigation. The wreckage of the three planes was being assembled in command centers near the involved airports. It occurred to everyone in the room that with the cause of the crashes now apparent, the safety agency's activities were rendered academic. There would be no finding of design-induced or pilot error, nor would they look for evidence of metal fatigue, instrument malfunction, or a runaway aircraft-control surface. Missiles had brought down the planes. No doubt about that. Crash site evidence was conclusive.

Still, NTSB had to go through with much of its regular examination of the crashes as though any of those causes could have been at play. Mullin, well aware of what others were thinking, ended his brief presentation: "Even though we all know what caused those aircraft to crash, determining the attitude, altitude, and angle of attack will be useful in painting a more complete picture of what happened."

"Peter is right," Harris said. "We're trying to pinpoint the exact location of each of the shooters by determining the angle of attack, as with an angle of entry."

Justice's liaison with local law enforcement spoke next.

"We're getting feedback on an hourly basis from police departments and emergency crisis centers across the country," he said. "New York has activated its center in the World Trade Center. They're monitoring subways, water supplies, and sewage systems. All known terrorist and kook groups are under heightened surveillance. Hawaii, Chicago, and Los Angeles have gone to emergency status, too. The problem is, they're all stretched thin because they don't know what they're guarding against."

"The Pentagon's liaison office with civilian emergency crisis authorities is swamped too," Harris added.

"Known terrorist groups?" Cammanati asked Harris. "Still no one claiming credit?"

Joe Harris ran his hand over his shaved head and grimaced. "No. We've got our list of possibles. I believe they were sent over to you about an hour ago."

"We got it," the Justice Department representative said, "and we're distributing it to state attorneys general.

They'll disseminate to local law enforcement in their states."

"The president is concerned that local cops don't start fingering individuals or groups just because they're of a certain ethnic persuasion," Cammanati said. "Racial or ethnic profiling big-time."

"We're worried about that, too," Harris said, "but there's not much we can do about it short of taking control of every police department in the country."

Harris turned to the CIA representative at the meeting. "Want to tell us, Sam, what progress, if any, your people are making with foreign terrorist organizations?"

"It's all input at this point," he said. "We've been keeping tabs on the leading groups for years, but no intelligence has come through pointing to any single one as a prime suspect. We're working every group we can, Sheik Abdel-Rahman's followers, the mujahideen, the Islamic Jihad, Hamas, the Muslim Brotherhood, the Algerian groups, El Noure, Bachir Hannaqui, the FIS, Osama bin Laden. Nothing tangible yet."

"We've got a major problem," the FAA's emissary said. All eyes went to him.

"This is raising hell with the airlines. Passengers are canceling left and right, domestically and internationally. They're facing—the airlines—an economic disaster of unprecedented proportions. And it would be even worse if these missile throwers had hit a heavy, a 747 or—"

"Can't say I blame those passengers," the assistant attorney general said. "I'm flying to New York later today on one of those puddle jumpers and I'm not looking forward to it."

The FAA rep ignored him. "The point is, as long as there's a nut out there with some sort of homemade rocket launcher—"

"Three nuts," someone corrected.

"One nut, three nuts, thirty, it doesn't make any difference. Those responsible had better be brought to justice before we have a crippled airline industry."

NTSB's Peter Mullin silently thought that the FAA spokesman was acting true to form, more concerned with the airline industry's economic health than what his agency was charged with, keeping the skies safe for the millions of passengers who depended on it.

"The missiles," the attendee from Justice said. "They were Russian? Chinese? Homemade?"

"Unofficially Russian," Harris said. "Weapons men from Wright Patterson in Ohio and the Naval Air Warfare Center in California are on their way to work with the Pentagon's weapons guys."

The meeting accomplished little, as far as State's Colonel Barton was concerned. No one seemed to have an inkling of who might have been behind the missile attacks, and judging from the comments made by the people in the room, there wasn't any breakthrough on the horizon. Still, he reminded himself as he left with the others to return to his office at State, it had been only a day since the three planes fell from the sky, hardly time to build a case against anyone or any group without a voluntary, prideful confession.

The FBI's Harris and National Security Advisor Cammanati stayed behind. When they were alone in the room, Harris pulled two pieces of paper from a briefcase at his feet and laid them in front of Cammanati. Cammanati picked up the first and read it over half-glasses.

"SA-7 Grail—9M32—Shoulder-fired surface-to-air missile—Entered Soviet service in 1966—Optical sight—IR seeker activated after sighting—Four feet long—20 pounds—Range 45 to 5,600 m—Speed,

Mach 1.95—2.5 kg high-explosive fragmentation warhead, 5½ pounds."

Cammanati laid the paper down and looked at Harris. "There's no question about this?" he said.

Harris shook his head. "The Pentagon says the missile fragments from the New York site were large and in surprisingly readable shape."

"What about the others—Boise, San Jose?"

"I got a preliminary report on the Idaho missile just before the meeting. Same batch."

"Batch?"

"There's a batch number on them. These guys weren't too bright. If you're going to use a gun, file the serial number off before you do. They didn't bother eradicating the batch numbers."

"Soviet-made," Cammanati said to himself, standing and going to the far end of the room. He faced the wall for what seemed to Harris to be minutes, turned in a few seconds, slowly shook his head, and asked flatly, "Who else knows this?"

"Just those who need to. The CIA. They'll have to be brought into it. The Soviet involvement. Same with State. We're out of the picture when it involves a foreign power."

Cammanati cocked his head. His expression said he knew better. The Federal Bureau of Investigation might be limited under its charter to investigating domestic crime, but that seldom stopped it from poking into international cases, to the chagrin of the CIA.

Harris didn't comment further.

"I'm meeting with the president and some of his cabinet when I leave here," Cammanati said. "I'll take your notes with me. The other piece of paper—I didn't read it." He went to Harris and picked up the second sheet. On it was a list of names:

Aryan Nation
Christian Identity
CSA
The Freedom Alliance
Americans for Justice
Silent Brotherhood
The Jasper Project
Nazi National Alliance
Rally for America
The Ku Klux Klan

"Suspects?" Cammanati asked, shoving the two sheets into his briefcase.

"Right."

"All domestic right-wing groups."

"Mainly. Hate groups, homegrown."

"You have information that points to one of them?"

"Information? No. But we do have an ongoing investigation that might result in useful info."

"How soon?"

A shrug from Harris. "Probably not soon enough to please you and the president—or the FAA and the airlines."

Cammanati displayed a rare smile. "Commerce marches on, Joe," he said ruefully. "Tell me about this ongoing investigation."

"No can do, at least not yet. Too much at risk."

"Christ, how much more could be at risk than what we've got now? Talk to me, Joe. I'm here because the president of the United States wants answers."

"And maybe a dead undercover agent, too?"

"You have someone undercover with some of these groups?"

Harris nodded.

"Which ones?"

"Compromise our agents, Tony, and you compromise what might be the answer to this. If the president wants a briefing, I'm sure Justice will oblige."

"That's encouraging."

"That's necessary."

"I assume Justice approved these undercover operations."

"Assuming anything in this town is a tricky exercise, but you know that as well as anyone. Things okay with you, Tony?"

"They were until yesterday. I'll get back to you."

Joe Harris went outside to Pennsylvania Avenue before returning to his office in the Hoover Building. He was a smoker other smokers envied, able to limit himself to five or six cigarettes a day, none on some days. He lit up and walked to the corner of E Street, where hundreds of tourists were lined up for the FBI tour, one of the most popular in Washington. Not long ago, the tour had been suspended after the Bureau received what it considered to be credible threats against the facility. But it resumed when security, already tight, was further beefed up, and thousands of visitors filed through every day, learning that G-man stands for Government Man, and that the FBI stands for Federal Bureau of Investigation but also that the *F* stands for Fidelity, the *B* for Bravery, and the *I* for Integrity. The tour always ended with a dazzling firearms demonstration by a Bureau sharpshooter. Always a bull's-eye. A shame things didn't work that smoothly in real life.

Harris agreed with most Washingtonians, at least

those who cared about such things, that the buff-colored, concrete-aggregate building named after J. Edgar Hoover ranked high on the city's list of ugly edifices, a prime example of the school of architecture known as New Brutalism.

He snuffed the cigarette out, dropped it in a trash container on the corner, and cast a final glance at the tourists. Everyone in Washington, DC, was hot in summer, but there was no hotter-looking creature on earth than a tourist waiting in line for a tour.

He welcomed the blast of air-conditioning as he entered the building and went to his office, where his secretary told him that the director wished to see him. "Where have you been?" she asked.

"Outside for a smoke."

"It sounds urgent. Why don't you just quit?"

"This place?" He laughed.

"You know what I mean."

FBI Director Russell Templeton was in his spacious office with top aides when Harris walked in. Harris liked working for Templeton better than he had for his predecessor, a much older man who, as far as Harris felt, was more of a political hack than a dedicated law enforcement officer worthy of leading the Bureau. What he especially admired was Templeton's willingness to stand up to the attorney general, whom Harris lumped in with the former FBI director as but another of the previous administration's misguided appointments.

"How'd the meeting go?" Templeton asked once Harris had joined the others in a circle of chairs around the director's desk.

"All right. Nothing new. I gave Tony Cammanati the information about the missiles."

"What did he say?"

Harris ran his hand over his head, on which stubble

was reappearing. "He's taking it to the president who, no surprise, wants this solved yesterday. I mentioned to him—general terms only—the ongoing investigation into right-wing hate groups." Harris turned to the special agent to his right: "Scope?"

The agent looked to Templeton for a signal that he could respond. Instead, the director gave the answer. "Scope is due to report in tonight." He raised his eyebrows at the agent to Harris's right, a silent call for affirmation.

"That's right, sir."

"How long has it been since he last gave a report?" Harris asked.

"A week," the agent replied in a pinched voice, leaning to his left to come closer to Harris. He was a small man with a narrow face and disproportionately large ears. "The Elephant Man," they called him when comparing notes over a beer or on the golf course. He was a Bureau "handler," responsible for training and maintaining special agents who worked underground, infiltrating groups of interest to the Bureau because of possible criminal activity. "He reports on a weekly basis." He sounded defensive, as though Harris were challenging the reporting schedule.

"Tonight," Harris said.

The Elephant Man nodded.

"When do we bring the other agencies into the loop on the missiles?" Harris asked.

"That's not our call," Templeton said. "I had a confirmation from the attorney general that we're to release nothing about the missiles until directed to by her. She'll get the word from the president."

Harris turned to his right again. "Has Scope reported anything in previous contacts that indicates he might know something about these missiles and whose hands they fell into?"

"No."

Harris didn't believe him.

Templeton stood and stretched, straining the buttons on his blue button-down shirt. "I assume that by tomorrow, we'll be getting together with the Company's people and State. Naturally, we'll cooperate fully with whatever agency the president dictates, but that doesn't include Scope's activities. Unless, of course, we're ordered to from up top. We'll meet here at seven tomorrow morning."

A representative from public affairs said, "The press? They know it was missiles that brought down the planes. The more we stonewall on this aspect of the case, the more we—"

Templeton, who almost always spoke in soft, measured tones, snapped, "They *think* they know. Anyone leaks anything to that bunch of vultures will end up providing a human target for the firearms demonstration. See you at seven!"

12

Joe Potamos was hotter than Sixteenth Street's pavement as he entered the Carlton.

He'd come from the *Post* after an argument with his editor, Gil Gardello, over Potamos's continuing assignment to develop human interest sidebars on the crash of the Washington-bound Dash 8. Of the thirty-six passengers aboard the plane, fourteen had been Washington-area residents.

He was crossing the elegant hotel's lobby in the direction of the bar when a voice stopped him.

"Hey, Joe."

The voice belonged to *The Christian Science Monitor*'s Godfrey Sperling, a familiar face at the Carlton, whose early-morning interviews with DC's political bigwigs in the Crystal Room were known as "Sperling breakfasts."

"How are you, Joe?" Sperling asked.

"I've been better. You?"

"Better than you, it seems. What are you chasing these days?"

"Grieving widows and fatherless kids. It's inspiring. You?"

"The Speaker's stonewalling of campaign reform legislation. I'm interviewing him here tomorrow."

"Yeah, well, that's great, Godfrey. That's a . . . excuse me, I'm meeting somebody."

The brief conversation only served to raise Potamos's internal temperature, despite the air-conditioning. There was a time when he, Joe Potamos, Frank Potamos's prodigal son, hotshot political reporter on the nation's second-most-important newspaper, would have been sitting down with Speakers of the House and other DC politicos with the power to block good legislation, or to ram through pork that benefitted no one except their hometown voters.

But that was then.

He muttered a few choice scatological comments as he entered the bar, where homicide detective Peter Languth, a drink in his hand, was talking to Nathan Yu, the bartender.

"I was getting worried," Languth said as Potamos took a stool next to him.

"Worried about what," Potamos said, "that I wouldn't show up and you'd have to pay for your own drinks?"

Languth leaned away from Potamos: "Oooh, the tiger is loose. What's the matter, Joe, that piano-playing girlfriend of yours play 'The Party's Over'?"

"Hello, Nathan," Potamos said to the barman. "Skim milk." To Languth: "No, she just keeps playing 'The Man I Love.' "

Nathan placed a Rob Roy in front of Potamos, who raised it in Languth's direction. "To my father, may he rest in peace. If he'd been more forceful, I'd be happily whipping up burgers swimming in grease and loving every minute of it. What's new on the Canadian, Wilcox, who got it in the park?"

Languth drew on his drink, a Black Velvet, dark porter

with champagne. He wiped his mouth with the back of his hand and said, "Assailants unknown."

"Yeah, fine, but what's your read on it?"

Languth finished his drink, motioned for Nathan to refill it, and shifted his bulky body on the stool so that he faced Potamos. "Why're you asking?"

Potamos hunched his shoulders and leaned his elbows on the bar. "I'm a reporter, for crissake."

"Yeah, but why are you so curious about this stiff?"

"I have a gut feeling about it, that's all. He was killed with a knife in the side, right?"

"Right."

"Not in the chest, not in the back, in the side."

"Yeah. So?"

"His wallet was intact, nothing taken, credit cards, cash, nothing."

"You okay, Joe?"

"No. Where was Wilcox coming from when he got it? Where had he been that night?"

Languth seemed to lack a neck, which made his shrugs less obvious. "I didn't catch the case after he was found. Cox did."

"What did Cox say? Where had Wilcox been?"

"I don't know. No, maybe I do. Cox said something about the deceased coming from some affair at the State Department, something about fishing rights."

"Fishing rights?"

"Yeah, fishing rights. A flap between us and the Canucks over fish."

Potamos grunted, finished his drink, and asked Nathan for another: "A little sweeter this time, huh?"

"What's new with your friend Bowen, Joe?"

Focusing on the murder of the Canadian trade rep, Jeremy Wilcox, had cooled Potamos off. The mention of

George Alfred Bowen stoked the furnace again. "You could've talked all night and not mentioned him, Pete."

"Yeah, I know it's a sore spot with you, but you never really talk about it."

Potamos looked into Languth's wide, flat face and tried to see inside his head.

When Potamos was covering the State Department, he functioned in a world that didn't include DC cops like Languth. But after his demotion to general-assignment reporting, with rape and murder and assault replacing diplomatic niceties, he found himself bonding with cops, including the plodding Pete Languth. In a sense, Potamos's temperament was more in line with the gritty world of a police officer than the striped-pants, cutaway-coat crowd, and he quickly came to appreciate the way cops spent their days and nights, wallowing in criminal human garbage that DC's more genteel citizens escaped from at night by fleeing to their suburban sanctuaries.

Although they were markedly different in every way, and seemed always to be at odds with each other, it was Potamos's appreciation of what Languth did for a living that initially forged a friendship of sorts. Languth loathed the press but soon recognized in Potamos a different breed of reporter, scornful of his profession's abuses, often disgusted with its excesses, yet dedicated to being the best.

They weren't friends in a social sense, never got together simply to enjoy each other's company. Their conversations always revolved around some aspect of their jobs. Languth was married with four grown children, Potamos twice divorced and with kids he seldom saw. Potamos enjoyed music and theater and books. Languth's idea of high culture was an imported beer while watching "professional" wrestling on TV. What they *did* share was a distrust of people. They both made their living asking questions, and had come to the conclusion that people lie more often than they tell the truth. Maybe that was why Potamos liked the lumbering, plodding, sarcastic detective. Potamos believed him, even when he didn't like what he was saying. Believing what people said in Washington, DC, was worth something.

"Did you really hit the guy?" Languth asked.

"Bowen? Yeah, I hit him," Potamos said.

George Alfred Bowen was one of the country's leading political columnists and commentators. His syndicated three-times-a-week column was carried across the country in more than two hundred newspapers, and his program on CBS, *As I See It,* was for aficionados of Sunday-morning talking-head shows. He was one of three columnists at the *Post* whose politics weren't compatible with the paper's liberal management, but whose presence on its editorial pages provided the expected balanced approach to opinion.

Bowen was a conservative Reagan Republican, no secret about that; he wore that credential on the sleeve of his double-breasted blue blazers. His was the arrogance of a fashion model in a group of senior citizens.

He was sixty-four years old. His silver hair flowed past his ears and hung with studied casualness over his shirt collars. He was corn-silk thin, and tall, and his reputation as a connoisseur of fine wines and haute cuisine was as familiar as his political views. Because he was powerful, he saw no need to disguise what was an abrasive and insensitive personality, nor did he make an attempt. Indeed, that abrasive personality and high-energy, loud voice seemed to give him credibility. Those who demonstrated friendship did so because it was prudent; the women in his life, four ex-wives, gave credence to the Kissinger thesis that power was a potent aphrodisiac.

Had he not been George Alfred Bowen, he might have had trouble finding someone with whom to have dinner.

When Potamos joined the *Post* after six years with *The Boston Globe*, where he had made a name for himself covering that city's often unfathomable political life, he was cautioned to stay clear of Bowen, and he did.

Until that night almost two years ago when staying away from him wasn't possible.

Potamos had been covering Congress for the paper, and doing a good job of it. But when a reporter assigned to the *Post*'s State Department beat suffered a heart attack and was placed on disability leave, Potamos was asked to fill in for him. At the time, he'd been working on a story involving a Missouri congressman who was alleged to have accepted illegal campaign contributions from a Japanese businessman to sway opinion on the House International Relations Committee's Asia and Pacific Subcommittee, which he chaired. Although Potamos now had a new news beat, he continued on his own time to delve into the congressman's campaign-fund assertions.

George Alfred Bowen had been chasing down that story, too. If Potamos had known that, he might have been expected to back off and leave the scoop to the preeminent political columnist.

But backing off had never been Joe Potamos's style. When he was told by his bosses that Bowen had what he considered to be a proprietary interest in the brewing scandal, Potamos just pushed harder and dug deeper until, through a friend in the House—a Greek-American representative from Boston—he nailed down the proof he needed and wrote the story.

Potamos was in his editor's office discussing the story when Bowen entered the newsroom. He usually walked with studied nonchalance. This night, he moved with purposeful strides, his praying-mantis body bent forward, mouth set in a hard, straight line, muscles in his cheeks working, eyes narrowed. He went directly to the managing editor's office, ignored Potamos, and threw down on the editor's desk an advance copy of Potamos's story, which was due to hit the street the next morning.

"What is this garbage?" he yelled.

The managing editor held up his hands. "Calm down, George. Joe came up with the goods, that's all. It's a hell of a good story."

"It is trash," Bowen said. "I have been working on this story for months, and you know it. I'm this close to breaking it." He demonstrated by holding two talonlike fingers an inch apart.

"George . . ." the editor said, getting up and coming around the desk in an attempt to placate their star columnist. As he did, Potamos stood to leave. Bowen spun around and blocked the doorway. His face was red with anger, and he visibly shook. "You little greaseball bastard, you don't know what you're writing about. You don't know anything."

Potamos hadn't expected the outburst, even though Bowen's temper was legendary. Being called a greaseball brought back an instant memory of high school. When another student had called him that, Potamos punched the student in the face, knocking him down.

"You pathetic little hack," Bowen said, voice rising. "Your story is junk. Your source is crap. You don't mess with George Alfred Bowen!"

Other staffers in the newsroom inched closer to the office. Potamos's hands tightened into fists at his sides. His breathing was heavy; he snorted through his nose like a bull. He looked up into Bowen's distorted, smoldering face. "Get out of the way," Potamos said. Bowen placed his hands on Potamos's chest and pushed. As he did, Potamos saw Bowen's face disappear in a blinding white light. The next thing he remembered was being held down in a chair by two other reporters.

He squeezed his eyes shut and shook his head, opened his eyes and looked down at his right hand. It hurt. Voices buzzed around him like a swarm of hornets. "Get the police," he heard someone say.

"Hell, no," someone else said. "No police."

"You okay, George?"

Potamos looked to his right; the blurred scene came into focus. George Alfred Bowen was slumped in a chair. His half-glasses, tethered to him by a thin strap, were broken. A tiny trickle of blood came from his nose. People hovered over him.

"You idiot!" The managing editor's face was inches from Potamos's. "You bloody idiot. What did you hit him for?"

"Hit him? I—I don't know. I don't remember."

Two security guards had been summoned from their position in the lobby.

"We called for an ambulance," one said.

"Jesus," the other said. "Who hit Mr. Bowen?"

"Potamos."

"How come?"

Bowen stood unsteadily with the help of others.

"Why don't you sit until the ambulance comes?" a woman suggested.

"I don't need an ambulance," Bowen said.

As he came to the door, he stopped, turned, and glared down at Potamos. "Write your obituary, Potamos. You're dead!"

". . . and so I punched the bastard and that was that," Potamos said to Languth.

"You're lucky he didn't press charges," Languth said.

"Maybe it would have been better if he did. Hey, Nathan, I'll have one more."

The bartender had been standing alone at the far end of the bar reading the new issue of the *Washingtonian*, which had been delivered that day. He came to Potamos and Languth and laid the magazine on the bar. "Mr. Potamos, look at this."

The story on the open page was a roundup of Washington's top society pianists. The first profile was of Roseann Blackburn, Potamos's friend. The color photograph showed her dressed in a gown and sitting at a gleaming black Steinway.

"You know she was gonna be in the magazine?" Languth asked.

"She mentioned something about a writer and photographer months ago. I didn't know when it was running."

"Hey, you're mentioned," Languth said, who'd pulled the magazine closer to him.

Potamos retrieved the magazine and read the final paragraph:

When she isn't pleasing the ears of well-connected Washingtonians with the melodies of Cole Porter, Duke Ellington, or Mozart, Ms. Blackburn soothes the savage breast of *Post* reporter Joe Potamos, who played his own dissonant chord two years ago when he allegedly assaulted political pundit George Alfred Bowen.

"You're famous, Joe," Languth said, laughing and slapping Potamos on the back with a hand the size of a catcher's mitt.

"My fifteen minutes."

"At least you kept your job," Languth said.

"Yeah, they didn't release me, just sent me to the minors."

"You know what I always wondered, Joe?"

"What?"

"How come you didn't pick up and get the hell outta DC, hook up with another paper someplace. You could've gotten another job, right?"

"Right."

"So? How come you didn't?"

"Because I don't run from anybody or anything. You run, the bad guys win. Every day Bowen sees me, he feels that shot to his nose again. I like that. I also like DC. Enough of an explanation?"

"You havin' another?"

"No, but go ahead. I've got to go." Potamos stood and placed his American Express card on the bar.

"You put this on the expense account?"

"Sure. Getting sloshed in a fancy bar with a homicide detective who tells me nothing."

"Joe."

"What?"

Languth brought his lips close to Potamos's ear. "You want the scoop on the Canadian in the park?"

"Yeah."

"Meet me here tomorrow, six o'clock."

"You buyin'?"

"Hell, no. I'm the seller, you're the buyer."

"You'd better be selling something good. I'll be here at six." He turned to Nathan. "Thanks, buddy. See ya."

"Say hello to your lady."

"Shall do."

Potamos paused in the lobby to call Roseann. He got the machine, then remembered it was Friday, the night of her regular stint at the Four Seasons Hotel. He stopped in a stationery store and bought the last six copies of the

Washingtonian, hailed a taxi, and went to the Four Seasons, where Roseann was seated at a grand piano in the center of the hotel's opulent lounge. Well-dressed, well-heeled men and women sat on overstuffed chairs and love seats in pockets of partial seclusion throughout the grand space. Roseann saw Potamos enter, smiled, finished "Summertime," left the piano, and gracefully crossed the lobby to him.

"Hi, babe," he said, kissing her cheek.

She saw the magazines, laughed, and kissed him on the mouth. "You saw it and bought all these," she said. "You are so sweet."

"Yeah, well, I figured you'd want to send a couple to your mother, other people."

"I do, I do. I'm almost finished. Another ten minutes."

"I figured we'd catch some dinner someplace."

"Love it. Good day?"

"The same. I'll wait outside. A little too rich here for my blood, or bank account."

She joined him outside twenty minutes later and they went to Bacchus, near Dupont Circle, a favorite spot when they were in the mood for Lebanese food. Instead of a full meal, they opted for a variety of appetizers, *mezze,* and beer, and settled back as the small dishes were brought in succession—hummus topped with pine nuts and ground meat, eggplant with pomegranates and sesame paste, stuffed grape leaves, and phyllo dough filled with piquant sausage and cheese. Roseann looked across the table and smiled. Potamos seemed relaxed; she loved being with him at times like this, when the edge was off.

"You weren't mad they mentioned you and Bowen in the piece?" she asked, picking up a radish and taking a bite.

"No, of course not. It's no secret what happened. The piece should get you plenty of work."

"Bill Walters called," she said. Walters owned Elite Music, Roseann's booking agent. "He said the same thing."

"Yeah, well, that's great."

"He wants me to start taking jobs out of the area."

"Yeah? Like where?"

"Not far. Fancy resorts in West Virginia, Delaware, maybe even some of the better piano bars in New York."

"Makes sense to me, as long as you remember Joe Potamos when you're on Broadway."

She placed her hand on his. With all his bluster, all his cynical, tough-guy persona, his dyspeptic view of the world, especially since the incident with Bowen, she knew a painful vulnerability and lack of confidence were an inch below the surface.

"When I'm on Broadway—why would you think I'd be on Broadway? I'm just a saloon piano player."

"The Four Seasons; some saloon."

"I'll never be on Broadway. And as for forgetting Joe Potamos, that's as likely as forgetting the C scale."

His mood picked up as the appetizers and bottles of beer kept coming. She knew he'd been drinking earlier in the day, which he confirmed by telling her he'd met Languth at the Carlton Hotel: "He's getting me some stuff on the Canadian who was murdered."

"Canadian? Oh, in the park."

"Yeah."

"Why do you want more information about him?"

"I don't know. This guy wasn't mugged. It was no street robbery, nothing like that."

"How do you know?"

"Instinct."

"Why do you think he was killed?"

"No idea. But I want to know. *Have* to know. I don't write unfinished stories. Maybe what I get from Languth will give me some answers."

"I hope so."

They finished their meal with strong coffee and a shared piece of lemony yogurt pie. When they were finished, Potamos asked, "Ready?"

"Uh huh."

They stopped to chat with one of the restaurant's owners before venturing out onto Jefferson Place. Inside, it had been quiet. The moment they opened the door, they were confronted with a noisy, angry group of a half-dozen young men who'd surrounded a well-dressed, dark-skinned couple who'd left Bacchus ten minutes earlier. One of the young men was the loudest and most vocal: "Why don't you get the hell out of this country and go back with the rest of your raghead terrorists!" he screamed. "You don't shoot down Americans, you bastard, and get away with it."

The man and woman were terrified. She crouched behind him as he tried to reason with them. "We know nothing of the planes being shot down," he pleaded, his hands held in a defensive position, his voice breaking.

"Let's show 'em," another man yelled.

The leader closed the gap and held up his fist.

"Hey!"

Potamos pushed through the men and confronted the leader. He'd pulled a small, sophisticated point-and-shoot camera he always carried with him and aimed it at the attacker's face. "Joe Potamos, *Washington Post*. You want your ugly face in the paper tomorrow?"

For a moment, Roseann thought Potamos would be physically assaulted. But the young man backed away, mumbling obscenities. The group dispersed, grumbling.

"Thank you, thank you," the man said, pumping Potamos's hand.

"Yeah, yeah, it's okay. Buncha jerks, that's all."

"We know nothing about any planes. We have lived here for ten years. We love this country."

"I'm sure you do. Have a nice night."

Later that night, Potamos and Roseann lay in bed with Jumper at their feet.

"That's just the beginning," he said.

"What is?"

"Looking for scapegoats. Pick on anybody who looks different, like that couple. You look like you come from some Arab country, you're automatically a terrorist. Some stuff came over the wire this afternoon, same kind of stuff happening around the country."

"That was gutsy what you did, Joe. I thought they were going to turn on you."

"So did I."

"Good night."

"Good night, babe."

They kissed and she turned over, her feet pushing Jumper and bringing forth a groan from the sleeping dog. Potamos stayed awake for a long time, thinking about nothing and everything. His final thought was a growing question: Should he ask Roseann to marry him?

He fell asleep before he had to answer it.

13

The Next Morning

It was as though the world had suddenly ceased spinning. It was one of those moments in American news—or what passed for news in America. No revolution, no incursions, no deaths of heads of state or movie stars, not even a B-plus scandal in Washington.

"In other news today . . ."

What news? The downing of the three commuter aircraft, and the involvement of shoulder-launched surface-to-air missiles, was the *only* news.

Television programmers engaged in a fierce competition for relevant guests to discuss the horrific crimes against innocent American citizens. Retired generals were interviewed about missiles, their range, speed, and destructive capability. Spokespeople from Justice, State, the FBI, ATF, and the administration ran from studio to studio answering the same questions over and over, reassuring the public while at the same time inadvertently heightening its fear that other such attacks could be imminent. The afternoon talk shows paraded every available, anxious-to-appear psychiatrist and psychologist before their cameras:

INTERVIEWER: "What's the psychology of someone so filled with hatred that he would target civilian airliners?"

ANSWER: "That's hard to say without having the opportunity to examine the perpetrator, to see what sort of background, childhood, life experiences might have impacted his adult actions."

INTERVIEWER: "How can people conquer what is now a natural fear of climbing aboard a commercial airplane?"

ANSWER: "There isn't much anyone can do except to adopt a fatalistic attitude. Because the victims were chosen at random, we're all possible victims. But life is a random exercise. We never know whether we'll be in the wrong place at the wrong time. Terrorists don't discriminate."

INTERVIEWER: "What are family members of those who died in the attacks feeling at this moment?"

ANSWER: "Shock, sadness, remorse, anger—yes, extreme anger."

Wally Watson's wife, Celia, succumbed to incessant pressure and agreed to appear on a local talk show.

INTERVIEWER: "How is the family holding up?"

ANSWER: "We're doing the best we can under the circumstances. Wally—that was my husband—is missed very much." She began to cry.

INTERVIEWER: "If you could come face-to-face with the person who shot down the plane with your husband on it, what would you say to that person?"

ANSWER: "I would say . . . I would ask why."

INTERVIEWER: "Yes, indeed, *why* is the question all America is asking. We'll take a brief commercial break. When we come back, we'll ask this courageous lady what the future holds for her and her family now that her husband is no longer with them."

The story multiplied, fed on itself. CNN devoted two hours to the activities of local police across the country. San Jose's police chief was among those interviewed:

INTERVIEWER: "What's the mood here in San Jose?"
ANSWER: "The mood is somber and concerned."
INTERVIEWER: "What is your department doing—what *can* your department do to allay these fears?"
ANSWER: "Well, we know that incidents like these aren't going to happen every day. The citizens of San Jose are being encouraged to go about their daily activities in a normal manner."
INTERVIEWER: "Including getting aboard airplanes?"
ANSWER: "Yes, that too. Look, I don't want to minimize what's happened. We've gone to full alert in our emergency crisis center as a precaution, and known hate groups are being sought out and questioned. But—"
INTERVIEWER: "Do you have information we don't have that a domestic hate group is behind these attacks, not a foreign terrorist organization?"
ANSWER: "No, but every potential source of information is being pursued. Thank you."

Warren Forrester held the APB his office had received as its subject, Zachary Jasper, approached.

WANTED—CAUTION—FOR QUESTIONING—JASPER, ZACHARY—SEX/M—RAC/W—POB/IDAHO—DOB/020752—HGT/601—WGT/290—EYE/BRO—HAI/BLACK—MIS/EXTRM PARANOID—AFFIL W/KNOWN HATE GROUPS—FOUNDR THE JASPER PROJECT—HEVLY ARMED—LV/RANCH, NORTH WASH, CALLED JASPER, NRST CTY BELLINGHAM (TWN/BLAINE)—RANCH POP APPROX 30.

Jasper wore a black T-shirt. Despite being the largest size available, it was stretched thin over his massive body. An unfurled American flag was emblazoned on its front. On the back, in white letters, was CSA, which stood for the Covenant, the Sword, and the Arm of the Lord, a militia group whose survival training school was considered among the best in the amalgamation of such groups across the United States. Jasper had been given the shirt after completing a refresher course there, and wore it with pride.

Huge, sunburned arms, covered with tattoos, bulged against the shirt's short sleeves. His hair was black and shaved daily into a buzz-cut. He wore a leather vest over the shirt, dark blue jeans—waist size forty-eight—leather sandals over bare feet, and a thick gold chain around his neck. A sizable, custom-crafted medallion, on which a lightning bolt cut across a shield containing a large red letter *J,* hung from the chain.

At first glance, Jasper might have been considered a fat man. He wasn't. He was a *big* man, muscular and hard, including his large belly. The only thing that mitigated the imposing figure he presented were round, rimless glasses that were absurdly small on his broad, flushed face.

He walked down the long road to where the six FBI special agents dressed in suits stood next to three unmarked sedans they'd driven to the remote area known as Jasper, Washington, a name given it by its only permanent resident, Zachary Jasper. Flanking him were six younger men, none of whom were armed. The deal struck by phone the night before called for Jasper to surrender to the agents the next morning, and that no weapons were to be carried. The firearms carried by the agents remained in their shoulder holsters beneath their suit jackets, although their eyes scrutinized the approaching men carefully, seeking any sign that the agreement might be breached.

Jasper and his entourage stopped ten feet away.

"Mr. Jasper," the lead agent, Warren Forrester, said.

"Hello," Jasper said. "Here I am, just as I promised."

"That's good, Mr. Jasper. Ready to come with us?"

"Yes. I'm being questioned only. Is that correct?"

"Yes, sir, that's correct."

"I'm not being arrested. I have witnesses here."

"You don't need them, Mr. Jasper. We keep our word."

Jasper got in the backseat of one of the cars, and the three vehicles and six agents left the area. They drove to Bellingham, ninety miles north of Seattle, fifty-seven miles south of Vancouver, and pulled into a parking lot behind the city's police headquarters. Jasper was led inside and down a long corridor to a general-purpose room at the east end of the one-story building.

"Hello, Zachary," Bellingham's police chief said as Jasper entered the room.

"Allan," Jasper said, going directly to a table, pulling out a wooden armchair, and sitting heavily. Agents took the remaining four chairs. The two others stood. The police chief left the room and closed the door. A Sony cassette recorder sat on the table. One of the agents turned it on, saying, "We'll be taping this, Mr. Jasper, for your sake and ours."

Jasper laughed gently. "For *my* sake? I don't think so."

The lead agent said, "You know the chief of police, I see."

"Allan? Sure, I do. Nice fella. We don't bother him, he doesn't bother us."

It struck the agents that this bear of a man, dressed like a Hell's Angels biker, was surprisingly well spoken. A few of them knew, however, that Jasper had been a political science professor in California before shucking that persona and taking the right-wing road that led him to form the Jasper Project, a hundred-acre ranch in a heavily wooded area outside Blaine, Washington, north of Bellingham, a busy port of entry between the United States and Canada. It was Jasper's dream to establish a colony for white Christians, insular, secure, self-contained. Most of the people living at the ranch had come from other parts of the country, lured there by Jasper's promotional materials promising a white, God-fearing nirvana.

"Mind if I smoke?" Jasper asked, pulling a pack of cigarettes from his vest.

"Prefer that you didn't," he was told.

"Go right ahead," Forrester said, tossing a critical look at the antismoking member of his team. Another agent brought an ashtray from a table and placed it in front of Jasper.

"All right," Jasper said, "you want to know if I shot down those three planes. Right?"

"We'd like to know if you have any information that would help us find who did, Mr. Jasper."

Jasper ran a hand over his chin and frowned. "You're aware I could consider this harassment," he said, smiling. "You've got me here because I and my people aren't especially fond of you and the whole damn government you represent."

"No one's harassing you, Mr. Jasper," Forrester said. "You came voluntarily."

"I'm glad you've taken note of that," said Jasper. "I know nothing about those planes being shot down. I'm as appalled as anybody at what happened."

"How many people live with you at the ranch?"

"That's none of your business, no insult intended. I'm here to answer your questions about those planes. Nothing else."

"Discussing weapons you have at the ranch would be fair game, wouldn't it?" Forrester asked.

"No."

"Weapons brought down those planes, Mr. Jasper."

"Soviet-made SAMs, as I hear on TV."

"Do you have any missiles at the ranch?"

A dismissive laugh this time. "Now, why would I have missiles on a working ranch? Hell of a way to shoot a deer or a rabbit. Maybe overkill."

"You could help us, Mr. Jasper," Forrester said. "You get around the circuit."

"The 'circuit'? You mean other groups that share my dislike for the government and all it stands for?"

A simple nod, and a small smile, from the agent.

Jasper sat up straight and leaned his elbows on the table. "Let me tell you something," he said, his voice demonstrating the first sign of pique since he had sat down. "I may hate the Jew-nited States of America and its fascist government. I may be a white supremacist. I might be all those things. But I don't approve of innocent American citizens being slaughtered by some foreign terrorist group."

"Why are you so sure it was a foreign group?"

"Had to be. You know how they are."

" 'They'?"

"Yes, foreigners."

They talked for another fifteen minutes before Jasper was escorted from the building, placed in one of the cars, and driven back to his ranch, where two of the young men who'd accompanied him waited. This time, they cradled rifles in their arms.

Forrester said as Jasper was about to depart the vehicle, "You'd make me very happy, Mr. Jasper, if you'd invite me inside to see this ranch of yours."

Jasper's tongue worked the inside of one cheek before

he responded, "That sort of invitation is usually called a warrant."

"I'd rather not go to the trouble of having it printed. You know, just a friendly visit."

"You know what Harry Truman said: 'If you want a friend in Washington, buy a dog.' Sorry, but I'm not in the mood for a party. It was a pleasure meeting you. We'll have to do this again sometime."

"I'll look forward to it."

Forrester called a number from a secured radio telephone in the car as he and the driver drove away from the ranch: "Forrester. We just dropped Zachary Jasper back at his ranch."

The agent on the other end of the call sat in a large room at FBI headquarters in San Francisco that had been designated and equipped as the western-sector command center for investigating the downing of the aircraft. She'd been taking calls all day from teams assigned to seek out and question known right-wing militia groups.

"Anything?" she asked.

"No. Claims to know nothing. I'd like a warrant to go in."

"No can do, at least at this stage. Justice is doing its usual blinders-on act, turned down a blanket request to search all known hate group locations. No probable cause."

"I thought—"

"Careful. That can get you in trouble."

"I thought they were getting info from inside Jasper's so-called ranch."

"Be a good soldier, Warren. It's not for us to question wisdom at the top."

"Christ," Forrester said into the phone, loud enough

for the driver to turn and raise his eyebrows. "What are they waiting for, another plane to come down?"

"No, they're operating on the theory that it was the act of a foreign terrorist group."

"What do they back that up with?"

"Looks like the administration wants it that way. You're heading for Portland?"

"Yeah. We have the two groups to check out there."

"Keep in touch."

As Special Agent Forrester and his colleagues headed for Portland, Oregon, to check out two known white supremacist groups, one comprised of neo-Nazi skinheads, the other led by an aging minister who used his self-consecrated church as headquarters, Mac and Annabel Smith watched the news on TV in their Watergate apartment. A special report was in progress about a rash of bias crimes that had sprung up across the country in response to the assaults on the aircraft. The window of a clothing store in Detroit, owned by a Pakistani family, was smashed by a chanting crowd; two black teenagers, the sons of a Nigerian diplomat, were attacked on Mass. Avenue. An Arab man in Houston was chased by a club-wielding gang and forced into a busy street, where he was struck by a car and taken to a hospital. His injuries were reported as not being life-threatening.

The anchor's report ended with:

"The president himself has asked the American people not to take the law into their own hands or judge people by their national origins. Every resource of the federal government is being utilized to determine who was behind the callous destruction of civilian commuter planes that took the lives of eighty-seven men, women, and children."

Mac switched off the set. "Doesn't take much, does it, to turn loose the posse?"

"Inevitable," Annabel said, "and unfortunate. I'd better pack."

"Oh, that's right. You're off to New York tonight."

"I'm really excited about seeing those pieces Mr. Relais has up for sale."

"I'm sure you are. What shuttle are you taking?"

"The seven-thirty."

He drove her to the airport in time for her flight to New York and dropped her off in front of the busy terminal. They embraced. "I'll be back tomorrow afternoon," she said. "If all goes well, I should be able to catch a flight around three."

"I'll be teaching."

"I know. A taxi will do just fine."

"Provided you find a driver who knows how to get to the city from the airport."

Annabel didn't respond. She couldn't help but reflect on Mac's comment about DC's cab drivers. Most of them were foreign-born; their reputation for not speaking good English or knowing their way around Washington was as established in the minds of visitors and residents as was the confusion of the city's system of traffic circles and one-way streets, thanks to Pierre L'Enfant, who designed it in 1791 "like a chessboard overlaid with a wagon wheel."

Stereotypes.

Cab drivers wearing turbans.

A store owner with dark skin.

Anyone different.

Someone to look down on, feel superior to.

She'd ridden the Metro that day and realized she was especially wary of foreigners carrying packages. Not

Americans. Just foreigners. She felt slightly ashamed. And justified.

What was the world coming to?

Homicide detective Pete Languth, too, was pondering the fate of the world as he sipped his Black Velvet at the bar in the Carlton Hotel waiting for Joe Potamos to arrive. He'd come from a particularly grisly double murder, a domestic dispute that got out of hand, and as inured as he was to violence and its predictable aftermath, this one got to him.

"You're late," Languth said to Potamos when he walked in at six-fifteen. Nathan, the bartender, delivered a Rob Roy without being asked.

"Right, I'm late," Potamos said. "You know any editors?"

"Editors? No. Why should I know editors?"

"There aren't any good ones anymore. I work for an idiot. Name's Gardello. I just left him."

"You hit him, Joe?" the big detective asked, chuckling at the question.

"No, I didn't hit him," Potamos said, laughing, too. "You come up with anything on the Canadian, Wilcox? Gardello told me to get off the story, stick with human-interest stuff on the grieving widows from the plane crash."

"So why do you want this?" Languth asked, sliding a thin file folder along the bar. Potamos opened it and glanced at its contents.

"This all you have, Pete?"

"Hey, how about showing a little gratitude? That's the case file. They wouldn't be happy I copied it for you."

"Yeah, sorry. Thanks. Anything you know that's not in this?"

"You *are* buying, right?"

131

Potamos slapped his American Express card on the bar.

Languth waved for another drink, turned to Potamos, and said, "The deceased, one Jeremy Wilcox, was working on some sorta treaty on fishing rights."

"You already told me that."

"Don't interrupt. Because you're so interested—why? I don't know and don't care—and despite the fact you're a hardheaded Greek with no common sense, I called a friend who knows another friend who knows somebody who knew the deceased. He was supposedly a trade type at the embassy, but maybe he wasn't."

"Meaning? Nathan, one more, please, a little sweeter this time."

"Meaning he might have really been a spy type."

" 'Spy type.' What the hell does that mean?"

"You know, making like he's here in the States to negotiate fishing treaties, but maybe working for some Canadian intelligence agency."

"No kidding? Who is this person who knows that?"

"I wrote it down inside. I didn't know they had one. An intelligence agency. The Canadians."

"Everybody's got an intelligence agency."

"Yeah, but I can't figure why the Canadians would want to spy on us. We're friends, right?"

"Everybody spies on us, Pete, and we spy on everybody. Remember Israel?"

"What about it?"

"They got caught spying on us, and we're friends. Do you think Wilcox got it because he was a 'spy type'?"

Languth shrugged his massive shoulders. "I don't know," he said, "but it's not being considered a street crime. Maybe having something to do with politics, or a rub-out. Drugs, maybe, some sorta criminal thing he got himself involved with."

"Hmmm," Potamos said as he tasted his second drink, gave Nathan a thumbs-up.

They talked about other things until a half hour later, when Languth announced he had to leave.

"Thanks for the drinks, Joe."

"Yeah, sure. Thanks for this stuff," Potamos said, tapping the file folder.

"Why don't you drop it, Joe?" Languth said, standing. "Follow orders. Your editor says drop it, you drop it, save yourself another headache."

"You might have a point. I'll think about it. We'll catch up." *Career advice from a cop?*

Potamos read what was in the folder as he finished his drink, paid, left the hotel, and went to Roseann's apartment. She was gone when he arrived, but Jumper gave him a wet greeting. After walking her, Potamos wrote a series of notes on the computer. Although there wasn't much useful information in what Languth had given him, there was enough to spur his interest. Besides, Gil Gardello's order not to follow up was motive enough to keep going.

14

"Well, well, well," Bill Lerner said as Pauling knocked and paused outside his office door in the American embassy, a nine-story yellow-and-white building on Novinskiy Bulvar. "He returns to the scene of the crime."

Max Pauling grinned and stepped inside. He'd arrived that morning at Sheremetevo II Airport on a British Airways flight from London, after flying there from Washington. He had declined the airline's food so when he checked into the Metropol Hotel, a long block from the former KGB headquarters and across the street from the Bolshoi, he ordered *blinchiki varenem*—small pancakes with jam—and coffee from room service, then showered, changed his shirt, and went to the Kremlin, a five-minute stroll and one of his favorite sights in the world, before hailing a taxi to the embassy. He was happy to be back.

Lerner came around the desk and enthusiastically shook Pauling's hand. Although he was a section head in ECO/COM, the embassy's economic and commercial office, like Pauling he, too, answered to a different and distant superior, in Langley, Virginia.

Lerner was tall, six feet four, a loosely jointed man with unruly reddish-brown hair and a face comprised of folds, sags, pouches, and putty-colored half-moons beneath his eyes. He was no fashion plate; he wore cheap suits and shirts that hung haphazardly from his angular frame, and drab wide ties of no known color.

"What crime did I leave behind?" Pauling asked.

"The names escape me, Max, but I do remember they were attractive. Coffee?"

"Speaking of crimes . . . no, thanks."

"You're at the Metropol?"

"Yeah. Living well is the best revenge. Who said that?"

"The Duchess of Windsor."

"I guess she knew. What's new here? I miss anything in the past year?"

"Of course you did," Lerner said, returning to his swivel, high-back office chair and laying one long leg over the other, displaying short black socks and an expanse of white leg. "What was a confused situation when you left has become more confused. Your Russian friends—"

"What Russian friends?"

"The ones with the funny noses. Your unsavory contacts in Russia's leading industry, the underworld, are thriving."

"Including arms sales?"

"Oh, yes, especially arms sales. Since you've rudely turned down my offer of coffee, would vodka be more to your taste?"

Pauling glanced at his watch. "Noon. A little early for me, even if this is Russia."

Lerner unfolded himself from the chair and went to the window. "Lovely day, isn't it?"

"Are we going for lunch?"

135

"Yes."

They left the building, stopping on their way for Pauling to exchange greetings with others with whom he'd worked, and walked up the busy boulevard in the direction of Moscow's zoo. Pauling knew from years of having worked for Bill Lerner that leaving the embassy had more to do with security than hunger. Lerner defined paranoia when it came to discussing sensitive matters within the building, and for good reason: The Soviets had attempted to install bugs in it during its construction; such Cold War mentality died hard.

They entered a small park that divided the boulevard and went to a *shashlik*, a kiosk offering barbecued meats and fish, freshly baked bread, and a small selection of vegetables.

"Hello, hello, Mr. Lerner," the elderly man in the kiosk said. His wife looked up from her food preparation and smiled sweetly.

"Privet," Lerner said, returning the greeting.

"A new favorite restaurant?" Pauling asked.

"Yes. Zagat hasn't discovered it yet. They're friends, occasionally helpful ones."

Pauling smiled and peered into the kiosk at the food cooking on the grill. "Smells good."

"Might I recommend the *pirozhki* and *khatchapuri*? He has a touch with them."

Pauling laughed. Lerner spoke excellent Russian and took considerable pride in it. Pauling had become almost fluent during his seven years in Russia, although he was not, and would never be, up to Lerner's standard.

Lerner placed the order and led Pauling to a bench a few feet from the kiosk. The park was busy with lunchtime workers from nearby office buildings. Two uniformed city police leaned against a utility pole on the opposite side. It had warmed considerably since Pauling arrived in

Moscow that morning. He removed his tan sport jacket and loosened his tie.

"What did you learn before leaving Washington?" Lerner asked as though not caring what the answer was.

"Nothing, except that they were Soviet-made missiles."

"We know more than that now," Lerner said, "but you've been traveling, wouldn't be up to date."

"Tell me."

"According to what we've been told, they—I'm speaking of the missiles, of course—they were SA-7, shoulder-fired, infrared homing after optical sighting, range—I don't have all the specs with me. They're back in the office, complete with batch and serial numbers."

"Narrows it down to a hundred thousand or so," Pauling said as the kiosk chef's wife appeared carrying two paper plates with ravioli-like stuffed grape leaves and slabs of hot cheese bread overflowing their edges.

"*Pivo, pazhalsta,*" Lerner said to her.

"*Da, pivo,*" Pauling said, also in the mood for a beer.

"It won't be quite as daunting as you think, Max. The batch number was intact on one of the missile fragments. Should help compress the process some. We're having dinner tonight with Elena. She's looking forward to seeing you again."

"I meant to ask about her. You're still with her?"

"In a manner of speaking. Different apartments, getting together when the need arises, which is less often as I get older. Our *friendship* is still between us, of course."

"Of course. She still work for the Central Bank?"

"Yes. But you can catch up on us tonight. I have a lead for you, Max."

"Good. Who?"

"Well, speaking of banks, a banker. A crooked one, successful because he *is* crooked. Very well connected in the district committees, the Central Committee, Council of Ministers—the usual criminal chain of command. Answers to the mafia, but that's nothing new in Russia, is it? You'll have to get to him through one of the names in your little black book."

"That could take a while."

"I believe I can narrow it for you, perhaps as early as tonight, after dinner. Check in with me at the end of the day. Until then, nothing has changed at the embassy. It's still a sieve. Our Russian nationals at the embassy profess loyalty to us, or at least wave off any thought that they might tell tales out of school. Don't believe them. I don't. Enjoying the *pirozhki*?"

"I like the bread better," Pauling said, taking a swig of beer from the bottle as he admired a stylishly dressed woman who sauntered past, her eyes playing with his.

"You're officially assigned to me and ECO/COM, as usual. Everything comes through me—as usual. You're to have no contact with Langley, none with Barton at State. You'll keep me informed of every move, Max, and I'll pass along what information you develop to the appropriate people back home. And, Max, as a personal favor to me, try to control your impetuous impulses for as long as you're here."

"Sometimes those impulses paid off."

"Yes, and sent me in search of antacid."

"Tom Hoctor told me the same thing."

"To curb your impulses?"

"Yeah. I had a pleasant couple of days with him at Langley."

"So I understand. We've been in daily touch."

"Good. I didn't learn anything I didn't already know, but it's always nice to see Tom. I wish the Company would fix the air-conditioning, though. Sometimes you wonder about who's running things. When they built the building, the air-conditioning contractor said he needed to know how many people would be working in it to come up with the right amount of AC. They wouldn't tell him. National security. So he puts in a puny unit and everybody sweats. Brilliant."

Lerner smiled. He knew the story. He also knew that Pauling enjoyed telling it as an example of inept leadership to anyone who'd listen.

"You'll have my complete support, Max, money, resources, whatever you need to find out how those missiles left here and ended up in whoever's hands. I suggest you stay in the hotel for a few weeks. The regular routine, seeking a suitable place for our new staff member to live. Hopefully, you won't be here long enough to have to find more permanent quarters."

Pauling grinned. "Should I be offended that you want me out of here so fast?"

"No. The seriousness of the mission dictates that."

"What if I can't trace the missiles to who ultimately used them against the planes?" Pauling asked.

"Then at least identify who here in Russia sold them. Hopefully, it will be a private party, organized crime, a morally bankrupt businessman—anyone but the Russian government."

"And if it *was* the Russian government?"

"I prefer not to think about that. We should get back. Your old office is vacant, although I don't suppose you'll be spending much time there."

Pauling stood and returned the smile of another young woman wearing a miniskirt and a tank top that exposed her bare midriff. The prostitutes were dressing better these days, he thought. So much had changed in Moscow since the dissolution of the Soviet Union and this new Russia's commitment, as painful as it was, to democracy, capitalism, crime, and prostitution. Western fashion had captured the women, cell phones and sport cars the men.

The problem, he knew only too well, was that behind this flashy facade of economic prosperity in the city, there was a vastly wider country on the verge of economic collapse. And where the money flowed in the cities, you could count on organized crime to control the spigots. Pauling and Lerner retraced their steps to the embassy, but instead of accompanying Lerner inside, Pauling hesitated at the entrance gate manned by an armed, uniformed Marine.

"Not coming?" Lerner asked.

"No. I want to get my bearings again, Bill, maybe make a few contacts. What time is dinner?"

"Eight. The Anchor in the Palace Hotel."

"I know it."

"I'll be there at eight. Elena will join us a little later, a chance meeting." A wan smile.

Pauling understood.

Lerner's four-year affair with Elena Alekseyevna was conducted quietly and with pragmatic discretion. Sleeping with a Russian woman was not encouraged for embassy male employees, especially those in sensitive positions like Bill Lerner. In fact, more than one libidinous male had been sent packing for succumbing to a Russian woman's wiles.

Lerner's superior in ECO/COM knew of the affair and, while not condoning it, chose to ignore it beyond cautioning Lerner on occasion to keep it low-key. Other supervisors might not have been quite so sanguine. But Lerner's boss and his wife had been extremely close to Lerner and his wife, Jackie, and with him went through the agony of her long, painful battle with breast cancer, which eventually took her life.

Lerner knew that he would one day have to face a decision about Elena, should his boss be transferred and a new one assigned. Until then, he reveled in the closeness he and Elena had forged, and viewed each day with her as a gift.

Pauling watched his old friend disappear beyond the guard station, then slowly walked away. As tiring as the long trip from Washington had been, at that moment he felt no fatigue. The past year in Washington had been like retirement, the days predictable and tedious, the lack of action and challenge wearying.

It was different in Moscow, and he welcomed the difference. Here, there was the element of tension, indeed of danger, puzzles to be solved, individuals to outfox, a need to be quick on your feet when someone you turned on decided to turn on you. He'd drunk vodka with Russian killers, and frolicked among the hookers and influence buyers with crooked Russian businessmen, whose approach to doing business, and to life, was not much different than that of Russia's organized-crime managers.

As he continued to walk, he thought of his most recent conversation with Doris about who he really was. He was glad he no longer felt the need to deny to his ex-wife that facing the challenges and dangers of his job was more satisfying than the challenges and, yes, dangers of a different sort, of being a husband and father. No more guilt, no more wondering whether something was wrong with him for not responding to family the way "normal" men were supposed to. Like Bill Lerner and his precarious need for Elena, Max Pauling needed something most "normal" men didn't.

So be it!

He paused to peruse a display of cell phones in a store window. As he did, he saw a reflection in the window of two young men in suits, smoking, observing him from across the street. Or were they observing him? Like most people in his business, he'd developed an instinctive sense of when someone was paying him too much attention. Was he being followed so soon? Good to be back in business.

He drew a deep breath, stepped away from the window, and picked up his pace. Might as well get some exercise, he thought—for himself and whoever might be tagging along.

15

". . . and so it is with the greatest of pleasure that I am able to stand here today, side by side with my able and honorable counterparts from the United States, to announce that after a long but pleasant round of negotiations, an agreement has been reached that is fair and equitable to both countries."

The Canadian minister of trade went on to explain the details of an accord reached on what had been a contentious issue between the United States and Canada— direct access to U.S. ports and markets by Canadian fishing vessels. His remarks completed, the negotiator for the United States stepped to the podium and said the requisite nice things about the Canadian negotiators. A small gathering of press in the second-floor briefing room took dutiful notes while former secretaries of state— William Rogers, Dean Rusk, Cordell Hull—kept unmoving eyes on them from their framed portraits on the wall. When the briefing was concluded and press kits handed out, reporters for whom State was a regular beat went to their cubicles in the press court to file their stories.

Two hours later, fifty or so members of Canada's embassy staff, led by the Canadian ambassador, traveled from the chancery on Pennsylvania Avenue to the State Department to join fifty invited American guests at a reception to celebrate the success of the negotiations. Roseann Blackburn, who'd been booked just that afternoon by her agent to provide background music for the occasion—"Johnny Johnson was booked but the jerk hurt his wrist in a tennis game this afternoon"—made sure she rehearsed "Canadian Sunset" before leaving the apartment, and had run through "New York, New York" after being told it was the Canadian ambassador's favorite song.

"What, nobody ever write 'Toronto, Toronto' or 'Montreal, Montreal'?" Potamos had said before she left for the job.

They'd argued that afternoon. Potamos, knowing he'd been less than a pleasant companion the past week, had planned to make it up to her that evening, starting with cocktails and the spectacular views of the White House and the Mall from the Sky Terrace on the roof of the Hotel Washington, then dinner at the romantic Coeur de Lion, and capping off the evening at Blues Alley, where jazz pianist Pete Malinverni, one of Roseann's favorites, was appearing with a trio.

"We don't have to make it such a big evening," she'd said in response to his disappointment that she'd taken the last-minute job. "I'll be home by eight, eight-thirty. We can grab a quick bite someplace and still catch a set at the club."

"Sure," he'd said, turning on the computer and logging on to AOL to check his e-mail.

She came around behind him and kissed his head. "I'll be back before you know it."

He turned, looked up at her, and smiled. "Just go on and play your gig. You're right, we'll skip the big dinner and

144

catch Malinverni at Blues Alley when you get back. Besides, I've got all this e-mail to answer." He raised his lips to hers. "You're delicious," he said when they disengaged.

"You taste pretty good yourself," Roseann said happily. "Got to scoot. Thanks for understanding."

Roseann knew he'd meant well, wanting to treat her to a special evening out. Earlier, she questioned whether she should have taken the job, considering the plans Joe had made for them that evening. Bill Walters, her agent at Elite Music, had been persuasive: "I really need you for this one, Roseann," he'd said. "I'm in a bind. They're in a bind. Besides, there's some nice opportunities brewing for you. We'll get together next week and discuss them."

So she said yes, acting out of her freelance musician's sense of survival: You didn't turn down a paying job because you never knew when the next one would come along.

Now, as the taxi went toward Foggy Bottom, she was pleased, and relieved, at Joe's easy reaction. She always played better when things were good between them.

"You play beautifully."

Roseann had just finished "Night and Day" and was about to begin another when the middle-aged man, who'd been standing behind her, complimented her.

"Thank you," she said, smiling.

"Nobody wrote better music than Cole Porter."

"One of my favorites," she said. "I love playing him. Any particular tune of his you'd like to hear?"

" 'Easy to Love'?"

"Sure."

"I'm glad to hear it."

"Glad to . . . ? Oh. I was referring to the song, not to . . ."

"I'm sure you were."

As she started to play, he came around and leaned on the grand's closed lid, watching her intently, listening closely to the music and never taking his eyes from her. She always played with more passion when she knew someone was really listening; others at the reception, as expected, paid no attention to her. When she ended on a dissonant minor chord, he quietly applauded.

"Thank you," she said. This was a handsome man by any definition—square jaw, lively blue eyes, wide, comforting smile. A gentle man, Roseann thought, easygoing, pleasant to be with, probably a good listener. Unlike . . .

"How late are you playing?" he asked.

She glanced at her watch: "Another hour."

"Free for dinner when you're through?"

"I, ah—no, I'm sorry, I'm not."

It wasn't an easy answer for her to give.

"Sorry you're not. I'm Craig Thomas." He handed her a business card: CRAIG THOMAS, PUBLIC INFORMATION OFFICER, THE CANADIAN EMBASSY, WASHINGTON, DC.

"I'm Roseann Blackburn," she said.

"I know," he said.

She laughed. No one at such gatherings ever knew the name of the pianist providing background music, or cared.

"I read about you in the *Washingtonian*."

"Oh, I forgot about that."

"Very flattering piece. Or maybe just accurate."

"Yes . . . I mean . . ."

"You won't be offended if I say you're even more attractive than your picture?"

"No, I'm not offended. Thank you."

She realized she'd better start another song and had played the first soft notes of "Memories of You" when he asked, "Having dinner with your reporter friend?"

She kept playing and cocked her head. "You really *read* the piece, didn't you?"

His laugh was easy. "I like keeping up with what's going on in the city." He plucked one of her business cards from a glass on the piano, put it in the pocket of his gray suit jacket, and said, "Your playing is the highlight of my evening, Ms. Blackburn. In fact, my week. These events can be deadly dull. Enjoy your dinner, and thanks for playing my request."

She watched him join a group of people a few yards away, and was tempted to catch his eye again and accept his invitation. It had been a stressful week with Joe; a pleasant evening in a restaurant with this Craig Thomas was appealing. It wouldn't be cheating to simply go to dinner, nothing more than that. But she didn't follow through. Joe expected her home right after the job, and she was looking forward to enjoying the music with him at Blues Alley.

She flipped through a small notebook in which hundreds of song titles were arranged by composer and chose "I'm Always True to You in My Fashion." Cole Porter said it all.

16

Diplomatic Security Special Agent Bruce Wray sat behind the wheel of the long, blue diplomatic sedan in front of "Main State," as the State Department building is called by those who serve it. A second vehicle, identical to the first, was parked directly behind. The radio in Special Agent Wray's car was tuned to an all-news station, the volume low.

Inside the building, Elizabeth Rock conferred with staff in her warm, wood-paneled inner office, light from lamps giving life to the burnished boiserie. Multiple photos of her daughter and two grandchildren, the Secretary of State with numerous heads of state, plus memorabilia testifying to her lifelong love of baseball provided an eclectic background for the meeting.

"These are the latest briefing papers, Madam Secretary," her confidential clerk said, handing her a file folder, which she placed on a growing pile.

Rock turned to Eva Young, her chief of staff. "The president is still in the meeting?"

"Yes, ma'am, with Director Templeton and Mr. Hoctor. Mr. Cammanati says it's due to break any minute."

Rock looked up at a stunning antique clock on the

148

wall, a gift from her daughter. "You'd better call flight ops and tell them we're running late," she instructed her COS.

Her executive assistant entered the room to inform Rock that the assistant to the Russian ambassador to the United States, Nikolai Sorokin, was on a secured line.

"Excuse me," the Secretary said, standing to go to a small room off her office to take the call. "Fourth call today from the charming, insufferable Counselor Sorokin," she said over her shoulder.

In her absence, those at the meeting relaxed and exchanged small talk until Rock reappeared. She hadn't even resumed her seat when her chief of staff opened the door: "The president, Madam Secretary."

Rock took this call at her desk.

"Yes, Mr. President . . . No, I'm running late, should be leaving here in ten minutes . . . What? . . . Oh, yes, sir, the meetings in Moscow are set." She laughed at something the president said. "I wouldn't miss them, Mr. President. Thank you."

She hung up and said, "He wants me to be sure and get back in time for the play-offs."

Her assistant secretary for public affairs, Phil Wick, silently thought that considering the severity of what was happening, and the gravity of the Secretary's sudden trip to Moscow, the president should be thinking of things other than baseball. Wick hated baseball, something he kept to himself.

"Ready?" her chief of staff asked.

"Yes, unless you have something else for me, Eva."

Nothing was offered.

"Let's go then."

Special Agent Wray had been notified on his cell phone that his passenger was on her way. He stood erect at the open car door and watched her exit the building, trailed by members of her staff and two uniformed security guards.

"Good afternoon, Madam Secretary," Wray said sharply.

"Good afternoon, Bruce. Any score?"

"Two-nothing," he said. "Yankees. Top of the third."

"Is Ripken playing?"

"No, ma'am. Erickson's pitching."

"Plenty of innings left," Rock said, climbing into the backseat, where she was joined by Phil Wick and Eva Young. Wray closed the door, got in behind the wheel, and slowly pulled away, followed by the second car, containing two armed diplomatic-security special agents. They made their way to the Capital Beltway and took it until reaching Prince Georges County, Maryland. Soon, the monstrous water tower at Andrews Air Force Base came into view. After being checked through security at the main gate, and joined by a military-police vehicle, they proceeded to where the Secretary's designated aircraft awaited her arrival, a converted pre-jumbo-jet 707 especially reconfigured to provide comfort, communications, and efficient working areas. The seal of the United States was boldly displayed on its tail.

Secretary Rock, Assistant Secretary for Public Affairs Wick, and Eva Young climbed the movable boarding stairs, returned a greeting from an Air Force major, and entered the aircraft. In the cockpit, the three-man crew, Air Force veterans, went over their preflight lists while ground maintenance personnel readied the plane for takeoff.

Already on board in the passenger cabin—actually a series of cabins created for specific functions: the Secretary's bedroom, bath, and small private office; a conference room; a communications center manned by Air Force technicians; lavatories; a press center; and other designated areas—were three men. They'd removed their suit jackets and sat at the small conference table on which pads of paper, materials from the briefcases they'd carried aboard, and a pitcher of ice water and glasses rested. They stood and greeted the Secretary.

"Please, sit down," she said. "I'll be back in a few minutes."

As Rock went to her private quarters, Wick joined the men at the table.

"The Secretary's looking well," Mike McQuaid, special assistant on terrorism to President Ashmead, said.

Wick frowned. "She handles pressure well."

"How are *you* holding up?" Herbert Shulman asked. Dr. Shulman was the highest-ranking civilian in the Air Force's Weapons Division, which reported directly to the Directorate of Special Programs, his area of particular expertise shoulder-launched missiles.

"Just fine."

"This should be like a minivacation for you," McQuaid said through a small laugh. "No press to coddle."

"I was thinking just that," Wick said, standing. "Excuse me." He retreated to the press center, where he sat alone. Usually, the seats were filled with journalists invited to accompany the Secretary on her many trips abroad. But this wasn't travel as usual. Wick had spent the day fielding questions from the press about the purpose of this particular trip. Despite his programmed denials—"The Secretary is going to Moscow to congratulate the new Russian minister of foreign affairs, Mr. Orlov, and to establish a working relationship with him. That is the only reason for the trip!"—the press were convinced that Secretary Rock was heading for Moscow because of the aircraft downings, and they let Wick know they knew. Some had become testy, prompting a few angry responses from the assistant secretary. He was glad the day was over and that the plane's press center was empty. With any luck, he'd be able to catch up on some of the sleep he'd missed since the attacks on the planes.

Elizabeth Rock was also grateful for a few moments of solitude. She stood in the private bath off her bedroom and looked at herself in the recessed mirror. This bathroom had been the subject of controversy after she'd been confirmed seven years ago. She'd taken an active role in the renovation and decorating of her office at Main State, and of the aircraft in which she would travel the world. She'd chosen Italian marble for the aircraft's lavatory and the bath off her office, the cost raising eyebrows among members of Congress already critical of the administration's spending policies, and journalists writing about it. Shades of Pentagon-ordered nine-hundred-dollar toilet seats and hundred-dollar ashtrays, they said. The flap eventually blew over, and Rock, sixty-four years old, widowed at thirty, with a Ph.D. in political science and a succession of increasingly important diplomatic jobs on her résumé, had her wood-paneled office and Italian-marble baths to enjoy.

As she leaned against a short wall, closed her eyes, and allowed her cheek to touch the cool marble, the 707's commander taxied to the end of the runway and then applied full thrust to the engines. Rock knew she should take a seat and buckle up, but she didn't move. No one would come looking for the secretary of state and insist she sit. A minute later, the Boeing four-engine aircraft was airborne and headed across the Atlantic on a new, important mission of many important missions.

Before the planes had been shot down, she'd been mired in days and nights of diplomatic game playing, feting heads of state large and small, gregarious and dour, friendly and antagonistic. Strange, and wearying, this business of diplomacy, she sometimes thought. She'd read Isaac Goldberg's *The Reflex* and jotted down one of his observations about diplomacy: "Diplomacy is to do and say the nastiest things in the nicest way." Once, when she'd recited that line to a friend at dinner, he'd retorted with something Adlai Stevenson had said on the subject: "A diplomat's life is made up of three ingredients, protocol, Geritol, and alcohol."

All of it true; so much ceremony, disingenuous rhetoric, accommodation of those not deserving of being accommodated, speeches—always a speech to give, an award to bestow, or a plaque to graciously receive.

But then there were those times when the froth of the job gave way to substance, when brokering a peace between a small country's warring factions took hard-nosed skill and attitude. Those were the times when the stakes were high for America, and the secretary of state's resolve matched that of others in the government charged with preserving and protecting the nation's sovereignty and vital interests.

This was one of those times.

She returned to the conference room and rejoined the three men. "Sorry to keep you waiting," she said. "I appreciate you joining me on this trip at the last minute."

"We've all had our bags packed and under the desk since it happened," McQuaid said.

"I know," Rock said grimly.

The Secretary turned to Dr. Shulman, the weapons expert from the Pentagon. "Why don't you begin."

He adjusted half-glasses, consulted typewritten notes, and began the briefing with, "The fact is, Madam Secretary, that the three planes were caused to crash by missile strikes, Russian-made missiles, a type generically known as MANPADs."

"Which means?" Rock said.

"Man Portable Air Defense Systems, shoulder-launched missiles."

"Go on."

She knew what MANPADs were because she'd been briefed more than once on the type of missiles used in the attacks. But she wanted to hear it again before the meetings in Moscow. It was as though that by hearing it repeatedly, some spark of understanding might emerge to help her understand how and why anyone would shoot down commercial aircraft carrying the most innocent of civilians—men, women, and children living ordinary yet important lives, lives that no other person had a right to take from them. Finding who was responsible for these inhuman acts, and bringing them to justice, had come to consume her, as it had everyone else involved in the investigation.

Shulman continued.

"Actually, Madam Secretary, our own Stinger missiles are the most common example of MANPADs; there are probably more of them in the hands of terrorist groups than any other type. Our estimate is that tens of thousands of Stingers have ended up on the world weapons underground."

"That's a lot of missiles," Rock said.

"Yes, it is," Shulman said. "We don't know how many missiles have been used to bring down civilian planes over the years—Stingers, French Mistrals, Soviet SA-18s and 14s—they're all available on the black market—but we know that some have."

Rock pulled a State Department report from her briefcase before he could continue. "This report goes back almost ten years," she said. "The intelligence agencies and terrorism experts were deeply concerned back then that these MANPADs would be used to bring down civilian planes."

She consulted another piece of paper prepared for her prior to leaving Washington and read from it: "Twenty-five commercial planes attacked by missiles between 1978 and 1993. Six hundred people killed in those attacks."

The third man at the meeting now spoke. He was Tom Hoctor, third in command of the Central Intelligence Agency's counterterrorism task force and Russian desk, and Max Pauling's boss at the Company. "Most occurred in Third World countries, Madam Secretary," Hoctor said, "and a few breakaway states from the old Soviet Union."

"We're not a Third World country," the Secretary said, lips drawn into a thin line, dark eyes that had stared down dictators across negotiation tables narrowed. She turned to Shulman, the Pentagon's weapons expert. "You say tens of thousands of our own missiles, the Stingers, have ended up on the black market. How many Russian SAMs do you estimate are in those same hands?"

"Easily as many, Madam Secretary. Once the Soviet Union fell apart, any semblance of weapons control collapsed, too. If you had the right connections, you could buy Russian SAMs, and worse, as easily as buying cases of Russian vodka."

Hoctor added, "It's compounded, Madam Secretary, by the situation in China, Poland, other countries who bought thousands of SAMs from the Soviet Union. They're a good source of weapons to terrorists, too. Poland does a brisk business with Colombian drug lords, and we have information that China recently sold SAMs to an organized-crime syndicate in Sicily."

"I find it strange," she said, "that no one has claimed

credit for the attacks. Isn't that what these terrorist groups want, after all, credit and publicity for their twisted aims?"

"Give it time," McQuaid said. "Someone will."

They continued to brief her for almost another hour. Toward the end of the meeting, the Secretary fell silent, her eyes on the tabletop, her mouth moving almost indiscernibly as she processed what was on her mind. She looked up, slowly shook her head, and said, "No matter how successful we are in bringing whoever did this to justice, they've won, haven't they?"

The men said nothing.

"They proved their point. The dislocation is complete. No matter what security is put in place, no matter how diligent we are, they're able to kill us. We fortify our embassies, ring the White House with concrete barriers, run luggage through sophisticated electronic machines, issue warnings about travel to foreign hot spots, do every damn thing we're capable of doing and they still . . . kill us." A rush of air came from her. "They didn't go after an enemy, someone in government whose policies are contrary to theirs. They went after the easiest targets, people who didn't give a damn about their politics or grievances, didn't give a damn about them at all, just Americans who happened to be flying to visit a parent or attend a graduation or—"

She realized she might shed tears, which she would not do, not in anyone's presence.

"Excuse me," she said, forcing a smile. "Time for dinner, and this secretary of state is hungry. Thanks for all your insight."

While Hoctor, Shulman, and McQuaid joined the Secretary's staff and security people in the press center for dinner served by Air Force personnel, Secretary Rock retired to her private quarters to take dinner alone, which included a glass of Rombauer chardonnay, her favorite, which was flown in from the boutique California vineyard especially for her, and was always on hand when she traveled.

Later, as the plane continued its flight over the Atlantic Ocean, the Secretary and Tom Hoctor sat in the conference room. Hoctor, a small, wiry man with a quick, wide smile, bald pate, narrow face, and a right eye that drooped slightly at the outside corner, filled Secretary Rock in on what initiative was under way in Moscow to identify the source of the SAM missiles that had downed the three U.S. commuter planes. Her request to be briefed about this had been debated at CIA headquarters in Langley, Virginia. Hoctor's boss was against it for security reasons, but he was overruled by the CIA director, who instructed Hoctor to inform the Secretary before arrival in Moscow. Rock and the CIA director had forged a good working relationship, something that could not be said for the previous Secretary and director. Establishing rapport with the heads of other agencies was one of Secretary Rock's strong suits, an attribute President Ashmead appreciated.

"I've met Mr. Pauling," she said.

"So he told me," Hoctor said.

"Yes, an awards ceremony. We got to talk a little afterwards. An impressive man."

Hoctor saw what he thought might be a mischievous glint in the Secretary's green eyes, and smiled.

"I appreciate being brought up to speed," Rock said, ending their meeting. "I think I'll try to catch a nap before we arrive."

"Good idea, Madam Secretary."

"If a nightcap will help you sleep, ask one of the cabin attendants."

"I appreciate the hospitality."

A few minutes later, a snifter of cognac in his hand, Tom Hoctor leaned his head back and smiled. That damn Pauling, he thought, able to generate a gleam in even the sixty-four-year-old eyes of a female secretary of state.

17

The main house on the Jasper ranch in Blaine, Washington, was large and sprawling. The central portion, constructed of twelve-inch-thick concrete blocks, had once been a stable. Over the fourteen years since Zachary Jasper had purchased the spread from its previous owner, he'd extended the basic structure through a series of haphazard additions, giving the house a modular look, boxes tacked on to other boxes without apparent concern for architectural niceties. Outbuildings had been constructed, too, seven in all—a barn; a new stable for the ranch's half-dozen horses; a woodworking shop; a bunkhouse accommodating a dozen people; a cabana of sorts next to an in-ground concrete pool Jasper had poured himself; a one-story clapboard building in which the ranch's arsenal of weapons was stored, maintained, and secured; and the most recent project, a two-story log building containing eight apartments, four up and four down.

The number of people living at the ranch fluctuated from month to month. Three women had resided there with Jasper over the fourteen years; the most recent, June, who at twenty-four was half his age, had been with him for three years. Her predecessor, a teenager, had borne him a son, and had taken him with her when she left five years earlier. The first "Mrs. Jasper" had been legally married to him when he moved the family to Blaine. They'd had four children together, three daughters and a son, Zachary Junior, who'd returned to live with his father when turning eighteen.

As of this morning, there were thirty-one residents of the ranch, many of them families that had responded to Jasper's marketing of the ranch as a bastion of white Christian values, with future plans to expand into the neighboring states of Oregon, Idaho, Montana, and Wyoming: "We will be the ten percent solution," Jasper said in his brochures. "One day, one tenth of the United States will be free of the mud people, the Jews and the blacks and the other minorities who are destroying our precious United States of America."

Jasper's stated goal of establishing a white Christian homeland in the Pacific Northwest was not limited to printed material. He held daily meetings with those who'd responded to his message, at which he slipped into the role of preacher, quoting the Bible to substantiate his beliefs and demanding adherence to his philosophy. This morning, over a big breakfast cooked by the women in the commune, he pontificated to others at the large, round kitchen table, including a young couple who'd arrived a week earlier with their eleven-year-old son, and who were staying in one of the apartments in the log house.

". . . and you've taken the first important step to creating a proper environment to bring up your youngster," he said, patting the boy's arm. "The way this country is bein' run into the ground by the Niggrows and Jews and other non-Americans, there won't be much left for your son by the time he's grown up and startin' his own family. The Zionist Occupation Government has this country in a greedy stranglehold, make no mistake about it. The antiwhite federal government and the mongrels won't let decent young white men like your son be heard. See, it's like this—and listen close to what I'm saying— Eve was seduced by the serpent and bore a son by him, Cain, who slew his brother, Abel. After that, Adam, the first white man, passed on his seed to another son, Seth, who became the father of the white race, God's chosen people. Cain's descendants are the Jews, who come from the seed of Satan. You read the book of Genesis while you're here, see that I'm right."

The boy turned to his father and said he wanted to go swimming.

"You listen to what Mr. Jasper has to say," his father said sternly. "You heed his words. And there's plenty of chores to do before you think about swimming."

The mother shifted in her chair, avoiding Jasper's eyes. She hadn't wanted to leave their trailer home in Southern California, pick up what roots they had to come to live in this place, with these people. But her husband hadn't asked her opinion or their son's. He'd been fired from a job as an automobile mechanic for initiating a fight with a black mechanic whom he perceived to be receiving preferential treatment. Two days later they were on the road, heading to, as he told his wife and son, "a place where the damn niggers don't matter and don't get special treatment."

"You go on out and take your swim," Jasper said to the boy, who eagerly left the table and disappeared through the screen door. "Make no mistake about it," he told the parents, "we're in a war, and we're getting ready for it. Luke 22:36 says, 'He that hath no sword, let him sell his garment and buy one.' "

Two other men sat at the table during Jasper's speech

to the newly arrived couple. One was Jasper's son, Zach, a surprisingly thin young fellow, considering his father's girth. The other, Billy Baumann, was a squarely built man of approximately forty, bare-chested, with sculptured pectorals and abdominals, and hard arms. He wore camouflage fatigue pants with flap pockets, and high black lace-up boots.

"You see," Baumann said to the couple, "Zachary is doing a remarkable thing in the interest of bringing Jesus Christ back into our lives and breaking the hold the Zionists and minorities have on this country. We're affiliated with dozens of groups across the country, good, God-fearing white people like us who are tired of laying down like beaten puppy dogs. We're getting ready for the grand fight, which will come. You can count on that and be a part of it."

"Another book I'll be giving you to read is *Essays of a Klansman* by Louis Bream," Jasper said. "He's got a point system in there for Aryan warriors like yourself, points for doing certain acts. Give you an example. A man will achieve special status in the eyes of the white God when he earns himself one point. You kill a Jew, that's a sixth of a point, same with a nigger, and so on. Kill that lily-livered president we got, and you get your whole point right away."

"Excuse me," the wife said, quickly leaving the table and the house.

Jasper laughed. "Sometimes it's hard for the women to get comfortable with what their men are fixing to do in the name of Jesus Christ. But she'll soon enough come around when she realizes you're doing what a good father should do, pull this country out of the gutter and get it away from the mud people."

"She wants to leave," the husband said, avoiding Jasper's eyes. "Wants to go back to California."

"Well, then, you tell her as the man of your household that she'll be doin' no such thing."

Billy Baumann stood and slipped into a green T-shirt that had been hanging over the back of his chair. "I'd better make the run into town," he said. "We're running low on things."

"Yeah, you do that, Billy," Jasper said. "On your way, swing by that house owned by that connivin' bastard, Howard. He still owes us for the help we gave him clearing that field. You tell him I want what he promised."

"That's twenty minutes out of my way," Baumann said. "I wanted to get to town and—"

"Just do what I say, Billy."

"Okay."

When Baumann was gone, Jasper said to the young husband, "Billy's the sort of man we're recruiting in every state, every day. You go on now and join up with your pretty little wife. Sit down and read the Scriptures together, and some of the other literature in your apartment. *The Turner Diaries* is one fine book, and tonight's movie after dinner is *Birth of a Nation*, one of the greatest motion pictures ever made. Ever see it?"

"No."

"Mr. D. W. Griffith, who made that fine movie, had it right all the way back in nineteen hundred and fifteen, how the Ku Klux Klan, no matter what others say, were the avenging angels of the white race."

"I'll look forward to seeing it, Zachary."

"And be sure your wife and boy are here to see it, too."

"Yes, sir, they will be."

Jasper went to where the women were finishing up the cleaning of breakfast dishes and complimented them on a fine breakfast. He kissed his wife on the cheek, slapped the back of his large hand against her buttocks, and stepped outside onto the porch that ran the length of the main house. The compound was busy with men handling chores, with some of the youngsters pitching in. It was a fine morning, Jasper thought, as he looked up into a pristine blue sky and drew a deep breath. He planned to spend it doing an inventory of the arsenal of weapons housed in the building dedicated to their storage, an enjoyable job. Jasper loved guns, had since he was a small boy growing up in rural Missouri. Later that day, he was scheduled to survey property a few miles away as a possible site for a satellite ranch to house others who'd communicated with him over the Internet in response to material he'd sent them. Two other smaller ranches had been established over the past fourteen years, and Jasper was proud of the expansion he'd managed to bring about.

The sound of a pickup truck caused him to turn. Billy Baumann waved as he slowed down to allow two mixed-breed dogs to cross in front of him, then gunned it and headed his red truck in the direction of the ranch's main entrance, waving to Jasper on his way. Jasper returned the gesture, stepped down off the porch, and took long strides to the weapons building, where two men dressed in jeans, blue denim shirts, and wide-brimmed hats leaned against it. Jasper pulled a ring of keys from his pocket, undid a large padlock, and swung open the doors. The men disappeared inside, reappearing a minute later. One carried a thirty-thirty-caliber rifle with a telescopic sight. His colleague held a Heckler & Koch Model 94 assault rifle, a nine-millimeter semiautomatic carbine whose sixteen-inch barrel had been sawed off to just under a foot in length. Jasper watched them climb into a tan ten-year-old Mercedes four-door sedan parked at the side of the building, and kick up dust as they left the compound.

* * *

As Billy Baumann headed down the road leading to the ranch, he passed a gray sedan parked on the shoulder, facing the main gate. Two men in suits occupied the front seats. Billy slowed as he approached, laughed, extended a middle finger, then accelerated past them. The driver of the car laughed and waved. They were FBI agents, one of two teams assigned to twelve-hour shifts to monitor traffic to and from the Jasper ranch since the three commuter airliners were attacked. The agent in the passenger seat held a camera with a long lens and a spiral-bound notebook. He hadn't bothered photographing the truck because they already had a half-dozen pictures of it, and of Baumann driving it. He noted the day and time in the notebook, leaned his head back, and closed his eyes. The boredom of such surveillance assignments was fatiguing. He opened his eyes and checked his watch; nine hours to go until they could return to their spartan motel room in Blaine and resume the game of chess they'd started the night before.

Five minutes later, the tan Mercedes approached. This vehicle, too, had been photographed on other occasions, but the agent squeezed off another shot to document the car's two occupants. "Making the beer run into Blaine?" he muttered to his partner.

"Probably. Not much other reason to go there."

Baumann continued for eight miles until turning off on a narrow, rutted dirt road running alongside a fast-moving stream. He drove slowly. Puddles dotted the road from rain the night before, and vegetation was thick on both sides, growing up and over the country lane like a canopy. He checked his watch. He was running late, which was why he hadn't wanted to make the detour to the small farm owned by Howard, last name unknown. He'd met the farmer once when he and a dozen other men from the Jasper ranch spent a day

165

clearing a field. Jasper had said it was a neighborly thing to do: "Got to be good to our neighbors, Billy Boy," he'd said. "The man seems like a decent, God-fearin' man, like us. We give him a hand, he'll do something for us. We've got to stick together as white men, like the niggers and Jews do."

As far as Baumann was concerned, Howard was a crazy old man with only half his teeth, and lips and beard stained from the chewing tobacco that caused one cheek to perpetually bulge, like a growth. But he wasn't about to disobey Jasper's order, get on his bad side. Jasper came off like a friendly patriarch, always talking about caring for his flock and making sure his values were heeded. But Baumann had seen the other side of him when he severely beat a man for getting drunk in town and saying bad things about the ranch's founder.

The road narrowed even more as Baumann approached Howard's small, ramshackle farmhouse. It looked like a set from *The Grapes of Wrath*. An overweight black Lab raised its head on the porch, barked once, and resumed its supine position. Baumann stopped the red truck by the porch. Two dilapidated floral love seats stood in the midst of pieces of rusted farm equipment, automobile tires, and two discarded floor lamps without shades.

Baumann rolled down his window and shouted, "Howard?"

No response came from the house.

"Damn," Baumann muttered as he prepared to leave the truck and go to the screen door in search of the farm's owner. But he glanced in his rearview and saw the tan Mercedes slowly moving along the dirt road in his direction. At first, he wondered why Jasper would have sent others from the ranch to remind Howard he owed a favor for having his field cleared. But that question was immediately replaced by the realization that the two men in the car were not coming for that purpose.

Baumann didn't hesitate. He rammed his left foot down on the clutch, slapped the gearshift into reverse, backed in a tight circle, and kicked up gravel and dirt as he headed down the road past Howard's farm, eyes darting between the mirror and the constricted road in front of him. The Mercedes had stopped; Baumann saw the two men talking with animation. Then, they began to follow.

Baumann knew the road would soon become a flat, relatively straight stretch before twisting up through a hill that, once navigated, would bring him back to the stream and eventually to the main road he'd turned off. He ran through the gears, gaining speed and keeping a watch on the Mercedes, which seemed to have trouble keeping up. Good, he thought as the road leveled out and he could accelerate even faster.

Minutes later, he arrived at a juncture where the road swung hard left and began its ascent up the heavily forested hill. He downshifted to gain traction and torque, but couldn't gain speed because of the road's rain-filled holes, and the rocks. A glance behind: The Mercedes, too, had started up the craggy incline. They'll never keep up with me, Baumann thought as he continued to shift gears in response to the terrain. But as he swerved right to avoid a large boulder that blocked half of the road, the truck's rear wheels lost their grip and skidded left off the road and backward down a shallow incline, stopping with a jolt against a large Douglas fir. The impact dazed Baumann for a moment, and he shook his head and squeezed his eyes shut against it. The sound of a vehicle on the road thirty feet above brought his head up. He reached beneath his seat and yanked open a flap of fabric held tight against the seat with strips of Velcro, creating a compartment. His right hand came up with two small items that he shoved into the flap pockets of his fatigues, then with an Ingram MAC-10 machine gun, with limited accuracy over any distance, but capable of gruesome results at close range. This model was a forty-five-caliber version that could fire nine hundred rounds a minute, fifteen bullets a second.

Baumann opened the door and rolled out, hitting the ground as the first shot from the thirty-thirty-caliber rifle hit a rock with a loud ping a foot from his head. He looked up the slope and saw the two men, permanent members of Zachary Jasper's sect, standing on the road, weapons aimed at him. Another shot, this from the sawed-off nine-millimeter, tore bark from the tree beside him.

Baumann crawled military style, propelled by his elbows, until reaching a sharp, ten-foot drop-off. He glanced back; the men had started down after him, widening the distance between them to maneuver him into a crossfire. He allowed himself to slip over the lip of the drop-off and slid down to a muddy ravine. He scrambled to his feet, slipped to his knees, then pulled himself up to firmer ground and quickly moved through a grove of saplings in the direction of the assailant with the thirty-thirty, who suddenly appeared at the top of the drop-off. Baumann brought the MAC-10 up into firing position and squeezed the trigger, sending a dozen bullets into the man's midsection, tearing it open, the shots clustered together as though the victim had been a target on a firing range. He'd been leaning forward, searching the forest for Baumann, when the fusillade hit. He pitched forward, the thirty-thirty preceding him, spun in the air, and tumbled to Baumann's feet, his mouth wide open as though to protest what was happening, his torso almost torn in half by the salvo from the MAC-10.

Baumann straightened as he heard the second man call

for his partner. The voice came from behind, the opposite direction. Using trees as handholds, Baumann hauled himself up the embankment, reached the crest, and crouched behind a large rock. He saw nothing . . . until two birds suddenly flew out of a bush, and Baumann saw what had sent them into flight. The second man had darted from the bush and behind a tree. He called again for his partner; Baumann sensed from the voice that he was scared, on the verge of panic. Let him make the next move, he told himself, the MAC-10 cradled in his right hand, ready for use. He remained in that frozen position, not allowing the perspiration running down his face to cause him to move, controlling his heavy breathing, eyes unblinkingly fixed on the bush, waiting, waiting . . .

The Heckler & Koch semiautomatic assault rifle came into view first, followed by the tentative steps of its owner from behind the bush. Baumann's eyes widened as the man approached where he lay, head swiveling in search of his colleague. When he was no more than ten feet away, Baumann slowly reached down, picked up a stone, and, when his assailant looked away, tossed it in an arc directly behind his foe, who spun around and started shooting at the sound. Baumann sprung from behind the rock and tackled the shooter, propelling his weapon and hat into the air, and pitching him face-first onto the ground. Baumann brought his hand back and slammed the ammo clip of the MAC-10 into the side of the fallen man's head, did it again, and again, until there was no movement beneath him. Now allowing his breath to flow naturally, and wiping sweat from his brow with the back of his hand, he searched his unconscious enemy for keys, picked up the assault rifle, and struggled up the incline to the road. He looked into the Mercedes. The keys were on the seat. Smiling, he slid behind the wheel, started the engine, and drove up the winding, rutted road until reaching the summit, then down to where the road joined the two-lane highway. He pushed the aged Mercedes to its limit, roaring past the few, slower-moving vehicles he encountered, until reaching the small town of Blaine and the intersection of Route 5, which he took south until a little more than an hour later, when he reached the northern fringes of Seattle. He pulled into the parking lot of a sporting goods and clothing store, bought jeans, a belt, a lightweight plaid shirt, white athletic socks, and a pair of moccasins, changed into his purchases in a changing room, transferred what he'd been carrying in his old clothing to the new, paid, left, and drove to Sea-Tac, Seattle-Tacoma International Airport. He checked the departure board. Good! A flight to Washington's Dulles Airport was scheduled to leave in two hours. He bought a first-class ticket with a credit card, went to the airline's VIP club, settled in a corner away from other passengers, and placed a call. It was almost noon in Seattle, three o'clock in Washington, DC.

The secretary in Sydney Wingate's office in the J. Edgar Hoover building answered the secured line. "This is Mrs. Wales," she said.

"I need Wingate," Baumann said. "It's Scope."

She went to the open office door and said to the special agent behind the desk, Sydney Wingate, the Elephant Man, "Scope on the SCI line." She backed away and closed the door as Wingate picked up the secured extension on his desk.

"Scope?"

"Yes. They blew my cover. I'm heading back."

"When?"

"Now." He gave the details of the flight.

"You're bringing what you have with you?"

"Affirmative. I've got it all."

"Come directly here."

"Okay."

"Skip" Traxler, known to Zachary Jasper as Billy Baumann—known to his handlers at FBI headquarters in Washington as "Scope"—hung up, went to a restaurant in the main terminal, where he had shrimp bisque, a salad, crusty French bread, and a local microbrewery beer, bought a paperback novel at a bookstore for the flight, and read in the departure lounge until his flight was called.

18

Pauling was glad Lerner had chosen the Anchor restaurant in the Palace Hotel because it featured American-style seafood dishes. He'd never become especially fond of Russian food during his seven years in Moscow, although the caviar was to his liking, and there were certain lamb dishes he enjoyed at the better restaurants. He'd learned early in his assignment not to order chicken: "The Russian method of slaughtering chickens is starvation," his American embassy friends often said.

Lerner was enjoying a scotch when Pauling joined him at a corner table as far removed from the dining room's bustle as possible. Pauling was served a Bloody Mary, which he raised in a toast: "Good to be with you again, Bill."

"The feeling is mutual, of course. Did you have a pleasant afternoon?"

"Very. I don't know why the Russians insist on cramming enough furniture for two rooms into one, but the bed's comfortable, and the shower actually delivers hot water. I took a nap."

"A sure sign of aging."

Pauling laughed and shook his head. "I've always enjoyed naps, short ones, twenty-minute battery chargers."

"I used to enjoy naps, but now I'm afraid I'll miss something," Lerner said in his soft, measured voice. "Our titular leader, Secretary Rock, is in town."

"So I've read."

"She impresses me. Her name is apt."

"A no-nonsense lady. I met her once. She looks you in the eye and doesn't let go. Where's Elena?"

"She'll join us shortly. You haven't made plans for after dinner, have you?"

"No."

"Good. I've arranged a meeting."

Pauling's eyebrows went up. "You aren't trying to find me female companionship, are you?"

"No, Max, I gave up pimping when I gave up naps, at least pimping for Americans. I think you'll find the meeting useful."

"Good. I'll look forward to it."

Lerner looked beyond Pauling to see Elena Alekseyevna crossing the dining room in their direction. He stood, kissed her on the cheek, and said, nodding at Pauling, "Recognize this stranger, Elena?"

She broke into a wide smile as Pauling stood, grasped her hands, and kissed her on both cheeks. "You look wonderful, Elena."

"Thank you, Max. You look fine, too."

"Don't flatter him," Lerner said, holding out a chair for her. "He naps now."

Elena looked quizzically at Pauling.

"Ignore him," Pauling said. "Come on, catch me up on what you've been doing since I left—and be sure to include how my leaving devastated everyone."

They chatted about many things over the caviar, and the *zhulienn*, a small casserole of mushrooms and sour

173

cream served in individual metal dishes, and the Dover sole flown in from England. When cups of strong, black coffee had been served to accompany vanilla *morozhenoe*—Pauling had forgotten how good Russian ice cream was—Elena said she had to leave.

"So soon?" Pauling said.

"Yes. I have an early meeting tomorrow, and unlike you, Max, I didn't have time to nap today."

Pauling laughed and stood. "Wonderful seeing you again, Elena. I hope we can do this again many times."

"We'll make a point of it." She kissed Lerner on the lips, glanced about the dining room, and left the table.

"Beautiful as ever," Pauling said, watching the gentle sway of her hips as she navigated the tables and disappeared from view. Elena Alekseyevna was more handsome than beautiful, Pauling knew: tall and sturdy, chiseled features, minimal makeup, and salt-and-pepper hair worn short, businesslike. She usually wore tailored suits, as she had that night, befitting her middle-level position at the Central Bank.

When the two men had resumed their seats and ordered more coffee, Pauling discerned an unmistakable sadness in Lerner's eyes. "You okay?" he asked.

"Yes, of course."

"I envy you. She's a fine woman."

"That she is." Lerner made a show of drawing a deep breath, sitting up straight, and smiling. "Let's finish up, Max, and go take a bath."

Pauling hadn't cultivated a liking for *banyas,* Russian public baths, which were as much a part of the national culture as borscht and vodka. He'd been to them a dozen times when living in Moscow, always at a Russian's invitation. Most deal meetings had taken place in hard-currency bars and restaurants owned by organized crime, or secluded rendezvous points on the docks, or in dachas, summer country homes popular with those city dwellers who could afford second homes, which included the political elite, plus stars of movies, organized crime, and crooked business.

But this night it was the baths, the Sandunov Sauna, one of the city's most popular.

"You don't have to come in with me," Pauling told Lerner as they approached the building on Neglinniy Pereulok. "Tell me who the guy is and go catch up with Elena."

"Oh, no, Max, wouldn't miss it. Things have been dull since you left. Besides, this gentleman is comfortable with me. We've—" He laughed. "We've bonded."

"This is the banker?"

"Yes. I originally called him just to ask whether he'd consider meeting a friend of mine. That's you, Max. But when he said tonight was convenient for him, I thought you'd want to take advantage of it."

Lerner paid the admission fee and they were directed to a changing room, where they handed their valuables to an attendant, who asked whether they'd brought bathing suits, towels, shampoo, and sandals.

"Nyet," Lerner answered.

The attendant assigned them small, curtained changing rooms and handed them the necessities they'd neglected to bring, including plastic robes. Each was also given a *venik,* a bundle of birch twigs with which to hit themselves, allegedly to get the blood flowing. They changed and met outside their cubicles.

"We shouldn't be here on full stomachs," Lerner said.

"Yeah, I remember," Pauling replied, feeling silly in his outfit.

"And no more than five minutes at a time in the sauna. Hate to have you pass out on me."

175

"Worry about yourself. Where are we meeting this guy you've bonded with?"

"The sauna. Ready?"

"Sure."

The sauna, a large room with three tiers of benches—the bottom level was the least hot—contained a dozen towel-clad men. Pauling's dislike of Russian saunas came back to him—the steam, the heat, the smell of aftershave lotion and toilet water and perspiration permeating the room as it sweated out of the bodies. *Bodies,* he thought as he and Lerner went to an empty space on the lowest bench, next to an overweight man smoking a long, thick, black cigar. Fat bodies, Russian bodies, expanded by all that grain and sugar and fats and oils and potatoes and greasy meat; what was the statistic? Russians have a 70 percent higher caloric consumption than Americans, and America wasn't a poster nation for svelte.

"Lerner," the fat man with the cigar said.

"Mr. Miziyano," Lerner said, extending his hand, which the banker shook halfheartedly. "Let me introduce you to my friend, Pauling."

Miziyano scrutinized Pauling before saying, *"Zdrastvuti."* Pauling returned the noncommittal greeting.

"So, Yuri, things are well?"

"Da." He struggled to his feet from the low bench and waved for Lerner and Pauling to follow him. They left the sauna and went to a small room with a table and four chairs. A bottle of vodka in a bucket of ice, and four glasses, sat in the table's center. Miziyano barked an order at an attendant for food to be brought to the room. The men sat, and Miziyano poured their drinks. *"Na zdrovia,"* he said, raising his glass.

"Yes, cheers," Lerner said.

They made small talk until a platter of snacks had been delivered. Once the attendant had left and shut the door, the corpulent Russian banker said, "So, your friend here, Mr. Pauling, is interested in missiles."

"Certain missiles," Pauling said.

"Yes, certain missiles," Miziyano repeated. "The ones that shot down your planes."

"Those missiles," said Pauling.

Miziyano grimaced, finished his vodka, and refilled his glass, not bothering to offer to do the same for Lerner and Pauling. "A dreadful thing what happened to your airplanes, Mr. Pauling. Tragic. My heart was sickened when I read about it."

Lerner glanced at Pauling, who he knew didn't have much patience with self-serving rhetoric.

"What do you know about those missiles, Mr. Miziyano?" Pauling asked.

A shocked expression crossed the Russian's broad face, and he placed his hands on his chest. "What do *I* know about these missiles? You insult me."

Pauling smiled. "Not my intention, sir," he said, "but I understand we're here with you because you *do* know something—or *someone* who might know."

Miziyano shrugged and transferred food from the platter to his mouth. "I know many people," he said, "and they know many things."

Pauling stood up, as if to go. Lerner said to the Russian, "Maybe this isn't a good time to discuss this, my friend."

Miziyano smiled and gestured to the room. "What better time? I would be willing to introduce you to a gentleman who might be able to shed some light on this matter, these missiles."

"*Might* be able to?" Pauling said.

Miziyano nodded and ate again, took a swig of his vodka. "Come, come, drink up," he said.

"When can we meet this gentleman who might know

something about the missiles?" Pauling asked, sitting down, and wincing against the heat of the vodka as it slid down his throat.

"A day? A week? I will let you know. Of course, he will have to be compensated for his time, huh?"

"Of course," Lerner said.

"How much?" Pauling asked, his voice now with an edge.

Another shrug from the Russian banker. "Let's talk in round numbers. Your government is very anxious to find out about these missiles. I am right?"

"Yes, you are right," Lerner said.

"Well, then, the information—if this gentleman is willing to provide it—will cost dearly."

"Round numbers," Pauling said.

"For the gentleman who provides to you the information? Two hundred thousand, although I am not certain if that would be his price. For me?" A low, guttural laugh. "My friend Lerner and I can talk about that at a later date."

Pauling started to say something sharp but Lerner cut him off. "A good starting point, my friend. You'll call?"

"*Da*. Good to see you, Lerner. Always a pleasure." He ignored Pauling.

"A shower, then home?" Lerner said to Pauling.

Miziyano laughed. "Shower? The baths, Lerner, always the baths."

They left the room, ignored his advice and showered, dressed, and walked up the street. There was a fine mist in the air creating halos around street lamps as they walked in silence until reaching a Metro stop.

"I'll leave you here, Max."

"We can share a cab."

"No, I prefer the Metro. Almost as good as Washington's, clearly superior to New York's. Join me, Max?"

178

"No. I'll enjoy a walk. Bill, I assume coming up with a million bucks isn't a problem."

"No problem at all. The entire budget of the United States is at our disposal. So to speak."

"Good night, Bill. Thanks for the sauna."

"My pleasure."

Lerner took a few steps down into the Metro station when Pauling stopped him. "Bill, do you think our fat friend played a role in selling those missiles to the bastards who used them?"

"Possibly. Money was involved, and he is, after all, in the money business."

"So he collects from both ends."

Lerner came back up the two steps. "Max, shelve your feelings. I've opened the door for you. Now you can hobnob with your people and get to the bottom of it."

" 'My people'?"

"The criminal types to whom our fat banker friend owes his Mercedes and fancy dacha, his whores, and his pinky rings. Large, weren't they?"

Pauling smiled. "I didn't see his girlfriends. Go catch your train, Bill. I'll see you in the morning."

19

Roseann Blackburn slammed the door to her apartment and came down the stairs with purpose. She stopped and looked back when the door opened.

"Look, you know I didn't mean it," Potamos, wearing shorts, said from the top of the stairway.

"Then you shouldn't have said it," she snapped.

"So forget I said it," he said, hands extended in a gesture of surrender.

"That's so typical of you, Joe; say something nasty, then say forget you said it. I'm late."

"We'll have dinner after the gig?"

"*You'll* have dinner after the gig! Or before. Frankly, my dear, I don't give a damn!"

She waved down a cab and ten minutes later was seated behind the gleaming black Steinway grand in the large lobby of the Four Seasons Hotel, playing an uncharacteristically dark version of "It Had to Be You." She finished that song and had just started "My Funny Valentine" when her eyes went to a cushioned chair across the room, near the bar. Seated in it was Craig Thomas, the Canadian embassy's public information officer. He raised his glass and smiled.

She was booked to play two forty-five-minute sets at the Four Seasons. At the end of the first, she went to the bar for her usual diet soft drink. Thomas sauntered up to her.

"What happened to Cole Porter?" he asked pleasantly.

"He's alive and well. Next set."

"How have you been?"

"Fine."

"It's Craig, Craig Thomas."

"Oh, I remember your name."

"I wouldn't be offended if you hadn't. How's your journalist friend?"

"Joe? He's as good as ever."

"Look, Ms. Blackburn, I'm not the aggressive type, the 'I won't take no for an answer' type. I'm Canadian."

The comment struck Roseann as funny, and she laughed. "Canadians aren't aggressive?" she said.

"On occasion, I suppose. Maybe this should be one of them. Free for dinner?"

"No. Well—"

"Just a pleasant, nonaggressive, hands-off dinner. To put it simply, I'd like to know more about you."

"Not much to know. I play the piano and . . . all right."

"A preference in restaurants?"

"No. I'll leave it to you. I'd better get back."

"I'll be here. 'I Concentrate on You'?"

"If you insist."

"The song."

"I know what you mean."

She finished the final set with a long medley, which brought polite applause from Thomas and two or three others. As she stood, closed the keyboard cover and saw him approaching, she had a fleeting moment of doubt. But when he arrived at the piano, smiled, and said, "Ready?" she simply said, "Yes."

20

State's officer in charge of educational outreach programs to area universities concluded his brief remarks and stepped away from the podium in the smallest of the eighth-floor diplomatic reception rooms. The forty people in the audience applauded, including Mac and Annabel Smith, and Jessica Mumford, who'd invited them along with a few other friends she felt might appreciate the moment and its meaning.

The event was to honor professors of international affairs and diplomacy whose students had interned at State over the past year. Jessica, as an adjunct professor at George Washington, had one such student, a young Egyptian exchange student she held in high regard.

"Must be satisfying to see your students go on to successful careers in diplomacy," Annabel said.

"No more so than seeing Mac's law students succeed," Jessica said.

"The stakes are different," Mac grumbled.

He'd become depressed over the past few weeks, and Annabel recognized it because she, too, had been out of sorts, feeling a vague, nagging discontent that was always

183

there even when events surrounding her were happy and positive. Like most of the country, she mused.

The downing of the three commercial planes with the loss of dozens of lives, and a sense of the loss of control, had set the nation on edge, although few were introspective enough to realize why their mood had changed. Not that the terrorist attacks had sent the population scurrying to bed and under the covers in fear of another attack. As with the World Trade Center bombing, it was business as usual, it seemed, across the country—except that it wasn't. Outwardly, perhaps; but inside, every American was a mix of rage and fear, confusion and anxiety. Depression—anger turned inward—was the way the shrinks explained it on the chatterbox TV and radio talk shows.

In Congress, the White House, and every other agency, federal, state, and local, the outrage was expressed daily in speeches, press releases, and appearances on those same talk shows for which the attacks were the subject of choice, the only subject, it seemed, worth exploring. Whether out of true sorrow, posturing, or genuine mystification, the country couldn't get enough of it, even though there was little new to get—the same video clips, the same sound bites played over and over while the talking heads tried to come up with different ways to say what had already been said.

"I'm so glad you could come," Jessica said to the Smiths as they prepared to leave.

"Thanks for the invitation," said Annabel. "Join us for dinner?"

"Love to but can't," Jessica said. "I'm going directly from here to my office, catch up on things. It's overwhelming."

"The attacks?"

"Yes. The paper piles up. The questions don't go away."

Annabel stepped into the ladies' room before leaving for dinner, and Jessica accompanied her. While brushing their hair and touching up makeup, Annabel asked about Max Pauling.

Jessica's response was a sardonic laugh. "Max who?"

"I shouldn't have asked," Annabel said.

Jessica touched Annabel's arm. "Don't mind me," she said. "Max is away."

"On business, or flying somewhere for fun?"

"State business."

Jessica leaned against the edge of the counter and seemed to deflate. "Funny," she said, "how the men in my life always seem to 'be away.' Skip—you met my ex-husband, didn't you?"

"Once, briefly."

"Skip's work with the Bureau had him off somewhere ninety percent of the time. I knew that would be the case when I married him, but wasn't mature enough to know how much I'd resent it. When I met Max—it was right here at State, at a reception—"

"I know. I remember how taken you were with him, although you tried to be aloof about it."

"You saw through that? Yes, I was taken with him. If he'd still been stationed overseas, in Moscow or some-place else, my antenna would have gone up. But he'd been assigned to DC, a desk job, like me."

"This latest trip—only temporary, I assume?"

"I'm sure it is. But do you know what, Annabel?"

"What?"

"It's not temporary in Max's mind and heart. He's been gone from the day he arrived in Washington. He hates being here."

"But didn't hate being here with you."

185

"No, I'm sure not, but he—a man like that—*men* like that are only happy when they've escaped the mundane, when they're being challenged by something or someone few of us encounter." She looked up at the ceiling, then at Annabel and smiled. "Max told me he once had a boat. That was early in his marriage. He said he'd take his wife and kids out for pleasure rides and never enjoyed it. It was only when he was alone and the weather was foul that he liked to take the boat out, navigate through the fog, challenge himself. Know what I mean?"

"I think so."

"Like Skip. They're capable of loving, and they do love, but we're more of a biological necessity for them. They love themselves more—especially when in danger. Max told me his former wife, Doris, is involved with an accountant. Smart lady."

Annabel considered Jessica's comments to represent an overly harsh evaluation, and her unstated characterization of accountants to be too general, but didn't express her feelings. Instead, she said, "Well, time to leave. Wish you could join us, and sorry you can't make our party next Saturday."

"Me, too, Annabel."

As they walked from the rest room, Jessica said brightly, "Maybe that's why I love birds so much, Annabel. They're predictable, and always entertaining. They stick close to their nests."

Annabel rejoined Mac. They said good night to Jessica, rode the elevator down to the lobby, took note of the extra armed security guards at the doors, and headed for a Pan-Asian dinner at Germaine's. It was after they'd arrived home at their Watergate apartment that Annabel recounted her ladies'-room conversation with Jessica.

"She ought to look for a man elsewhere," Mac said

while rubbing Rufus behind the ears. "Hang around IRS hearing rooms, or attend accountants' conventions."

Annabel laughed.

"What's funny?"

"Suggesting Jessica look for an accountant. Max Pauling told her his ex-wife is dating one."

"Smart lady."

"That's what Jessica said. Know what, Mac?"

"What?"

"I'm sorry for Jessica, and happy for me."

21

Roseann Blackburn and Craig Thomas had driven from the Four Seasons to the historic Tabard Inn, on N Street NW, in Thomas's car. He offered to drive her home after dinner but Roseann declined, and Thomas knew why. She didn't want to run the risk of her boyfriend, Joe Potamos, seeing her arrive in another man's car.

The taxi ride gave her a chance to ponder the evening, and, more important, what to tell Joe about how she'd spent it.

They'd started with a drink in the inn's lounge, then moved to the brick-walled outdoor garden with colorful umbrellas over the tables, and sculpture that was, surprisingly, artistic rather than merely decorative.

"So, Roseann Blackburn, tell me all about yourself," he said after he perused the wine list and ordered an Oregon pinot noir he could vouch for.

"Everything?" she said lightly.

"No, be selective. What's it like playing the piano in places like the Four Seasons? Does it ever get—well, boring?"

"Sometimes, but whenever it does, I focus on the

188

music and try to play a tune differently than I've ever played it before, find some new chord to use, a change of tempo. Music never bores me."

"I took piano lessons as a kid but they didn't take. Where are you from? When did you start lessons? Did you start with classical music? Were your mom and dad musicians?"

And so it went for the next two hours, scores of questions gently asked over crab salads, lobster and rosemary, a hefty loaf of raisin pumpernickel bread, and blackberry brulée tarts. At one point, Roseann wondered whether she should be annoyed at so many questions but she wasn't. This was obviously a man who was sincerely interested in other people, a man filled with natural curiosity. It felt good talking about herself. She was basically a shy, private person, secure only when a piano separated her from the rest of the world. But everything about Thomas exuded kindness, especially his eyes.

They lingered over coffee. Roseann said, "I've been babbling away about myself, something I never do." Then, unexplainably, she began to cry, softly.

"I'm sorry if I've upset you with all my questions," Thomas said.

"No, no, you didn't upset me," she said, dabbing at the corners of her eyes with her napkin. "It's just that . . ."

"It's just that what?"

"Things have been topsy-turvy lately, not going the way they were supposed to go."

His smile was comforting. "Obviously, your musical life isn't in turmoil. Your boyfriend?"

She nodded and swallowed against further tears. When he didn't respond, she said, "I'm absolutely nuts about him, madly in love, but sometimes I wonder why."

She spent the next five minutes talking about her relationship with Potamos, its ups and downs, highs and lows, the happy times and those other times, like tonight, when she wanted to drop a piano on his thick head. When she'd finished, she blew a stream of air at an errant strand of hair that had fallen over her forehead, smiled, then laughed and said, "I can't believe I've done this."

"Had dinner with me?"

"No, talked like this about Joe and my personal life to—to a stranger."

"I understand," he said, motioning to their waiter for the check. "If I'd known how much in love you were with him, I wouldn't have asked you to dinner."

"I'm glad you did. I'd better go."

"Sure. Drive you home?"

"No, I'll take a cab, thanks."

They went to the bar, where Thomas told the maître d' a taxi was needed for the lady.

"I understand your friend Potamos has an interest in a murder that occurred not long ago," Thomas said casually as they waited.

She thought for a moment, then replied, "Oh, the Canadian, the man who was killed in the park."

"Yes. Jeremy Wilcox. He was a friend of mine."

"Oh? I'm sorry."

"We worked pretty closely at the embassy."

"That's right, he did work there. I never even thought about that. Joe has been trying to find out more about it."

"So I hear. I might be able to help him."

"Really?"

"Yes. There's an aspect to it that no one knows, at least outside of a few of us at the embassy. Have him call me." He handed her his business card.

"I already have one," she said.

"I thought you might have tossed it in the trash the

190

minute you left the reception. I'm serious, Roseann. I'd like to talk to Mr. Potamos."

"All right, I'll—"

The cab arrived. Roseann shook Thomas's hand. "Thanks for a lovely evening, although I didn't intend to have you end up playing shrink."

"I enjoyed every minute of it. Safe home."

She had the cab drop her two blocks from the apartment, in front of a convenience store that carried Joe's favorite ice cream flavor—peanut butter chocolate—and bought a half gallon. He was at the computer when she arrived.

"Hey, I was getting worried about you," he said, getting up and kissing her.

"I went out for a bite with friends. Here." She handed him the ice cream.

"Hey, thanks."

Later, in pajamas, they sat up in bed eating ice cream.

"I love you, Joe," she said.

"Even though I can be an idiot sometimes? Or because for a few minutes a day I'm *not* an idiot?"

"Maybe that's *what* I love about you."

"Lucky me."

They put their empty dishes on the night table and made love. After, and when what had been left of their ice cream had melted into cold soup, Potamos let Jumper lick from the bowls while Roseann went to the bathroom.

How do I finesse this? she thought as she looked in the mirror. He'll be pleased to have a lead on the murder story, but I'll have to tell him about going to dinner with Craig.

Tomorrow, she decided. It can wait until tomorrow.

"Joe, I didn't go out to dinner last night with friends. I went out with a man I met at the State Department when I played that reception a few days ago."

Potamos had been reading the paper and enjoying an English muffin and coffee. He lowered the paper and looked at her across the kitchen table. "You went out with this guy?"

"Yes. He was at the Four Seasons, and you and I were fighting, and . . . he's with the Canadian embassy, in public information. He says he was a good friend of the embassy person who was murdered, the one you've been digging into, and says he can tell you some things that no one else knows about the murder."

"Yeah? What's his name?"

"Thomas."

"Thomas what?"

"Craig Thomas. And, Joe, all we did was go to dinner and talk. He's a gentleman. We shook hands when I left the restaurant. Here's his card. He wants you to call him."

"I will. You have a thing for this guy, Roseann?"

"No, Joe, I have a thing for you."

He considered pressing her about Thomas and their dinner together but thought better of it. She'd been honest with him, and he was sure there wasn't more to it than she'd said there was. Besides, he reminded himself as he stood up, he was lucky she was there at all, considering how he'd been acting. He touched the back of her neck as he passed her chair, felt her fingertips on his hand, and went to the phone.

22

"You're confident about this?" Russell Templeton asked.

"Yes, sir," Sydney Wingate, one of the Bureau's handlers of special agents working undercover, responded.

FBI Director Templeton sat at a round table in his office with Wingate and with Joe Harris, head of the Bureau's counterterrorism division. "Joseph?" Templeton said, looking at Harris, to whom Wingate reported.

"It looks solid," Harris said. He consulted a computer printout. "We've had someone inside five—no, make that six militia groups. Recently, I'm talking about. These are the six our intelligence indicated were most active and likely to mount some sort of an attack in the near future. It's a crapshoot, as you know. With more than five hundred identified hate groups in the country, and damn near fifteen hundred web sites, you hope you choose right. In this case, it looks like we did."

"The Jasper Project."

"Yes, sir. We got lucky in another way. They blew Scope's cover a day ago. He's fortunate to be alive. But he is alive—very much so—and got out of there with the goods."

"Where is he?"

"We've got him secluded in Virginia, one of the safe houses," Wingate said. "He's finished his report, and I've seen the documentation he brought with him. He's done a hell of a job."

Templeton glanced at a paper on his desk and read aloud from it, paraphrasing: "Traxler, Donald, nickname 'Skip,' sixteen years' service with the Bureau, plenty of commendations, nothing negative in his file. Divorced, no children, former wife with State Department, teaches part-time at GW. Worked undercover past eleven years, speaks fluent Spanish, passable German, psychological profiles negative." He stopped reading and grimaced as something on the paper stopped him. "What's this report from the psychiatrist?"

Wingate said, "Not too bad. It was after his last undercover assignment in New York. The debriefing psychiatrist passed him, but commented that he felt Traxler was prone to taking greater risks than prudent, and tended to be scornful of authority. Not an unusual profile for someone in his line of work. It's high-risk to begin with."

Templeton picked up another sheet of paper. "This shooting death of a member of the Jasper group—Traxler?"

"Yes, sir," Wingate replied. "As I said, his cover was blown and he had to shoot his way out. They sent two men from the ranch after him. He killed one, disabled the other. Our agents in the area have things under control with local authorities. Assailant unknown. They won't push it."

"Will Jasper push it?"

"Unlikely. He's already gotten the word out in the community that it was a hunting accident. Wouldn't look too good to his followers that he had an FBI agent in his compound for almost six months and didn't know it."

Templeton sat back, rubbed his eyes, and took in Harris and Wingate. "Is Jasper and his organization national?"

"National?"

"Yes. The three aircraft downings occurred in three diverse geographical areas—New York, Idaho, California. They've got followers in all those places?"

"These militia groups are forming alliances every day, sir. The networks they're establishing make them especially dangerous."

"So we might be talking about groups other than Jasper's."

"Affirmative. But Jasper is the point man. Scope's nailed that down."

Templeton sighed. "All right," he said. "If what Scope says is true, and if his proof holds up, I'll take it to Justice. Until then, it stays strictly with us. No leaks. I want a personal briefing by Scope at three this afternoon, all of it laid on the table. Be here, too. Any questions?"

"Just one concern," Harris said. "State has an operative in Moscow trying to run down the source of the missiles. Barton at State briefed me on him. Should we coordinate with them?"

"I don't see why," Templeton said. "If we've got the ones who used the missiles, how they got them is of secondary importance. I want an immediate mobilization order issued, all regional resources moved into place within striking distance of Jasper's ranch. Quiet but fast. Get an authorization for aircraft, as many as we need, to move manpower and armaments out there, tactical units, the mobile communications center, firepower necessary to make damn sure it goes without a hitch."

Harris ran his hand over his shaved head. "A little premature, sir, without Justice's okay?"

"With what you've told me, getting the go-ahead from Justice won't be a problem. Everybody wants action, including the White House—*especially* the White House. I want every scrap of intelligence we have on Jasper and his ranch, who's there, what weapons they have, number of women and children—they have women and children, don't they?"

"Yes, sir," Harris said. "Everything you're asking for is in Scope's report. I'll have it here by noon."

"Good. No mistakes. This won't be another Waco!"

23

That Same Day

"You've reached the public information office of the Canadian embassy. No one is available to take your call at the moment. Please leave your name, number at which you can be reached, and a brief message, and your call will be returned as soon as possible."

"This is Joe Potamos from *The Washington Post.* I'm calling Mr. Thomas, Craig Thomas. Please have him return my call at his earliest convenience." Potamos gave the numbers for both his Rosslyn apartment, and Roseann's.

Potamos hung up, sat at the piano, and picked out "Chopsticks," slowly, with his index finger. Roseann had left the apartment to meet with her agent; Potamos was due in a half hour for a story conference with Gil Gardello. He continued to doodle at the keys until he realized there wasn't any way he could make the conference on time. He tried Craig Thomas's number again before leaving but received the same recorded message.

"You be good," he told Jumper, gently holding her snout and peering into her soulful brown eyes. He was out the door when he heard the phone ring, rushed back to the apartment, and snatched up the receiver.

"Joe, it's Roseann. I wanted to remind you we're having dinner tonight with Bill and Jane Mead."

"Yeah, right. Thanks."

"Aren't you supposed to be at a meeting?"

"I would be if I wasn't on the phone with you." He knew it was an edged comment the moment he said it, and apologized—into a dead phone.

Gardello's story conference was in full swing when Potamos arrived at the *Post*'s Fifteenth Street headquarters, and he received a disgusted look as he joined the six other beat reporters in the cramped office. Potamos looked around. He was easily the oldest in the room, with the exception of Gardello, who was approximately his own age. Gardello outlined stories that were to be pursued over the coming days and assigned them to each individual reporter. The last assignment went to Potamos: Investigate reports of a growing rift between the District's school board and the superintendent of schools.

Potamos said nothing while Gardello wrapped up the meeting with a moment's pep talk on the importance of local news. Potamos was the first on his feet and was headed for the door when Gardello stopped him: "Stay a minute, Joe."

"What's up?" Potamos asked when the two were alone.

"You heard my assignment about the school board and super, right?"

"Right."

"You have any problem with it?"

"Problem? No, I don't have a problem."

"You didn't look especially interested."

Potamos shrugged. "What do you want me to do, Gil, break out the champagne?"

"Sit down, Joe."

"I have to get out of here," Potamos said, "get cracking on the story, maybe do street interviews with kids, ask them how they feel, who they think is right, the superintendent or the board."

"Sit down, Joe!"

Potamos slumped in a chair.

"I want you to listen to me, and listen hard. You are hanging on here by a thread, a goddamn thread. You are a disruptive force at the paper, and you've rubbed damn near everybody wrong, top to bottom. Lately, I've been spending more time than I want to saving your Greek ass, and I don't like it. I've got better things to do. I'm all through warning you, Joe. Either straighten up and fly right, beginning with the school board story, or you're not journalism, you're history."

"Okay. I'll do the school story."

Gardello's tone softened. "I like you, Joe, I really do. You've got a lot of talent, lots of street smarts and good sense when somebody's pulling your chain. But I can't keep covering for you, damn it! What's with this Canadian thing you've been chasing down?"

"What Canadian thing?"

"The guy who was murdered in the park. Wilcox. Jeremy Wilcox."

"What about it?"

"You've been poking your nose into it even though I told you—what, a week ago?—to drop it."

"Where do you hear that?"

"My boss, Joe, who got it from somebody she knows, only I don't know who that somebody is and I don't care. I *do* care that my boss cares, and wants the story to stay where it is, another unsolved DC murder."

Potamos sat up straight and showed his first spark of interest since arriving. "Somebody's putting the arm on this paper to drop it?"

Gardello swiveled in his chair and looked away.

Potamos chewed his cheek before saying, "Gil, if this

is just another unsolved DC murder, why would someone care that I keep looking into it? On my own time, I might add."

"I don't care when you're doing it, Joe, I'm telling you to stop."

When Potamos didn't respond, Gardello added, "I mean it."

"Yeah, I know you do, and I appreciate everything you try to do for me. Okay, I'm off the case. Who cares that some Canuck trade rep gets whacked in a park? Not me. Anything else?"

"Somehow, I don't get the feeling you're totally sincere, Joe."

"Sincere? My middle name. Thanks, Gil. I'll keep you informed on the school board story. *Ciao.*"

Gardello watched through his glass door as Potamos left, made his way through the newsroom, stopped to exchange greetings with a few people, then disappeared in the direction of the elevators. The anger the editor had displayed during their brief meeting had been for show. What he'd really felt was sadness and frustration. The truth was, he liked Joe Potamos and wanted to save him from himself, keep him around, play some small role in resurrecting his career at the *Post.* It was a salvage job he wasn't sure was possible, but he knew he'd keep at it until he succeeded, or Potamos went down in a flaming, self-induced crash.

Potamos stopped at his Rosslyn apartment to pick up some fresh clothes, then went to Roseann's, where the answering machine was blinking; the digital readout indicated there were nine messages. Ordinarily, he wouldn't have bothered replaying them; virtually all would be for her. But he pushed PLAY and listened. The first seven calls were for Roseann. The eighth was a woman who asked for him.

"I'm calling Mr. Joseph Potamos. I would like very much to speak with you. I presume you know what this is about. I'll try you again at another time."

Potamos replayed the message. "Damn!" he muttered. Why didn't she leave a number? She sounded Canadian, judging from her pronunciation of *about,* which became more nearly *aboot.* He called the number on Thomas's business card again, received the same recorded message. He listened carefully to see if the woman's voice on the embassy's outgoing message was the same as on Roseann's answering machine. He thought it was. He left a message. "This is Joe Potamos from the *Post.* I'm trying to reach Mr. Craig Thomas, or a woman who might have responded to my previous message. Please call me."

Again he left both numbers.

He sat in front of the computer, pulled up a database he'd created of his Washington contacts, and scrolled to names from the District's school system. The name of an administrator whom Potamos knew to be an alcoholic, and for whom he'd done favors in the past, appeared. Potamos jotted down his office and home numbers. He wasn't in his office but he reached him at home.

"Walker, Joe Potamos from the *Post.* How are you?"

"All right."

"I need to talk to you."

"About what?"

"About the hassle going on between the board and the superintendent."

"I don't know anything about that."

"Sure you do, Walker. Dinner? My treat."

"I, ah—"

"You owe me, Walker."

"I suppose so."

Potamos made a date for them to meet at six at

Martin's Tavern in Georgetown, where the prices were low, the food good, and where they usually shaved the bill for him. He walked Jumper, splashed water on his face, wrote a fast note for Roseann saying he was out on an assignment, and left. He was determined to do a good job on the school story if only to get Gil Gardello off the hook with his boss, a driven woman with ambition in her veins and a heart made of brass. But as he rode in a cab to Georgetown's oldest tavern, his thoughts turned to Canada and the small Foggy Bottom park in which Jeremy Wilcox had been murdered. A harmless-seeming man is murdered, a knife in his side, in a park. His job is innocuous enough, probably important, but one like a thousand others. Not much is known about the man, and it appears few will mourn him. There is heat on to close the books. But a human being remains dead, a knife user walks, and no one cares. Or no one has turned up yet who does.

Why hadn't Thomas returned his call? The Canadian was the one who initiated contact through Roseann, said he wanted to talk to Joe.

Had Thomas taken Roseann to dinner because he wanted a line to Joe?

Who was the woman who called? Why hadn't she left a number? Did *she* have the story Thomas had mentioned to Roseann?

And why was someone putting the arm on the paper to unpursue the Wilcox murder?

Walker Appleyard drank vodka with orange juice. Buying drinks for a guy with a drinking problem caused Potamos only minor and fleeting guilt. He was there to get a story, not play Bill W. When Appleyard finally opened up, Potamos had enough leads on what was happening inside the school board and in the superintendent's office to form the basis for the story.

He raced back to Roseann's apartment to see whether anyone had called him. No one had. The only message was a note from Roseann on the kitchen table: *At dinner with Bill and Jane Mead. Hope you had a pleasant evening. Why don't you and Jumper stay in Rosslyn tonight. Witnessing her master's murder might upset her. R.*

24

The director, Joe Harris, and Sydney Wingate listened intently, making only an occasional written note but saying nothing to interrupt Special Agent Skip Traxler as he presented his report on the months spent undercover with Jasper. He spoke for forty-five minutes, using a series of photographs, sketches, and an audiotape to illustrate the points he wished to make. Included in his evidence that the Jasper Project was behind the missile attacks were copies of maps and charts, including aeronautical charts of Boise, Idaho, San Jose, California, and Westchester County airport, New York, he'd managed to photocopy before being forced to flee the ranch.

He concluded, "I think that covers it. Happy to answer any questions."

There was silence in Templeton's office until the director said, "A most impressive job, Agent Traxler. You're to be commended."

"Thank you, sir."

Templeton had watched Traxler make his presentation with a sense of pride. The forty-year-old special agent looked the way Templeton wanted FBI special agents to look—military bearing, physically fit, hair close-cropped, clear-eyed, dressed conservatively in a gray suit, white shirt, and muted tie. In the days when only accountants or lawyers were acceptable candidates to become special agents, there was that sense of a military unit. But as criteria for admission to the Bureau broadened, so did the style of its agents, resulting in the demise of the "IBM look"—dark suits and white shirts were now being replaced by the more casual attire of the new, Silicon Valley generation.

The director referred to his notes. "That audiotape you played," he said. "It's not very audible."

"It was recorded under difficult circumstances, sir," Traxler said. "But I think the thrust of it comes through loud and clear. Jasper intends further attacks."

"But it doesn't specify what form those attacks might take," Templeton said.

"True, sir, but considering that he masterminded bringing down three civilian aircraft with innocent victims aboard, it's reasonable to assume, I think, that future attacks will be similar in nature."

"Let me see those pictures," Templeton said to Harris, who was staring at them. He handed them to the director, who adjusted his half-glasses and squinted as he took a close look. "These shots of the weapons storage shed," he said to Traxler. "You say those bags on the shelf are the ones used to transport the missiles to California, Idaho, and New York?"

"Yes, sir."

"And they're empty."

"Yes, sir. There are only two of them. The one used to transport the missile to California never came back to the ranch."

"I'm a little confused, Agent Traxler. You say the missiles were carried from Jasper's ranch to California, New York, and Idaho by members of his group, but that those same people weren't necessarily the ones who actually fired them at the planes."

"That's correct, sir. Jasper is affiliated with other groups around the country. I've included the names of the ones I know in my report. It's my understanding that members of those splinter groups used the missiles supplied by Jasper, but I can't be certain of that."

"Who actually transported the missiles from the ranch?"

"Page seven, sir. Those names are listed there."

Templeton sat back, removed his glasses, and frowned.

"How did the three missiles end up in Jasper's hands, Skip?" Harris asked. "You say they were smuggled into the country by Chinese arms dealers. How did Jasper make the contact with these dealers?"

"I don't know," Traxler responded. "I tried to find out but didn't want to push it. I sensed I was walking on thinner ice and wasn't about to blow my cover." He smiled. "As it turned out, my cover *was* blown, but you know about that."

"What blew it?" Templeton asked.

A shrug from Traxler. "I don't know specifically. Lots of times it isn't any one thing. You just know that they're looking at you in a different way from when you managed to infiltrate."

"And fortunately you recognized it when you did and were able to get out in one piece," Sydney Wingate said.

"Wasn't hard to recognize it," Traxler said, smiling. "Jasper sent two of his people after me with guns. I got the message."

Wingate asked Traxler, "As far as you know, Skip, they don't have any other missiles in their possession."

"Correct," Traxler replied. "At least I didn't see any."

"You say the missiles came through Chinese arms dealers."

"According to Jasper."

Templeton came forward, elbows on his desk. "When did you learn of the missile attacks on the civilian aircraft, Agent Traxler?"

"When? After the fact, sir. If I'd known in advance, I would have passed the information along to—" He looked at Wingate and almost said Elephant Man. "To Agent Wingate, sir. Jasper kept the operation very much to himself. It was only after the planes had been attacked that he talked openly about it, bragged about it, to be more accurate. He had the TV on day and night after it happened and damn near cheered as the news reports came through at how successful the attacks had been, the number of people dead as a result. Those times were the toughest for me. I wanted to shoot the bastard right there in the lodge."

"I can understand," said Templeton, "and I applaud your restraint." He turned to the others. "Anything else?"

"Jasper gives the impression that he's a reasonable man, sir," Traxler said. "Former college professor, Bible reader, which he uses to bolster his claims, a father figure on the ranch. But beneath that veneer is a madman. He once told me that if the government ever attacked and tried to take the ranch from him, he'd kill every man, woman, and child there before he went down."

After a few moments of silence, Templeton said, "Thank you for coming here, Agent Traxler, and for your superb job of infiltration under what were obviously difficult circumstances."

"I was honored to be chosen to do it, sir."

Traxler stood.

"Agent Traxler has requested an extended leave, sir," Wingate said, "and I've granted it. He'll remain in the safe house for a few more days, then go to a place of his choosing. Naturally, we'll be in daily contact in the event he's needed again."

"Good," Templeton said, coming around the desk and shaking Traxler's hand.

When Traxler was gone, Templeton said to Harris and Wingate, "I've arranged a meeting with the attorney general at five. He's been briefed on what Traxler's report contains, and the nature of this briefing. If he now agrees, and the president does, too, and criminal charges are brought, we'll make our move. In the meantime, we're continuing to position ourselves for a possible assault on the Jasper ranch. Naturally, we'll want to resolve it peacefully, have Jasper and his people give themselves up. But if they don't . . ."

"We're ready for that possibility, sir," Harris said.

"Yes, we must be ready to move. Thank you, gentlemen, for a fine job. I wish Agent Traxler had better information on the other groups involved in this, Jasper's partners."

"That'll come," said Harris, "through Jasper once he's in custody. As I said this morning, sir, we got lucky. More than five hundred hate groups around the country and we placed Scope in the right one."

"I don't believe in luck," Templeton said. "The Federal Bureau of Investigation does not believe in luck. We make our own good luck. Excuse me. I have calls to make."

25

Two Days Later
Moscow

Max Pauling had used his first five days back in Moscow
to settle in at the United States embassy, occupying the
office that had been his the year before, until he was reas-
signed to Washington. It was one of six such offices in
the ECO/COM division under the leadership of William Lerner, ostensibly to foster trade and commerce, in
reality providing intelligence to the CIA on Russian industry, legitimate and, increasingly, not so legitimate. He
spent part of his time in the Russian city poring over
reports generated by others in the division, and com-
muniqués from CIA headquarters in Langley, Virginia,
channeled through Lerner. He found most of the information to be of little use. A more productive exercise was
reestablishing contacts with sources in Moscow's nether-
world, men and, more recently, women who knew more
about Russia's economic and industrial landscape than
those in official capacities, and who were willing to sell
what they knew for the right price. Pauling quickly
learned from calls he made, and two lunches, that infla-
tion was alive and well in every sector of the Russian
economy, including the price of information.

Lerner had been away for the past two days at a

conference in Ryazan, a hundred and fifty miles south-east of Moscow. He walked into Pauling's office the morning after his return. A front had pushed through Moscow the previous night bringing a cold, drenching rain to the city on the broad Moskva River, home to more than nine million, and the unchallenged political, cultural, criminal, and economic center of all things Russian.

Lerner shook water from his raincoat and hat.

"You're making puddles on my floor," Pauling said.

"Better your floor than mine." Lerner hung the coat and hat on a coat tree and took a chair across the desk.

"Good trip?" Pauling asked.

"Excruciatingly boring," Lerner replied, "but that's expected. How are you doing?"

"Fine."

"Making progress?"

Pauling nodded. "I'm—"

Lerner held up his hand and raised his bushy, grizzled eyebrows. "Free for lunch?"

"Yes."

"Good." Lerner stood and retrieved his coat and hat. "Sorry for the puddles, Max. One o'clock?"

"I'll be here."

At one, they took a taxi to Tren-Mos, on Ostozhenka ul, where Lerner was greeted by the owner, an American from Trenton, New Jersey, who'd opened the restaurant in 1989 in partnership with a Russian businessman. They were seated at a small table partially hidden from the rest of the dining area by a waist-high planter filled with flowers. A portrait of George Washington looked down at them from the wall above. A waiter who'd been working tables in the front of the room was dispatched by the owner to handle Lerner and his guest.

"Like being back home," Pauling said, taking in the

rest of the red-white-and-blue decor, including flags from the fifty states.

"A pleasant change," Lerner said. "My friend named it Tren-Mos for Trenton and Moscow."

"Very democratic."

"Yes. I hadn't thought of it that way. We can talk here. Too wet for the park."

"Better food, too. I've set up a meeting with the guy your banker friend passed to you."

"Good. When?"

"Tonight. I may put in for combat pay. We're meeting at a disco. The Red Cat."

"Disco not your musical cup of tea, Max?"

"You know it's not. I brought six tapes with me, Ellington, Basie, Ella, Benny Goodman, Artie Shaw, and a vintage Miles Davis. My desert-island collection. We're meeting at eleven."

"Not past your bedtime?"

"Sure it is, but I'll manage, catch a nap."

Lerner chuckled. "Ah, yes, a nap. How did you reach this gentleman who's fond of discotheques?"

"I called the number you gave me before you left, got a woman who thought she spoke English. She gave me another number. He was there."

"What did you say to him?"

"I told him the banker suggested I call and that I would appreciate a chance to meet with him in person."

"Did he balk, ask questions?"

"No, but I had the feeling the banker prepped him that a call would be coming. I'm sure he knows exactly what this is about."

"I asked Mr. Miziyano for some background on this individual. He said he was a man of honor—"

"Of course."

"A man of honor who could prove to be helpful in

your business venture, provided you could come to terms."

"Two hundred thousand."

"That seems to be the asking price. Of course, others will have to be taken care of, too."

"Like your fat friend."

"And probably others. That's not your concern."

"What do I tell him about the money? Tonight, I mean."

"That you'll have to discuss what he has to offer with others." Lerner smiled. "Your superior."

"I'd like to give him the sense that I have more authority than that, Bill."

"I've received final authorization for the money. Two hundred thousand. A bargain, actually, especially when you consider money is no object. If they demanded a million, they'd have it—provided their information is correct. You'll have to make that judgment on the spot, Max. You'll have the money with you; your discretion whether to turn it over."

"I somehow don't think they'll let me leave without handing it over."

"It's out of my hands."

Translation: You're on your own, Pauling, no ties to anyone, nothing to fall back on except your own wits and experience in dealing with such people. In a sense, he preferred it that way. He had infinitely more faith in himself than in his employers, as well-meaning as Bill Lerner and the others might be.

"Any more questions?" Lerner asked.

"No."

"You'll see Sutherland before you meet."

"Of course."

"Good. Ah, our burgers and fries have arrived." He turned to the waiter: "Ketchup, please."

212

* * *

When Pauling walked into the Red Cat discotheque, he was engulfed in an orgiastic, undulating phantasmagoria. Music blared from six-foot-high speakers throughout the room, the thundering bass notes coming up from the floor and assaulting his legs like a jackhammer, the deafening, discordant scream of guitars and shrill voices numbing the senses. The vast dance floor was packed with gyrating men and women, mostly young, but with a few Pauling would have assumed had outgrown the disco craze.

This was music? He scanned the room. He'd been told to seek out the club's manager, who would be at a raised podium on the north side of the club, from which the man could oversee what was going on. Pauling spotted him and skirted the dance floor. As he got closer, he saw that the manager was flanked by two large men in black suits holding fully automatic AK-47s. Subtlety wasn't in the Russian vocabulary, he thought as he closed the gap and looked up at the manager, a thin man with a beaked nose and a forehead that sloped back into baldness. The two bouncers eyed Pauling, then one nudged the manager, who looked down.

"Misha Glinskaya," Pauling shouted over the music's din.

The manager frowned and narrowed his already narrow eyes.

"Glinskaya," Pauling repeated, louder this time and hoping he had the pronunciation of the mafioso's name right. "He's waiting for me."

The manager leaned close to one of the bouncers and said something into his ear. The heavyset man with the automatic weapon came down off the platform and motioned with his head for Pauling to follow. The bouncer didn't bother trying to avoid the dancers. They gave him

213

wide berth as he walked through them, Pauling close behind, until reaching a door manned by another AK-47-toting man, who stepped aside and allowed the bouncer to open it. Beyond the door was a large room with concrete-block walls, a high ceiling with black metal industrial beams, and no windows. Two men played pool; six others sat at a table playing cards. What Pauling especially noticed was the relative silence of the room compared with the clangorous pandemonium outside.

His eyes went to a couch on his left, along the wall. Seated on it was a young Russian man wearing a double-breasted white jacket, black slacks, a teal silk shirt with the top buttons undone, and black alligator loafers. Pauling noted he wasn't wearing socks, like a trendy Beverly Hills or East Hampton yuppie. The man smiled and motioned for Pauling to join him.

"Pauling?" he said.

"*Da.* You're Glinskaya?"

"Yes. Speak English, huh? I speak good English."

"Fine." Pauling took in the other men in the room. "Can we go somewhere a little more private?" he asked.

"We are fine here. My friend tells me you are seeking information."

"Your friend would be the banker, Miziyano."

"It is not important who my friend is. He tells me you are interested in buying some missiles."

Pauling was taken aback for a moment, both because he hadn't expected to be identified as a weapons buyer, and because the young Russian had said *missiles* as though he were talking about shoes or tennis racquets.

"He is wrong?"

"Maybe not. Actually, I'm interested in finding out about someone else who might have bought some missiles from you a while ago."

As Glinskaya laughed, Pauling saw that the Russian

had a false eye that never moved. "I am not in the business of selling missiles, Mr. Pauling. You have been given false information."

"Then maybe you know somebody who might have sold missiles to this friend of mine."

"I might. Would you care for a drink? Vodka?"

"No. Look, I don't have much time to play word games, Mr. Glinskaya, and I don't care whether you sell missiles or your mother does. I'm looking for information and I'm willing to pay for it."

The Russian looked for a moment as though he might be offended at what Pauling said. But then he laughed and said, "Ah, the American way of doing business, aggressive—what is the term?—proactive, no time for a pleasant drink. It is not our way of doing business, Mr. Pauling."

"Then we've both wasted our time," Pauling said, standing and realizing two men from the card table had left the game and stood a few feet from either side of the couch. The bulges in their suits were not, Pauling knew, growths, although they were undoubtedly malignant.

"Your government is willing to pay a lot of money for the information, I am told."

"Yes, a lot of money—for *good* information."

Glinskaya calmly reached in the breast pocket of his jacket, pulled out a small slip of paper, and handed it to Pauling. At first, all Pauling saw were a series of numbers. But then the meaning of them became only too evident. There were two sets of numbers, one preceded by *Serial* #, the other by *Batch* #—the same numbers he'd been shown by Lerner designating the three missiles that had been used to down the American planes.

Pauling looked down at the mafioso and nodded.

"Two hundred thousand, U.S., huh?" Glinskaya said flatly.

Pauling nodded.

Glinskaya stood and slicked back dirty-blond hair on his temples. "Now, we will have a drink together and discuss how and when you will be able to meet with my friend. Come. I become—what do you say?—agitated when my hospitality is refused."

26

That Night
Washington, DC

"Look, Roseann, if this guy Thomas shows up at your gig, give me a call and I'll head right over," he said as she was leaving for her engagement at the Four Seasons.

"Okay," she said, "but I don't expect to see him."

"Just in case. I'll be here."

"All right," she said, stopping on her way out the door to admire the three dozen long-stemmed roses he'd bought her as a peace offering for blowing the dinner date with the Meads. It was a good thing he'd brought three dozen. A dozen wouldn't have done it.

Strange, she thought as she worked her way through a medley of Michel Legrand, that her boyfriend was hoping the man she'd gone out with showed up again. She understood, of course, that for Joe it was business, and that there was nothing quirky about it. Still, it was amusing, and she thought she might try and write a song about it.

She played a major B chord instead of the minor going into the bridge of "What Are You Doing the Rest of Your Life?" and grimaced, looked around to see if it had jarred anyone's ears as it had hers. Not to worry. As usual, it seemed that the music was only a distant melodic cushion under conversation. Then again, there was the occasional customer who seemed to be listening, at least with one ear, and Roseann looked for such a person in the room, someone like Craig, who'd appreciated the music. Or had he? Had he feigned interest in Cole Porter in order to ingratiate himself? She dismissed that cynical thought as she segued into "I Will Wait for You" and continued to scan the room in search of a music lover. She found her, she thought, in a short, chunky blond woman seated alone at a small table between the piano and the service bar. Being alone helped, Roseann knew. If there was no one to talk to, you might as well listen to the piano player. The woman returned Roseann's smile.

She continued playing until a surreptitious glance at her watch said it was time for a break. The blond woman stopped her on her way to the bar.

"You play beautifully," she said.

"Thank you."

"I love Michel Legrand. Do you know 'You Must Believe in Spring'?"

"Yes, I do. I'll play it next set."

"Join me? May I buy you a drink?"

"I, ah—sure. Thank you." She stopped a waitress and ordered a Diet Coke.

"I'm Connie Vail," the woman said, extending her hand and breaking into a wide smile.

"I'm Roseann Blackburn."

"Yes, I know."

Must have seen my photo and name on the easel in the lobby, Roseann thought.

"Do you know Oliver Jones?" Connie asked.

"The Canadian pianist? I've never met him but I have some of his recordings. He's wonderful."

"Oh, yes, he is. We're quite proud of him."

"You're Canadian?"

"Yes."

Roseann's soda was served along with a second white wine for Connie Vail. She raised her glass: "Here's to good music."

"I'll always drink to that," Roseann said with a laugh.

An awkward silence ensued, and after a short time Roseann decided to leave the woman to freshen her makeup and hair in the ladies' room. Connie seemed to sense that she was about to depart and said, "Would you be offended to know that I didn't just happen to stop in here for a drink this evening?"

"Why would I be offended?"

"I came to see you."

"Really?"

"Yes. I suppose I'm still not being completely honest. I was hoping your friend the reporter, Mr. Potamos, would be here with you."

"I see. You don't happen to know Craig Thomas from the Canadian embassy?"

Connie nodded.

"My friend Joe Potamos has been trying to reach him. He took me to dinner a few nights ago and gave me his card, asked me to give it to Joe."

"I know."

"Do you also know why he hasn't returned Joe's calls?"

"Ms. Blackburn, Craig is out of the country and probably will be for some time."

"He told me he had a story for Joe, something to do with the murder of a man from the Canadian embassy."

"Jeremy Wilcox."

"That's right. You knew him?"

"Yes, quite well."

Roseann hesitated, thought for a moment, then asked, "Do you know the story Craig Thomas was going to tell Joe?"

"Yes."

"I'll call him and have him come here."

"No, not here, Ms. Blackburn. Could I meet him someplace private and quiet, where we can really talk?"

"How about my apartment? We have a dog but—"

"I get along quite well with dogs."

"Will you stay until I finish the next set? It's my last. Forty-five minutes."

"Of course. 'You Must Believe in Spring'?"

"My first song."

Roseann took a detour to a pay phone outside the ladies' room.

"I'll be right over," Joe said.

"No, Joe, she doesn't want to meet here. I'm bringing her back to the apartment."

"You sure she won't take off?"

"Not likely, Joe. She really wants to talk with you. She drinks white wine. Why don't you buy some before we get there."

"What are we having, a party? You want caviar and pâté, too?"

"Absolutely. We never have caviar. Be there in an hour."

27

"Jessica, it's Annabel."

"Hi."

"Interrupting anything important?"

"Just getting my gear ready for the trip."

"What trip?"

"Canada. This weekend. My bird-watching group. The annual trek into the wilds in search of *Lanius excubitor*, among others."

"I always wondered what happened to them," Annabel said, unable to stifle a giggle.

"Better known as the northern shrike," Jessica said, not offended. "People confuse it with a mockingbird but it has a facial mask, and a heavy, hooked bill. We're only going for three days."

"Feel like some dinner? Mac and I decided to abandon the kitchen and eat out. Join us?"

"Love to, Annie, but too much to do. Between work and getting ready for the trip, I don't seem to have time to breathe, let alone have a leisurely dinner with friends. Rain check when I get back?"

"Sure. Has your gentleman friend returned yet?"

"No, and just as well. He views me and my bird-watching friends as a little kooky." There was silence on the other end. "Do you?"

"Do I what?"

"Think we're kooky?"

"Of course not. I get as excited over a Teotihuacán urn as you do over a . . . what was that loggerhead bird you mentioned? Sounds like the official bird of Congress."

"*Lanius excubitor.* A northern shrike."

"Right. A northern shrike."

"Teoti—?"

"Teotihuacán. A Mexican culture. Some wonderful pre-Columbian art was created by them. I'll let you go. Have a great trip, Jess, see lots of rare birds."

"Thanks. It'll be good to get away from the insanity around here."

Annabel hung up and turned on the TV news. The downing of the three commuter aircraft continued to dominate, although other world events had forced the networks and all-news cable channels to find time to cover them, too. With official information about the investigation virtually nonexistent, speculation was the basis for newscast after newscast, and news-oriented talk shows. And the Internet had spawned hundreds of web sites and chat rooms in which the wildest rumors and theories made the rounds, some ending up as fodder for the fact-starved mainstream press. Without anything solid to report, the media and repetition and speculation fueled the national paranoia, and a growing sense that the White House, CIA, Pentagon, FBI, Justice Department, and every other agency charged with bringing the terrorists to justice weren't up to the task. One report claimed that Secretary of State Rock was in Russia laying the groundwork for a declaration of war against the former Soviet Union, according to "reliable sources."

Other "reliable sources" pointed the finger at Iraq, Iran, Pakistan, China, or domestic hate groups such as Aryan Nations, the Silent Brotherhood—the list went on and on.

"We've learned on good authority that . . ." Annabel turned off the TV and stood on the balcony overlooking the Potomac, her hand resting on Rufus's head. From that peaceful vantage point, all was well, the lights of Georgetown and Rosslyn giving dimension to the buildings in which people went about their lives. Yet Annabel knew that everyone's sense of well-being and calm, like her own, had been assaulted by the missiles and, no matter what, that sense of peace would never be fully restored, just as the lives lost could never be.

"Damn you!" she muttered to whoever had sent those missiles up on their deadly trajectories. The potency of the feeling of doom that had suddenly consumed her caused her to cry silently. She wiped her eyes, gave the folds of the dog's neck a squeeze, and returned inside her Watergate apartment, closing the sliding glass doors to the balcony as though to shut out any evil lurking outside.

28

Three Days Later
Blaine, Washington

"This is Roberta Dougherty reporting live from Blaine, Washington, on the Canadian border. I'm standing near a ranch owned by Zachary Jasper, head of the so-called Jasper Project, a militant antigovernment, white-supremacist group suspected of having played a role in the downing of three American commuter airliners almost three weeks ago. The Federal Bureau of Investigation and the ATF have moved a sizable contingent of armed men and assault equipment into the area in anticipation of some sort of military action against the ranch and its occupants. We've learned from reliable sources that the FBI has obtained a warrant to enter the ranch and search for possible evidence linking the Jasper Project to the aircraft downings. We've also been told that Jasper, the head of the group, has refused to accept the warrant and to allow the government to enter the property, setting up a potential siege and armed conflict. We'll keep you abreast of developments in this increasingly tense situation."

The camera pulled back to reveal a virtual army lined up along the road leading to the ranch's main entrance.

SWAT teams in flak jackets and helmets, carrying high-powered rifles with scopes and automatic weapons, flanked a dozen vehicles, including two armored personnel carriers with weaponry mounted above the bulletproof windshields. A three-bedroom RV, rented from a nearby recreational-vehicle rental company, had been established as a command center. Dozens of FBI agents wearing windbreakers bearing the agency's seal in large letters on the back stood with other special agents in suits. The ranch was kept under constant surveillance through two large telescopes and binoculars. State police had been brought in to establish a perimeter behind which onlookers and the press were corralled.

Inside the main house, Zachary Jasper stood in the kitchen, phone in hand. On the other end of the line was the FBI's Joe Harris, who'd flown to the scene to take personal charge of the operation. Standing next to him was a hostage negotiator who'd accompanied Harris from Washington.

". . . and I'm telling you, Mr. Harris, you've got no right coming on this property, warrant or no warrant," Jasper said in a measured voice. "You're looking for a damn scapegoat because you've got nothing else on who shot those planes down."

"Look, Mr. Jasper, you're setting up an ugly situation here," Harris said. "You've got innocent people in there who are going to get hurt if you don't listen to reason."

"That's right, Mr. Harris, women and children in here who haven't done a damn thing except stand up for their rights as free, white citizens of this country. And I'll tell you this, sir. Every person here, right down to the youngest, is ready to fight for their birthright."

The negotiator had been listening to the conversation on a set of earphones attached to the battery-powered phone Harris held. They looked at each other without expression before Harris said, "Mr. Jasper, I'm putting you on with Special Agent Simone." He heard the click of the phone being replaced in its cradle.

"Keep trying," Harris told Simone. "Keep calling until he picks up again."

Harris entered the command center and used a direct line to Director Templeton's Washington office. "It's Harris, sir," he said.

"What's the status?"

"No movement yet. He's holding firm but it's early."

"Is he just demonstrating bravado or does it look like he's getting ready to defend the place?"

"Hard to say, sir. The surveillance agents report having seen men with weapons leave the main house and disappear into other areas of the ranch. We've established posts behind and to the sides of the ranch. They're in position and have just started reporting their sightings." He went on to recount his conversation with Jasper.

"Keep negotiating, Joe. I want to see this resolved peacefully."

"Yes, sir."

"The president wants it resolved peacefully."

"We're all in agreement on that, sir."

President Ashmead met with his cabinet and select members of his inner circle in the Situation Room on the first floor of the White House. They were joined shortly after convening by FBI Director Templeton and State's director of counterterrorism ops, Colonel Walter Barton, who arrived together. Ashmead sat stoically as National Security Advisor Tony Cammanati chaired the meeting, turning first to Templeton for an update on the Jasper ranch situation. Templeton reported what Joe Harris had told him from the scene. Others at the table asked questions of the FBI director, most focusing on whether the agency's manpower and equipment were sufficient to conduct a swift, clean assault on the ranch, should that be necessary.

After everyone had had their say, the president asked Barton for a status report on State's efforts in Moscow to trace the source of the missiles.

"That effort, Mr. President, is being coordinated through the CIA. It's our people but they don't report to us. Frankly, I find it an awkward situation and not terribly productive."

Ashmead drummed his fingertips on a yellow pad. He'd heard it before, State's complaints about the clumsy system of their operatives at embassies around the world reporting to CIA handlers back in Langley. He understood the concern. At the same time, it was a system in place long before he took possession of the White House, and he saw no reason to interfere with it. Secretary of State Rock had raised it with him a year ago, although she hadn't lobbied for change, simply mentioned it during conversations about State's internal structure and embassy operations, and what could be done to smooth out some rough edges.

Templeton offered, "Finding out who provided the missiles is, of course, extremely important, Mr. President, but it should not be the priority. As we're all aware, missiles are for sale everywhere by underground arms dealers. What we've got to concentrate on is identifying those who would use them here in the United States and putting them out of business. Groups like the Jasper Project are always looking for ways to spill innocent blood and disrupt the country."

There was obvious truth to what the FBI director said, although Ashmead also knew it was part of a continuing battle for dominance between the FBI, whose jurisdiction was domestic, and the Central Intelligence Agency, whose mandate was overseas. The seemingly constant, petty infighting between agencies and even among his own staff—everyone vying for attention and favor, at times putting those needs ahead of more vital national priorities—was an ongoing source of irritation for this hands-on president, whose patience with what he considered trivia could be as thin as tissue paper.

He was also aware that State's Barton and the FBI's Templeton had deliberately been kept out of the loop when it came to the State Department's efforts in Moscow to trace the missiles to their source. Through personal, twice-daily phone briefings with Secretary Rock, or Ashmead's special assistant, Mike McQuaid, he knew that a seasoned CIA operative named Max Pauling was working undercover in the Russian capital. He'd been told, too, that the CIA had dispatched a senior officer named Hoctor to manage Pauling's effort through the embassy.

Secretary Rock's purpose in flying to Moscow was officially billed as a goodwill trip to meet with the new minister of foreign affairs, Leonid Orlov, who'd replaced Igor Ivanov, with whom Rock had forged a particularly good relationship. In reality, she was there to assure senior Russian officials behind the scenes that the United States was not looking to make an international incident out of the discovery that the missiles had been Russian-made, and to ascertain what cooperation might be forthcoming from the Russian government in tracing them.

"We're ready to go, Mr. President. All we need is for you to give the word," Templeton said.

Ashmead turned to his attorney general. "Give it to me," he said. "What's your read on this?"

"We should establish a deadline for Jasper," he replied, "and stick to it."

Cammanati said, "There could be considerable political ramifications, Mr. President, if things go sour."

"Those eighty-seven people in the airplanes who lost their lives weren't thinking about politics," Ashmead growled. "I've made my position clear to everyone involved, that I want a peaceful resolution, and continue to. But there comes a point when . . . There comes a point when the American people lose patience with killers like Jasper, and I lose patience, too. Give Jasper and his people forty-eight hours to come out peacefully. Use that time to try every negotiating trick in the book. But if that doesn't work . . . Well, if negotiations fail at the end of forty-eight hours, do what you have to do, and use all necessary force to accomplish it."

29

Max Pauling awoke at ten in his room at the Metropol
Hotel, beating the wake-up call by fifteen minutes. He'd
forced himself to take the nighttime forty-five-minute
nap. Now, wide awake, he remained on his back, eyes
open wide, arms stretched to the sides, the city's lights
through the open windows creating shifting patterns
over his naked body.

After drawing a series of slow, measured breaths, he
swung his legs over the side of the bed, stood, and went
to a window. Things had moved faster than he'd expected, engendering conflicting emotions. If things went
as planned tonight, his assignment to Moscow would
come to an end. That was good, of course, except that it
also meant he would be sent back to Washington, which
was also good in some ways—Jessica and his Cessna
coming immediately to mind—but bad in other ways,
the potential for a dull daily existence at the State Department and reporting to Colonel Walter Barton top-
ping the list of negatives.

When he left Washington for Moscow, he'd assumed
his task of identifying the source of the missiles would be
long and arduous, characterized by false turns and dis-

appointments. That hadn't turned out to be the case. Lerner had so effectively paved the way through his banker friend, Miziyano, that Pauling found himself having only to run local CIA checks on Miziyano and the mafioso Misha Glinskaya, and to make a few informal queries about them through old "friends" in Moscow's criminal underbelly—and, of course, follow through with the exchange of money for names. Piece a cake.

But he also knew that having things go smoothly was a recipe for complacency. Complacency was dangerous. Complacent agents working underground seldom survived long enough to grab the pension and live out their final years in the sun, on some island. Although he was not introspective by nature, being on assignments like this generated changes in Pauling that were readable to him. He was aware of how leaving Washington and arriving in Moscow had altered his perceptions of things, and of himself. In Washington, it was as though his senses had shut down, like those of a hibernating animal secure in its winter burrow. Unless you were a politician attuned to subtle shifts in the political wind, there was no need to be on the alert, look over your shoulder, put everyone and everything to the test. It was like dying, he sometimes thought, the body put on idle until finally running out of gas.

But on assignment in Moscow and elsewhere, where death, if it were to come, would be swift and sudden, the animal, *this* animal named Pauling, was never more alive, senses operating at peak frequencies, eyes narrowed, mind questioning what wouldn't be worth questioning at a desk back at Main State. He was out of his hibernation, reborn, and the predators were everywhere.

Since arriving in Russia, he'd scrutinized every step he took, and steps taken by others. That afternoon, among many of his thoughts, profound and occasionally whimsical, was why, more important *how*, Lerner had so effortlessly laid the answers in his lap so quickly. He answered by reminding himself of Lerner's long experience in Moscow, and the professional that he was, one of countless dedicated and skilled American men and women representing their country far from home, blessedly removed from Washington's penchant for political meddling, getting the job done and proud of it. But it had been too easy, and it wasn't over. If something bad could happen, it would. "You're always expecting the worst," Doris had said with some regularity before the divorce. She was right. And he was still alive.

As he dried himself vigorously after setting the shower to the hottest temperature he could stand, his thoughts went to his friend and CIA mentor, Tom Hoctor, who he'd learned was in Moscow with the secretary of state. Why hadn't Hoctor made contact? Surely, Pauling reasoned, Hoctor hadn't accompanied Secretary Rock as part of her diplomatic mission. Presumably, he'd come to Moscow to oversee the CIA's stake in the investigation of the missiles' origins. Hoctor had made it clear to Pauling at Langley prior to Pauling's departure for Moscow that he, Hoctor, was in charge of the operation. But he'd also instructed Pauling to report only to Lerner, who would be the conduit of all information between Moscow and Langley. Another convoluted, broken chain of command.

Pauling dressed in jeans, a navy-blue T-shirt that hugged his torso, white athletic socks, sneakers, and his multipocketed tan vest. It was a fair night in Moscow, although low clouds moving quickly over the city promised rain by morning. He searched his carry-on bag on the floor of a closet and pulled from it a nine-millimeter Austrian Glock 17 semiautomatic. He checked the clip, slipped the weapon into the vest's largest right-hand pocket, then removed two small, spring-loaded devices attached to tiny glass ampules from the bag and placed them in one of a half-dozen pockets on the left side. He then pulled out two slightly longer ampules and also slipped them into his left pocket. Each spring-loaded ampule contained prussic acid. He'd been given them, and the Glock 17, that afternoon by Harold Sutherland, a longtime embassy employee (read CIA) who spent his days behind a locked door in the embassy's basement. The sign on the door read TECHNICAL ASSISTANCE, a benign promise considering the sophisticated instruments of death the room contained, some personally invented by the CIA's Sutherland, an acknowledged technical genius. Sutherland's final words to Pauling were "Make sure when you trip the spring, Max, that the prussic acid goes up somebody else's nose, not your own. But if it does, break one of the other ampules under your nose and breathe in the nitro, fast!" Pauling had been trained in the use of prussic acid, and the antidote, nitro, but appreciated the reminder.

The final item removed from the bag was an envelope containing twenty ten-thousand-dollar bills, which he slipped into an inside vest pocket and zippered it closed. He pulled a slip of paper with a phone number written on it from his jeans pocket, said it aloud a few times, then burned it in an ashtray.

He rode the elevator to the opulent lobby, went into a bar off it, and sat alone sipping bottled water with lime. At eleven-fifteen, he stepped out onto Teatralny Proezd. The streets in Theatre Square were busy as more than two thousand people spilled out of the Bolshoi Theatre after enjoying a performance by the world-famous ballet company bearing its name, joining hundreds of others, many tourists, coming to and from the impressive light show on the Kremlin's towers, a five-minute walk from the square.

Pauling got into the first taxi in a long line of them and told the driver to take him to Gorky Park. Traffic was sluggish, but the driver took less congested side streets until pulling up in front of the House of Artists, home of the Russian Artists' Union, directly across the street from the entrance to the park. Muscovites were out in droves there, too, enjoying the 275-acre park, Moscow's most popular recreation center. It struck Pauling as he watched the vibrant street scene that the resiliency of the Russian people, gripped as they were in a brutal recession exacerbated by Yeltsin's decision to devalue the ruble, was to be admired. He doubted if the majority of Americans, certainly those whose lives were basically free of hardship, would fare nearly as well if faced with similar adversity.

He checked his watch: eleven-fifty. He crossed the road, entered the park, and strolled along its tree-studded walkways. A jazz concert was in progress in the ten-thousand-seat open-air Zelyony Theatre, and the giant Ferris wheel that dominated the horizon was in action, its tinkling music and the shrieks of delight from children blending with the jazz band to create a surprisingly compatible sound.

He continued to walk until reaching a boating pond and stopped beneath a tree at its edge. Another glance at his watch: a few minutes before midnight. He was sure he had the right place. Lerner had told him to wait by the tree closest to the stand-up cafe on the north side of the pond.

A minute later, he saw Glinskaya emerge from behind the cafe. The young Russian mobster wore a black, Italian-cut suit and black-and-white shoes. Two other men were with him, one on either side. When they were closer, Pauling recognized them from the back room of the Red Cat.

"Pauling, on time, huh?"

"Of course. I keep appointments . . . and promises." Pauling looked for another person to join them, the arms dealer Glinskaya was supposed to deliver. When no one did, he said, "Missing someone, aren't we?"

The Russian smiled, shrugged.

Pauling made a show of looking at his watch. "Are we talking here, or are we going someplace else?"

"The impatient American way," the Russian said.

"Maybe you haven't noticed but it works," Pauling said.

Glinskaya's face hardened, and Pauling regretted his flippancy. But then the slick man smiled and nodded vigorously. "I like you, Pauling. Direct, huh? You are always direct." He looked about; the only people near them were his two colleagues, who stood a few feet away. "You have the money?" he asked.

"Yes." Pauling pressed his right elbow against the Glock 17 in his pocket. "It stays with me until I have what I'm paying for."

Without a word, Glinskaya pulled an envelope from the breast pocket of his suit jacket and handed it to Pauling. "Go ahead," he said. "What you want is in there."

Pauling looked at the envelope.

"Read it," said Glinskaya.

The Russian's two men moved closer to Pauling, taking up a position on either side. Pauling got the message: Read what was in the envelope but don't think about walking away without paying.

Where they stood was in deep shadow. Pauling removed the single sheet of paper from the envelope, squinted, then slowly moved into a shaft of light from the cafe. The two men moved with him, as in a ballet.

The note was written in English, good English. It was fifteen lines long, the sentences properly punctuated, capital letters where they should be. But Pauling wasn't focusing on the note's syntax or style. It was what it said that had his full attention.

"So, Pauling, you are satisfied?"

"Who wrote this?" Pauling asked, moving back closer to Glinskaya.

"The one who knows."

"Who?"

"No, no, Pauling, that is not important. I asked him to meet with us. He refused. But I convinced him to write down about the missiles, who he sold them to. Believe me, Pauling, this is the man who sold the missiles that shot down your planes. Now, you give me the money and I will give to him his share for the information."

If Pauling had even a fleeting notion of not paying, he knew it wouldn't work. He now knew the truth—if what was in the note was truthful. Time to pay up. He unzipped his jacket's inside pocket, withdrew the envelope containing the two hundred thousand dollars, and handed it to Glinskaya, who pocketed it without bothering to count what was in it.

"We made a good deal, huh?" Glinskaya said pleasantly, slapping Pauling on the arm. "Come on, I'll buy you a drink."

"No, thanks," Pauling said, remembering the number he was to call once the transaction was completed.

"Pauling, again, I get agitated when you say no to my hospitality. Come on, one drink. To celebrate."

"All right," Pauling said.

"There is a good bar close by. I, ah, am a partner in it. You will like it. Real liquor and real women available for a price. Maybe you will take a liking to one."

Pauling didn't respond, simply fell in step with Glinskaya as his two goons followed close behind. They left the park through the main entrance and walked a block along Krymsky Val until reaching a narrow alley leading to another street. Glinskaya entered the alley but Pauling stopped. Glinskaya turned and said, "Hey, Pauling, come on. The bar is on the next street. We take this, what do you call it, this shortcut?"

Pauling still hesitated, but the two men in suits nudged him into the alley. He slipped his hands into his jacket pockets and fingered the Glock 17 in the right, the prussic acid vials and nitro ampules in the left.

The alley was not as deserted as Pauling initially thought. There were a few small shops, an occasional open door to a ground-floor apartment revealing the life of its occupants, and three vagrants with their backs against a wall, two asleep, the third muttering in Russian and extending a tattered paper cup. Pauling was surprised when Glinskaya dropped coins into it.

They reached the street at the end of the alley, a commercial thoroughfare lined with bars and restaurants with gaudy neon lights heralding their names. Pauling had been on that street before during his seven-year stint in Moscow. Many of the bars were owned by organized crime, and he'd met with contacts in some of them.

"Over there," Glinskaya said, motioning with his hand for them to follow. His bar was a hundred feet down the strip, on the same side of the street where the alley emptied out. They reached it and Glinskaya pointed up at the flashing sign in Russian, which Pauling translated: THE GOLD COIN. While Glinskaya proudly indicated the sign, and Pauling and the two henchmen briefly looked up at it, the first shots crackled, one after the other, automatic-weapons fire, four guns, four shooters in a black Mercedes that had pulled up to the curb simultaneous with their arrival.

Pauling instinctively threw himself to the ground, knocking over a flower seller, an elderly woman, on his way down. His right hand came out of his pocket holding the Glock 17 but he held fire as he tried to take stock of the situation. Passersby screamed and tried to get out of the way. Pauling saw Glinskaya lying in a heap on the sidewalk. One of his men was down, too. The other returned fire but a barrage of shots from the Mercedes sent him stumbling back, arms flailing as he went through the bar's plate-glass window, sending a shower of glass inside and to the sidewalk.

Pauling's immediate thought was that he'd happened to be at the wrong place at the wrong time, in the midst of a Russian mob hit. Did the men in the car know he wasn't part of Glinskaya's mob? Or was he the target? A street lamp stood between Pauling and the car, not enough to prevent anyone in the vehicle from shooting at him, but enough of a barrier to hinder a clear view. Pauling came to his knees, raised the Glock with both hands, and trained it on the Mercedes, which he expected would roar away, its job done. Instead, three of the four doors flew open and the men who'd gunned down Glinskaya and his henchmen came through them, AK-47s in their hands. Pauling didn't hesitate. He and the Glock were no match for them, and he knew it. The older woman he'd knocked down was gone, and those who'd been in front of the Gold Coin when the attack began had either scattered or were on the sidewalk moaning and pressing hands to their wounds. Pauling looked back over his shoulder; an alley ten feet away separated Glinskaya's bar from another. He rolled in that direction, six or seven turns, then sprang to his feet and took off down the alley. A flurry of shots ricocheted off the walls, whizzed past his head, skipped up from the concrete at his feet. He ducked, zigzagged, considered returning fire but decided distance was a better defense.

He reached the end of the alley, ducked out of it, and looked back. They were in pursuit, big men, lumbering along, yelling things in Russian at one another. Pauling could have revealed himself and opened fire, certainly taking down one or two. Instead, he ran to the corner, dodged traffic as he crossed the wide boulevard to a taxi, whose driver sat smoking a cigarette. Pauling opened the back door, tumbled in, slammed the door, and told the driver in Russian to get moving, fast.

"*Nyet,*" the driver said, adding he was on break.

Pauling put the Glock to his head. The driver tossed his cigarette out the window, started the engine, and pulled away. Pauling looked back through the grimy window. The three men were trying to navigate the traffic as they hurried in the taxi's direction. Pauling yelled at the driver to take a sharp left onto another street. A minute later, he let out a long stream of breath, wiped perspiration from his brow with the back of his hand, and slipped the Glock into his vest pocket.

"Where are we going?" the driver asked over his shoulder, lighting another cigarette.

"Just drive awhile," Pauling said. "Don't worry, I'll pay you."

They continued in a westerly direction until reaching the beginnings of Moscow's outskirts, grim, gray buildings lining the street, streetlights dim or not working. The promised rain had started, now just a mist, certainly to become heavier as the night progressed. Pauling considered a number of times instructing the cabbie to let him off at any corner containing a public telephone, but he wasn't ready to leave the security of the taxi and be out alone on the streets of Moscow. Eventually, after responding to the driver's question—"You're a convict?"

"No, but I was almost a dead man"—he gave the driver Bill Lerner's address, in the other direction, in central Moscow. Twenty minutes later they pulled up in front of the four-story apartment building that had been Lerner's home for sixteen years. Pauling pulled out a wad of rubles and handed them over the seat to the driver, who thanked him profusely. As he watched the taxi pull away and turn a corner, he couldn't resist a smile. It might have been a traumatic trip for the driver, but it was probably the most lucrative fare he'd have all year. He also had a fleeting, absurd thought as he approached the building entrance that maybe he should have tried to retrieve the money from Glinskaya before bolting the scene. To keep for himself? Or to return to the United States government?

That he was lucky to be alive was more on his mind as he stepped into the foyer. Broken tiles on the floor hadn't been replaced, and graffiti on the walls was fading; Russian building management at work.

There wasn't an intercom, so Pauling started up the stairs to the third floor, moving slowly, his hip aching from when he'd flung himself to the sidewalk. He'd realized during the cab ride that a bullet had grazed his cheek, causing a tiny rivulet of blood to drip down onto the shoulder of his jacket. It was now dry, but had started to sting.

He heard a noise from the next level up and stopped, leaned against the wall, and slowly pulled the Glock from his vest. An older man said something in Russian and was answered by an older woman. A door slammed shut. All was quiet again. Pauling continued up the stairs, one slow step at a time, until reaching the small, third-floor landing. Lerner's flat was one of two, the one to the left. The phone number Pauling had memorized came to mind. It wasn't Lerner's phone.

He was about to knock on the apartment door when he heard the phone ring from inside. He brought his ear close to the door and listened, heard a muffled man's voice say something, then the phone being replaced in its cradle. Had the voice sounded like Lerner's? He couldn't be sure. It was too brief.

Pauling knocked. Shuffling inside, someone moving. Pauling realized he still held the Glock 17, slipped it into his pocket, and knocked again. The knob turned, then stopped.

"Bill? It's Max Pauling."

The door opened.

"Tom?" Pauling said, face-to-face with his CIA mentor, Tom Hoctor.

"Come in, Max."

Pauling stepped into the apartment and Hoctor closed the door behind them. The flat was as Pauling remembered it to be, appropriately small—this was Russia—and cluttered. Lerner was an inveterate reader; books were everywhere, covering tables and kitchen countertops, piled on the floor, and overflowing from floor-to-ceiling bookcases on two walls of the living room.

"What are *you* doing here?" Pauling asked.

"Waiting for you," Hoctor said, going to a window and parting the curtains to look down on the street. "Why didn't you call the number you were given?" he asked Pauling, who stood in the middle of the living room.

"I had other things on my mind. I was improvising. A few unexpected events."

Hoctor turned from the window. He looked even smaller and slighter than when Pauling last saw him at Langley. He was dressed in suit and tie; he always seemed to be. Light from a floor lamp created a sheen on his bald pate, and Pauling noticed that his friend's perpetually drooping right eye was sagging a little lower than usual.

"Did you get the information?" Hoctor asked.

"Yes." Pauling handed him the envelope Glinskaya had given him. Hoctor opened it and read the note. That an expression of shock crossed his narrow face didn't surprise Pauling. He'd been shocked, too, when he'd read it.

"Do you believe it, Max?"

"Yes. It's detailed enough."

"Information provided by Russia's less sterling citizens."

"I trust them as much as I trust the spin doctors in Washington."

Hoctor placed the envelope in his pocket. "Ready to go?" he asked.

"Where's Bill?"

Hoctor lowered his head and slowly shook it.

"Something's happened to him?"

Hoctor nodded toward the small bathroom. "In there."

Pauling went to the open door. Lying on the floor was Bill Lerner. He was dressed in baggy slacks and a sleeveless summer undershirt. He was barefoot. His eyes were open, rolled back into his head.

"Jesus," Pauling said, turning to Hoctor, who was again peering through the curtains.

"Obviously a heart attack. He was there when I arrived."

Pauling knelt next to Lerner's lifeless body and touched his fingertips to his throat in search of a pulse. There was none. He looked up at Hoctor, who'd come to the door.

"We must go, Max."

Pauling's eyes said it all, that he didn't believe Lerner had died from a natural heart attack. Prussic acid? That was one of its advantages, killing people and making it look like a coronary to less probing medical examiners. Hoctor met his hard stare, right eye sadly lower on the outside corner, chin on his hand, index finger on his lips.

"Let's go, Max."

"Was he compromised, Tom?"

A shrug from the small man in the suit.

"Elena? Does she know? Was she—?"

"We make our choices in this world, Max, and live with the consequences. The only choice you have now is to come with me. The plane is waiting."

"What plane?" Pauling said, getting to his feet.

"Secretary Rock's plane. She's a nice lady, but she has no patience for people who are late."

Part Three

Part Three

30

Zachary Jasper stood with residents of the ranch in the main house's large kitchen, except for men who'd been posted outside as lookouts. The government forces surrounding the ranch had begun training powerful spotlights on the house for the past thirty-six hours, accompanied by nonstop music blaring from huge speakers mounted on truck beds. Sleep had become impossible. Nerves were frayed, tongues sharp.

They'd said the Pledge of Allegiance, modifying it to read "One Aryan nation under God." Now Jasper addressed them from in front of the massive stone fireplace. A large flag with a swastika hung above him. He was impassioned, red in the face, hands trembling as he attempted to instill in them the courage to stand up to whatever was in store.

"We are God's blessed and courageous martyrs," he yelled, "whose sacrifice will ensure us a permanent place on the right hand of Jesus Christ himself, the white man's savior and protector. We have right on our side, God's blessing in our fight against the evil forces out there."

He scanned the room. Some of the men shouted agreement with what he said, others sat passively. The children's faces mirrored their confusion and fright, which was to be expected, Jasper reasoned. But it was the women in whom he was most interested. His wife, June, stood proudly next to him, a deer rifle in her hands, hatred written on her face. He noticed that some of the other wives appeared staunch and ready. But not all. Patty, the young woman with the eleven-year-old son who'd recently traveled to the ranch with her husband from Southern California, stood near the door, arms wrapped about herself, lips pursed tight. Her son pressed against her side, abject fear in his eyes. Her husband had been dispatched by Jasper to be one of the armed lookouts.

Jasper directed his next words at mother and son.

"As long as this alien evil occupies our beloved land, hate is our law and revenge our duty."

Hands went up in the Nazi salute.

"Saint and martyr rule from the tomb of greatness," he shouted, paraphrasing Blake, then turned to O. Henry: "There is no happiness in life so perfect as the martyr's life!" O. Henry's irony was missing. He switched back to Blake, reading from a handwritten card: "The bitter groan of the martyr's woe is an arrow from the Almighty's bow."

More salutes and shouts of encouragement. He narrowed his eyes and glared at the young woman by the door.

"We will fight the Jews and blacks who send armed men to our door this night, lay down our lives for that cause we believe in with all our hearts and souls. We have thousands of brothers and sisters across the land who watch us in our moment of truth and who stand ready to take up arms to further our cause. We have been called by Jesus himself to this place and time to take a stand and to let our white brethren know that we are willing to die for white Christian justice."

Jasper stepped down from his faux pulpit and went from person to person, delivering heavy-handed slaps on backs and kisses on the women's cheeks. He turned to the frightened newcomer, Patty, but saw only her back as she and her son left the room. Jasper followed and watched as they stumbled down the porch steps and ran in the direction of the main gate, two hundred yards away, she holding his hand and pulling him along behind, falling herself and struggling to her feet. Jasper pulled a walkie-talkie from his belt, pushed ON and barked, "Stop that woman headed for the gate. Stop her, damn it!"

Joe Harris and other special agents stood outside the gate at the forward surveillance post.

"Who's that?" Harris asked as the woman and her boy came into view, their frantic flight bathed in light from the huge, truck-mounted spots.

"They're headed for the gate," an agent said.

Harris and others watched as Patty and her son continued to close the gap between themselves and freedom. He and other agents left the surveillance post and started to run to the gate, where two of Jasper's armed men watched the mother and son approach. Jasper's voice crackled from their walkie-talkies: "Stop that woman!"

Mother and son were within fifty feet of the gate when the sentries decided to take action. Ignoring the armed federal force, they stepped into the light with the intention of grabbing the runaways.

"Let them go," Harris shouted, trying to override the pulsating music from the speakers. "Don't interfere with—!"

The rifle's report was lost in the drums and wailing guitars, but its effect was clearly visible. Patty pitched face-first to the ground as the bullet tore into her back, between the shoulder blades, piercing her heart and killing her instantly. Her son fell, too, not from a gunshot but from the pull of his mother's hand as she collapsed.

He got to his knees and looked down at her. As he did, everything suddenly became silent; Harris had ordered the music be killed. The special agent in charge of the siege was now joined by a team of sharpshooters wearing helmets and flak jackets, and brandishing M-249 fully automatic weapons capable of firing more than a thousand rounds a minute.

It took a moment for Joe Harris to realize that the fleeing woman had been shot. "Who fired?" he yelled. No response from anyone within earshot. He immediately turned his attention to the boy, who was now on his feet, obviously in a daze.

"This way, son," Harris called. To Jasper's sentries at the gate he said, "Touch that kid and you're both dead."

The sentries turned and looked down the barrels of a half-dozen automatic weapons held in firing position by the sharpshooters.

"Come on, son, this way," Harris shouted, trying to inject compassion and hope into his voice.

The boy looked back at the main house. A dozen people had come from it, shrouded in light as they stopped halfway to the gate. He looked at Harris, who had now come within ten feet of the gate and Jasper's armed men. "You touch that kid and—"

To Harris's relief, the sentries lowered their weapons as Patty's eleven-year-old son ran in his direction, climbed over the gate, and was snatched into the air by two of the marksmen. Everyone slowly backed away from the ranch entrance to the forward surveillance post, where Harris crouched and placed both hands on the boy's shoulders. "You okay, son?"

"My momma. Is she . . ."

Harris straightened, took the boy's hand, and led him to the command post in the RV. Once inside, he sat him at a small Formica table and took the chair opposite.

"We'll do everything we can to get your mom out of there," he said, knowing she was dead but not wanting to acknowledge it until having had a chance to question the boy about conditions inside the ranch: "How many people in there?" "How many men, women, and children?" "Does everybody have a gun?" "Did you see bigger guns, rockets, hand grenades?" "What does Mr. Jasper say about this situation?"

It was the last question that brought this response from the boy: "He says he's goin' to kill everybody. My daddy's in there, too."

"Okay, son," Harris said, taking the boy into one of the vehicle's three bedrooms and assigning an agent to watch him. "Don't you worry," he said as he left, "you'll be all right."

He returned to the living room, where the communications center had been established. "Get me the director," he told a tech-support agent. A minute later he was on with Director Templeton in Washington.

"The situation's changed, sir," he said hurriedly, and went on to explain what had just happened.

"You're sure none of our people shot the woman?" Templeton asked.

"Yes, sir." Harris was confident in his answer, although he'd assigned an agent on his way back with the boy to question everyone at the site.

"Keep this line open," Templeton said. "I'll confer with the attorney general and the president; be back to you within the hour."

"You did what you were told to do," Zachary Jasper told the man who'd gunned down Patty. With them was her husband, who'd watched the slaying of his wife.

"My boy," he said.

"He'll be all right, don't you worry." What Jasper

didn't add was that if he'd been the one doing the shooting, he would have killed them both.

"That wife of yours would have told them everything about us," Jasper said to the husband. "Put us all in harm's way. We couldn't have that, could we?"

"No, sir," the husband replied, looking at the floor and fighting tears.

"Your boy hasn't been here long enough to tell them much. Didn't see much, was too busy playing. That's right, isn't it?"

"Yes, sir."

"Now, you two keep your eyes open. No tellin' what this might cause those bastards out there to do."

He returned to the main house, picked up a phone, and dialed the number of a radio station in Bellingham. The call was answered by a receptionist, who put Jasper through to the news director.

"This is Zachary Jasper, head of the Jasper Project. You know all about what's going on here at my ranch?"

The news director glanced at a recorder on his desk programmed to automatically tape all incoming and outgoing newsroom calls. The tape was running.

"Of course I know, Mr. Jasper, I've had reporters out there since the siege began. Why are you calling?"

"Your reporters tell you about how the FBI just shot and killed the young wife of a loyal, decent, God-fearing man at the ranch?"

"The FBI did? Our reporter just called in, said it appeared that someone at the ranch shot the woman."

"That figures, doesn't it? Are you running an independent news organization or one run by Jews in the government's pocket?"

The news director, Eli Cohen, withheld the reply he was tempted to make, asking instead, "Can you verify that it was the FBI who did the shooting, Mr. Jasper?"

"You've got my word on it. What the hell do you think, I'd be stupid enough to kill one of my own?"

"I'll follow up on this, Mr. Jasper. Give me a number I can reach you at."

"I'll call you."

Jasper hung up.

Thinking that it was a shame that the bigoted Jasper hadn't been the one killed, the news director contacted his on-the-scene reporter and told her what Jasper had said. "Try to get a statement from the FBI, Mindy. Maybe Jasper's right. Keep on it."

FBI Director Templeton got back to Joe Harris in twenty minutes.

"The attorney general and the president have given the okay, Joe, to advance the schedule. Tell that bastard Jasper he and his people have six hours to come out peacefully. If they don't, use all necessary force to end this thing. We can't stand by while this madman kills innocent women and children. Tell him to send out all the women and children and we'll give him and his men more time. If he refuses, move!"

31

"How awful!"

Jessica watched the news in her Foggy Bottom apartment with her friends and fellow bird-watchers Cindy and Horace, who'd returned from Canada with her after spending a few days in search of uncommon species and photographing them. Upon arrival in Washington early that afternoon, Jess took everyone's undeveloped rolls of film into a local one-hour processing service on her way home, including two rolls shot by Cindy on a similar trip six months earlier that she hadn't gotten around to having processed.

They'd decided to extend the trip by having Chinese food at Jessica's apartment that night and going over the pictures. A dozen envelopes containing the prints were piled on a coffee table in the living room. Jess had called in the takeout order, and they were about to begin going through the photos when their attention was diverted by a special TV report on the siege in Blaine, Washington.

"Tension has increased dramatically here with the shooting of a young woman inside the Jasper com-

254

pound that's been under siege by federal authorities since yesterday. There are conflicting reports about who killed the woman, whose name was Patty Davidson, and whose eleven-year-old son, Mark, escaped. FBI spokesman Special Agent Joseph Harris, who's in charge of the operation here, denies vehemently that any member of the siege team killed Ms. Davidson, and insists that she was shot by someone inside the compound. At the same time, Zachary Jasper, whose Jasper Project, an antigovernment, white-supremacy group, is accused of being involved in the missile downing of three commuter aircraft almost three weeks ago, has claimed in a call to a local radio station that the woman was gunned down by FBI marksmen. Whether this incident causes the siege team to step up its announced deadline of forty-eight hours for Jasper and his people to surrender peacefully remains unknown at this moment. When informed of the woman's murder, President Ashmead stated, 'Killing all those innocent men, women, and children on the planes, and now this senseless slaughter of a member of Jasper's cult, reflects on the cowardice of Jasper and his followers, and their total disregard for human life.' Aside from the denial by Special Agent Harris, no statement has been forthcoming from FBI headquarters or the Justice Department."

"If this Jasper character was involved in shooting down those planes, they should go in and blow him and his crazy followers up," said Horace, a retired actuary who'd spent his professional career at the General Accounting Office.

"God, no," said Cindy, a tall, angular woman who permed her brunette hair in a 1940s style, and who worked as a secretary in a ten-term congressman's office on Capitol Hill. "Killing more people won't solve anything."

"Only way to stop people like him," said Horace in a pinched, nasal voice testifying to chronic sinus problems. "We ought to round up all the nuts and put 'em on an island someplace, get 'em out of society before they destroy it."

Jessica liked Horace as a bird-watching companion as long as they didn't discuss politics; his were to the right of John Birch's, just below Ivan the Terrible's.

"Have you heard from Max?" Cindy asked Jessica, changing the topic.

"No." She was glad the delivery of the food spared her from having to say more.

"Well, now, what say we take a look at what we got," Horace said after they'd eaten, hiding a small belch behind his hand and yawning. "Flying always makes me tired."

"There's no jet lag between eastern Canada and Washington, Horace," said Cindy, winking at Jess.

Horace ignored the dig and opened the first of the envelopes, one of his, and began explaining every aspect of each of the pictures: the name of the bird, his camera setting, and his state of mind at the moment he pushed the shutter button. His painfully slow commentary was mitigated by the pictures themselves—in fact, he'd shot a lovely series of a rose-breasted grosbeak, which was joined at the end of his roll by another bird he claimed was a black-headed grosbeak.

"Can't be," Cindy said, using a magnifying glass provided by Jess to examine the picture more closely. "Black-headed grosbeaks don't come that far east or north. Strictly the Southwest."

"And I'm telling you it's a black-headed grosbeak,"

said Horace. "If you're jealous because I spotted it and managed to get a picture, say so, Cindy."

Cindy sighed and sat back as Horace finished going through his twenty-four shots. Now, it was Cindy's turn. Of the group, she was acknowledged as the best photographer. She certainly had the best equipment, including a telephoto lens the size of a small cannon. Although she hadn't seen an especially impressive array of birds, her photographs of what she'd come across were professional quality.

"Where did you shoot this sequence?" Jess asked, referring to a set of three prints that had caught a pair of Canada warblers feeding in underbrush. As was usually the case, Cindy had gone off on her own during the trip, not to be seen again until the end of the day.

"A beautiful ridge I discovered six months ago," she said. "It overlooks a gorgeous valley right on the border, just north of Plattsburgh. I sat up there for an hour. Aren't they beautiful?"

"They certainly are," agreed Jess, speaking of the pair of warblers, the male with its distinctive black necklace on its yellow breast, the female's necklace less distinct.

An hour later, they'd gone through the pictures from this more recent trip, and Cindy turned to an envelope containing the six-month-old material. She'd asked Jess to have three sets of prints made from that period: "One for you, and one for Horace," she said, handing envelopes to both. They opened the third envelope and went through the pictures, which represented brilliant photographic work.

"These are stunning," Jessica said, pulling one of the prints from the batch and admiring it. "I'll have it blown up and framed, add to my collection on the wall. Thanks so much."

Cindy started to put the set back in the envelope.

"Wait a minute," Horace said, pulling a couple of shots from the pack. "What are these? Looks like birds of a different feather."

Cindy laughed. "Oh, just forget those. I saw this group of men down in the valley and couldn't resist taking a few shots of them."

"We've got a Peeping Tom here, Jess," Horace said, chuckling.

"A Peeping Tomasina," Jess corrected, looking more closely at the men in the photos. "What were they doing?"

"Beats me. Running around in the valley. Probably some male bonding group." Cindy looked up at a clock on the wall. "Oh, speaking of running, I've got to run. The congressman's an early-morning guest tomorrow on C-SPAN. Wants me to go with him to the studio."

"I believe it's time for me to leave, too," said Horace, standing stiffly and arching his back. "Lovely evening, Jess."

"Great trip," Cindy said. "Dinner was fine, too."

They left after dividing the cost of the photo processing and the meal. Alone now, Jessica cleaned up the remains of the dinner, removed her makeup, washed her face, brushed her teeth, dressed for bed, and settled on the couch. She was tempted to turn on the television again but decided not to. The news from Washington State was too depressing to watch before trying to sleep. Instead, she briefly browsed through the latest copy of *The Washington Monthly*, felt her eyes closing after ten minutes, and went to bed. Her final conscious thoughts were of Max. What was he doing at the moment, who was he with? A woman? His pal Bill Lerner? Some Russian lowlife?

"I miss you, Pauling," she muttered as she turned on her side, fluffed up the pillow beneath her head, and allowed sleep to take hold. *Come home.*

32

Early Morning
Moscow

Hoctor led Pauling to a car that had been parked around the corner from Bill Lerner's apartment. The young Russian driver said nothing as Pauling and Hoctor got in the rear seat. "Sheremetevo," Hoctor said.

The 707 with the seal of the United States of America on its tail was bathed in light at Moscow's international airport, twenty miles outside the city. It was parked away from the main terminal, an area specially designated for the aircraft of foreign dignitaries, and had been there since Secretary of State Rock and her party arrived. It was surrounded by a dozen uniformed, armed Russian soldiers, supervised by diplomatic security special agents assigned to the Secretary, some of whom had flown with her from Washington, others from the American embassy in Moscow. The Air Force crew had been billeted in a former Soviet military barracks a mile outside the airport. Now, six hours after they'd been alerted they'd be leaving, the pilots busied themselves in the cockpit preparing to depart; cabin stewards had provisioned the aircraft and awaited the arrival of the passengers, most notably Elizabeth Rock. A bottle of Rombauer chardonnay chilled in an ice bucket in her private quarters.

Pauling and Hoctor's car was stopped at a gate by two Russian soldiers and an American security officer. He greeted Hoctor by name but still asked for identification. Pauling's temporary ID card from the embassy indicated he worked in the ECO/COM division. They were waved through.

They hadn't spoken for the entire ride from the city to the airport, nor did they say anything now as the driver maneuvered the car close to the 707's boarding stairs. Hoctor was first out; Pauling hesitated, then joined him on the tarmac. Moving lights in the distance caused them to turn. Secretary Rock's black limousine, followed by four other vehicles, came to a stop at the foot of the boarding stairs. The Secretary got out, spoke to a few people, and went up into the aircraft.

"Time to board, Mr. Hoctor," a security man said.

"Max," Hoctor said, touching Pauling's arm to indicate they were to go to the stairs.

When he didn't follow, Hoctor turned and glared at him.

"I want to know what happened to Bill Lerner," Pauling said.

"And you will, Max, but not now. You've done a good job. Don't screw it up by being obstinate."

They bounded up the stairs, ignored the salute of the uniformed Marine at the top, and entered the plane. Pauling glanced to his left, into the cockpit, where the three-man crew, dressed in blue Air Force flight fatigues, were still calmly going through their preflight routine. The Secretary's chief of staff, Eva Young, greeted Hoctor as they moved through the aircraft to the conference table, where Mike McQuaid and Air Force weapons expert Dr. Herbert Shulman were seated. Leaving the area as they arrived was Phil Wick, who, as State's assistant secretary for public affairs, was a familiar face on TV. Hoctor started to introduce Pauling when Rock entered.

"Madam Secretary," Hoctor said. McQuaid and Shulman stood.

"Please, sit," Rock said, plopping a thick file on the table and taking the seat reserved for her.

"Madam Secretary, this is Max Pauling," Hoctor said.

"Yes, I know," she said. "We've met before."

"Yes, ma'am," Pauling said, extending his hand across the table.

Rock locked eyes with him as she took his hand, dropped it, opened the folder in front of her, and quickly read a secured e-mail Eva Young had handed her on the way to the airport. She looked up from the document and said, "The situation with the Jasper Project has changed. Dramatically!"

"How so?" Shulman asked.

McQuaid started to respond but the secretary cut him off. "One of the members of Jasper's group, a young woman, has been shot and killed," she said, "by someone inside the compound."

"That's verified?" Hoctor asked.

"Yes. The schedule for an assault on the ranch has been moved up. Six hours." She looked at her watch. "Five hours now."

"Madam Secretary," Hoctor said, "maybe you'd better let Pauling here report on what he's come up with."

Everyone paused as the sound of the jet's engines being fired up broke the relative silence of the conference room.

Rock turned to Pauling and cocked her head, an invitation to speak.

"I managed to trace the source of the missiles, Madam Secretary," Pauling said.

"Oh? You work fast."

"In this sort of operation, speed counts, as you know," Pauling said.

"Obviously, the source was Russian."

"They were made here," Pauling said, "and sold through the Russian so-called mafia. Arms dealers."

"To the Chinese."

"That's not what my informants told me."

"The FBI's undercover agent who infiltrated the Jasper ranch reported that the Chinese were involved, didn't he?" She directed the question to McQuaid, the president's terrorism man.

"Yes, ma'am. That's what we've been told by Director Templeton."

Rock said to Pauling, "You're saying the FBI is wrong."

"Not my place to say they're wrong. All I'm doing is reporting what I learned from my Russian informants."

"Maybe we should just let him tell us what he's learned," McQuaid said.

"Go ahead," said Rock, sitting back.

"Could I have that paper, Tom?" Pauling said to Hoctor, who pulled it from his pocket. Pauling read it, cleared his throat, and said, "I was handed this note by my Russian contact. He'd been given it by the arms dealer who sold the missiles. According to him, missiles from the batch used in the attacks on the planes were sold to a Canadian buyer. They were brought into the U.S. on a Canadian fishing vessel, specifically to Bath, Maine."

"And transported out to Jasper in Washington?" Secretary Rock asked.

"No, ma'am. The Canadian buyer told the arms dealer the missiles were going to a right-wing group in upstate New York, Plattsburgh, New York, to be precise, on the Canadian border. A group called the Freedom Alliance."

"I'm not familiar with it."

"A small but particularly violent group," McQuaid said. "We've recently been taking a closer look at it."

"Is this Freedom Alliance tied to Canada?" Rock asked.

"Its members move back and forth across the border, Madam Secretary. Many of them live in Canada but are U.S. citizens."

The Secretary closed her eyes, opened them, and took in the men at the table one by one, coming to rest on Tom Hoctor. "What do you think?" she asked him.

"I think the FBI might be about to attack the wrong group," Hoctor said.

"Based upon the claim of a Russian thug?" Rock said.

"Yes, ma'am," Pauling said.

"Over the word of an FBI special agent?"

"Yes, ma'am."

"Do you have anything to substantiate this Russian's claim, Mr. Pauling?"

"First of all, it's information given to this Russian thug by the arms dealer who sold the missiles." He found himself becoming protective of Misha Glinskaya, whom he'd left just hours ago in a pool of blood on the sidewalk in front of the Gold Coin bar. It wasn't the first time he'd felt this way about a hoodlum he'd encountered while working the Moscow underworld. "I've no reason to doubt that the FBI undercover agent did come up with something at the Jasper Project, but that doesn't mean the agent was right. At the very least, the information I've now brought to the table is worth further investigation, and reason for the Bureau to reevaluate its planned action against Jasper. Second—"

They were interrupted by the captain's voice over the PA system. "We're beginning our taxi to the runway, ladies and gentlemen. Please prepare for takeoff." The engines whined louder, and the aircraft began to move.

McQuaid spoke: "Frankly, Madam Secretary, I'm unconvinced by what Mr. Pauling has said."

"Will the president share that view, Mr. McQuaid?" Rock asked.

"Yes, ma'am, I'm sure he will. It doesn't make any sense to take the word of a Russian lowlife over a dedicated, veteran FBI undercover agent."

"Anyone else?" Rock asked.

"Not for me to say," Dr. Shulman said.

"Mr. Hoctor?"

"It's reason enough to hold off any action against the Jasper Project until the stories are sorted out."

"Mr. Pauling?"

"I just told you what I learned, Madam Secretary," he said. "What's done with it isn't my call."

The Secretary stared at Pauling like a trial lawyer deciding whether to ask another question of a witness. Pauling's eyes remained fixed on hers, not challenging but silently testifying to the truth of what he'd said.

"I don't know what credence to give the source of your information, Mr. Pauling, and I'm having trouble weighing it against what the FBI says. But I do know that if what you say has any validity, a monumental mistake might be in the making."

She pushed a button on the wall behind her. Eva Young opened the door. "Yes, ma'am?"

"Get me the president."

33

Joe Potamos got off the plane at Reagan National Airport and climbed into the first available taxi outside the terminal. The flight from Vermont had been delayed an hour, something to do with a malfunctioning warning light in the cockpit. It seemed like ten hours to Potamos.

The driver took him to his condo in Rosslyn, where he checked messages on his machine, emptied his overnight bag on the bed, rammed a change of clothes back into it, and went downstairs to hail another taxi, this time going to Roseann Blackburn's Capitol Hill apartment. He went up the stairs two at a time and burst through the door. Roseann was at the piano, her attention divided between finger exercises she was doing and the television. The all-news cable channels had been covering the siege at Blaine almost continually, interrupting the growing crisis only for commercials.

Roseann got up and greeted him with a tender kiss and a hug while Jumper climbed up the back of his leg. "How was the trip?" she asked.

"How was the trip? *How was the trip?* The trip was . . . the trip was incredible. Your buddy, Connie Vail, was right, baby, on-the-nose right. Craig Thomas was in

Burlington, just like she said he was." Potamos made two fists, pumped them into the air, did a turn in the middle of the living room, and collapsed on the couch. "I have got the story of the year, Roseann. Of the decade." He stood, straightened, and addressed her as he might from a podium: "Ladies and gentlemen of the Pulitzer committee, I am both honored and humbled by your having bestowed this coveted award on me. I want to thank my father, Frank, and my mother and—"

"Joe," Roseann said, laughing, "calm down and tell me what happened."

He responded by pulling a red director's chair up in front of the TV set. Joe Harris, FBI special agent in charge of the Jasper ranch siege, had just begun a press conference, one of two scheduled that day.

"The situation here continues to be without resolution," Harris said into the bouquet of microphones. "We have been in constant contact with Mr. Jasper, and we continue to urge him and his people to leave the ranch peaceably. As of this time, he has refused to comply with that order. His posture at this juncture is one of defiance. I'm afraid that's all I have to report at this time."

"You've got the wrong guy, buddy!" Potamos said to the screen.

A reporter asked whether it was true that the timetable for an assault on the ranch had been pushed up, and that the assault was imminent.

"I have no comment about that at this time," Harris said, the powerful TV lights catching the perspiration on his shaved head and creating what looked like a halo above it.

"Joe, Gil Gardello's been calling while you were gone," Roseann said. "He's called at least four times."

"You didn't tell him where I was?"

267

"No. You told me not to. Aren't you going to tell me what happened with Craig Thomas?"

"Yeah, sure, I am, but I have to make a call first. A couple of calls, okay, babe?" He pecked her on the cheek as he went into the kitchen and took the receiver from a wall phone.

She followed. "It wasn't that group in Washington who shot down the planes?" she asked.

He shook his head. "Nope. The FBI's about to blast the wrong people."

"Shouldn't you be calling the FBI, the attorney general, the president?"

"I—Gil, it's Joe."

Potamos held the phone away from his ear, then brought it back to his mouth. "Hey, Gil, back off a little, huh? I really don't need abuse from you. Especially now."

"Joe, where the hell have you been?"

"Vermont. I was a little early for the changing of the leaves, but—"

"You're fired, Joe."

"Ah, come on, Gil, here I am sitting on the story of the century and—"

It had gone from year to decade to century, Roseann thought as she sat at the kitchen table listening. "What story?" Gardello asked.

Potamos laughed. "You know that party going on out in the boondocks of Washington, the Jasper ranch?"

"Of course I do. I'm looking at it on TV right now."

"What would you say, Gil, if I told you I had proof that those crazies at the Jasper ranch didn't have a damn thing to do with shooting down those commuter planes?"

"Where did you get *that*?"

"From the horse with the mouth. You remember that

Canadian trade rep from their embassy who got whacked in the park, the story you told me to drop?"

"Yeah."

"Well, it's a good thing I stayed with it. The guy who was stabbed in the park, Jeremy Wilcox, wasn't about to win the Canadian good citizenship award. He made some extra pocket change greasing the skids for arms dealers to sell to groups in this country, Canada, too. Paperwork went through him and he made sure there weren't any hitches. Been doing it for a couple of years before certain associates he thought were his friends—Russian guys with funny noses—decided not to be friends anymore."

"Where did you get this, Joe?"

"Oh, suddenly there's interest. I'd better not say any more. I'm fired, remember?"

Gardello ignored him. "Where did you get it, Joe?"

"A fella named Craig Thomas. He put the make on my girlfriend, Roseann and—"

"Joe!" Roseann said, coming up out of her chair. He quieted her with a smile and a wave of his hand.

"This guy Thomas—"

"Hold on a second, Joe," Gardello said, his attention going back to the small television set hanging from the wall. "There's something breaking out in Washington."

Potamos stretched the phone cord so that he could look into the living room. A reporter was standing on a low rise, from which he had an overview of the federal forces outside the ranch.

"We get a sense here that something is about to happen. Behind me, armored vehicles that have been stationary for most of the day have now started to move into positions closer to the ranch."

The sound of helicopters was heard.

"These ATF and Washington State choppers have also

gone into action. The SWAT teams seem to be spreading out along the front perimeter of the ranch. Officials here won't confirm whether they're poised to make a move on Jasper and his people, but something's up. Back to you, Ray, in the studio."

Potamos heard his name being yelled through the receiver. "See that, Gil," he said, bringing the phone back to his mouth, "we're watching a major scandal in progress."

"Who else have you told?" Gardello asked.

"Nobody, but I'm about to. The FBI, the attorney general, hell, maybe the president himself."

"Come in, Joe. We can call from here."

"*We?*"

"You're still an employee of this newspaper, damn it."

"If I heard right, *former* employee. Look, Gil, I know I've been a pain and you're one of the white hats, and I appreciate you've been saving my ass and all that, and I don't have a beef with you. But here I am sitting on the kind of scoop I've wanted all my professional life, Gil. *Every* journalist worth his salt looks for this break, getting inside, digging out the truth with his fingernails, not the way the spin doctors want the truth to appear to be, but the *real* truth." He looked to Roseann, whose satisfied grin and emphatic nod of her head were energizing— as if he needed it.

"Look, Joe, why don't we sit down and—"

"Gil," Joe said, slowly and without the passion of his previous words, "I've got some sorting out to do, got to figure what to do with this. Yeah, I owe you and the paper, and I'd love sticking it under Bowen's pompous, WASP nose, but give me some time. I need some time."

"Do your thinking here in my office," Gardello said.

"Maybe I will. I'll get back to you."

He hung up and let out a sustained sigh.

"Joe, please, come down to earth and tell me what's going on," Roseann said.

"Okay." He joined her at the table. "Connie Vail works for Craig Thomas, but you already know that. Everything she said here at the apartment three days ago panned out. By the way, there's more to their relationship than just working together. They've had a thing going for years, according to Thomas. Anyway, I don't blame her for being afraid for his life—hers, too, if the same creeps who killed Wilcox in the park find out she knows what's been going on." He leaned across the table and covered her hand. "Roseann, Wilcox and maybe a few others in the Canadian embassy have been conduits for Russian arms sales to North America for a couple of years now. Nice deal they had going. Our government keeps a pretty tight lid on ships and planes coming into the country from other places, especially the obvious ones—Middle East, South America, Greece, Turkey, the Balkans. But we don't take as hard a look at stuff crossing the border from Canada. Hell, they're our best friends, right? Allies, neighbors, we talk the same language, look the same. You know that fishing treaty we just signed with the Canadians? Man, the trade group Wilcox was involved with pushed hard for that. Guess why."

"To have easier access to American ports."

He blew a kiss across the table. "Right you are, Rosie, my beautiful, bright, and talented friend."

"You know I don't like being called Rosie."

"Yeah, sorry. Where was I? Right, so your friend Mr. Craig Thomas gets wind of what's happening and decides to blow the whistle, but subtle-like, leak it to the American press, aka Joseph Potamos, son of Frank Potamos, deceased Greek diner owner, rising star at *The Washington Post* until he punched George Alfred Bowen's lights out, and who happens to be in love with a ravishing piano player named Roseann Blackburn, who happens to have her picture in the *Washingtonian* and this Joseph Potamos is mentioned, which sends Mr. Craig Thomas in search of the disgraced journalist through this beautiful and talented Ms. Blackburn."

He sat back and recaptured his breath.

Another report could be heard from the TV: "It looks like troops at the Jasper ranch are ready to go in behind armored vehicles, including Washington State National Guard tanks that have been added to the arsenal."

"Thomas told you the missiles didn't go to that group?" Roseann asked.

"Right again," Potamos said, grabbing the phone. "The day after he had dinner with you, Thomas got hold of paperwork from Wilcox's files. Until then, he knew what was going on, sort of, but only the general picture. Once he came across a paper trail that traced specific shipments of arms, he knew he could end up like Wilcox. No wonder he took off."

"Who are you calling? The FBI?"

"Fat chance of getting through—or believed. I'm calling Jim Bellis at CNN."

"Why CNN? You don't work for them."

"I know, and I hate to stiff Gardello, but there's no time to do this through the paper. If Bellis will go on the air with it, it'll be out there right away and carry weight."

Bellis answered the call on his direct line.

"Jim, it's Joe Potamos."

"Hey, Joe, how are you?"

"Good, good. The FBI's about to attack the wrong group out in Washington."

"Say again?"

"Jim, that Jasper bunch out in Washington weren't the ones who shot down the planes."

"How do you know?"

"Look, there's not a hell of a lot of time to lose. I'm heading over to you. I'll call on the way from my cell phone, give you the details. But believe me, Jim, I know what I'm talking about."

"You can prove it?"

"Yeah, I can prove it, at least enough to get them to call off whatever they're planning to do in Washington."

"I'll be here."

"Back to you in a few minutes."

"I'll come with you," Roseann said.

"Good. Jumper been out?"

"An hour ago."

"Great." He rubbed behind the dog's ears. "Steak bones for life, Jump, for all of us."

34

That Same Morning
Washington, DC

The Air Force 707 carrying Secretary of State Elizabeth Rock and her party landed with smooth precision at Andrews Air Force Base. The Secretary, Mike McQuaid, Tom Hoctor, and Max Pauling got into a long, black official limousine with the flag of the United States flying from both front bumpers and were whisked to Main State.

Rock had spent the trip on a telephone. The more she heard, the angrier her expression became; uncharacteristic four-letter words issued from this genteel female secretary of state, just loud enough to cause her passengers to look away, or glance at one another.

Pauling shared her anger. Rock's attempts to reach President Ashmead from the plane had been unsuccessful the first few hours, although she had spoken with aides at the White House who promised to pass her information to the president. Eventually, Ashmead returned her calls.

"Mr. President, I assume you've been told what I told your aides," she said.

"Yes, but I'm not clear on what it is you're saying. You

have this State Department employee with you who claims to have information about the missile attacks on the planes?"

"Yes, sir, that's right. His name is Max Pauling. He's been working undercover in Moscow tracing the source of the missiles."

"We know they were Russian-made."

"Yes, Mr. President, but the assumption that they ended up in the hands of the Jasper group is wrong, according to what Mr. Pauling has uncovered."

"Uncovered? What's his source?"

"The arms dealer who sold the missiles, Mr. President."

There was silence on the other end. Ashmead, accompanied by National Security Advisor Tony Cammanati and Press Secretary Chris Targa, had placed the call from the Oval Office after being summoned from a diplomatic reception for the president and first lady of Guatemala. "An arms dealer?" he finally said, incredulity in his voice. "This Pauling believes what some arms dealer tells him? What, Russian? A Russian arms dealer? A criminal?"

The Secretary chose her words carefully. "Mr. President, I have every reason to believe that what Mr. Pauling has learned has an element of truth to it, at least enough so to call off the troops at the Jasper ranch until a further investigation can be conducted."

Another silence. "Elizabeth, we have evidence from the FBI itself that the Jasper Project was behind those missile attacks. They had an undercover agent there for months."

"All I'm urging, Mr. President, is that until this can be verified, the proposed attack on the Jasper ranch must be held off."

"I'll take it under advisement, Elizabeth."

"Sir, it's more urgent than that. What's the harm in waiting until—"

"Call me as soon as you arrive back in Washington, Elizabeth. Safe flight." The connection was broken.

"I don't know what her problem is," Ashmead said to Cammanati and Targa after hanging up. "She wants me to call off the action in Washington based upon what some Russian mafia guy told an undercover from State. Christ, we have inside information from the Bureau itself, from inside the group."

"Sir, the latest poll indicates that almost eighty percent of the public wants action taken, and taken now," said Targa.

Ashmead stood. "Chris, get hold of her public affairs secretary and tell him in no uncertain terms that State is not to issue any statements, answer any questions from the press without prior approval from this office."

"Right."

"The line remains open to Director Templeton, Mr. President," Cammanati said.

"No movement on Jasper's part?"

"No, sir. The concern is still that Jasper will kill more of his own people if this thing drags on, including kids."

"Shouldn't you get back to the reception, sir?" Targa asked.

"Tony, make an excuse for me. I need think time in here—alone!"

As Secretary Rock handed the phone to Eva Young, her face, youthful for someone sixty-four, with fewer lines than might be expected, was deeply creased, her mouth a tight, straight line. She turned to Pauling. "I want you to go over this again for me, give me as many tangible selling points as possible I can use with the president."

Pauling sighed, drew a breath, looked at Tom Hoctor, and started at the beginning—again.

This time, he went into detail—bloody, chilling detail.

35

Potamos was still talking to Bellis on his cell phone when he and Roseann got out of the cab in front of CNN's Washington studios on First Street NE. Bellis, a cordless phone to his ear, was waiting at the door when they arrived and quickly led them into the main studio, where a male and female anchor kept viewers abreast of what was happening at the Jasper ranch.

"Joe, if what you say is true, we've got a bombshell to report," Bellis said after taking them into a small makeup room off the studio.

"Yeah, I know, and it's an even bigger story if the feds go ahead and storm that ranch, blood and guts and all that, huh? How do we head that off?"

"You want to go on, tell the story? One of the anchors can interview you."

Potamos looked to Roseann for her reaction. The broad grin on her face mirrored the excitement of the moment, and the pleasure of having him go out front, on television.

"Let's go," Bellis said. "Next commercial break, I'll clue in the anchors." He picked up a phone on the makeup table, dialed the control room, and told the

278

executive producer of the segment being aired that Potamos had arrived, that the story had to be told, and that the entire CNN network should be alerted the interview was coming up and to clear the time.

Potamos suffered a moment of stage fright. Roseann sensed it and put her arm around his shoulder. "You'll be great," she said, kissing his cheek.

He checked for lipstick with his fingertips, said to Bellis, "Don't I get made up?"

"It wouldn't help," Bellis said.

"Thanks," Potamos said. "I'm ready."

Secretary Rock had taken detailed notes during Max Pauling's second recounting of events leading to the information he'd gathered from the Russian. Now, as she led her contingent into Main State, she mentally went over what she would say to the president. Members of her staff were in her outer office watching TV news coverage of the Blaine standoff when the Secretary arrived. Commercials were playing.

"New developments?" she asked.

"Looks like they're getting ready to go in, Madam Secretary."

She turned to her chief of staff, Eva Young. "Get me the president."

As Eva entered the Secretary's office to place the call, the face of one of CNN's anchors filled the screen. The camera pulled back to reveal Joe Potamos sitting next to her.

"Welcome back to our continuing coverage of the dramatic events unfolding in Blaine, Washington, where a large force of FBI, ATF, and local law enforcement agents seem ready to storm the ranch owned by hate-group leader Zachary Jasper. Seated with me is *Washington Post* reporter Joe Potamos, who has just returned from meeting with a man he claims can prove that the Jasper group was not involved with the fatal downing of three commuter aircraft more than three weeks ago. Mr. Potamos, welcome."

"Yeah, thanks for having me."

"Your appearance is last minute," so I don't have specific questions for you, she thought. "Suppose you start at the beginning and tell us what's behind your claim that the Jasper Project was not tied to the missile attacks."

"Yeah, well . . ."

Potamos looked frightened, and a little confused. Roseann, watching from the control room with Jim Bellis, made a fist and shut her eyes: Come on, Joe, do it! she said to herself.

"Well, it started when I was covering a murder here in DC, Foggy Bottom, in a small park across from the Lombardy Hotel. I saw right away that the deceased was Canadian because he had this tie on with little Canadian flags. Anyway, I was there with a buddy, a police lieutenant, homicide detective Pete Languth, and we were . . ."

"Is this being videotaped?" the secretary of state asked an aide.

"Not here, ma'am," he replied. "The press center."

Another aide started to speak but Max Pauling hushed her with a raised hand. For a moment, it didn't seem real to him, hearing this reporter saying the same thing he'd been claiming, that the missiles came from Russia through Canada—and not to the Jasper Project but to a binational hate group located in Plattsburgh, New York, on the U.S.-Canadian border. Everyone stood transfixed as Potamos wove his tale, becoming more confident as he went, animation creeping into his voice, hands gesturing, pausing

280

for slight dramatic effect. The anchor said little, asking only occasionally for more details.

"The president's not available, Madam Secretary," Eva Young said, rejoining the group.

"Not available?" Rock snapped. "I'm not some county chairman, or kook. Get Tony Cammanati, the first lady, anybody in the White House, and do it now!"

The interview, more a Potamos monologue, lasted seven uninterrupted minutes. A commercial for a depilatory abruptly replaced the two on the screen.

"Mr. Cammanati is on the line, Madam Secretary," Eva Young announced. Rock entered her office and slammed the door.

National Security Advisor Tony Cammanati took Rock's call in his private office in the White House. "Welcome back, Madam Secretary," he said pleasantly.

"Thanks. Tony, have you heard what this reporter, Potamos, just said on CNN?"

"Yes, I did."

"He corroborates what our undercover agent came up with in Moscow."

Cammanati said nothing.

"Did you hear me, Tony? We now have it from two different sources, *very* different sources, that the Jasper Project was not behind the missile attacks."

"We have it, Madam Secretary, from—"

"For God's sake, Tony, it's been years. Call me Lisa."

Cammanati's laugh sounded forced. "We have it, Lisa, from two very tainted and suspect sources. As I understand it, your guy got it from a Russian thug, a mafioso or mafiotsky, or whatever the hell they're called, and this reporter, Potamos, he's—"

"He's a journalist, Tony, with *The Washington Post*."

"No, he's not. We checked. He was fired. He's also the one who punched George Alfred Bowen a few years back. Remember?"

"Yes, I remember that incident. Not a bad idea. This is the same one?"

"Yes, ma'am—Lisa, the same one. The point is—" The Secretary looked up at the TV set in her office. The federal and state forces were in place at the ranch. "—the president's in an extremely difficult position, as I'm sure you can appreciate. He has solid evidence from a veteran FBI undercover agent who risked his life infiltrating the Jasper organization. You're asking him to discard that source in favor of stories concocted by a Russian thug and a disgraced former reporter. Justice has signed off on the Bureau's source and the action being contemplated. We've got Jasper shooting his own people, for crissake, a young woman trying to get the hell out of that snake pit. The families of the victims of the plane crashes are demanding a private meeting with the president. They want blood. So does the rest of the country."

"Tony, I understand what you're saying, and I do appreciate the decision the president has to make. But *two sources*, Tony, no matter how sullied they might be— isn't that reason enough to hold off for a time to get to the truth? What if these so-called tainted sources are right, and the FBI is wrong, and troops go in and kill Jasper and some of his people, including women and children? And do you know the political ramifications that will have for the administration?"

"Sure, I do. I also know that taking swift, decisive action will put to rest all the rumors and speculation about foreign powers being behind the missile attacks. Those missiles are throwing this nation into panic, Lisa, panic and terror and maybe chaos. All the terrorist attacks are coming to a head in this one episode."

Rock's sigh was loud enough for Cammanati to hear over the phone.

"I'll talk to the president again, Lisa. That's all I can promise."

"And I appreciate it, Tony. Please let me know what he says."

"I will. Glad to have you back."

She slowly replaced the phone into its cradle, lowered her head, and closed her eyes. A wave of fatigue had suddenly overwhelmed her, as though the reserve energy tank on which she'd been running had been ruptured. But the television caused her head to snap up and her eyes to open wide. It started with a single report, loud, amplified by microphones picking up the sound, every sound. Then, multiple gunshots, rifles.

"They're shooting at the troops," Hoctor said from the other side of the door. "They're going to make a fight out of it."

The sound of a bigger weapon firing erupted like a volcano from the TV inside Rock's office, something heavy and lethal. She watched as the tanks rolled up to the main gate of the ranch and stopped.

"Tear gas," Rock muttered. "Where's the tear gas?"

There was a lull in the sound. In the background, smoke spiraled up from a corner of the main house where the shell had hit. Two armed men who'd been near the gate suddenly turned and ran toward the house. A barrage of small-weapons fire crackled from the television speakers; one of the men could be seen falling to the ground; the other disappeared near the house.

"Good God," Rock muttered as a reporter began describing the assault over a cacophony of guns being fired. Helicopters came in low over the compound, spraying it with machine-gun fire. Distorted commands through powered bullhorns added to the reporter's audio scrim.

Wide-eyed witnesses on the other side of the door looked on with disbelief and morbid fascination: Pauling, Hoctor, McQuaid, and members of the Secretary's staff.

Pauling walked slowly through the reception area, the broadcast sounds of the carnage in Blaine, Washington, fading behind him. He considered for a moment going to his office, or to the press room to watch other accounts of the action. Instead, he left the building, crossed Twenty-third Street to the Columbia Plaza apartment complex in which Jessica Mumford lived, sat at an outdoor table under an umbrella, and watched people come and go from the apartment building and the small shops strung along one side of the large, open space. A twin-engine commuter plane flew low over the courtyard on takeoff from National, and Pauling thought of his Cessna parked at the airport, ready to go, to take him away to anywhere except Washington, DC.

But a heavy reality set in. They'd be looking for him back at State. Heavy-legged, he retraced his steps.

As he did, FBI Director Russell Templeton concluded his conversation with the president of the United States and swiveled in his chair to face the dozen men in his office.

"The president," he said, "has assured me he has initiated a total blackout on any information coming out of State about this so-called undercover investigator Pauling. But that doesn't deal with that son-of-a-bitch newspaper reporter going public, on CNN, damn it! Pick him up, detain him. If there's any truth to what he's saying, he's a material witness to a crime. And I want to know everything about him, every dirty magazine he's ever read, every woman he's ever slept with, how much he drinks, whether he uses dope, if he's ever missed a child support payment to an ex-wife, ever kicked a dog or picked his nose in public—*everything!*"

He directed his final words at Sydney Wingate, the Elephant Man, Special Agent Donald "Skip" Traxler's handler. "Where is Agent Traxler?" he asked.

"On leave, sir. You know he was—"

"What I know is that I'd like to talk to him again, and quick. This is going to blow up into a major scandal. We put somebody inside a hate group, he gets the goods on that group, and we do what we're expected to do, take action. Then State sticks its nose where it doesn't belong, helped by the CIA, of course, and they come up with a crazy story from a Russian con man. Worse, this jackass reporter gets himself on TV with another crazy story, gets his fifteen minutes of fame, and whips the public and the press into a further frenzy, with us on the receiving end of it—again, of course. Let's cut the legs out from under this."

Colonel Walter Barton was on the phone when Pauling walked into his office.

"What the hell is going on?" Barton snapped, placing his hand over the receiver.

Pauling sank into a chair. "What's going on," he said, "is one hell of a big mistake."

"The Secretary's office is on the line, looking for you."

"Well, tell them they've found me."

"Hoctor from CIA wants you, too."

"It's nice to be wanted—Colonel."

"He's here," Barton said into the phone. "What? Yes, I'll have him report there now." He hung up.

"Where do I report first—or next, Colonel?" Pauling asked.

Barton ignored the sarcasm. "Get up to the Secretary's office, on the double."

"Sure."

"You haven't spoken to anyone outside of the chain of command, have you, the press, anybody like that?"

Pauling slowly shook his head as he pushed himself out of the chair and went to the door. He paused, his hand on the knob, and turned. "Know what just occurred to me?"

Barton stared at him.

"It just occurred to me, Colonel, that my source in Moscow says four missiles were sold to that group on the Canadian border in upstate New York."

"And?"

"And, Colonel, only three of them have been used. Have a nice day."

36

Like millions of Americans—and countless viewers around the world—Mac and Annabel Smith sat for a time transfixed in front of their television set as the events in Blaine, Washington, played out in real time, a video war game with blood-and-flesh people and live rounds, Academy Award–worthy sound effects, the black hats and white hats pitted against each other as in a classic western, with occasional tension relief provided by commercials.

But the script failed to provide a seamless story line. There were too many back stories, as they say in Hollywood, getting in the way of the main tale of good triumphing over evil, justice being served, the proverbial happy ending.

"Do you believe that *Post* reporter, Potamos, and his claims?" Annabel asked her husband.

"I don't know, Annie. If he's right, the FBI's got a lot to explain."

"They haven't identified the undercover agent, have they?"

"No, and they won't—unless, of course, some enterprising investigative reporter digs out his name."

"I was thinking of Jess Mumford," Annabel said.

"Her ex-husband, Skip—what is it, Traxler?"

"Uh huh. I'd hate to be in his position—the one who provided the information on the Jasper group, I mean—if they attacked the wrong people based on his faulty information."

"That'd be a heavy weight to bear. Have you spoken with Jess lately?"

"No. Think I'll call."

She returned to the den a minute later. "Busy. I'll try again."

Annabel's second call to Jessica Mumford's apartment reached a clear line, but no answer. Jessica heard it ringing but didn't move to pick up. The call she'd just completed had left her shaken.

"Ms. Mumford, this is FBI Special Agent Sydney Wingate," he'd said.

"Yes?"

"I work closely with your former husband, Special Agent Traxler."

"Has something happened to him?"

"Oh, no, ma'am, nothing like that. He's been on extended leave and we need to speak with him on agency matters. I thought he might have been in contact with you."

"With me? No, we haven't spoken for . . . no, I haven't heard from him."

"If you should, Ms. Mumford, I'd appreciate a call." He gave her his direct number at the Hoover Building.

"All right, although I doubt he'll call me."

"Thank you."

* * *

288

The call itself was upsetting enough for Jessica. No one from the FBI had ever contacted her before concerning her former husband, and the inherent message wasn't lost on her. She knew that agents of the FBI were never out of touch with their superiors, *never*, no matter where they were or the reason for being there.

Was Skip hurt and unable to contact the Bureau? Or dead, his cover blown and the victim of a group he'd infiltrated?

TV coverage of the assault on the Jasper ranch played in the background. She knew now that an FBI undercover agent had provided the information leading to the attack. Had Skip been that agent?

When will you ever learn? she asked herself, staring vacantly at the screen. When would she allow—indeed, insist—that her mind override her heart? Traxler, now Pauling, the two significant men in her life, restless and adventuresome, their passions inflamed more by danger than a kiss, off doing what they loved best and unconcerned that those who cared about them worried, speculated, chewed nails and ate too much out of anxiety. She knew—her *mind* knew—that to allow such men's fire-eating, daredevil, flying-without-a-net existence to dominate the lives of those mired in more mundane lives back home was, if not futile, self-destructive. But tell that to the *heart*.

She forced herself to disconnect from the TV by picking up some of the photographs Cindy had taken six months earlier, from the duplicate batch she'd given Jess as a gift, and examined them through the magnifying glass she kept for that purpose. The birds depicted in the shots were beautiful, but this particular photo didn't contain brightly colored birds in their natural habitat. It was one of two Cindy had taken of the group of men in the valley on the U.S.-Canadian border. Jessica kept changing the position of the magnifying glass to make the figures as large as possible.

The ringing phone caused her to flinch. She took another look at the photo before going to the kitchen and answering.

"Jess, it's Max."

"Where are you?"

"In Washington."

"When did you get back?"

"Today. I flew back with . . . it doesn't matter. I'd like to see you."

"Now?"

"Later today? Tonight?"

"Yes, of course. I have the day off, at least for now. Max, I'd like very much to see you."

He managed a laugh. "I'm glad to hear that. Dinner?"

"Here at the apartment. There's something I want to show you."

"What is it?"

"I can't go into it over the phone. What time?"

"I'm not sure. I'm at State, will be the rest of the day, maybe evening, too. I'll call again when I know."

"All right. Max, is the Jasper thing the reason you're back?"

"Tonight, Jess. I have to go."

She looked at the clock; tonight couldn't arrive fast enough.

Joe Potamos and Roseann Blackburn were secluded in a small conference room a floor above the studio where he had just told the world that federal authorities were attacking the wrong hate group. His friend, Jim Bellis, fielded calls on the room's only phone.

"Everybody and his brother want to interview you, Joe," he said, "the nets, other cable operations. Geraldo, Brian Williams, Wallace, Jennings, everybody. We want you on in an hour, a special report built around you. They're putting it together now. Tonight, you're on Larry King, and another special right after Larry."

Potamos put up his hand. "Wait a minute," he said. "I'm no TV star."

"If it's money you're concerned about, don't worry. That's taken care of."

"No, it's not the money, Jim, it's just that it didn't change anything, did it? They're still going ahead and blowing up that ranch. What'd they do, kill everybody there?"

"No confirmed casualty reports, Joe, but—"

"Jesus."

"Joe," Roseann said, "you can't feel responsible for what happened. You did the best you could."

"Yeah, yeah, I know, but—"

Bellis took another call, handed the phone to Potamos.

"Who is it?" Potamos asked.

"Your editor at the *Post*. Gardello, something like that."

"Gil?"

"Joe, what are you doing?"

"What do you mean, what am I doing?"

"Now, at this very moment."

"I'm catching my breath."

"I want the story from you, Joe, all the space you want, all the help you need. And don't throw back in my face that I fired you. You're still on the payroll. Besides, like you said, you owe me for all the times I've covered for you."

"Look, Gil, I'm in no mood to—"

The door opened and four men in dark suits were framed in the doorway.

"Can I help you?" Bellis asked.

"FBI. Mr. Potamos?" They entered the conference room.

Potamos looked up. "Yeah, I'm Joe Potamos."

One of the agents showed his identification. "Please come with us, Mr. Potamos."

"What for?" He spoke into the phone. "Gil, I gotta go."

"Joe, listen to me—"

Potamos handed the phone to the lead agent. "It's my editor at the *Post*. Tell him I can't write the story because I'm otherwise occupied."

The agent frowned, handed the phone back to Potamos, who hung up.

"Am I being arrested?" Potamos asked.

"No, sir, but we do want to talk with you."

"About the mistake you guys just made?"

"Sir, just come with us."

"He hasn't done anything wrong," Roseann said.

"Who are you, ma'am?"

"Roseann Blackburn. I'm his—"

"She's my fiancée," Potamos said. "Where are we going?"

"Headquarters, Mr. Potamos. The Hoover Building."

One of the other agents touched Potamos on the shoulder, his message clear.

"When will he be back?" Bellis asked. "He's doing Larry King tonight and—"

"Go home," Potamos told Roseann as he accompanied the agents to the door. "Take care of Jumper. I'll call as soon as they're done with me."

Bellis picked up the phone and called down to the studio. "Get a crew out front and do it fast! The FBI's taking Potamos out. Grab it!"

Part Four

37

Fifteen minutes after returning to State, Pauling was summoned by Colonel Barton to a conference room across from Secretary Rock's office suite. Present were Mike McQuaid; the CIA's Tom Hoctor; an undersecretary of state for Russian affairs, Stuart Zweibel; and assistant secretary for public affairs, Phil Wick. Conversation ceased when Pauling entered the room, the sudden silence unsettling. Barton pointed to a chair and Pauling took it. Everyone was in a suit, with the exception of Barton, who wore his full military uniform; Pauling still wore the jeans, navy-blue T-shirt, sneakers, and photojournalist's vest he'd worn when meeting Misha Glinskaya.

"Max," Barton said, "we're all aware you've been through a tough couple of days. I want you to know how appreciative everyone is of your dedication to your assignment and the professional way in which you carried it out."

Pauling grimaced and recrossed his legs. Platitudes from Barton were never either spontaneous or sincere, in Pauling's experience, and he wondered when the "first

297

say something good" portion of the meeting would shift to the hard stuff.

Barton continued. "As you know, Max, the events of the past few hours have created a sensitive situation for everyone involved. Do you know this reporter, Joseph Potamos?"

"No, sir," Pauling said.

"But your report supports, in some ways, what he's claiming."

"Which might give it additional credence," Pauling replied.

Barton's reaction to Pauling's quick analysis was an almost indiscernible pursing of his lips and a small movement of his shoulders, as though to subtly redistribute parts of his body.

McQuaid used the lull to inject himself into the conversation. "Mr. Pauling, the reporter, Potamos, is being interviewed by the FBI as we speak. Obviously, it would be imprudent to reach a decision before all the facts are known. In order for this unfortunate episode to receive a fair hearing, it's critically important that all information, from any source, be confined to those charged with getting at the truth."

McQuaid's expression said he expected an affirmative response from Pauling. He received nothing.

"Perhaps Assistant Secretary Wick will be able to better explain," Barton said, looking to Wick, who straightened from the slouch he'd been in and locked eyes with Pauling.

"Mr. Pauling, as of this moment, no one outside this agency knows about your claims that the Jasper Project was not behind the missile attacks on the aircraft. That's good, and we intend to keep it that way until there's been ample opportunity to evaluate what you say—in a formal, official way, I mean."

"That reporter sure poked holes in that plan, didn't he?" Pauling said.

"I'm sure the Bureau will get to the bottom of his claims," Zweibel, the Russian expert, said.

McQuaid chimed in: "In the meantime, Mr. Pauling, the president has issued a firm and unambiguous directive: There is to be no public discussion of any aspect of State's involvement until all the facts are known. Do you have any questions about that?"

"Sure," Pauling said, "but I doubt if I'll get any answers here." He looked at Hoctor, whose wan smile was that of a parent exhibiting patience with a petulant child.

Barton said, "Max, as I said at the start of this meeting, you've done an outstanding job. Of course, I never doubted for a minute that you would. I'm relieving you of your duties here at State, for an indeterminate period of time. Give you a chance to rest up and get over the ordeal you've been through. I understand there was gunfire involved. We're all thankful you managed to come through it unscathed."

Pauling remained stoic, expressionless.

Tom Hoctor, who'd been silent, now spoke. "You're coming home, Max, back to the Farm. Do some instructing on covert operations, slide back into the Puzzle Palace's way of doing things." "The Farm" was slang for the CIA's training facilities on a handsome estate two hours south of Washington; the Puzzle Palace, CIA headquarters in Langley, Virginia.

Pauling considered challenging the decision to transfer him back to the Central Intelligence Agency. He didn't, for two reasons. First, he'd be happy to get away from State and Colonel Walter Barton. Second, it would have been a wasted exercise. Besides, it might simplify his life, reporting to people at the agency to which he was actually assigned.

Barton stood, came around the table, and extended his hand. "It's been a pleasure working with a consummate professional, Max. Don't worry about paperwork. I'll take care of everything. I wish you well."

Pauling gave a limp handshake, said nothing.

"Let's go, Max," Hoctor said, smiling. "Good to have you back in the fold."

Hoctor and Pauling waited until the others had left the room.

"I'm going to my apartment, Tom," Pauling said. "I need a shower."

"Is that an editorial comment?"

"No. When do I report?"

"Immediately."

"In a day or two?"

"Max, let's take a walk."

They exited onto C Street, went to the corner, and headed up Twenty-third, passing Jessica Mumford's apartment building on their left. Pauling looked across the street and wondered what she was doing at the moment, whether he should simply tell Hoctor that his girlfriend lived there and that he was going to see her. He decided against it. He had questions, and Hoctor presumably had answers.

Hoctor talked about everything but the meeting from which they'd just come, the events of the past twenty-four hours, and the imbroglio that had developed over the deadly assault on the Jasper ranch. When they came abreast of a Chinese restaurant, the Magic Gourd, Hoctor asked, "Drink, Max?"

"Sure, and something to eat. I just remembered I'm hungry."

The restaurant was empty and they took a booth near the front window. Pauling ordered a beer and a platter of firecracker shrimp, Hoctor a white wine and hot-and-sour soup. The small man, Pauling's CIA mentor and friend, watched as Pauling concentrated his attention out the window to the street, body tense, fatigue adding extra crevices to an already craggy face.

Hoctor broke the silence. "Max," he said, "you obviously understand what that meeting was all about."

Pauling slowly turned to face him. "Yeah, I think I do. This whole thing is going to be kept under wraps, spun like cotton candy until you can't see the core for the candy. And that means keeping my mouth shut, saying nothing, as though Moscow didn't happen."

"But not forever, Max. Look, I'm not a fan of Ashmead's administration and policies, but I do understand the ramifications involved here. The Bureau has egg all over its face if they moved on the wrong people based upon an undercover agent's reports. Not that I care a hell of a lot about whether the FBI has to squirm a little. But they need time to figure it out, come up with a game plan. And, my friend, there is always the possibility that this Scope was right, and you and the reporter are wrong."

"Scope?"

"The Bureau's undercover agent's code name."

"Oh."

Hoctor picked up on Pauling's expression of recognition. "You know something about it, Max?"

"What? No. You were saying they, meaning the FBI and the administration, need time to sort it out. Fine. Just as long as I'm out of it."

"You are that, Max, out of it. You come back to Langley for a few days, then head for the Farm. I never could see you in State. Not your sort of people. Diplomacy's never been your strong suit."

"I'll need a few days before reporting."

Hoctor's look of displeasure spanned the table. "I'm to get you back to Langley posthaste, Max."

"To keep me mummified."

Hoctor nodded and rubbed at his drooping right eye.

"Sorry, Tom, but I've got things to clean up here before I go anywhere."

"Such as?"

"Such as a lady I'd like to see, and a plane I'd like to get some time in."

"Fly it to Langley, keep it there. I'll go with you."

"Maybe I will. The shrimp are good. Sure you don't want one?"

"No. Enough spice for one day. Max, if I cut you some slack, give you a day here in DC, do I have your word that you'll lay low, speak with no one about what happened?"

"The press, you mean? No fear of that. The networks are getting rich off it. Nothing like a little carnage to kick up ratings."

"Tell you what," Hoctor said, motioning for a check and pulling out his wallet. "Go see your lady friend, take a shower, have a good dinner, make love, go out to the airport and pat your plane on the nose, and meet me tomorrow at six at the Westin, on M. Have your bag packed. Know where it is?"

"The Westin? Pretty fancy. Sure it's government issue?" Pauling said, patting Hoctor on the back as they stood on Twenty-third Street. "Thanks, Tom. See you at six."

Hoctor started to leave, but Pauling stopped him by calling his name. Hoctor retraced his steps.

"Did you kill Bill Lerner?" Pauling asked casually, as though questioning whether Hoctor had seen a popular movie.

Hoctor hesitated before answering. When he did, Pauling searched his face for a sign that what he said was truthful.

"He had enemies, Max."

"Enemies?"

"Russians he became involved with through Elena."

"You knew about her?"

"Yes. His superior chose to ignore their relationship, but others in the embassy didn't. He posed quite a dilemma, Max. There was plenty of talk at Langley about how to handle the situation. I don't think they ever came to a resolution, but now they don't have to. He was in deep, as I understand it, with some banker types, one in particular named Miziyano."

Pauling didn't signify that he knew who Hoctor was talking about. "In deep?" he said.

"I don't know the details, Max, just that it seems Lerner was building a nest egg by doing favors for this Miziyano. He must not have done enough of them. Powerful, isn't it, the love of a woman? A shame that people in Lerner's position—my position or yours, for that matter—can't fall in love with the enemy. Some of them are more appealing than our own."

"Elena Alekseyevna wasn't the enemy, Tom. She loved Bill."

"And he loved her—too much."

"It wasn't a heart attack, was it?"

"I wouldn't know, Max. Enjoy your evening. I'll see you tomorrow. Discuss what's transpired with no one, and that includes this female friend of yours."

"Don't worry, Tom, the last thing I want to talk about with her is what happened."

Pauling watched Hoctor walk away, saunter, actually, as though he held a closed umbrella and was strolling a boulevard or boardwalk. It struck Pauling that despite years of working for and with Thomas Hoctor, Pauling didn't know the little CIA operative at all. Maybe that was the prime requisite for being in their business, being unfathomable to even your closest friends.

Had Hoctor killed Bill Lerner?

Would he ever know the answer?

When Hoctor was out of sight, Pauling pressed his elbows against the pockets of his vest, feeling the Austrian Glock 17 semi-automatic in the pocket on the right, the two small glass ampules of prussic acid and their spring-loaded activating devices in a left. He'd forgotten he still had them until sitting in the meeting at State. Having flown back on Secretary Rock's private aircraft, and being ushered into Main State as part of her contingent, precluded having to go through the usual metal detectors.

Should I walk back to Columbia Plaza and pop in on Jessica? he asked himself. His answer was to wave down a cruising cab and direct the driver to his apartment in Crystal City, across the Potomac from the District.

38

Joe Potamos burst through the door from the J. Edgar Hoover Building like a man who'd just been released from prison. In a sense, he had been.

At first, the FBI agents interrogating him were pleasant and polite, even went so far as to congratulate him on his journalistic skills and the scoop he reported on CNN. But when it came to the point where they wanted the name of the man he'd gone to interview in Burlington, Vermont, and he refused to give it, the atmosphere in the room had changed from compatible to confrontational.

"Look, Potamos," the lead interrogator, one of six agents in the cramped room, said, "you stated on TV that you got this story from somebody in Burlington. Obviously, this person was involved with the Jeremy Wilcox who was killed here in DC, an employee of the Canadian embassy. Why don't you just make everybody's life easy and tell us who he is?"

Potamos had deliberately not mentioned Craig Thomas or Connie Vail during his on-camera performance, and he wasn't about to give them up now. "That's privileged information," he said. "Shield law."

305

"Ever hear of national security?" another agent asked. "Ever hear of patriotism?"

"Patriotism?" Potamos repeated, snickering. "I figure being patriotic means telling the truth to the American people, no matter who's in front of the fan when the goop hits. Look, I'd like to leave. I came here voluntarily, didn't give you any hassle. But unless you're arresting me for sedition or espionage or for being unpatriotic, I'm out of here."

Potamos stood. The lead agent ordered him to sit.

"I want a lawyer," Potamos said.

"You don't need one," the lead agent said. "You haven't been charged with anything." He nodded at another agent, who left the room.

The door opened and FBI Director Templeton stepped into the room. Potamos recognized him immediately.

"Mr. Potamos, Russell Templeton," the director said, smiling and shaking Potamos's hand. "Please, sit."

Potamos's surprise at being confronted by Templeton was fleeting. "I was just leaving," he said. "Nice meeting you."

"Please, Mr. Potamos," Templeton said, "sit down and hear me out. I promise it will only take a few minutes. Strictly off the record. When I'm finished, you can leave and go about your business."

Potamos resumed his seat and Templeton stood over him. The director was taller than he appeared to be on television, and looked older than his reported age of forty-seven. A nice-looking guy, Potamos thought, as the director started speaking in a measured, calm tone.

"You're aware, Mr. Potamos, that the claims you've made on TV are in direct conflict with the information that led to the attack today on the Jasper Project."

"Yeah, sure."

"You cite information obtained from people you

306

refuse to name, yet expect us to assign more weight to your sources than the ones we've relied upon."

Potamos shrugged and held out his hands, palms up. "Look, Director, all I know is what I was told by people who are credible to me. I don't know who gave you your information about that nut Jasper and his cult—an undercover agent, right?—but it seems to me that you should at least be open to the possibility you and your agents made a mistake out at that ranch. Now, with all due respect, sir, I have a story to write, and I know you have a lot of work to do to sort out this mess. Why don't we just get on with our jobs and—"

"Mr. Potamos, I am asking you, as director of the Federal Bureau of Investigation, to withhold any stories or future TV appearances until I'm able to do exactly what you suggest, 'sort out this mess.' I assure you that if you agree to help me and the Bureau with this small favor, we'll work closely with you to ensure that you receive exclusive information, before any of your colleagues do. You can build on your scoop with validated information from the Federal Bureau of Investigation itself."

His expression said he'd just made an offer Potamos couldn't refuse.

Potamos stood. "Thanks for the offer," he said, "but I think I'll pass. Nice meeting you, sir. Keep up the good work."

His first steps to the door were tentative; would they stop him? They didn't. He left the room, fought the urge to run, made his way down to the ground floor, and exited onto Pennsylvania Avenue, where he hailed a cab. Ten minutes later he was running up the stairs to Roseann's apartment. She was on the phone when he entered.

"Hold on," she said, "he just walked in."

"Who is it?" he asked, noticing a pile of papers torn

from a small pad with names and phone numbers written on them.

"It's Gil Gardello," she said.

Potamos took the phone from her.

"The story," Gardello said. "What happened at the FBI?"

"Nothing. We broke bread and swapped recipes."

"Stay there, Joe. I'm on my way."

"Don't bother, Gil, I—"

The click of the phone being hung up was like the snap of a bullwhip in Potamos's ear.

"Joe," Roseann said, "all these messages are for you. The phone's been ringing off the hook."

He quickly scanned the slips of paper. "What's this one?" he asked, handing it to her. "There's no name."

"Oh, my flight information. Bill Walters called. He's booked me into the Cedars in Pennsylvania, outside Pittsburgh."

"When?"

"Tonight. A fancy dinner for a bunch of big shots, government and business types. The money's great, triple scale, and all expenses."

"Tonight?"

"I'm subbing. That's why it's last minute."

"I thought maybe—"

"What?"

"I thought maybe you'd be around with all this craziness going on."

"Oh, Joe," she said, kissing him, "I'll be back later tonight. The job's two hours. Fly there on a puddle jumper—only an hour flight—do my thing, hop the last plane back to DC tonight. Come with me, Joe. Get away for a few hours."

"Nah, can't. I've got all these TV shows to do tonight."

"You're going to do them?"

"Yeah. I'd better start calling everybody back."

"And I have to get ready. I leave for the airport in a couple of hours."

Potamos nodded and started dialing a number.

"Joe."

"What?"

"I'm really proud of you."

"Are you? Good. I'm proud of you, too. Go on, get your act together." He smiled as he finished dialing and waited for the Larry King show to answer.

He'd just confirmed to King's producer that he would show up that evening when Gil Gardello arrived.

"You've got a hell of a nerve," Potamos said.

"Joe, listen to me. I'm sorry about what happened earlier. I said you were fired to wake you up, that's all, get you to realize you were skating on thin ice. Bowen's been after management to can you ever since you popped him, and I've been going through hoops to keep you around. You're still a reporter for the *Post*. You're no TV star, for crissake. You're a print journalist and a damn good one. You're onto a big story, Joe, and like I said, the world is yours, all the support you need, unlimited expense account, researchers, whatever you need."

Potamos said nothing.

"There'll probably be a book, too, Joe, with a big advance," Gardello said. "Do a tour, talk shows, book signings."

Potamos saw that Roseann was standing in the bedroom doorway, a quizzical look on her face.

"And," Gardello said, his voice emphasizing that what he was about to say next was especially important, "George Alfred Bowen is already grousing about you having this story. Follow up on it with me and you'll hurt him a lot worse than a punch in the nose."

"Do it, Joe," Roseann said.

"Yeah, I'll do it." To Gardello he said, "But I do it my way, on my schedule."

"Of course, Joe. That's the way it'll be."

"Great." He turned to the bedroom. "Hey, Rosie, you're goin' to miss me on Larry King."

"Program the VCR."

Potamos looked at Gardello and grinned. " 'Program the VCR.' You know how to do that?"

"No, you?"

"No."

"You can get a tape from the show," Roseann said, emerging from the bedroom dressed in a black cocktail dress and carrying a small carry-on bag. "How do I look?"

"Sensational," Gardello said, meaning it.

Potamos explained where she was going and turned on the TV set. His interview with CNN was being replayed. Potamos turned in his director's chair and asked, "Do you think I should wear a blue shirt tonight, maybe get a haircut, a trim, before the King show?"

Her answer was to lean over the back of the chair, hug him, and say, "You look perfect the way you are, my handsome Greek." She straightened up. "Have to run. I'll be back by midnight. Nice to see you again, Gil."

"Same here. Play good."

"I'll try."

And she was gone.

39

"Max?" Jessica Mumford said into the intercom in response to someone buzzing from the lobby.

"Max?" the male voice said. "No. It's Skip."

Hearing his name and voice startled her. She managed, "What are you doing here?"

A laugh preceded his response. "I'm here to see you. Anything sinister about that?"

"No, of course not. I—"

"Hey, Jess, I may be your former husband but that doesn't mean I can't stop by to say hello to my ex-wife."

"Do you want to come up?"

"Unless you want to come down to the lobby."

She pushed a button releasing the downstairs inner door to the elevators. A minute later he knocked and she was face-to-face with him.

"Well, well," he said, "you're more beautiful than the last time I saw you."

"Really?" She didn't return the compliment. The man standing in the hallway was not the man she remembered from when they'd conducted their whirlwind courtship and ran off to cement their folly. Dissipation ruled his once boyish face. His hair had begun to recede and had

311

become curly, corkscrews growing haphazardly on top, shaggy and untended at his temples and over the back of his neck. He wore a lightweight yellow-and-brown plaid shirt, khaki pants in need of pressing, brown hiking boots, and a lightweight gray windbreaker.

He walked past her into the living room and took it in. "Very nice, Jess. Looks like you."

"Meaning?"

"Meaning it reflects you, the furnishings, the decorations, everything in its place. Perfect order, like birds in flight."

He went to a wall covered with framed eight-by-ten color photographs. "Ah hah," he said, "still tracking down our little feathered friends."

"Yes. The Bureau is trying to locate you. A Special Agent Wingate called."

"The Elephant Man."

"The—?"

"He has unusually big ears."

"Oh."

"Serving drinks, or should we go to a bar?"

"What would you like?"

"Still partial to bone-dry martinis, straight up?"

"Would you like a beer?"

"Sure, anything but a light," he said, sitting on the couch.

She went into the kitchen and looked in the refrigerator, where a lonely bottle of Amstel Light represented her beer stock. "All I have is light beer," she called.

"If I must," he said from the living room.

A bottle opener eluded her until she found one that had been put in the wrong drawer after dishwashing. She paused for a moment to choose an appropriate glass. As she started to open the bottle, she remembered that the photos she'd been examining through the magnifying glass were still on the coffee table in front of the couch. She came to the kitchen door. Traxler was holding the glass and peering through it at the picture from the top of the pile. He sensed her presence, looked at her, and asked, "Where did you get this?"

"What, that picture? Cindy Pearl took it."

"When did she take it?" His voice was suddenly heavier.

"I don't know, a few months ago." She came to the table and reached for the picture, but he held it away from her.

"You've been looking at this, Jess?"

"I—no, I was going to but—"

He looked up at her with hostile eyes, then took the shot of the men in the valley near Plattsburgh and put it in one of his windbreaker's pockets. There was no joy in his smile. "I wish you hadn't seen it, Jess."

"I'll get your beer," she said.

"Don't bother." He stood and came around the couch until he was between her and the apartment door.

What had been apprehension hardened into defiance. She locked eyes with him. "I did look at that photo, Skip. I saw you in it."

"I should be flattered, or concerned, considering what I do for a living, that you still know what I look like."

"I have things to do, Skip, and parrying with you isn't on the list."

"No, Jess, I think talking to me should be at the top of your list."

"Get out, Skip. Leave me alone. What you do with your life doesn't interest me, even if—"

"Even if *what*?"

"Even if you were the agent who infiltrated the Jasper group."

"Oh, yeah, I sure was that agent. Scope in action—again."

Her concern reappeared. She considered trying to change the subject, lighten the mood. But the heat his face and body language gave off caused her to realize that words wouldn't alleviate what was in the air.

"Was it really this Jasper group behind the missile attacks on the planes?" she asked, going to the sliding glass doors to her small balcony, which were partially open. "That reporter who's been on TV claims you attacked the wrong people."

"I didn't attack anybody. You believe this reporter, right?"

She shrugged and wrapped her arms about herself, leaned against the closed portion of the doors. "I don't know what to believe. The reporter claims it was a hate group up on the Canadian border, near Plattsburgh, where—"

"Where this picture was taken."

"Yes."

"And that fertile brain of yours has already written a script in which I'm the heavy, the bad guy, the black hat."

"No, that's not true."

"You've been hearing things about me."

"That isn't true, either. I just wonder why you would be out in a field with other men in the same area where this other hate group operates. Were you undercover there, too?"

"You might say that."

"Are the other men in the picture hunters? Guns in those bags?"

"You ask a lot of questions, Jess, always did. Let's take a ride."

"I'm expecting someone."

"Max."

"Yes, how do you—?"

"You said his name when I arrived."

"Oh, right. Yes, I'm waiting for someone named Max."

"A beau?"

"A friend."

"I see. Does he work with you at State?"

"That doesn't matter."

"Meaning it's none of my business. Come on, Jess, I didn't ask you to stick your nose into this."

"How have I done that?"

"This picture," he said, patting his jacket pocket. "You know, Jessica, I came by today to touch base with you. It's been a long time. We had our problems, that's no secret, but we were both young—impetuous youth, as they say. But I've been doing a lot of thinking lately about where I am in life and where I want to go. I'm through with the Bureau, through sticking my neck out for civil servant pay. I thought . . . I thought it might be time for you and me to get together again, try to make a go of it."

Jessica listened, wishing the buzzer would sound, announcing Max's arrival.

"You'll hear a lot of bad things about me, Jess, concerning the Jasper assault. Yeah, I was the one who infiltrated the group and brought back the evidence linking Jasper and his crowd to the missile attacks."

"Then it *was* the Jasper group behind the missiles. You should be proud."

"That's right. But sometimes you make mistakes. Easy to do in that circumstance."

"A mistake? About whether it was Jasper?"

"Uh huh. Not that it's a big deal if I did make a mistake. Jasper just represents another hate group put out of action.

They're all the same, Jasper, Freedom Alliance, Aryan Nation, Silent Brotherhood. Like the mob. What difference does it make if you put the wrong capo in jail, or kill the wrong godfather? They all have to go eventually."

His cavalier analysis of the situation was chilling to Jessica. Was he admitting to her that he had, in fact, made a mistake in fingering the Jasper Project, and was justifying it?

"I don't agree with you, Skip, but—"

"I don't give a damn whether you agree with me or not, and if your friend hadn't taken that picture, it wouldn't matter whether anybody agrees with me. What could they do to me for making an honest mistake, a slap on the wrist from those clowns at the Bureau, a reprimand, a bad report in my file? That doesn't matter because I'm resigning."

He pulled the photograph from his jacket, looked at it for what seemed a very long time, slowly shook his head, and returned it to the pocket. "But this changes things, Jess, this picture, and you knowing what's in it."

"Why? I don't understand. I don't know anything about it, Skip. You were on a hunting trip, fishing with friends?"

As she said it, she knew the gathering of men in that valley on the Canadian border was neither a hunting nor a fishing expedition. It was what the reporter spoke of on television, the right-wing hate group that had really been behind the missile attacks.

As though reading her thoughts, Traxler said, "Yeah, you're right, Jess."

"You were undercover with them? You were—you were *part* of them?"

He closed the gap between them and placed his hands on her shoulders. "I meant it, Jess, when I said I came here to see whether we could take a stab at getting together again, ride out whatever comes of this mistake I made. If I know Templeton, he'll smooth it over, spin it a hundred and eighty degrees to make the Bureau look good. It's just this reporter claiming we were wrong. A bloodsucking reporter against a decorated FBI special agent. There'll be some controversy, the do-gooders in Congress will insist on holding hearings, the press will sell newspapers, and it'll blow over. At least that's the way I had it figured until I came here and saw that picture of me with them. That changes things. *You* change things."

He tightened his grip on her shoulders. She shook loose, but there was nowhere to go.

"Let's take that ride, Jess. Give me a chance to explain things to you."

"I'm not going anywhere, Skip." She slid to her right. He stepped back. She thought for a moment that he might decide to leave—until his hand went into another of his jacket's pockets and came out with a small revolver.

"Put that away, Skip," Jess said, her quavering voice betraying her fear.

"No," he said. "I've been planning my future for too long to let you and one Kodak moment screw it up. Come on, Jess. You haven't seen our lovers' nest in a long time."

"Lovers' nest?" She realized then how far apart they had grown.

"Our cabin in the woods. We used to enjoy the ride there. Remember? Nice this time of year. I don't have a convertible anymore but—I'm losing patience, Jess. Don't underestimate me. I have no problem shooting you right here. We haven't seen each other in years, and the gun can't be traced to me." His eyes darted about the room. "I'd hate to mess up your neat apartment. We can talk on our way, maybe figure out how we can resolve this nicely, like two reasonable adults."

"All right," she said. "I . . . I need to go to the bathroom first."

"Go ahead. I hate to stop on the road."

Jessica started for the bedroom, paused, picked up the pile of photos, and went to the desk in the living room.

"You never change, do you?" Traxler said. "Always the neatnik."

She smiled at him as she made a careful pile of the pictures. When he looked away, she removed the second of two shots of the men in the valley from the middle of the pile, and shoved it in her blouse.

"I'll only be a minute."

Traxler followed her into the bedroom. "Hurry up," he said.

She entered the bathroom, closed the door, and tried to collect her thoughts, think clearly, make use of the few minutes she'd have alone. She pulled the photo from her blouse and laid it on the vanity. A pad of orange Post-its was on top of the toilet tank. She opened the medicine cabinet; a glass held a variety of eyebrow pencils, and a Flair pen.

"Come on," Traxler said through the door.

Jessica flushed the toilet and started writing: *Max— Taken by Skip to Gauley Bridge, W.V.—Cabin deed in desk—Help!*

She placed a towel on top of the note and photograph.

Traxler banged on the door, then opened it. She spun around. "I'm ready," she said.

"Yeah, so am I," he said.

As they went to the apartment door, Jessica in front of him, the gun pressed against her back, Traxler stopped and picked up her binoculars and bird book from a table.

"Why do you want those?" she asked.

"Maybe you can teach me to be a bird-watcher," he said, moving her forward with the revolver. "Better take your slicker, Jess. They're forecasting rain."

She pulled down her yellow rain jacket from a row of pegs in the entranceway and put it on. They went to the hall and she locked the door behind them. As she did, the sound of the phone ringing in the apartment was heard. It had to be Max, she thought.

"Come on, come on," Traxler said, pushing her toward the elevators. They exited the building and went to his rented silver-blue Ford Taurus. He held the door open for her, came around the other side, slipped behind the wheel, started the engine, and backed out of the space.

Pauling, showered and in a fresh pair of jeans, blue button-down shirt, and running shoes, listened to Jessica's outgoing message on her answering machine. Strange, he thought, that she wasn't home. She'd sounded anxious to see him. He tried the number three more times before deciding to drive there, use his key, and wait for her in the apartment.

The moment he stepped through the door, he sensed something wrong. He tensed, reflexively, eyes open a little wider and unblinking, ears tuned to the room's silence. Her purse was on a chair just inside it. She wouldn't have left without it. Her car keys were hanging on their usual hook in the kitchen. An unopened bottle of Amstel Light sat on the counter, next to an empty glass and an opener. She'd never leave it out.

He returned to the living room and noticed the sliding doors to the balcony were open. Jessica Mumford was meticulous about closing those doors before leaving, even for a few minutes.

He saw the desktop, picked up the photos, and flipped through them. Where are you? he wondered. He headed for the bathroom. Another dissonant sign struck him, a towel on the sinktop. Towels were always neatly hung, never left on the edge of the tub or the sink. He lifted the towel and saw a photograph, picked it up, and read the note.

It took him a few minutes to locate the photocopy of the deed to the cabin; Jessica had made it before handing the original over to Traxler as part of their divorce settlement.

He picked up the phone and dialed the number of the flight service facility at Reagan National Airport that serviced private and corporate aircraft, and was happy to reach a manager with whom he was friendly. "Bruce, this is Max Pauling. Can I get my Cessna fueled and serviced on the double? I'm heading out there now, should arrive in twenty minutes."

"Sure, Max. We're slow. That front coming through is keeping the VFR crowd grounded. Where are you headed?"

"Charleston, West Virginia."

"Rough weather forecast. Maybe you ought to—"

"Thanks, Bruce. Weather is getting rough all over. See you in twenty minutes."

40

That Same Evening
Penn Hills, Pennsylvania

"You play as if that song had just been written."

Roseann looked up into the smooth, familiar face of the Senate majority leader, Gary Jackson, senior senator from Pennsylvania.

"Thank you," she said, playing the final chords of a surprisingly up-tempo theme from *Gone With the Wind*.

"Are you from the area, one of my talented constituents?" Jackson asked.

"No, sir," she said. "Washington, DC."

"Really? Fairly far from home for a gig."

Roseann laughed. "You sound like a musician instead of a senator."

He grinned. "I was, played my way through college. Drums."

"That's wonderful," she said. "If we had a set here, you could sit in."

"Afraid my—what's the term?—afraid my chops wouldn't be up to it."

"Neither is this piano," she said. "I don't think it's been tuned since the Johnstown flood."

"Well, you certainly overcome it."

"Any requests, Senator?"

321

" 'Sweet Georgia Brown'?"

"Sure."

The discordant piano aside, the first of two sets went smoothly. Senator Jackson approached her again during intermission as she stood alone in a corner sipping a Diet Coke through a straw.

"Are you returning to Washington tonight?" he asked.

"Yes, sir."

"That last flight?"

"Yes."

"I'm on it, too. Care to ride to the airport with us? There's just myself and an aide. Plenty of room in the car."

"Thank you," Roseann said. "I appreciate that."

"Don't forget Rufus has a vet appointment in the morning," Annabel Reed-Smith said to Mac as he pulled up in front of the terminal at Reagan National Airport. She was catching a late-evening commuter flight to Philadelphia for a meeting the next morning with a pre-Columbian dealer.

"I won't," he said. "Give me a call when you get settled in the hotel."

"I always do, although I never really settle into a hotel. I'm only settled when I'm with you."

"Is that a comment on hotels? Or my daily ego builder?"

"Both."

They kissed. She left the car and entered the terminal.

Mac smiled as he watched her. He loved everything about his wife, including her legs and her walk, purposeful, yet with a charming tall person's awkwardness.

Sometimes you get lucky, he thought as he pulled away.

41

That Same Evening
Washington, DC

Max Pauling called the flight weather line the moment he rushed into the private and corporate flight operations center at Reagan National, and was told the weather between Washington and Charleston, West Virginia, was passable but deteriorating. He checked the charts covering the Charleston area, filed an IFR flight plan, and ran to his plane, where a ground service technician had fueled it and moved it to a tie-down closer to the ops center.

"Thanks," Pauling said, casting a wary glance at the sky before climbing into the left-hand seat, shutting the door, and running through his preflight checklist. He was cleared to taxi to an active runway parallel to the one handling commercial takeoffs and landings, and took his place in line behind two corporate jets. Five minutes later, cleared, after waiting not very patiently, he advanced the throttle. The small, single-engine plane rolled slowly forward, then accelerated until reaching sufficient speed to break gravity's tether and wobble into the sky, a brisk crosswind threatening to push the light aircraft off its path over the runway's center line. He banked right, following the air traffic controller's instruction, and climbed away from the airport and its traffic. He adjusted his heading, set his automatic direction finder to the Charleston radio frequency indicated on the chart strapped to the top of his right thigh, and engaged the autopilot.

The horizon ahead was clear, but low, black clouds preceding a front were moving in from the south, to his left. Now on course, and with the instruments guiding him to Charleston, he was able to sit back and reflect on what had sent him running to his plane.

Until coming to Jessica's apartment and seeing her note, his thoughts had been exclusively on the events that had led up to his arrival, much of it emotional—Bill Lerner's death, the narrow escape on the street in Moscow, finding himself on the secretary of state's plane, and the ramifications of the information he'd learned about the missiles. But he'd always been good at compartmentalizing troublesome episodes in his life, pushing emotions to the side in favor of cognition. "Maybe if you'd let your heart in on a decision now and then," his former wife, Doris, once said, "we could work things out." He had tried for a brief period to do just that but was a failure. As far as he was concerned, emotions only clouded one's ability to make reasoned, rational decisions, whether they involved family or what he did for a living.

Was stripping away emotions something he'd learned, he had wondered, or was it hardwired in him? There was even a period when he questioned whether his lack of affect represented a psychological problem of some sort, a failure, a device to shield himself from the pain often inflicted by emotions. He wasn't comfortable grappling with that question, and when he and Doris decided to call it quits, he shucked not only the tension between them, but also any compelling reason to probe his psyche. He wasn't sure which had provided the greater relief.

Now, boring through an increasingly nasty sky toward Charleston, his only thought was of Jessica and the note she'd left.

He'd taken the photocopy of the cabin's deed with him in order to be able to find it once he rented a car, provided he could find a rental agency with available vehicles. He wore his vest again, with its multiple pockets, which he'd put on after showering and changing clothes at his apartment. If they'd planned to have dinner out, he would have worn a sport jacket. But Jessica had said they'd be eating at the apartment. He reached into a pocket and removed the Glock 17, checked its clip, and placed it on the right-hand seat. A sudden downdraft caused the Cessna to drop thirty feet, causing his lap belt to cut into his thighs. He checked his instruments, then returned his thoughts to the note and what it said: *Max—Taken by Skip to Gauley Bridge, W.V.—Cabin deed in desk—Help!*

Why would her former husband kidnap her? Pauling now knew that Traxler was the "Scope" who'd infiltrated the Jasper ranch for the FBI. Did absconding with Jessica have something to do with that? Or had Traxler done it for personal reasons, an outgrowth of their failed marriage? Ex-spouses or lovers could make for lethal company.

He pushed such questions from his mind as he turned to managing his intrusion into Charleston's airspace with air traffic control. He hadn't arrived any too soon. The weather had lowered to almost zero visibility. Rain pelted his windshield, and wind gusts buffeted the single-engine plane. He had to fight the controls as he flew a left-hand pattern in preparation for landing, first flying downwind parallel to the runway, banking sharply left ninety degrees, then making another ninety-degree left turn putting him on final approach. He maintained more power than normal to provide better handling as he passed high over the lights at the end of the runway and used half of it to put the plane down. Okay.

A ground controller directed him to the tie-down area for private aircraft, where he parked, killed the engine, shoved the Glock back into a vest pocket, and ran toward the terminal. He was soaked by the time he reached it.

"I need a rental car," he snapped at a young man behind the desk.

"Okay, but first take care of the paperwork. That's your 172 out there?"

"Yeah. Look, give me the papers!"

He filled out the form, slapped down a credit card to pay for the landing and tie-down fees, and followed signs at a trot in the direction of baggage handling, ground transportation, and rental car agencies. A uniformed woman with hair the color of nicotine read a magazine behind the Hertz counter.

"Hi," Pauling said. "Got any SUVs?"

She looked up and then smiled. "No, only full-size or compact."

"Full-size. And I need directions to Gauley Bridge."

"Where's that?"

"It's . . . southeast of here."

She prepared the forms; Pauling provided his driver's license and credit card and signed. She pulled a map from beneath the counter and studied it. "Here it is," she said, drawing a small circle around Gauley Bridge. "Never heard of it," she added uselessly.

"Yeah, thanks," Pauling said, grabbing the keys she'd given him and running to where the rental cars were parked. It was a maroon Chevy Caprice, big and boat-like. Pauling got behind the wheel, started the engine, turned on the interior lights, and studied the Hertz map until confident he knew the directions to Gauley Bridge.

It was raining harder now and the wipers, even at full speed, had trouble keeping up with the water. He navigated the airport roads to the exit, saw a sign for Route 77 that would lead southeast, and took it. There was little traffic, most of it coming from the other direction, the lights temporarily blinding him each time they assailed the windshield. He checked his watch and calculated how long it would take Traxler and Jessica to reach the cabin from Washington, assuming they were driving. He figured they were at least an hour away, probably longer considering the lousy weather. That pleased him. He wanted to reach the cabin before they did, know the terrain and layout, be there when they arrived. He was confident that Traxler wouldn't know that Jessica had left a note. That gave him the advantage of surprise.

He turned on the radio and tuned to an all-news station. After a series of commercials, and a report on a controversy over logging in West Virginia, the anchor broke in: "We go now to Washington, where FBI Director Russell Templeton is beginning a news conference."

"As you know, the FBI today took decisive action against a terrorist group in Blaine, Washington, known as the Jasper Project. Months of intensive investigation, including the infiltration of the group by members of the Bureau, provided irrefutable evidence of the Jasper Project's involvement in the missile downing of three civilian commuter planes almost a month ago.

"I stand here today to report another development in this tragic episode in our fight against those who would subvert our American way of life, and who have so little regard for human life. As part of our ongoing investigation of hate groups, we've worked closely with law enforcement agencies in other countries.

"Today, in the wake of the successful siege on the Jasper compound in Blaine, our agents, working in concert with Canadian investigators, have linked another group to the downing of those aircraft, one closely allied with the Jasper Project, the Freedom Alliance. This organization, headquartered in Plattsburgh, New York, on the Canadian border, has used the cover of that border for years, moving back and forth across it in order to avoid law enforcement on both sides. Acting as an extension of the Jasper Project, the Freedom Alliance played a vital role in smuggling the missiles used to bring down the civilian aircraft into this country.

"As we speak, the FBI, acting in close concert with our Canadian counterparts, have surrounded the Freedom Alliance's facility in Plattsburgh and are prepared to take action similar to that taken today against the Jasper Project. Sorry, but my statement will have to stand. No questions."

"Son of a bitch," Pauling growled, snapping off the radio with enough force to pull the knob from it. "That's how they're going to cover up the screwup—take credit for uncovering the Plattsburgh connection."

As he fumed, he missed the marked turnoff to Gauley Bridge, doubled back, took it, and drove slowly along a narrow macadam road until reaching a wooden covered bridge that gave the town its name. Pauling stopped a few feet from the bridge, flicked on the inside lights, and consulted the photocopy of the deed he'd taken from Jessica's desk. The bridge was noted on the property map; the cabin was on the other side, 640 feet to the north.

The Kanawha River ran behind it. He turned off the interior lights, crept across the bridge, emerged from beneath its wooden roof, and proceeded another fifty yards until reaching a break in the trees on his right. The large Caprice barely cleared brush on both sides as Pauling inched down a rutted path that had been washed out in spots, necessitating backing up and moving closer to bushes that scraped the sides of the car like fingernails on a blackboard. The outline of the cabin came into view in the headlights. Pauling stopped and studied the scene. A covered front porch ran the width of the building. It was one story, the door in the middle. Pauling then noticed that the road jogged to the right of the cabin and seemed to go behind it. He drove in that direction until passing the cabin on his left. Ahead of him was the river shown on the property map. He backed up, turned the wheel hard left, and maneuvered closer to the river, between two trees that would afford some cover for the car. He got out and approached the cabin, saw two wooden steps leading up to a back door. He went to it and tried the knob. Locked. A curtain over its glass portion obscured any view of the interior.

He went to the front of the cabin, his shoes coming out of the mud creating sucking sounds. He stepped onto the porch and opened a screen door, tried the handle of the solid inside door. It too was locked. Double-hung windows flanked the door. Pauling took out the Glock 17 and used the handle to smash one of the small panes of glass, reached through, turned the sash lock, and raised the bottom half of the window. He hunched over and stepped through the opening, his foot knocking over a small piece of furniture. Now inside, he strained to see in the room's darkness. He always carried a small flashlight in his vest and tried a few pockets until coming up with it. The narrow beam showed a light switch on the wall just inside the door, but Pauling didn't turn it on. Instead, he examined the space using the small light. It was one large room, with a Pullman kitchen at the far end. Next to it was the only door leading from the room. Pauling opened it and stepped into a cramped bathroom with a stall shower wedged into a corner.

He returned to the main room and looked through the window. No car lights—yet.

He used the time to see what else was in the room. A sleeper couch was on the front wall between the two windows. Battered green leather chairs occupied opposite corners. Above the couch, two fly rods rigged with reels and line hung from wooden pegs. In one corner, behind a chair, a gun cabinet contained four long guns, two rifles and two shotguns. Needs a woman's touch, he thought absently.

He turned from the couch and played the light over the back wall. An eight-foot-long wooden chest sat next to a wood-burning stove. Pauling went to the chest and lifted the lid. Inside was an arsenal. Machine guns, grenades, what appeared to be a dozen handguns, two bulletproof vests, and hard and soft cases. He picked up an empty soft-sided case, approximately five feet long, made of canvas, with a heavy zipper. He dropped it into the chest, was about to close the lid when he saw a small pile of what appeared to be maps in a corner. He pulled them out and examined them. They were aeronautical flight charts for Boise, Idaho; San Jose, California; Pittsburgh, Pennsylvania; and Westchester County airport in New York.

He held the charts in one hand as he closed the lid and went into the small kitchen area, stopping on the way to unlock the cabin's rear door and to slide open one end of a curtain covering the glass a few inches. He kicked broken glass from the front window under a chair, spread out the worst of his muddy footprints with the sole of his shoe, and sat on a tall wooden stool in front of the sink. The wind-whipped raindrops hitting the windows sounded like the marching of toy wooden soldiers, and the wind whistled down the chimney. He pulled the pistol from his vest pocket, turned off the pen-light, and waited.

42

How many different emotions can one experience in a compressed period of time? Jessica wondered.

When she left the apartment with Traxler, she was shaking with fear. All the vague, unstated intimidation she'd suffered when they were married now took on a reality that gripped her with physical force, sickened her, made her hands tremble, legs go weak, voice crumble.

But after an hour in the car, she found herself gaining resolve. The helpless, hapless victim now began to think, to process the predicament in order to devise a way out of it. A calm set in as her former husband drove too fast; his speech was accelerated, too. He rambled, a jumble of thoughts going in many different directions, seldom connecting, with no beginning, middle, or end.

Midway through the trip, he abruptly fell silent after delivering a monologue about putting himself first for a change—"If I don't look after me, make me numero uno, nobody else will. I've been laying my life on the line for years to make some bureaucrat look good and . . ." The muscles of his cheeks worked as he focused on the road, eyes narrowed, hands tight on the wheel.

"You don't have to keep going, Skip," Jessica said.

"You can pull over and we can talk. Or you can let me out right here."

He didn't respond.

"It doesn't matter to me what happened at that ranch out in Washington. I don't know anything about what you did there, or why. The picture Cindy took—you have it. I don't want it. I don't have any use for it. Whatever it means, just tear it up, burn it. Let's turn around and go back. I'll get the negative from Cindy and—"

"Shut up!"

He put on the radio. An all-news station was in the midst of replaying Director Templeton's press conference:

". . . we've worked closely with law enforcement agencies in other countries.

"Today, in the wake of the successful siege on the Jasper compound in Blaine, our agents, working in concert with Canadian investigators, have linked another group to the downing of those aircraft, one closely allied with the Jasper Project, the Freedom Alliance. This organization . . .

"As we speak, the FBI, acting in close concert with our Canadian counterparts, have surrounded the Freedom Alliance's facility in Plattsburgh and are . . ."

Traxler turned it off.

"Those are the men you were with in Plattsburgh?" Jessica asked. "In the picture?"

"Right," he said.

Should she ask more, try to learn *why* he was there? It didn't seem to matter what she knew or didn't know. Simply having seen a photograph of him with those men—and his knowing she'd seen it—had caused him to pull a gun and kidnap her. The question she now asked herself was whether probing him for answers would ease his apparent, irrational need to silence her—or fuel it.

Fighting to think clearly, she decided that at this juncture it was better to engage him rather than allow his silent thoughts to fester.

"Skip, whatever's happened in your life, I'm no longer a part of it. We weren't right for each other and recognized it. I've gone on with my life and you've gone on with yours. Why don't we just leave it at that?"

He sneered as he said, "You never did get it, Jess, never understood what I was all about, what I was going through."

"Of course I did. Working undercover was dangerous. You were under constant pressure. I worried about you every day you were away working."

"That's really sweet, Jess. I'm touched."

"I wasn't trying to 'touch' you, Skip. I'm just telling you the truth."

He drew deep breaths as though trying to keep himself under control. "You don't know what it was like," he said, not looking at her.

"No, I'm sure I don't," she said. "How could I? I didn't live the life you led."

"You bet you didn't." Now he turned to her. "Know what the worst part was, Jess?"

"What?"

"Watching the scum I was with living high and thumbing their noses at people like me. Oh, they didn't know who I was. I was good, Jess. The best." He began veering into the oncoming lane and swerved back, the maneuver startling Jessica into momentary silence.

She was afraid her resolve, manifested in the flat, calm voice she'd been using, might wane, and forced matter-of-factness back into her tone. "I still don't understand why you've done this, Skip," she said as waves of water hit the windshield from oncoming vehicles, causing her to wince each time they slapped the glass. "I don't wish you any harm."

"But you can *do* me harm, Jess."

"How? What would I do? Why would I do it?"

"You and that stupid bird-watching."

She reached across the seat and touched his right arm. "Skip, I didn't take that picture. I wasn't there. Are you concerned I might take the photo to someone, some law enforcement agency? That would never cross my mind. What would be the purpose, to show that my ex-husband . . ."

He slowly turned his head and fixed her in the sort of stare that froze her when they were married. "Go on," he said, allowing a trace of a smile to touch his lips. "You were about to say that your ex-husband was photographed with a bunch of rednecks up on the Canadian border, right-wing, government-hating, white supremacists who don't mind shooting down civilian planes to get the country's attention. Right, Jess? Was that what you were about to say?"

"No."

His right hand came off the wheel and shot across the seat, gripping her wrist and squeezing. She backed against the passenger door. "You're . . . hurting me," she said, trying to pull free.

He relaxed his grip and leaned forward, squinting, to see through the sheets of water on the windshield. She rubbed her wrist. As she did, a rage welled up in her of an intensity she couldn't recall ever feeling before.

"What did you do, Skip, get involved with those rednecks in upstate New York, forget who you were and become one of them?" She had no idea whether that was what had happened, but her anger now dictated.

"What I did," he said, "was to get a piece of what's owed me."

"*Owed* you? What were you owed?"

"Money. For years of sticking my neck out, getting paid off with a slap on the back by some fat-cat bureaucrat and a nice letter in the file. I learned a lot from hanging around with the lowlifes, Jess. The FBI. Fidelity, Bravery, Integrity," he said scornfully. "Put the mobsters behind bars. Get the drug dealers off the street. You know what, Jess, this country's on one fast slide to oblivion. In the sewer. The politicians steal us blind, the cops in every city are on the take, we blame Mexico and Colombia for the drug problem but the problem's right here, the users, the market those countries feed. You have any idea how much money from drugs some of the right-wing groups, left-wing groups, no-wing groups make? Millions." He snickered. "Those guys up in Plattsburgh have been bringing drugs into this country for a couple of years now, right across the Canadian border, waltz it in like loaves of bread. That's how they finance their crazy schemes. They praise the Lord while they're selling crack out the back door."

"And you?"

"And me *what*?"

"You're praising the Lord, or in this case law and order, while you're taking some of that dirty money? Is that what you're saying?"

"You hear what Templeton said before, Jess?"

"Yes, I heard. That group you were with in Plattsburgh was involved, too, in the missile attacks."

"Of course."

His cold admission of it—more important, that he knew—was like a blow to her chest. She said nothing for a moment, the countryside flashing by her window distorted by the rain, her mind distorted by him. Finally, she said, "The people out in Washington, the Jasper people. Were they involved too, or was that the 'mistake' you mentioned."

Anger visibly flared in his face, then sagged into an expression of frustration, annoyance at her lack of understanding. "None of it matters," he mumbled, barely audible above the sound of the car's engine and the swoosh of water beneath the tires. "Who cares who did what, or who gets it? I'm through. I did what I said I'd do, got my money and I'm out of it."

"Who cares?" she repeated loudly, incredulous. "*Who cares?* What about the people on those planes? You could have stopped it, couldn't you?"

"No, I couldn't," he said, exiting the highway and taking a two-lane road leading to Gauley Bridge. "I didn't know the Freedom Alliance was going to target civilian airliners. All I did once it happened was to point a finger at the Jasper Project, make sure the Bureau looked the wrong way." His laugh was ironic. "Worked out fine, didn't it? Two hate groups down, including the right one. Justice prevails."

"What are you going to do with me?" she asked.

"Like I said, go bird-watching with you."

She stared at him.

"Only you're not going to bring any pictures, or anything else, back," he said, turning onto the narrow road leading to the covered bridge.

43

That Night
Pittsburgh

Roseann and Senator Jackson talked music on the limo ride from the Cedars, in Penn Hills, Pennsylvania, to the airport in Pittsburgh. He wanted to know everything about her—her childhood, her musical training and ambitions, and her influences.

She felt embarrassed talking so much about herself and after a while began asking him questions.

"I considered staying at the Cedars an extra day to get in some golf," he said, "but I've got to be back in Washington in the morning. I'm the ranking member of the Judiciary Committee. We're going to have an emergency meeting on this Jasper ranch fiasco. You've kept up with it?"

She swallowed and looked out the window. Knowing he was waiting for an answer, she said, "Yes, I have. I . . . the man in my life has something to do with it."

"Oh? Who's he?"

"Joe Potamos. He's a reporter for—"

"You don't have to tell me about Mr. Potamos," the senator said. "He'll be a prime witness before the committee."

"He will?"

"Yes, he certainly will. He told a remarkable story on TV today. Do you know how accurate his account is?"

"Me? No, I don't know anything about it, except that Joe is an honest person. He wouldn't make anything up."

"I'm glad to hear that," Jackson said.

The rest of the ride was consumed by his questions about Joe, and she was glad when they pulled up in front of the Pittsburgh terminal.

The senator and his aide, a young woman named Marie, and Roseann were escorted to a VIP lounge, where they were told the flight to Washington was delayed because of weather. "The equipment should be here in a half hour," the pleasant woman at the desk said. "Sorry for the delay, Senator."

"No problem," he replied, smiling. "You can't fight Mother Nature."

He excused himself from Roseann. "I'm afraid Marie and I have some reports to go over before tomorrow."

"That's all right," Roseann said. "I brought a book."

As the senator and his assistant went to a secluded corner of the lounge, Roseann settled into an overstuffed chair, opened her book, and picked up where she'd left off. She thought of Joe, wondered how Larry King had gone, and how he'd react to being a witness before a senate committee. She kept her smile from becoming a giggle.

How exciting; he'd hear it from her first. She couldn't wait to get home.

The pickup truck was red and new. It was an extended-cab model, with a small bench seat behind the twin buckets used by a driver and front passenger.

Its driver was a small, wiry man wearing a red-and-black flannel shirt over well-worn jeans, and rubber, ankle-high boots. His hair was gray and matted, slicked down with some sort of gel, and pulled into a small ponytail.

His lights were off as he parked the truck in a heavily wooded area a mile from the southern end of the Pittsburgh airport's north-south runway. He reached behind and pulled a heavy, five-foot-long canvas bag from the rear bench, grunting against the weight. He laid the bag on the passenger seat and unzipped it, began to remove the contents piece by piece, handling them with care, running his fingers over them, a gesture of admiration.

The sound of a plane taking off caused him to look up into a clearing sky. The plane passed directly above him, then banked to the east, the shriek of its engines fading into the night.

He got out of the truck, went around to the passenger side, opened the door, and lifted the missile and its shoulder launcher from the seat. He walked a hundred yards to a clearing in the trees that he knew well from having been there a number of times over the past two weeks. A fallen tree provided a seat, which he took. He checked the mechanisms on the launcher, took a small, thin cigar from his shirt pocket, lit it, drew a sustained, calming breath, and waited.

44

Pauling saw the headlights through the cabin window. He got up from the stool and went through the rear door carrying the Glock 17 in his right hand. He'd left the aeronautical charts in the kitchen; no time to go back for them.

The rain had effectively stopped, leaving a fine mist in the air. Behind him, the sound of the flowing river provided a misleading sense of peace.

He stood on the top step and peered through the gap he'd created in the curtain. The approaching vehicle's lights continued to flash into the cabin, then disappear as the car bounced over the bumpy, pitted road. He heard the engine, then its shutdown. A car door opened and closed. Another door opened; "Come on, come on," a man's voice said. The second door slammed shut. Footsteps on the front porch, the door being unlocked, swung open with force; "Come *on*," the man's voice again. Would he notice the broken windowpane? Pauling wondered. Evidently not. The door was closed and the cabin was suddenly illuminated by two overhead fixtures suspended from rough-hewn beams in the ceiling.

Skip Traxler and Jessica Mumford stood facing each other in the center of the room. She wore a yellow rain

341

slicker Pauling had seen her in many times before, part of her standard bird-watching gear. He searched her face for what she was feeling and thinking. He saw anger in her eyes. Pauling felt no such anger at the moment. He'd cleared his mind of anything and everything to make room for the decisions he'd have to make.

Traxler held a revolver pointed at the floor. Pauling had seen him in pictures in Jess's apartment, never in person. This was "Scope," an undercover FBI agent and her former husband. The question of why he'd done this came and went, unanswered. It didn't matter. There'd be plenty of time for those questions. For now, disarming Traxler and getting Jess out of harm's way was the only question to be acted upon.

Pauling sized Traxler up physically. Same height, squarely built, fit and strong was the assessment. Pauling had him outmanned when it came to firepower. The Glock was a semiautomatic, Traxler's revolver less puissant.

They moved out of his view. He pressed his ear to the door but only the incessant flow of the river reached him. He considered going to the front of the cabin and looking through one of the windows, but Traxler might hear him. As he pondered his next move, Traxler said loudly, "What the hell?" Pauling looked through the gap in the curtain. Traxler stood by the front window Pauling had smashed. Traxler looked around, eyes wide, mouth determined. Pauling stepped off the side of the steps and crouched in the darkness. The back door opened. "Unlocked," Traxler growled to himself. Pauling was certain he'd see the car beneath the trees, but if he did, he didn't react. He slammed the door shut.

Pauling immediately straightened, went around the side of the cabin, stepped onto the porch, took careful, silent steps to the nearest of the two windows, and looked through it. Traxler had herded Jessica to the closed rear door. Her back was to him; his revolver was trained on her. Pauling strained to see what Traxler held besides the revolver. Binoculars? A book of some kind?

Pauling knew he had to act. It appeared that Traxler was about to take Jessica out through that rear door. If he went in the direction of the river, he'd see Pauling's rental car. Pauling tensed until he saw Traxler open the door and push Jess through it into the night. He left the porch and hugged the side of the cabin until reaching the back corner. A full moon, obscured until now, cast light on the area between the cabin and the river, then was hidden again behind low-moving black clouds. But in that brief moment, Pauling saw that Traxler was prodding Jessica to the riverbank. He stepped away from the cabin and moved in their direction, taking long strides, trying to be silent and swift at once. He hesitated; Traxler had suddenly stopped when he saw the Caprice parked beneath the trees. Jessica continued to walk to the river, creating ten feet between her and Traxler.

Pauling sprung, feet churning in the mud as he hurtled at Traxler, crouched low, closing the gap, only a second until contact. Traxler saw him but not in time to do anything with his weapon. Pauling's head rammed into the FBI agent's stomach, causing the revolver to pop from his hand as he went over backward. Pauling pounced on him and they rolled down a slippery slope to the river, clutching each other, over and over, until a tree stopped them. The jolt caused the Glock to slip from Pauling's hand and land a few feet away.

Traxler twisted free of Pauling's grip and reached for the gun, but Pauling grabbed his wrist. They struggled to their knees. Traxler made another try for the Glock but Pauling drove a fist into his face, felt his nose break. Traxler let out a tortured moan as he got to his feet. Pauling was on all fours, about to get up, when Traxler's foot smashed into his side, sending him tumbling. Traxler desperately looked for the Glock, saw it, went to his knees and reached for it in the mud, found it, turned and pointed it at Pauling, who was up on his knees facing Traxler, a broad target. Pauling braced for what was sure to come. Jessica appeared from nowhere and flung herself at Traxler. He collapsed beneath the weight of her unexpected attack but held on to the Glock, twisted free, then slipped in the mud, his feet going out from under him and landing on his stomach.

Jessica jumped on him. So did Pauling, but not before frantically digging into the pocket of his vest and coming out with the ampule of prussic acid. He brought the device up to Traxler's broken nose and activated the spring. The ampule shattered, releasing its deadly contents—into Jessica's face.

She shrieked as the acid entered her nostrils and then fell away from them, rolling on the ground, her fingers at her nose as though she could tear the acid from it.

Pauling saw what had happened. He brought his fist back and pounded it against the side of Traxler's skull, again and again, pounding him until he was limp. He jumped to his feet, ran to where Jessica lay on the ground, pulled the vial of nitro from his vest pocket, held it beneath Jessica's nose, snapped it in two, and shouted, "Breathe, Jess. Breathe, damn it!"

She looked up at him with frightened eyes as the prussic acid began to act on her heart, constricting the arteries, shutting off blood supply. But the nitro took effect. Her hands, which had been clutched against the pain in her chest, relaxed, and her breathing became less labored.

"You okay?" Pauling asked.

"I think so."

Pauling got up and returned to where Traxler was beginning to recover from the pummeling he'd received. He picked up the Glock, grabbed Traxler by the front of his shirt, and pulled him to his feet.

"Let's get inside," Pauling said as the rain began to come down hard again. He shoved Traxler down into a chair, brought the stool and aeronautical charts from the kitchen, and sat in front of him.

"So here's the infamous Scope," Pauling said, "FBI undercover hotshot. You don't look so hot to me, buddy."

Traxler glared at him.

"He told me what happened, Max," Jessica said from where she stood behind him. "He said—"

Pauling cut her off. "These charts, Traxler. Boise, San Jose, and Westchester, where the three planes were shot down."

Still no response.

Pauling waved the fourth chart in front of his face. "Tell me about this one," he said.

Traxler wiped a rivulet of blood from beneath his nose and managed a grin. "Who the hell are you, anyway?" he asked.

"Somebody who'd enjoy putting a hole in the middle of your head," Pauling said. "This Pittsburgh chart, is that where the fourth missile is going to be used?" He took Traxler's lack of a reply to be affirmative. "When?" he asked. "These handwritten numbers on the charts—dates? The number on the Pittsburgh chart is today's date. Is it being used today, tonight?"

This time, when Traxler didn't say anything, Pauling grabbed his face and squeezed hard, pressing the heel of his hand against the FBI agent's nose. He put all the fury and loss and sadness of Bill Lerner's death, the woman at the Jasper ranch, the victims of the plane crash, even the slain Russian into his grip. Traxler whined from the excruciating pain and slipped down in the chair. Pauling stood, yanked him up to a sitting position, and brought his face within inches. "When?" he repeated with vengeance. "Tonight?"

Traxler's nod was almost imperceptible.

Pauling stepped back and asked Jessica, "There a phone here?"

She shrugged, started to look for one. "No," she said from the far end of the room.

"You have a cell phone?" Pauling asked Traxler.

"Go to hell."

Pauling brought the back of his hand against the side of Traxler's face. "Where's the nearest phone, Traxler?"

Silence.

Pauling handed the Glock to Jessica: "Keep it on him, Jess, and don't be afraid; if he moves, use it." He went to the kitchen and rummaged through several drawers, coming up with a roll of gray duct tape. He returned to the main room, shoved Traxler against a wall, and taped his hands behind him. "Let's go," he said.

They exited through the rear door and went to Pauling's rented Caprice. Traxler was stuffed into the backseat, and Pauling used more tape to secure his ankles and mouth. Jessica, still holding the Glock, got in the front passenger seat while Pauling backed out from beneath the trees, clipping the sideview mirror against one and knocking it off. "Going to be an expensive rental," he grumbled, coming forward again, then going into reverse and clearing the obstacle. He could barely see, but he managed to reach the road in front of the cabin.

45

**That Same Night
Pittsburgh**

"Your flight's ready to board, Senator Jackson," the VIP lounge's hostess said.

"Great," he said. "Thanks."

Roseann saw Jackson and his aide stand, and put her book in her carry-on bag. Jackson waved for Roseann to join them, and they left the lounge and went to the boarding gate. Airline ramp personnel held large golf umbrellas with the airline's insignia on them over the passengers as they crossed the tarmac and went up the short flight of stairs into the twin-engine turboprop. Jackson asked if he could sit next to Roseann. She couldn't refuse, although she hoped he wouldn't ask more questions about Joe. She was afraid she'd say something that would get him in trouble.

"Welcome aboard, ladies and gentlemen," the captain said in a deep Southern accent through the intercom. "Sorry for the delay tonight but the weather hasn't been very cooperative. But we'll be on our way in a few minutes and get you good folks back to Washington in short order. Just settle back, kick off your shoes, make sure those seat belts are nice and snug, and we'll get goin'."

Roseann and Jackson smiled at the captain's down-

347

home safety announcement. One of two flight attendants came down the narrow aisle to make sure seat belts were fastened, and took her seat next to the other attendant in preparation for departure.

They taxied to the end of the active runway. Roseann looked out the window and saw flashing lights on what appeared to be emergency vehicles. What's that all about? she wondered, her natural fear of flying kicking in. Senator Jackson saw it, too, and leaned across her to get a better view.

The captain's voice was heard again: "Ah, ladies and gentlemen, seems like we're goin' to have us another short delay. I'll keep you posted."

"What's wrong?" an elderly woman behind them asked.

"I don't think we'll ever get off the ground," a man said in a disgruntled, booming voice.

Jackson stopped a flight attendant. "Is there a mechanical problem?" he asked.

She ignored his question and entered the cockpit.

More lights could be seen outside the plane, and then the sound of helicopters was heard. They passed directly over the aircraft, powerful floodlights turning the area into daylight.

"Something's going on," Jackson said to Roseann.

What they couldn't see, or know, was that an army of FBI special agents, state police, and ATF officers had converged on a clearing a mile from the end of the runway and captured a man with a SAM missile on his shoulder that he was about to launch at the next departing flight.

"Well, folks, we're cleared now for takeoff," said the captain.

"It's about time," the passenger with the loud voice said.

The plane lifted off and they were Washington-bound.

It wasn't until they'd landed that Roseann Blackburn and the senior senator from Pennsylvania learned that the FBI's raid on the Freedom Alliance's headquarters in Plattsburgh, New York, had revealed a plan to use a fourth missile smuggled in from Russia to down a civilian airliner in Pittsburgh that night, the man wielding the deadly weapon a member of a Pennsylvania right-wing hate group loosely affiliated with the Freedom Alliance group. The information was relayed to Senator Jackson and those with him by an aide who'd come to the airport to pick him up.

Roseann's legs went to jelly when she heard. Jackson offered to have her driven home, but she declined the offer and called her apartment.

"Hey, babe," he said, "were you on that flight from Pittsburgh?"

"Yes, I was," she said, starting to cry.

"Easy, Rosie," he said. "Where are you?"

"The airport."

"Here?"

"Uh huh."

"You sit tight, grab a drink. I'll head out right now, be there in no time."

As she sat waiting for him, a Brandy Alexander in front of her, she looked up at the TV suspended behind the bar. Russell Templeton was giving a new statement just outside the Pittsburgh airport: "A tragedy has been averted this evening by swift action taken by the FBI and other law enforcement agencies. Information received this afternoon from a white-supremacist group in upstate New York led us this evening to converge on a position near the Pittsburgh airport, where . . ."

Roseann shuddered and closed her eyes. When she

349

opened them, Joe was at her side. She grabbed him and hugged hard, tears flowing, body shaking.

"Hey, it's okay," he said, taking a stool next to her. "Everything's okay now. Aristotle's here."

46

A Year Later
Albuquerque, New Mexico

Max Pauling glanced out the window of his condominium at the sound of a plane taking off. The condo overlooked the private airport where he'd been teaching flying for the past four months. He'd been reading after having taught two students that morning, and dozing.

Jessica came through the door carrying the mail. "For you," she said, handing him a letter. "From London."

He opened the envelope and removed the neatly typed single sheet of paper.

My dear Max,

I suppose you've been wondering whatever happened to me, although that might represent wishful thinking on my part. I've left Russia and have settled here in London. The change is dramatic, of course, but was necessary. I've achieved a position with an international bank, and have found quite a nice flat in an area known as Mayfair, a very fancy area although my flat is rather spartan, better reflecting my Russian experience.

I'm sure you think of Bill often, as do I. His death was unnecessary, but in this day and age, particularly in Russia, one can never be sure of anything. I think of Hesse when I think of Bill: "Strange to wander in the mist, each is alone. No tree knows his neighbor. Each is alone." That's so true, isn't it, Max? We are so painfully alone, from the beginning to the end.

Bill always said he was doing it for me, for us, but I suspect as with most things we do, he did it for himself. Very nasty people he involved himself with. Very nasty, indeed.

I worry that you might think poorly of me because of the way Bill died. I pray that isn't true, and I hope that one day when you come to London, you will be kind enough to call and say hello. I obtained your new address from someone at your State Department, who was kind enough to pass it along.

I won't bore you any longer, Max. I simply hope that all goes well for you and that you are happy.

Fondly, Elena

"Who's it from?" Jessica asked from the bedroom.

"Bill Lerner's lady in Moscow. She's living in London now. A good woman."

The phone rang.

"Hello?" Jessica said.

"Jess, it's Annabel Reed-Smith in Washington."

"Annabel, how are you?"

"Just fine."

"And Mac?"

"Tip-top. Still working, officially and unofficially, still partly nuts, partly wonderful. Catching you at a bad time?"

"No, but I will be leaving in a few minutes. I've joined a bird-watching group here in Albuquerque and we're going up into the mountains this afternoon . . ."

Her voice faded into the background as Pauling picked

up the book he'd been reading, *The Vipers,* a nonfiction account of the FBI's deadly mistaken assault on the Jasper Project in Blaine, Washington, and the role played by an undercover FBI agent, Skip Traxler, in this tragic episode in American history.

He turned the book over in his hands. Looking up at him was a photograph of the author, Joseph Potamos, whose brief bio read: "Veteran print journalist with *The Washington Post,* now a political reporter for CNN, Mr. Potamos lives in Washington with his wife, Roseann, a professional pianist, and their mixed-breed dog, Jumper."

He placed the book on the table, closed his eyes, and allowed his thoughts to wander along the lines of Joe's story. The reporter was good, had gotten most of the story, but not all.

Traxler had been indicted for providing false information to a government agency, and for the kidnapping of his former wife. He was awaiting trial.

The surviving members of the Jasper Project had filed a massive civil lawsuit against the FBI and related agencies for the assault on the Jasper ranch.

A Senate hearing on the event had uncovered the FBI's attempts to cover up what had really happened at the Jasper ranch. Director Russell Templeton, while maintaining his innocence of any knowledge of the cover-up, retired.

Retired.

Pauling, too, had walked away, along with Jessica, who'd decided to move with him to New Mexico and give their relationship a serious try. He'd had to promise that his days working undercover were behind him, and he meant it—when he said it. It wasn't as hard as he thought it would be, although it hadn't been that long since he walked away from life on the edge. As far as Jessica was concerned, going up each day with student pilots in a small, single-engine plane should be danger enough. Maybe so.

His reverie was interrupted by a kiss on the forehead.

"I have to go," Jessica said.

"Yeah, I know. Be careful, huh? You don't know these mountains. Might be snakes."

"Wouldn't be anything new. Plenty of them in Washington—and elsewhere. Odd birds, too."

He laughed gently, brought her head down with his hand, and their lips met.

"Annabel and Mac send their best."

"That's nice. Great pair. He's a top-drawer lawyer— and occasional undercover man himself. She's a beauty, and brainy." He sighed. "Know what I wish?"

"What?"

"I wish we'd been the ones to blow the whistle on that guy with the missile in Pittsburgh. Kind of a wasted exercise, wasn't it, driving like a madman in the rain looking for a phone when the Bureau already had the info from those wackos in Plattsburgh?"

She smiled and shook her head. "It doesn't matter," she said. "It doesn't matter."

"No, I suppose it doesn't. There'll be more."

"More what?"

"Terrorism by domestic groups. That they were able to work together the way they did—Idaho, California, New York, Pennsylvania, even Canada—doesn't bode well."

"I don't want to think about it, Max. I just want to think about peaceful things, like birds, the mountains, the clean air and blue sky . . ."

"I know. Go. Soak it up."

"I will."

She started to leave, paused at the door, and looked back. He'd closed his eyes again, and she wondered what dreams he would have this day. She knew the sort of reckless life he'd led was a powerful narcotic, not easily conquered. Like the alcoholic, you took it a day at a time, hoping tomorrow wouldn't provide temptations too powerful to ignore. And like the alcoholic's caregiver, you did what you could to offer an attractive alternative to the addiction.

She blew him a silent kiss.

He opened his eyes and smiled, then waved her from the room.

MURDER IN THE WHITE HOUSE

The First Capital Crimes Novel

by
Margaret Truman

In a town where the weapon of choice is usually a well-aimed rumor, the strangling of Secretary of State (and accomplished womanizer) Lansard Blaine in the Lincoln Bedroom is a gruesome first.

In death as in life, Blaine is a power to be reckoned with. Only a few highly placed insiders had access to the Lincoln Bedroom that fateful evening. And one of them was the president. . . .

> "The plot builds up to a superb denouement.
> One wonders if all is fiction."
> —*Time*

MURDER ON CAPITOL HILL

by
Margaret Truman

Between them, Senator Cale Caldwell and his blue-blooded wife wielded as much power on Capitol Hill as the law would allow. Sadly, it wasn't sufficient to protect him from a killer, even surrounded by his friends at a champagne reception in his honor.

The senator's death could benefit many people—among them a bitter political adversary, an ambitious talk show host, and a master of spin who makes even murder look good.

"A good old-fashioned mystery."
—*Cosmopolitan*

MURDER AT THE LIBRARY OF CONGRESS

by

Margaret Truman

In the depths of the U.S. Library of Congress toil thousands of researchers, chasing down obsessions, breakthroughs, and new contributions to human intelligence. But when amateur D.C. sleuth Annabel Reed-Smith enters this stately American institution, she discovers a hornet's nest of intrigue and murder.

After a renowned scholar is bludgeoned to death among the scholarly stacks, Annabel suspects that buried in the library are secrets some people will do anything to keep silent. . . .

"Truman has settled firmly into a career of writing murder mysteries, all evoking brilliantly the Washington she knows so well."
—*The Houston Post*

MURDER AT THE
NATIONAL GALLERY

by

Margaret Truman

When the senior curator at Washington's famed
National Gallery finds a missing painting by the
Renaissance master Caravaggio, he mounts a
world-class exhibition—and plots a brilliant
forgery scheme that will stun the art world.

But an artful deception suddenly becomes a
portrait of blackmail and murder—as gallery owner
and part-time sleuth Annabel Reed-Smith and
her husband go searching for clues in the heady
arena of international art.

"A thrilling chase."
—*Publishers Weekly*